Summer sucked in her breath. *Oh!* If not for her injured arm, she'd have socked the rotten polecat in the nose. "Well, you've found me, so go back and tell my sister I'm fine."

His smile faded. "You're not fine."

"I'm fine enough. Waco isn't that far. I'll walk the rest of the way. I'll not let the whole town think I've been rescued by the *great* Jesse Slade."

Another wicked smile tugged at his lips. "But I did rescue you, Summer."

She propped her hands on her hips. "You most certainly did not. You um…you just happened to arrive the exact moment I lost consciousness."

He sighed and tipped his hat back from his forehead. "Actually, the bullets from my gun dismounted three of the bandits."

She scowled. "I had things under control. Besides, I'm very capable of walking to town on my own now." She took several steps forward and dizziness blurred her vision. She swayed, and tilted toward the ground. Two strong arms grabbed her by the waist and pulled her upright.

"You bullheaded little twit. That does it." He picked her up and carried her to the horse, then let her feet drop to the ground and held her by her uninjured shoulder. "You ain't walkin'."

She slapped at his hand. "I'm not going into town with you."

"You're as ornery as an old mule." He paused, his heated gaze boring into hers. She liked neither the look, nor the silence.

"You listen to me, Miss Persnickety. I don't care what you like or don't like, I'm takin' you to town."

"I--don't--like." She grinded her teeth with each word.

"To--damn--bad." He mocked her. "You have two choices. You can get on that horse willin'ly, or I'll hog-tie you and put you there myself."

Her mouth dropped open and her mind scrambled frantically for several seconds.

He produced a cocky grin. "Time's up."

Champagne Books Presents

Holding Out For A Hero

By

Phyllis Campbell

Champagne Books
www.champagnebooks.com
Copyright © 2006 by Marie Higgins
ISBN 1897261357
August 2006
Cover Art © Chris Butts
Produced in Canada

Champagne Books
#35069-4604 37 ST SW
Calgary, AB T3E 7C7
Canada

Dedication

I want to dedicate this book to my very first hero—my father, Marvin Campbell—who I fashioned my heroine's father around. I wish my father could have lived to see this book published, but I know he was proud of me nonetheless. Dad, I miss you.

One

Texas, 1890

I should have taken the train.

Another bone-jarring jolt slammed Summer Bennett against the older gentleman sitting next to her. After two days of traveling in September's heat, her good humor had disappeared. The apology she felt obliged to issue refused to roll off her tongue, but when she looked at the man, she managed a smile.

Drawn and weary expressions on the other passengers' faces were testimony that they, too, were eager for the journey to end. The rickety old coach took its toll on all, not just in shortened tempers and dust-covered faces, but also in sheer physical discomfort.

She should have taken the train. Instead, she'd listened to her aunt and had gone on the stagecoach.

Summer rearranged her brown skirt and adjusted her sore backside on the seat, seeking a more comfortable position. She took out her miniature timepiece and flipped open the gold case. She gave a ragged sigh. Within one hour she'd be in Waco, Texas--her hometown.

"Summer, dear," said the silver-haired woman across from her. "What were you thinking when you offered to help the driver repair the wheel after it broke down?" Her withered hand fluttered against her chest. "Why, it's unheard of for a lady of your standing to do such a laborious, menial task."

Summer sat straight as possible in her seat, smiling at her

chaperone. A dear friend of her aunt's and a widow from Brownsville, Mrs. Whitaker had agreed to accompany her to Waco while on her way to Ft. Worth. Mrs. Whitaker should have known better than to bring that up. The woman knew Summer had always been a hoyden.

"Well, considering I used to repair wheels on the buggies rented from my pa's livery stable, I saw no harm in offering to assist. Like the rest of you, I want to get to Waco as soon as possible."

The other passengers in the coach agreed with nods and weary grins.

Mrs. Whitaker shook her head. "I would hate to think you wasted those five years at your aunt's school of etiquette. She would most certainly swoon if she knew you soiled your pretty dress on purpose."

Summer forced a laugh and tried to smooth out the many wrinkles in her skirt caused by the long journey and close quarters. "Yes, Aunt Lydia would certainly faint dead away. Although my aunt taught me etiquette, she knew she wouldn't be able to drive the tomboy out of me completely."

Mrs. Whitaker opened her mouth to reply, but before she could say another word, gunshots echoed in the distance. The others gasped and cried out, but Summer turned to peek out the window just as another shot broke the stillness. Pings from bullets shells ricocheted off the stagecoach near her head. Her heart plummeted, and she pulled inside.

The two older women screamed, crouching low, as did the elderly man seated beside her. Summer didn't dare risk sticking her head out again, but she couldn't bear not knowing what was happening. Three more shots rang out, closer this time. A blood-chilling death cry came from the driver as he fell from his high seat past the carriage window and hit the ground with a thud. She lost her breath. The stagecoach jerked unsteadily, rocking passengers to one side when a rear wheel rose off the ground.

"We ran over him," one of her elderly companions screamed.

Summer prayed for strength, then with shaky hands, pulled herself up and grabbed the door. Glancing out, six men on horseback rode toward them. They were some distance back, but gaining quickly as if the devil were on their heels. Red bandanas over the lower halves of their faces hid their identity.

One man remained on top of the coach. With the driver already down, the guard would need help controlling the team if he was to fight off bandits at the same time. Her chest tightened and she said a silent prayer. *Lord help us!*

On the floor, the wide-eyed passengers huddled together. They would be of no assistance. Without a second thought, Summer climbed out the window, clinging to the door. The vehicle swayed and she slipped. A small cry escaped from her throat.

"Summer? What are you doing?" Mrs. Whitaker wailed.

"Someone has to do something." Summer eased from her sitting position, then lost her hold on the door. With her heart pounding against her ribs, she slashed her hands through the air and tried to find something to grab onto. Another rifle fired, the bullet passed close to her head. The ground blurred beneath her and she screamed. Many hands grasped her feet, ankles, and skirt.

"Summer, you won't fall, we won't let you," Mrs. Whitaker shouted.

Summer braced her hands on the side of the coach and used all her strength to pull herself up to sit on the window's ledge. Snapping her head around, she looked over her shoulder. The bandits were closer. One hoisted a rifle to his shoulder and aimed. Summer gasped, and ducked. The bullet hit another mark and the lifeless guard fell from the driver's seat.

The horses raced out of control. A deep ache throbbed in her head. Someone must get hold of the reins and keep the coach from upsetting. If the bandits didn't kill them, an overturned coach could easily do the deed.

She glanced at the passengers and clenched her jaw. It was left to her to stop the runaway coach.

Oh, why didn't I take the train?

~ * ~

For about the hundredth time in the past hour, Jesse Slade flipped open his pocketwatch and checked the time. He switched his gaze up the road while stepping out of the depot. Waco was quiet that afternoon, which made watching for the stagecoach nerve wracking. Although he thought he was wasting his time out in the blistering heat, he'd support his fiancée, Violet, as they waited for her younger sister to arrive from Brownsville.

His gut twisted when he thought about Summer Bennett. That girl's name had always left a bad taste in his mouth. He loved the Bennett family as his own, but Summer had always been the burr under his saddle. The hotheaded little tomboy competed with him constantly, and ignoring her had been almost impossible since she'd followed him everywhere, like a love-struck child. He chuckled. Yet he knew love was not the true emotion, when all she wanted was to get him in trouble.

But that had been five years ago, and he hoped to see some change. According to Violet, her aunt ran the finest etiquette school for young ladies in Texas. She'd also told him Summer was reformed of her hellion ways. He'd believe it when he saw it.

He swiped the back of his sleeve across his sweaty brow before squinting up at the sun. The stagecoach was late, and according to the stationmaster inside the depot office, it was presumed missing. Letting out a deep groan, he rubbed his forehead. Time to break the bad news to Violet.

He hooked his thumbs in his belt loops and ambled over to where she stood on the boardwalk. He purposely kicked the heel of his boots in the dirt, creating a cloud of dust behind him. "Violet, honey…um…somethin's happened to the stagecoach."

Violet's head jerked his way. "What do you mean?"

"Well, accordin' to the telegraph, the stage checked in at Big Springs five hours ago. They should've arrived here on schedule." Jesse flipped open his pocketwatch and checked the time again, then looked back up the road. "They're an hour late."

Violet flexed her hands against her stomach while glancing up the street. "What is the depot going to do?"

"Don't you worry, honey. They'll send out the sheriff sooner or later."

"Oh, heavens. This isn't good. What are we going to do, Jesse? This is going to worry my parents, and Pa shouldn't have any extra stress right now."

He gave her an indulgent smile. Violet was the type who worried about everything. Yet, this time she had good cause. Through her fear, she still held herself straight, not a hair out of place, wearing a fresh, wrinkle-free gray dress. And she never,

ever spoke in anything but gentle tones. Why, even now when she was so obviously upset, she made her plea softly. Violet was the perfect model for all women--female through and through, a little woman he'd be right proud to come home to. Yes, she'd make a fitting wife.

Using his knuckle, he lifted her small chin and looked into her brown eyes. "Don't you worry none. If it'll make you feel better, I'll go out lookin' for her. The stagecoach can't be far from here. It's probably just a small delay. Maybe a wheel came loose or somethin'. I'll find her."

Violet's eyes pleaded with his. "Oh, Jesse, do you mind?"

He laughed heartily. "Why should I mind?"

She gave him a slight smile. "That's right. You do things like this all the time, and the townsfolk adore you. How could I forget Waco's hero?"

He laughed again. "Well, I wouldn't go that far." He touched his finger to the tip of her slightly freckled nose. "I'll be back soon. If your ma happens by, tell her the stagecoach had a broken wheel. There's no reason to worry your parents."

She nodded, still wringing her hands. "Jesse…let me remind you, Summer might not be happy to see you. In her last letter, she sounded extremely upset about our engagement."

Jesse pinched the bridge of his nose, releasing a deep sigh. "Yeah, I know. She still thinks I'm not good enough for you." His gaze met with hers. "It'll be like old times, won't it?"

"Just don't say anything to set her off. She'll receive a shock once she gets home and sees what's happened to Pa. I'd hate for anything else to disturb her."

That's true enough. A small twinge of pity ran through him at the thought of how Summer would react when she saw her father again. "I'll do my best, Violet, honey." He squeezed her shoulders in a reassuring motion.

Jesse strode to his horse, mounted and galloped away from the small chattering crowd assembled around the depot. He could tell by their wide-eyed expressions that they wondered what catastrophe had occurred to the delayed stagecoach. They probably also wondered why a Texas Ranger traveled out to meet it.

He rode hard, only stopping to drink from his canteen. His thoughts remained on the hardheaded tomboy whom he should have turned over his knee five years ago.

An unconscious smile stretched across his face. That girl could drive him crazy. If it hadn't been for Violet, he would've wrung Summer's skinny little neck long before now. Lord, those two sisters were as different as sweet lemonade and corn liquor.

As he guided his horse over a rise, a gunshot rang through the air. He reined to a stop. Another rifle fired. He kicked his heels into the animal's flanks and urged the horse forward in the direction of the sounds. Arriving at the top of the knoll, he saw the stagecoach--and the group of riders shooting at it.

His heart dropped as he withdrew his pistol. He spurred his horse into a hard gallop. Moving in close enough, he aimed and fired at the nearest rider. His shot rang true as the rider tumbled to the ground in a motionless heap. Jesse turned his attention to the coach. Oh, good heavens--was that a woman in the driver's seat fighting off the bandits as they swarmed the stagecoach? She aimed her rifle and shot, killing the bandit while holding onto the horse's reins.

Although he admired her courage, that confounded woman would get herself killed.

Another rider climbed on back of the vehicle. Terrified screams came from inside. Aiming, he fired. The bandit fell backward. Jesse looked at the woman driver. She'd just blown a hole through a man right next to her. The man's limp body hung halfway off the coach, smacking against the wheel before falling into the dust.

She pulled the team to a stop then swung her rifle around, aiming at anything that moved. Another rider approached, keeping hidden behind the conveyance. Jesse kicked his horse into action. She didn't realize she was about to be ambushed.

With deadly accuracy, Jesse aimed at the remaining bandit and pulled the trigger. The bandit howled and fell from his horse. Jesse rode up to him, dismounted, and grabbed the man's weapon.

When the sounds of gunfire and whining bullets ended, the passengers peeked out the window. The door opened. Two older women and an elderly gentleman hobbled out. The woman in the driver's seat climbed down and surveyed the damage, still swinging her rifle about. They all looked dazed, but unhurt.

Where was Violet's sister? His heart plummeted. Was she injured? Worse yet, could she have been killed in the shooting?

Jesse walked toward them, but as soon as he neared, the younger woman brought up her rifle, pointing it at his heart.

"Whoa." He raised his hands to let the little lady see he was no threat.

Her dress had been torn, and her shoulder was caked with blood. A purple goose egg knotted her forehead, surrounded by scratches. Her hair had lost most of its pins, and the small auburn knot hung limply on one shoulder.

He tipped his hat. "Ma'am, I'm not going to hurt you." His eyes strayed again to her wounded shoulder. "I've come to help."

She seemed to stagger a bit, and Jesse instinctively moved to help. Her rifle flew up, stopping him in his tracks. When her gaze rested on his silver Ranger's star, she sighed and lowered her gun.

"My prayers have been answered. Thank the good Lord you've come," she muttered before her eyes rolled back in her head and she crumpled to the ground.

Jesse rushed to her and scooped her into his arms as fast as lightning. "Someone give me somethin' to stop the bleedin'."

A silver-haired woman handed him a lacy handkerchief. "The poor brave little thing," she murmured. "I hope she isn't hurt badly."

"It's a good thing you showed up when you did, young man," said the elderly gentleman. "Those bandits killed the driver and guard. We would all be dead now if it wasn't for you."

"What do you mean by that?" demanded the silver-haired lady, directing her question to the elderly man as she poked him in the arm.

Jesse used the handkerchief to staunch the flow of blood from the young woman's shoulder, but it wasn't helping much. He wished the older couple would stop jabbering so he could ask about Summer Bennett.

"You know as well as I do Miss Bennett here saved us all," the elderly woman continued. "We owe her our lives."

Jesse's eyes widened as his attention lifted to the couple. He shook his head as if he hadn't heard correctly.

"All I know," continued the man, "is that I saw this young man shoot that bandit there." He motioned to the one still alive, although moaning and groaning. "I saw it with my own eyes. He saved us."

Jesse cleared his throat. "Excuse me. Did you say Miss Bennett? Would that be…Summer Bennett?"

"Why, yes," the woman asked. "Do you know her?"

He frowned. *Unfortunately, I do.* He looked down at the woman in his arms. Her hair unkempt, her clothes torn and disheveled--well, that certainly fit Summer Bennett. *But why is she wearing a dress?* Jesse had never in his life seen her in a dress. Well, not counting church, of course. But even then she would rush home and change back into trousers.

On closer inspection, he realized she didn't look anything like the tomboy he knew. Her hair was darker, and gone were the freckles that had once decorated her nose. Her eyelashes, dark and thick, were long, and the delicate shape of her mouth had a bewitching curve.

What was he thinking? This was Summer, for heaven's sake. But it just couldn't be.

"Miss Bennett saw them bandits kill the driver and that's when she climbed out the window and up to the driver's seat," informed the silver-haired lady.

"She did *what*?" Jesse's voice rose.

"Well, we couldn't see much from inside the coach, of course. But I saw one bandit ride up right beside us, climb up next to her, and oh! He hit her in the head with the butt of his rifle." The woman pulled herself straight and tall. "But of course, Miss Bennett shot him before he could do worse."

Worse? Jesse's jaw hardened and he ground his teeth. As he examined her head, anger welled within him like he hadn't experienced since the irritating girl left to go stay at her aunt's fancy school.

The older gentleman stepped forward, looped his thumbs around his suspenders and rocked back on his heels. "If she did kill that bandit, it was just a lucky shot. This fella here saved us. Why Miss Bennett's just a *girl*. We're all lucky that the Ranger came along when he did."

Jesse bit his lip to suppress a grin. Good thing Summer

was out cold. She wouldn't like to hear that. But one thing was certain, she was no longer just a *girl*. While she'd been away, she'd blossomed into a beautiful young lady.

"Oh, fiddlesticks," said the older lady. "If you ask me, I think she deserves a ree-ward. Why, she saved our lives."

Reward my foot. Jesse inwardly seethed. What she needed was a good tanning of her fanny, and he planned to see it carried through the minute she was well enough. Not only had she foolishly risked her own life, it appeared those years away at the school for young ladies hadn't done her a bit of good. Despite the dress and the woman's figure, she was still the little hellion he remembered. An injured hellion, he reminded himself as he looked from the bruise on her temple to her wounded shoulder.

He glanced at the group. "I need to get her to a doctor, quickly. Will you folks be all right until the sheriff comes?"

"Oh, yes-sirree. We'll tie up the low-life robbers that aren't dead, so there won't be no more problems."

Jesse carried Summer to his horse. With help from the others, he situated himself in the saddle and cradled her in his arms. As he rode away, one thing struck him as odd. Of course it'd been quite a while, but he didn't remember Summer feeling so soft and womanly. He'd grown up thinking of her as a tomboy, but with her snuggled comfortably on his lap, he knew she'd gone through some major changes.

Jesse distanced his mind from the feel of the female on his lap. He'd get her to the doctor, but what worried him most was her reaction when she regained consciousness. A wave of foreboding swept through him. Cursing inwardly, he shook his head. He'd bet his boots Summer Bennett would be fit to be tied when she found out who her rescuer was, and the resulting fireworks should be a sight to see.

He scowled. *It'd be just like old times.*

~ * ~

The cloud of darkness parted in Summer's mind, opening a small light of awareness. Every muscle in her body screamed in pain, and she clenched her jaw. But protective arms surrounded her, and the swaying motion let her know she was on a horse, curled against a firm body. The man's musky scent enveloped her. Comforted her.

As the fog lifted, she shifted closer, her hand resting on a solid chest. Gentle fingers stroked down the side of her cheek and she nuzzled closer. A sharp pain shot through her head, throbbing with every beat of her heart.

She groaned and forced her eyes open, squinting against the sun. The full brightness of a Texas autumn afternoon flowed around her. Her head pounded, but she struggled against the soreness and the fog in her brain. Suddenly, her memory came rushing back. The stagecoach, the bandits, and especially the archangel of mercy who had come to her rescue.

The Ranger must be the one holding me. She let her body relax against the contours of his hard muscled body. Not too often did she like being protected and cared for by a strong, virile man, but at the moment she was reluctant to break the spell.

She dared a peek at his face. His deep blue eyes grabbed her attention. Kind eyes. Sunlight glinted off the golden tones of his light brown hair, his thick mustache, and long sideburns. He must have sensed her watching, for his square jaw changed shape and a soft smile bracketed his mouth.

Handsome.

Yes, very handsome. She couldn't have dreamed a better vision of a hero, and dream it must be because things this good just didn't happen to Summer Bennett. Safety and security spread over her like a warm blanket and she melted against him, closing her eyes while his long fingers continued their tender exploration. It was the first time in her life she had allowed a man to touch her like that--a soft stroke, a gentle caress--and the first time she had ever really relaxed in a man's presence.

She sighed. *Wonderful.*

"How do you feel, Summer?"

The soft baritone voice rumbling in his chest seemed oddly familiar. Summer frowned and took a second peek at his hair, his mustache, that incredible mouth. He gave her a full smile. Awareness tugged at her memory and a large knot formed in the pit of her stomach. When recognition came, it struck like a thick piece of wood right between her eyes and ripped through every nerve in her body like venom from a rattlesnake bite.

She jerked, moving off the comfortable nest she had made of his chest. "Jesse Slade?"

A crafty smile claimed his face. "The one and only, darlin'."

She widened her eyes. "Darlin'? I'm not now, nor will I ever be your darling, Jesse Slade." She couldn't believe her rotten luck. Her temper snapped, and she fought to move from his grasp. She batted his hands away. "Get your hands off me."

"Be still Summer or--"

"Let me go," she demanded.

"Tarnation, Summer." His hands moved to her waist. "You're as slippery as a wet weasel."

"Quit touching me and put me down."

Although he held onto her, she managed to slither from the horse.

"Of all the confounded-stupid-female stunts." He pulled to a halt and dismounted.

The moment her feet touched the ground, dizziness overtook her and she plopped down on her bottom. When Jesse reached for her, she slapped at his hands.

She glanced up at him from her undignified position and clenched her teeth. "*You*. Of all people, it had to be you." Holding onto a stirrup, she pulled herself to her feet and gazed into the heavens. "Why Lord? Why me?"

"There's no need to get your feathers ruffled," he snipped, looking at the blood oozing from her shoulder wound. "Look what you've done. You're bleedin' again."

She glanced at her shoulder. It was worse than she thought, but she'd die before admitting it to him. She was *not* riding into town perched on Jesse's lap for everyone to see.

"It's just a scratch." She lifted her skirts, grabbed an edge of her petticoat and ripped off a piece. It was bad enough that he had to rescue her, but why in heaven's name did he have to look so gol-darned handsome? This certainly wasn't the skinny, ill-tempered Jesse Slade she remembered. Well, the ill-tempered part still fit.

Jesse stood by the horse, arms folded across his chest as he tapped his foot. She brought up the strip of fabric between her free hand and chin and awkwardly fashioned it around her shoulder. Her head pounded worse than ever. She kept on, but the makeshift bandage tore apart. Out the corner of her eye, a self-assured grin stretched across his mouth.

"Oohh." She stomped her foot, causing another throbbing burst of pain in her head.

"Would you like some help?" Jesse offered with a self-assured grin she'd liked to slap right off his face. She knew the man enjoyed every second of her struggle, but she just couldn't ask this arrogant no-good for help.

"Course, I'd have to touch you," he needled.

She tossed him a murderous glare, but he ignored her. She tore off another strip of petticoat and began again, but fared no better.

"Summer, if you'd just use your head for once, you'd admit you need help."

She scowled and tried to think of another solution, but nothing came to mind. It galled her, but plain and simple, he was right. She couldn't bandage her shoulder by herself. Letting out a sigh, she nodded.

Jesse took the flimsy strip of fabric and covered the wound while she stood stiff as a board. The enticing scent of cedar and leather emanated from his body and stirred flutters in her stomach. The gentle touch of his hands as he bandaged her shoulder sent warm tingles over her skin. Her chest constricted, making it difficult to breathe. When he stepped away, the feeling disappeared and she wanted to sigh with relief, but she didn't for fear he'd hear.

He smiled. "That wasn't so bad, was it?"

She inhaled deeply and gave him an indignant look. "Maybe not for you."

"I was just trying to help."

"After making my life miserable all these years, why do you want to help me now?"

A mocking grin touched his lips. "Well now, I couldn't just let you bleed to death, could I?"

"Don't tell me you've grown a conscience?" She brushed the dirt off her skirt.

His eyes twinkled. "Actually, I promised Violet I'd find you. When the stagecoach was late, we knew somethin' was wrong. After all, I had to rescue my future sister-in-law from harm."

Summer sucked in her breath. *Oh*! If not for her injured arm, she'd have socked the rotten polecat in the nose. "Well, you've found me, so go back and tell my sister I'm fine."

His smile faded. "You're not fine."

"I'm fine enough. Waco isn't that far. I'll walk the rest of the way. I'll not let the whole town think I've been rescued by the *great* Jesse Slade."

Another wicked smile tugged at his lips. "But I did rescue you, Summer."

She propped her hands on her hips. "You most certainly did not. You um…you just happened to arrive the exact moment I lost consciousness."

He sighed and tipped his hat back from his forehead. "Actually, the bullets from my gun dismounted three of the bandits."

She scowled. "I had things under control. Besides, I'm very capable of walking to town on my own now." She took several steps forward and dizziness blurred her vision. She swayed, and tilted toward the ground. Two strong arms grabbed her by the waist and pulled her upright.

"You bullheaded little twit. That does it." He picked her up and carried her to the horse, then let her feet drop to the ground and held her by her uninjured shoulder. "You ain't walkin'."

She slapped at his hand. "I'm not going into town with you."

"You're as ornery as an old mule." He paused, his heated gaze boring into hers. She didn't like the look. "You listen to me, Miss Persnickety. I don't care what you like or don't like, I'm takin' you to town."

"I--don't--like." She grinded her teeth with each word.

"To--damn--bad." He mocked her. "You have two choices. You can get on that horse willin'ly, or I'll hog-tie you and put you there myself."

Her mouth dropped open and her mind scrambled frantically for several seconds.

He produced a cocky grin. "Time's up."

Two

Jesse made Summer's options clear, but the stubborn twit just wouldn't listen.

He was an honorable man, and when he made a promise, he stuck to it. When he made a threat, it didn't matter what gender he threatened, he would not cower, especially before a female.

Horrified whispers and startled gasps from the townsfolk followed their progress as his horse plodded down Main Street. He didn't have the slightest twinge of guilt. He'd promised to deliver Summer Bennett to her sister, and he was going to do just that. Although, he hadn't originally counted on surrendering his package hog-tied.

She had left him no choice. Not surprisingly, she protested when he tied her hands and feet, but he quickly remedied that problem. Of course, she'd mumbled for quite awhile with his bandana stuck in her mouth, but eventually the ride into town became more tolerable. At least she sat atop the horse with a straight back and her chin raised in indignation.

"Well, here we are, darlin'." He exaggerated the endearment. "Home sweet home."

As he dismounted, her murderous scowl shot at him. Outwardly, Summer looked cold and rigid, but knowing her, inside she burned like the fires of Hell. Wisely, he kept his laughter to himself. After tying his horse to the hitching post, he glanced into her heated stare. He'd have to watch his back, because this little filly was already plotting revenge.

Nothing he couldn't handle, though.

He leaned back against the post and crossed his arms over his chest. What should he do with the little wildcat? No matter how much the thought of leaving her bound and gagged might appeal to him, he didn't have a choice. He had to untie her.

As he studied her, straddled across his horse in an undignified fashion, he once again took note of the major changes that had occurred since he saw her last. Curse his hide, but she actually looked like a female. She'd even made an effort to dress presentably, and it had almost worked.

Her little yellow jacket was torn, and the brown skirt was now a tattered rag, trailing a scrap of petticoat underneath. The once fancy hairdo had fallen to become nothing but unmanageable tangles framing her face. The poor thing was as dirty and scratched as an orphan.

He shook his head. What a mess.

Muffled noises came from the irritated woman as she did her best to wiggle out of the ropes. Chuckling, he straightened and stepped over to his horse, staring up into her angry hazel eyes.

"If you promise to be a good girl, I'll untie you."

Her eyes widened as she nodded in desperate appeal.

"Your sister's over yonder somewhere. I'm sure she won't appreciate seeing her sister all tied up."

Summer agreed with another nod.

"It's nice to see your aunt was able to teach you how to act like a female." He untied her feet, then lifted her off the horse and set her on the ground. "We'll get along a lot better now that you've learned how to cooperate," he added as he released her hands.

Immediately, she ripped the gag from her mouth and kicked him hard in the shin.

"Ouch!" He hopped around on one foot. "Why you li'l--"

"...scum-sucking, mule-headed, son of a motherless...goat," she screamed.

He drew a deep breath and calmed his temper as he tested his leg. "I suggest you quiet down, Summer. If you haven't noticed, you've drawn a crowd."

"Me?" she yelled. "Why, I haven't done a doggone thing."

"Unless, you want the whole town knowin' you're a shrew, you'd better simmer your boilin' kettle."

She hardened her jaw and turned her head, looking toward the curious spectators crowding the boardwalk. Huffing, she crossed her arms over her chest. She pretended to ignore him, but he could tell she secretly watched him tend the horse. Out of the corner of his eye, he noticed her gaze skim over his braced legs, down his thighs. When he wound the dusty rope he'd used to tie her hands, her attention switched to his long sleeved russet shirt that pulled tightly across his upper arms and chest.

He held himself from grinning openly. His appearance must have sparked an interest in the li'l filly. Of course, he'd changed quite a bit since she'd last seen him.

Off in the distance Summer's name rang out, which took her gaze away from him and toward the middle of the street. He wished her attention still roamed over him. The little tomboy looked at him as if he were a real man. She'd never done that before...and why hadn't Violet ever looked at him that way?

Summer snuffed her anger when she heard her sister. Jesse watched her scan the streets, finally seeing the newly built stores along the boardwalk with wide curious eyes. Things had really changed in Waco since she was a li'l tomboy running around giving him trouble. There were more houses and certainly more people.

When she saw her sister, she clapped her hands together. "Violet," she cried joyfully, stretching out her arms as her older sister ran to her.

"Thank the good Lord." Violet kissed Summer's cheek, then pulled back slightly. "Look at you. Gracious, you've grown into a woman...and you're wearing a dress."

"And you're pretty as spring flowers, just like always."

Violet laughed and hugged her sister again. "Did my eyes deceive me or did I see you tied up a few minutes ago?"

Summer glared accusingly at Jesse. "Yes, you could say I was embarrassingly affixed to the horse, thanks to your *fiancé*."

Violet propped her hands on her slim hips. "Why, Jesse Slade. I can't believe you'd do such a thing."

Jesse pushed his hat off his forehead. "Well, now, your sister wouldn't listen--"

Summer sobered her expression. "Violet, you can't be serious about marrying this in-bred cowboy. Why, he had absolutely no concern for my welfare and tied me up like some pig to be slaughtered. He has no manners at all."

Violet gave Jesse a reproachful look. "Jesse Slade? Do

you have an explanation?"

He glanced at his sweet Violet and his anger cooled slightly. "My dear, we'll talk about that later. Right now we need to get your sister over to Doc Gill."

Summer's wounds finally captured Violet's attention, and she sucked in her breath, her hand flying to her chest. "Let me have a look at you." Her gaze travled over Summer.

"I'm fine, really."

"Jesse is right." Violet's arm linked around Summer's waist for support and walked toward the doctor's office. "What in heaven's name happened to you?"

Jesse cut in, "She--"

"You, stay out of this," Summer warned, sending him a glare over her shoulder. "I'll tell the story."

Jesse shrugged and fell into step behind the girls.

"You tell me exactly what happened, dear Summer," Violet commanded in a sweet tone.

Summer's gaze flew back to her sister. "It was just the most frightening experience of my life," she began dramatically as they continued to walk. "Gunshots came from everywhere it seemed, and suddenly the driver was shot dead and fell from the stagecoach."

Violet gasped. "Oh, my."

"The bandits popped shots at us right and left and we dodged bullets to keep from being killed. Then…"

Jesse rolled his eyes as he listened to Summer's rendition of the story. The woman jabbered like a magpie, only pausing long enough to take a deep breath now and again. But he couldn't seem to keep his eyes off the gentle sway of her crooked bustle. *Mercy*!

"Once I slowed the coach, I noticed the rifle by my feet. By this time, the bandits were upon us, so I grabbed the gun and fired," Summer continued.

"Don't forget the part about your head," Jesse interjected.

She shot him another piercing glare over her shoulder. "Well, you see, I was busy shooting bandits and didn't notice one climbing up next to me. He took his rifle and hit me in the head."

Violet inhaled deeply. "Oh, gracious, no."

Jesse chuckled. "Yeah, I bet it really rung your bell, Summer."

Once again, Summer treated him to one of her glares, then turned back to her sister. "Yes, it hurt, but I shot the man right in the heart before he could do worse. Within minutes, I had all six of the bandits lying on the ground."

Jesse loudly cleared his throat, getting her attention. She rolled her eyes. "Jesse arrived at the scene just at the right time and helped with disarming the bandits."

He continued to listen to the story in disgust. Why, the little minx made it sound like an adventure. Didn't she realize she could've been seriously injured?

Violet's eyes widened. "Did you kill them all?"

"Only a few. I think the others were just knocked unconscious from the fall."

"Oh, Summer. You're so brave." Violet hugged her sister again.

It was hard for Jesse to hold his tongue while Summer hammed it up for Violet, boasting like a peacock fanning its feathers. But listening to her made him think, and as he seriously considered what had happened, his annoyance evaporated. Maybe she did deserve a little praise. Given the circumstances, she'd had little choice than to do what she did. But he still didn't like the idea of the fool woman pulling such a dangerous stunt.

He shook his head. Who else but Summer Bennett would put herself in such a life-threatening situation?

Jesse opened the door to the doctor's office and ushered the girls inside. "I'll be waitin' for you across the street at the Low Down Saloon," he said, but the sisters were so involved in conversation he doubted they even heard.

He crossed the street and entered the drinking establishment.

"Afternoon, Slade," Parley Cyrus, the owner of the saloon greeted. "Do ya want yer usual?"

"No. Promised Violet I'd quit drinkin'."

Parley shook his head. "What men will do fer their women is beyond me." He paused. "Ya don't look so hot, there." Jesse took off his Stetson and swiped his fingers through his thick hair. Setting the hat on the counter, he leaned his hip against the bar. "It's been one confusin' day."

"Saw ya high-tailin' it out'a town earlier."

Jesse nodded. "The stagecoach was robbed." He paused, held up a hand then corrected, "Actually, almost robbed."

Parley smiled wide, showing his crusty brown teeth. "Done it again, didn't ya, Slade?"

"No, Cyrus, I didn't." Jesse glanced briefly out the window toward the doctor's office across the street.

"Ya didn't? Then who did?"

"Miss Summer Bennett."

A cynical expression crossed Parley's face, then humor struck. "Ya mean Marv Bennett's little girl?"

"Yes, the same."

"Has she come back from that uppity town down South?"

"Yes. Went to collect her at the stagecoach. Of course, that's when I found out she'd disarmed most of the bandits herself." Then he added with a low mumble, "The little fool."

Parley laughed. "Well I'll be. Why, that young'un hasn't changed a bit."

Feeling reluctant to describe just how much the young'un had changed, Jesse leaned his elbow against the bar and went back to staring out the window. The sensations his body had experienced from her curves pressed against him still tingled. Yes, Summer had indeed changed, and in more ways than one. He wasn't exactly sure if he liked it or not.

~ * ~

Summer frowned. Forced to stand and watch Jesse place a kiss on Violet's cheek before helping her up into the family's buckboard, Summer bunched her hands into fists. He turned to her, fidgeted as if wondering where to put his hands, then throwing caution to the wind, nearly squeezed the loving life out of her before plunking her bottom on the seat next to Violet. A pain shot through her shoulder and she grimaced. She glared at him as he climbed aboard.

"So, what did Doc say?" he asked as he slapped the reins. The horses took off toward the outskirts of town.

Summer sat up straight, smoothing the wrinkles on her dress. "It surprised the doctor that a woman of my delicate nature could have accomplished such a feat. Under the circumstances, he thinks my shoulder and head look pretty darn good."

"Delicate nature?" Jesse huffed under his breath.

Violet nudged him with her elbow.

"What?" Summer asked, but got no reply.

Violet squeezed his arm. "Doc Gill bandaged Summer's shoulder, and gave her some ointment for her wound."

Jesse glanced down at Violet, a smile tugging on his lips.

Summer boiled, watching the affectionate glances they exchanged. If it was the last thing she ever did, she would put a stop to this marriage. Anyone with half a brain could see they were a disastrous match. Why, it looked as if Violet had ganged up against her own sister just to please the lout.

As they passed through town, Summer noticed a number of new businesses: a hotel, butcher shop, barber shop, drug store, law office, several other stores and a newspaper office, and newly built saloons. The town had even refurbished the boardwalks and hitching posts.

She kept her eyes straight ahead and ignored her sister and Jesse, but now she had a moment to think, she found it strange that her mother and father hadn't come to greet her. After all, the house was just at the edge of town.

Jesse and Violet remained conspicuously quiet during the ride, Violet's forehead furrowed in thought. Jesse whistled an irritating tune off-key that drove Summer insane.

"Violet? Why didn't Ma and Pa come to get me?" she asked.

Her sister's head snapped toward Jesse, giving him an apprehensive look. He stopped whistling.

Something was very wrong.

"All right you two. Why are you acting strange?"

Violet sighed. "Summer, we need to prepare you for something before we reach home."

"Prepare me for what?"

"It's Pa." Violet's voice shook.

Summer's heart clenched. "What's wrong with him?"

"Six months ago, Pa fell from the hayloft. It damaged his legs, and he hasn't been able to walk since." Tears gathered in Violet's eyes. "He's lost a lot of weight. You won't recognize him. It's been bad. The livery's gone down hill. It's all we can do to survive. Jesse has been helping out when he can, but he just doesn't have time."

Summer breathed slower, trying to maintain the panic welling up inside her chest. "Why didn't anyone tell me before now?"

Violet shook her head. "I'm sorry. I know this is a shock, but there was nothing you could do so far away. We didn't want to worry you needlessly."

Summer took hold of her sister's hands. "Needlessly? But it's not needlessly. I could have come home and ran the livery."

Tears gathered in Violet's eyes. She lowered her head.

"Summer, your ma didn't want us to say anythin'," Jesse continued. "She knew you didn't have much time left at school, so she and your brothers and sisters did all they could to make things work."

Summer harrumphed in irritation. "How much are we set back?"

Violet shrugged. "The bank hasn't threatened foreclosure yet, but Pa's worried they'll call in a note for the property soon."

Summer's throat constricted and pain rushed to her chest, making breathing difficult. "Well, now I'm back, and I won't let that happen. The bank will *not* foreclose on Pa's livery."

Violet patted Summer's hand. "I knew you'd be strong about this, and you wouldn't let us down."

Summer's gut twisted. The reality of her father's business going under--confronted with the possibility of losing everything--left her in a state of shock. Suffocation swarmed through her lungs, threatening to stop her breathing completely. If she'd known sooner, maybe she could've done something.

"Ma! Pa! She's home!"

Dragged from thought by a familiar voice, she glanced up. Her two younger brothers dashed out the front door, followed by two younger sisters and her mother. Summer put aside her concern for her father momentarily and joined the joyous reunion.

She scanned the yard, the house. *Home.*

The old elm tree she'd climbed as a kid still stood guard over the front yard, and the two-story house looked as if it had been freshly white-washed. Windows sparkled against the sun, and a rainbow of flowers in the planter below the porch enlivened the entry and calmed her spirit.

Everything was exactly as she remembered.

Jesse pulled the team to a stop and set the brake as Nate, her twelve-year-old brother, halted just below her. She smiled down at him as his gaze combed over her in confusion.

"I don't believe what I'm seeing. Summer, you're wearing a dress."

She glanced at her youngest brother, Charles, standing behind Nate, and she nearly laughed at their awestruck faces. Her younger sister, Elizabeth, just two years younger than she, looked as pretty as Violet, and Emily at age fourteen, held that awkward gangly look, all arms and legs--with ponytails. Lillian Bennett pushed through her brood and looked up at her daughter.

"Well, I'll be." Lillian smiled. "I think you better tell us what happened with our little tomboy."

Summer laughed. "Aunt Lydia buried that ruffian back in Brownsville."

Lillian clapped her hands joyfully. "Oh, thank the good Lord."

Jesse helped Summer down from the wagon. Lillian gathered her daughter in her arms. They held each other for long moments, then Lillian pulled back, holding Summer at arm's length.

Ma hadn't changed. Still short, plump, and healthy looking. Her brown eyes sparkled with love as they gazed into Summer's. The only thing different was a few more strands of gray hair in the auburn knot at the back of her head. Most certainly from the stress of caring for Pa.

Ma smiled. "Welcome home, sweetheart."

"Oh, Ma. It's good to be home."

She lifted her head to see her brothers and sisters waiting for their chance to hug her.

Nate grabbed hold of her first. "Welcome home, Sis."

She cupped his face in her hands. "Look at how you've grown. You're at least six inches taller. So close to becoming a full-grown man. And what's this?" She rubbed her hands over his smooth cheeks. "A beard coming in?"

"Not yet, but I'm trying." He laughed. When he looked at her chest, his cheeks pinked. "You ain't exactly what I remember either."

Everyone else suddenly bombarded her and she had an

attack of the giggles. "Let me look at all of you.""

Both Elizabeth and Emily had Pa's dark hair, and Nate resembled Charles with cinnamon colors in his hair. Summer smiled as she hugged Charles. He certainly wasn't the crying little five-year-old she remembered. In fact, his ten-year-old body was too heavy for her to pick up.

Worry creased young Charles' brow. "Does this mean you ain't gonna play leap frog with us anymore?"

Summer bent and tousled his hair. "Well, if I can still fit into my britches, you bet, tiger."

"How 'bout sling-shot and fishin'?"

She tilted her head and grinned. "You just try and stop me."

After completing the round of hugs and compulsory teasing, Summer faced her mother. "Ma, where's Pa?"

The happy expression on Lillian's face wavered. "He's waiting for you in the parlor, dear."

Summer entered the house and familiar smells brought back a flood of memories. The nostalgic scent of Pa's pipe overwhelmed her with the homesickness she suffered when she first left home. She glanced across the hall to the parlor. The faded yellow curtains and the well-worn brown carpet brought comforting reminders of cold winter evenings when the whole family gathered by the fire.

Pa sat in his favorite over-stuffed chair, facing the hearth with his back to her. She could see that his grayish-black hair had thinned, leaving a bare spot on the top of his head. And as Violet and Jesse had warned, each leg was strapped with leather braces. Her heart pounded as she stepped into the room.

"Pa?"

"I'm here, Summer."

She ran to the front of his chair and knelt at his feet. "Oh, Papa, what happened to you?"

Marvin Bennett touched her cheek lovingly. "My dear, sweet, Summer. Come, give me a hug."

She lifted and embraced him.

"My little girl's finally home. I've missed you so."

"Oh, Papa, why didn't you send word that you needed my help?"

30

He gazed into her eyes. "Now, what good would that have done?" He patted her hand. "Let me look at you."

She smiled, then stood and did a little pirouette.

His brows creased. "Why are you wearing a dress, but still look as if you've been climbing trees?"

A laugh escaped her throat. "I had a heck of a time getting here, Pa."

"Tell me all about it."

The family gathered in the living room and Summer retold her story. For her father, she covered her worry and made her tale humorous. As she talked and joked with her brothers and sisters, her gaze wandered to the man who had set off her temper this morning. Jesse sat next to Violet with his arm casually resting on the back of her chair. His attention focused on Summer while a strange expression touched his face.

Out of all the people in the room, Jesse had changed the most. But it struck her odd to think of him as handsome, so muscular, so much more a man. And she didn't even mind the mustache. Her mind quickly brought back the image of him tying the horse to the hitching post earlier today. His clothes practically strained across the cords of his muscles.

She mentally shook out her thoughts and tried to think negatively.

She didn't have to work hard to assess his faults. For one, she didn't like the way he treated Pa. Instead of trying to pamper and care for him, Jesse's lazy, good-for-nothing backside melted to the chair as he allowed her ma to run her legs ragged. He even had the nerve to argue with Pa--though it was all in fun. She reminded herself to bring this flaw to Violet's attention. If Jesse truly cared for Pa, he wouldn't act like this.

The day passed slowly, and luckily her ma didn't need much help which gave her time to spend with her father. They talked about the business and he explained the new changes recently made to the livery stable before the accident.

"I'll get right to work tomorrow morning, Pa."

Marvin chuckled. "Oh, no, you won't. I'll not have you turning into a boy now you're home. I like seeing you in those dresses too much. Besides, you're at the age where courtship and marriage should be on your mind. If you go back to your boyish ways, I'm afraid we'll never get you married."

Summer laughed as she circled her arms around his shoulders. She rested the side of her face on his thin shoulder. "I haven't been back for very long and already you're trying to get rid of me."

"No, Summer. If I had my way, you'd never get married. I would keep you by my side as a little girl, forever."

Tears sprang to her eyes, and she struggled to hold them back. "I would like that very much."

"It's enough you're here with me now." He turned his head and kissed her cheek. "Besides, we'll make do in the livery. We've been doing just fine since the accident."

Summer held him tightly, knowing he was fibbing to her. She had missed him so much her whole body ached. He couldn't be crippled. He was too young, and his family needed him.

She didn't want her father to see her cry, but she was on the edge of tears and couldn't hold them back any longer. "I see my trunks are here, so I'd better go unpack."

She kissed her father quickly and ran upstairs to her room. When she reached her bed, she fell upon her pillow and let her tears flow freely. She lay for some time thinking about her father's accident and how the family would manage without his strength. Why would the Lord let this happen to their family, especially to a man who'd been so full of life? Answers didn't come right away, and while she cried, she noticed the frilly pink and yellow daisy bedspread. In spite of her disheartened mood, she smiled. She used to hate this particular cover because of the feminine colors, but now it actually appealed to her.

As she ran the fingers of one hand over the patchwork and dried her tears with the other, peacefulness settled over her. For five years, she'd shared a room with two other girls at the school, but now she would have her privacy.

Everything in her room was the way she'd left it--except maybe cleaner. The unused vanity Pa had purchased several years back, with hair brushes, ribbons, and perfumes beckoning her to make use of them.

She moved off the bed and stepped to the table. Her reflection shone back from the mirror and she nearly fell over. She looked horrid. Her clothes were torn, her face splotched with dirt, and matted hair framed her head. Since her brothers had brought up her trunks, she quickly unpacked. Nate and Charles hauled up some hot water for her to bathe in, and she spent the next little while tidying her appearance.

Within an hour, Summer pulled on the rose dress her aunt made for her over her freshly washed hair. She tugged it down over her hips and settled the bustle in place. Her fingertips traced the white lace around the neckline, stitching carefully sewn by her aunt Lydia who made certain it was perfect. Glancing into the mirror, she turned side to side and realized she looked like the lady her aunt had worked so hard at creating. She lifted the silver brush off the vanity table and pulled it through her hair, taking care not to touch the bump on the side of her head. Instead of the respectable bun, she arranged her hair by pulling back the sides and tying it with a rose-colored ribbon.

Summer approved of her new look, but still harbored the fear of dissatisfying her pa. She didn't want to fail him in any way, especially now. When she envisioned him downstairs, helplessness swept over her and her buoyant spirit faded. Moving to the window, she stared at the back lawn as her mind scrambled to think of a way to help.

According to Pa, he didn't need her at the livery stable, but Violet's opinion was different. Pa wasn't going to confess how bad business was, and she knew it was left up to her to straighten things out. Violet had never helped in the stable, and although Nate was getting older, he still couldn't do it all. Aunt Lydia had taught her bookkeeping, and the livery stable was in great need of an efficient hand--perhaps even a woman's touch. Of course, it meant forgetting most of the etiquette her aunt had drilled into her, but she didn't really want to go back to her tomboy ways. Not when wearing dresses made her feel pretty--like a lady. Perhaps she could do both. She could show Nate and Charles the necessities, and at the same time, work in the office and do the books. She could wear her pretty dresses in her pa's office.

With her mind made up and a good attitude about her future, she descended the stairs. Near the bottom, she found Pa trying to move from his chair to the roller-chair. His grunts and groans magnified the supreme effort it took. Her stomach churned at the sounds of him gasping for breath as he fell into the roller-chair.

"Marvin, we need to get you to bed so you can rest," Ma spoke softly.

Summer reached the bottom step and peeked into the room. Ma hovered over Pa, his weary hands drooping from fatigue.

Agony stabbed at her heart, and her eyes again blurred with tears. She couldn't watch anymore. She escaped through the kitchen past Jesse and Violet and out the back door before letting go of her emotions.

~ * ~

Jesse frowned as Summer whirled through the kitchen in a fit of anguish, her face drawn in grief. His heart went out to her. He stood at the sink basin next to Violet as he helped wash the vegetables. Not very often did he help, but Violet wanted everything special for Summer's homecoming dinner.

Violetturned to him, her forehead creased. "Jesse? Would you go talk to her? She needs some reassurance."

Panicked, he widened his eyes. "Me? She's not goin' to hear anythin' I have to say."

Violet touched his arm gently. "Summer's had quite an upset," she continued in softer tones, "and you're the only one free to talk to her at the moment. I'm about ready to put the kettle on."

"Where are your sisters? Your brothers are due back from the stable any minute. Can't we wait for them?"

"Jesse, she needs somebody now."

"But, she…I…we can't talk." His mind scrambled to think of a way out. "All we ever do is argue."

The corners of her mouth lifted into a grin. "Then it's time the two of you settled your differences. I don't want you constantly at each other's throats once we're married."

Jesse silently cursed, then stormed out the room. Women! Why did men fall all over themselves to please the fillies? The reason was beyond him. He understood Summer's turmoil, though. It tore at his heart to watch the man he loved like a father wither before his eyes, and feeling helpless wasn't his idea of aiding the man he idolized. True, he could ride with the Rangers and capture outlaws, but he couldn't do one thing to help Marvin.

Jesse slowed his progression when he caught sight of

Summer sitting in her childhood swing, staring up into the tall elm tree. As he studied her attire, he shook his head in disbelief. The rose-colored dress made her look prettier than a flower, and the sunlight gave her hair a reddish tint. He scratched his chin. Why in the hell was he noticing things like that? If someone asked him now what Violet was wearing, he didn't think he could answer.

But no matter what she looked like, Summer was the same disagreeable pain-in-the-rear she'd always been.

Still, she did look pretty against the sunset's backdrop. She'd left her hair long, hanging down with the sides pulled away from her face, and suddenly his fingers itched to feel the texture against his skin. Would it be as silky as it appeared?

Then he caught the drift of his inappropriate thinking. This was Summer, and he was engaged to her sister. Shame on him!

Through the calm evening, a small wind rustled through the canopied branches--only chirping insects interrupting the evening's silence. Yet, there was an unsettling in his heart that wasn't contributed to heartburn this time.

As he neared, she swung her head around and met his gaze. When she lifted her hazel eyes filled with unshed tears on him, he came to a halt. Her look of anguish pierced straight through him.

As a sign of truce, he gave her a smile. "Thought I might find you out here."

"Why? Is supper ready?" she snapped.

He sighed heavily, knowing whatever he did or said, he always brought out the worst in her. "No, not yet. Figured you might want some company."

A frown touched her mouth. "Well, you're wrong." She turned away.

Jesse stopped near the swing and shoved his hands in his pockets, watching as she battled with her emotions. She turned her head away, but he detected a shimmer of tears in her eyes. He leaned against the trunk of the tree. Within a few minutes, her ragged breathing eased.

"What are we going to do?" she whispered. "Do you know how hard it is to see Pa like this? He can't even move from one chair to the other."

"Your pa's a stubborn man. He'll soon be movin' better with his arms than he's ever done before."

"It's just so hard." Her voice cracked. "It's hard to see him so helpless."

Jesse wasn't used to comforting a woman, not even Violet, and so he didn't know what to do with her. He reached out and gently touched her shoulder, and she stood and launched herself into his arms. He sucked in a breath.

Kinda nice holding her when she wasn't kicking and screaming.

"Why did the Lord do this to him?" she asked.

"He didn't do anythin', darlin'. Your father just had an accident."

"But I want him back the way he was."

"So do I, darlin'. So do I."

Jesse tightened his hold and caressed her hair; silky as he had imagined it would be. A lump formed in his throat as he shared Summer's agony.

The more he stroked her hair, the more her body relaxed. Finally, she lifted her head and gazed into his face.

"Thank you, Jesse."

"For what?"

"For loving Pa."

He smiled. "I can't help it. He's like my own pa."

Her forehead burrowed. "I know I've never asked this, but where are your folks?"

He shrugged, and wiped away a tear from her cheek with the pad of his thumb. "My ma died when I was a baby, and since I never knew my pa, my older brother watched over me."

The warmth of her skin blended into his hand and set shivers down his spine. Her eyes widened and she stepped away. *Did she feel it, too?*

"Are you talking about Clint?" she asked.

"Yes, Clint, but he's nothin' like Marvin. Me and Clint have been through a lot, but I'll never forget the time I met your pa."

"You had a hard childhood. I'm sorry, Jesse."

"I'm not. Comin' here was the best thing that ever happened to us." He smiled wider. "Your pa treats me like one of his own sons."

"Pa loves you very much."

Jesse was touched by Summer's comment, but before he let sentimental emotion take him, he stepped back into the shadows. "I better go see how supper's comin', and if Violet needs any help."

"Jesse?"

He stopped and turned. "Yes?"

She shyly looked down at her hands. He wasn't used to her acting so reserved.

"I never did get the chance to congratulate you on becoming a Ranger. I'm certain it made Clint proud to have you working next to him."

Jesse chuckled. "Actually, I see less of my brother than before. Texas is a large state, and the gov'nor has Clint runnin' all over the place. Luckily, I've been assigned to stay around here."

Her smile returned. "So, how is that handsome brother of yours? Is Clint married yet?"

Jesse let out a bark of laughter. "No. I'm not even sure he's given his heart to anyone."

"How old is he?"

"He's five years older than me, so he's thirty-three."

"That's not too old."

"No. He's still in the prime of his life."

A tomblike silence fell upon them. Now his body was no longer pressed against the unsettling warmth of hers, he was again able to think clearly. One question prodded him--why in the world were they being nice to each other? The pleasant expression on her face proved she was up to something.

"When are you and Violet getting married?" Her sweet voice purred, which confirmed his suspicions. She was putting on some kind of show.

"We really haven't decided. Violet changes the date as often as she changes her bonnet. She's funny that way."

"Do you plan on fixing that flaw?"

He shrugged. "Only if I can."

Off in the distance, Violet's voice rang through the air, calling them to supper.

"Well, I guess we better go." He turned to leave, but

Summer stopped him by touching his arm.

"Jesse? Thank you for everything."

"Sure, darlin'."

"It was nice talking to you. I don't think we've ever really carried on a decent conversation before."

"No. Not unless it consisted of yellin' and name callin'."

She laughed lightly. "That's true. I was rotten back then, wasn't I?"

He moved closer and gently touched his finger to her nose. "You've changed into a lovely young lady, but there's still a childlike stubbornness to you."

"Yes, you're right." She paused for only a moment. "It's like I told my aunt before I left to come home, if I'm ever challenged to a sling-shot game, I'll not turn it down. Although I'm trying to become a lady, I still miss the games I used to play."

"Then, how about havin' one sometime?"

Her eyes widened. "A sling-shot competition?"

"Sure, that or any kind of competition."

Mixed emotions crossed her features, then she stood straight and lifted her chin a notch higher. "Name the place. I'll compete with you anywhere, doing anything you like."

It surprised him to see such confidence. Now he couldn't wait to prove her unequal to the challenge.

Three

Summer sat in the parlor receiving a horde of guests the next morning. The grandfather clock in the hallway rang ten times. Ten o'clock. The day was still early to get to the stable--if only her guests would leave. But she was happy to see the elderly passengers from the stagecoach. It thrilled her that they'd given her their thanks and praise. In fact, the whole town had heard about her bravery. Even the sheriff presented her with a small reward. When he patted her injured shoulder, she winced, but kept a smile on her face.

She glanced down at the fist full of coins. "Oh, my goodness, Sheriff. I didn't expect this."

"Well, Summer, you deserve it. We're all mighty grateful to you for what you did."

Summer smiled shyly, but the attention gave her ego a significant boost.

The last of her visitors walked out the front door shortly before noon. With a sigh of relief, she scurried up the stairs to her room. She found her boy's trousers in the bottom of one of her drawers. It had been a while since she was in the stable, and when she thought about getting back to her duties, anticipation hammered through her heart.

She slipped into her worn blue britches from five years ago, almost couln't close the buttons together. When she tried buttoning up her faded red shirt, she giggled over the way the fabric stretched tight across her bosom. This was certainly indecent, but she couldn't very well go to the stables to clean wearing a dress.

Forgetting the ladylike manners her aunt had drilled into her, she flew down the back staircase and out the door, running all the way to the livery stable. She enjoyed the freedom of her unbound hair as it flapped against her neck and back. She stopped when she came to the front of the stable. The chipped red paint on the barn aged the structure, but it still stood larger than life. A wooden sign painted in black letters hung high above the hay port: BENNETT'S LIVERY, HORSES BOARDED & BEDDED, RIGS FOR RENT.

Her heart ached from the years she'd missed away from the stable. But she was home now--and she'd make everything right.

She opened the front doors and peered inside. The barn reminded her of a tunnel, dark and cold, yet bright at both ends. When she walked inside, the horses' neighs welcomed her and brought her attention around. She hurried over to the animal's stall and smiled at Buck, her favorite of the boarded horses. The black stallion was tall, fifteen two, broad chested, and snip nosed. She reached up to stroke his mane.

"Hello, Buck, I've missed you so."

She buried her face against his neck. Buck nuzzled her with his nose and sighed aloud. *Yes, I've certainly missed this.* Tearing herself away from the horse, she stepped into her pa's office and picked up the ankle-length, brown leather apron hanging on the wall, then wrapped it around her waist. Now, where should she start?

The brightness from the morning sun shone through the dirty small paned windows, lighting the east side of the barn. Despite the obvious changes, things still seemed the same. Running her fingers over the roll-top desk, she noticed how scarred and rickety looking the drawers were from hard use. The room was cluttered with bridle rings, horseshoe nails, snaffle bits, horse liniment, and tack hammers. Years of use had worn the varnish from the back and arms of the chair. To the right of the desk sat a potbelly stove just as dusty as the rest of the office.

She let out a heavy sigh. So much work.

Deciding her first order of business should be dusting, she found an old rag and moved around the office swinging the cloth through the air, creating a dust storm. She sneezed, but continued wiping until the office looked halfway presentable, then realized it was going to be dusty no matter what she tried to do. This was Waco, for heaven's sake.

From out in the stable, Buck snorted again, and she wished she had the time to take him for a ride. It'd been so long. She glanced over at the animal and smiled. "You'll get your turn, don't worry."

The fast pace of shuffling feet stopped her. "Hello? Is anybody here?" somebody called out.

In hopes of helping her first customer, she ran to the front of the barn. When she rested her eyes on Jesse Slade, her enthusiasm dropped and her temper lifted a notch. She hadn't forgotten the way he brought her into town, and she wasn't about to back down from his bullying tactics. She had no idea why she was so soft on him last night by the tree, but she vowed *that* would never happen again. Just because she was a woman didn't mean she needed him…and she'd prove it. And just because he'd been nice to her last evening, didn't mean she'd changed her mind about him. He still wasn't good enough for her sister--and especially to be part of her family.

His gaze skimmed up and down her length. A lazy smile touched his mouth.

"Oh, it's you," he said.

She plopped her hands on her hips. "Of course it's me. Who else would it be?"

He leaned back against the wall, crossing one ankle over the other. He looked mighty handsome today, wearing the deep brown Ranger pants that perfectly hugged his legs. His beige shirt and leather brown vest molded over his chest, outlining his muscular torso. Her heart fluttered. It dawned on her this was hardly the reaction she wanted if she intended to make her dislike for him obvious.

He tipped his silver-belly Stetson to the back on his head. "Do you need any help? Since it's your first day back, I figured you'd need an extra pair of hands."

"Well, you figured wrong. I can handle things just fine."

He nodded. "How about takin' the horses out to be exercised?"

She shrugged. "Since there are only two horses today, I'll be all right."

"But, it'll be easier if I helped," he said with a smile.

"Jesse, don't you have anything better to do today besides

antagonize me? Have you forgotten I won't take that kind of treatment from you?"

He chuckled and rubbed his forehead. "How can I forget? My noggin was your favorite target to unleash your frustrations on when you used your slingshot to talk."

She couldn't help it--laughter erupted from her. She quickly covered her mouth to hide the mistake. Ladies weren't supposed to laugh so boisterously.

He shook his head. "Give it up, Summer. You don't need to be fussy around me. You can laugh out loud if you want."

"Yes, but I'm a lady now, and I'm supposed to remember my manners."

He grinned. "Didn't know you had any."

She lifted her brows. "Are you trying to provoke me?"

"It'd be like old times, wouldn't it?"

She studied his teasing grin. For some reason, the polite man she talked with last night had disappeared, replaced with the Jesse she used to know. This Jesse Slade she could handle.

"Jesse? Other than arguing with me and driving me to distraction, why are you really here?"

"I just want to help. Is that so hard to believe?"

"Yes."

"Why?"

"Because I know better."

He shrugged. "Fine, then. I came here to welcome you back home and…and to let you know how much I think you've changed."

Her brows shot up in surprise. "Did Violet put you up to this?"

He laughed. "No, not really. It's just a shock to see you all grown up."

"I wasn't certain you'd noticed."

"'Course, I noticed, and I'm not the only man noticin', either."

She grinned. "Really? Who else?"

"Just about every man in town."

She thought about that for a moment as she picked up the strap-brush and began stroking it through Buck's mane. She remembered the astounded look on most everyone's face when

42

they came to see her this morning. "I think I've shocked them. This morning the town acted as if I were some stranger."

"You are a stranger, Summer." He laughed. "And half the time, I don't understand what you're sayin'."

"Why?"

"Because you talk so educated."

She smiled. "Aunt Lydia taught me to speak proper English."

He folded his arms across his wide chest. "Well, nobody around here will know how to act with you this way."

The awkward conversation made her uncomfortable, and she couldn't meet his stare. "You're doing just fine."

"I am?"

"Yes." She turned and looked at his rugged features again. "It's almost like it used to be, yet...different somehow."

"Yeah, I know."

"You're being more polite. Before, you didn't care how badly you insulted me."

"I was only gettin' back at you for what you said to me."

She shrugged. "True. I wasn't very nice, either."

He gave her a soft smile and her heart melted.

"Neither of us were nice," he said.

She gazed at him a second longer, not believing how incredibly handsome he was. Of course, if the truth were known, she thought he'd been nice-looking five years ago. But now that he was older, he made her heart leap.

She stopped, suddenly realizing the inappropriateness of her train of thought. This was her sister's fiancé, for heaven's sake. And she wasn't supposed to like him.

Straightening her shoulders, she moved away from Buck and set the brush back on the self. "Mr. Slade, if you'd kindly leave, I have a lot of work to do."

He pulled away from the wall and walked beside her. "Come on, Summer." He bumped his elbow into hers. "Let me help you, if just for today. I know how much work there is for you, and I want to help you exercise the horses."

She lifted her chin and challenged politely. "Fine. You can saddle up Thunder, and I'll take Buck."

He flashed her his cocky grin before she moved to the

tack room and lifted a saddle. Jesse followed behind and copied her actions. She couldn't believe their conversation had turned sappy just a moment ago, and she promised herself not to fall in his trap again. Suddenly, an idea sprang to her mind that she just couldn't dismiss.

She flipped the saddle over Buck's back. "I have a suggestion," she added. "Let's not just exercise the horses, but have a race.."

"I don't know, Summer. You've been out of the saddle for a while."

She tilted her head and met his eyes. "It hasn't been that long."

His grin widened as he stepped closer to her. "Fine. We'll have a race, but will you promise me somethin'?"

Her heart leapt again from his nearness. Flipping up the stirrup, she grabbed the cinch. "What?"

"That you won't hate me when I win."

She did laugh aloud, propping her hands on her hips. "And what makes you so all-fired sure you're going to win?"

He shrugged. "I just think you're gonna be a little rusty is all."

She laced up the latigo, commenting over her shoulder, "Well, Mr. Slade, you think too much."

"Oohh, so mean."

Once the saddle was in place, Summer mounted then urged her horse forward into a trot until she was out of the barn facing down the road toward the end of town. Within seconds, Jesse was by her side.

"How far?" he asked.

"Until we reach Poppy's meadow."

"Deal."

Summer leaned over her horse's shoulders, her body crouched low as she tightened her knees. Out of the corner of her eyes, she noticed Jesse copying her actions--to annoy her, she was certain. She couldn't stop her smile from stretching from ear to ear. Jesse was right when he told her she'd been out of the saddle too long, but there was no way she'd forget how to ride a horse. To her, it was like getting dressed each day.

"Are you ready?" he asked.

"Count it down, Mr. Slade."

He laughed and shook his head. "You can back out any time, you know."

"Count it down," she repeated, "or I'll do it for you."

"On your mark," he began. Get set…"

"Go," she shouted as she kicked her heels into Buck's belly. The animal put his ears back against his head, apparently eager to be active again and took off down the street.

Jesse's laughter rang through the air behind her, but she concentrated on guiding her horse over the rutted road. There was no way she would let Jesse see how out of practice she really was. But within minutes, she began to doubt her ability to prevail when Jesse's horse raced neck to neck with hers. The wound in her shoulder throbbed along with her head, and she silently cursed. Angrily she growled and crouched closer to the horse, trying to ignore the pain.

She pushed Buck to run faster, but it seemed as if Jesse's horse was just as fast. Her heart burned with the knowledge this might be something she couldn't beat him at. No! She *had* to beat him. Losing was *not* a option.

Quickly mapping out the route to Poppy's field in her head, she remembered a back road. The road twisted sharply in a few spots, and there was a fence…and that way was quicker. It wouldn't be cheating if she took that direction. Besides, they hadn't made up any rules for this race, so maybe she should…

Adjusting the reins, she maneuvered the animal to the right, up a side trail. She laughed when Jesse remained on the original road. Now her goal was in sight. But just as she turned a corner, he cut through the trees and up the little hill. From the seriousness on his expression, he meant to catch up. She cursed under her breath.

Once again, the horses were neck and neck, and no matter how hard she tried, she couldn't break free. The road turned and she spotted the fence. It'd been a while, but if she jumped the obstacle, she'd come out ahead. Without a second thought, she pulled the reins sharply to the left and headed toward the fence.

The closer she came, the more confidence expanded in her chest. She'd show Jesse Slade once and for all. But within mere feet of the fence, Buck came to a dead stop. It happened so fast she didn't have time to think about grabbing his mane. She flew through the air at an incredible speed and landed flat on her stomach, spread eagle in a huge mud puddle. Pain from her head and previous shoulder injury sliced through her body, but she ignored the throb and concentrated on trying to peel her face out of the sticky goo.

"Summer," Jesse shouted as he rushed to her side, slushing through the mud. He stood over her, wrapped his arms around her waist and lifted her. Mud dripped disgustingly from the front of her body as she wiped at her eyes. Jesse used his handkerchief to gently remove the mud from her face.

"Are you all right?" he asked in a voice laced with worry.

If not for the great amount of embarrassment that came over her, she'd have laughed. She also realized this saved her from having to admit defeat for almost losing the race.

"I'm fine." She spat mud out of her mouth. Blinking, she focused on his furrowed brow, and worried eyes. He appeared genuinely distressed.

"Are you sure?" His hands moved to her shoulder to inspect the bandage from underneath her soiled shirt. "It doesn't look like you're bleedin'."

"I'm not."

He blew out a gush of air, then the corner of his mouth lifted in a grin. *Curse his hide.* He was going to rub it in. She just knew it.

"Summer? Why did you decide to jump the fence?"

"Because I knew I'd win."

"Didn't think you'd be the kind of person to resort to cheatin'."

"I wasn't cheating. If you remember right, we didn't lay down any rules."

He nodded, his grin expanding. "I'll remember that next time."

"Next time? Are you challenging me to another race?"

"No. I thought about doin' somethin' I know you can handle."

She gave him a scowl. "Like what?"

"How long has it been since you've been fishin'?"

"Not as long as you might think. I went once a week

while I stayed with my aunt."

"Then how about goin' fishin' tomorrow?"

She smiled, feeling better as the tension eased. It'd been a while since she'd shown him how well she could fish. She couldn't wait to show him now. "I'd like that."

His smile softened. "First thing in the mornin'?"

"The earlier, the better."

"Good."

Her heart sped at the thought of being alone with him again, but she couldn't allow that to happen. She didn't like the tingles spreading throughout her body whenever she caught his gaze.

"What do you say we bring Violet?" she asked. "In fact, maybe Pa would like to come with us, too?"

His smile widened and relief swept over his expression, making his face relax.

"That'll be great. I'll ask Violet tonight."

"All right. We'll meet at six o'clock in the morning," she replied with entirely too much excitement.

He gave her a wink. "It's a date."

~ * ~

It's a date? It's a date? Jesse's mind repeated as he paced the floor in the small cabin he and his brother shared. What was he thinking calling it a date? It certainly was not a date. Why would he want to court Summer when Violet suited him just fine? Of course, courting Summer wasn't such a far-fetched idea. She was a very beautiful woman. But it was hard to forget about her tomboy ways and how she always had to prove herself better.

A laugh rose in his chest as he remembered when he used to avoid her altogether. He'd duck behind a building when she came up the boardwalk in town. If she helped her father in the stable, he'd take a horse to be exercised.

So, if Summer really annoyed him when she was younger, why did he act like a smitten schoolboy now? Had her beauty completely knocked him senseless?

He shook his head. Impossible. Besides, no matter how her body had changed, she was just as obnoxious as she had been as a snot-nosed kid.

He moved to the window and looked out upon the signs

of early evening. The dusky velvet sky highlighted the descending sun. Thoughts of this afternoon with Summer eased and a smile claimed his face. It had been a long time since he'd been in a horse race. Summer had been a semi-good sport, an evenly matched competitor, but he had to admit he enjoyed more than just the race. He liked bantering back and forth and trading sly glances--a major departure from their usual exchange of insults.

Summer had changed, he'd give her credit for that. Perhaps there was a small amount of maturity peeking through her stubborn streak. Then he realized his inconsistent thinking, remembering how he'd struggled with her to hog-tie her back on his horse yesterday, and how his panic heightened when she was thrown from her horse during their race.

He rubbed a smudge off the dirty window, turning his thoughts to Violet. Now, there was a real lady. A sweet, genteel woman who always thought of others--so much like her mother. Totally uncomplicated and predictable. She'd keep his home immaculate. Yes, she'd be the perfect wife.

Boringly perfect.

And lately, he didn't know if he wanted perfection.

He growled. The stuffy cabin must be warping his mind. He shoved open the screen door and stepped out. Looking out over the peaceful landscape, land going as far as the eye could see, he tried to capture some peace for himself. The setting sun spread a deep golden red tint over the land. He took a deep breath of air, enjoying the breeze at the end of a hot day. Autumn wasn't very far away and he couldn't wait for the cooler temperatures.

In the distance, Clint galloped toward the cabin. Jesse's heart warmed when he thought of his brother. Clint looked like an older version of himself, same blue eyes, same build, except Clint's hair was slightly darker in color.

"Howdie, stranger," Jesse greeted as Clint tied his horse to the railing. "Didn't think I'd see you this soon."

Clint smacked the dust off his pants. "Well, I just completed the project I've been workin' on, and I couldn't wait to come home and tell you about it."

"Project? You've been workin' on a project?"

Clint laughed and removed his hat. He swiped his gloved hand over his sweaty forehead. "Actually, I've been buildin' somethin' for you. I planned on givin' it to you as a weddin' present, but that lovely woman of yours keeps postponin' the happy day, so I guess I might have to give it to you early."

Jesse moved closer to his brother. "Now you've got me curious. What is it?"

"Why don't I show you and Violet at the same time? In fact, why don't you round together whoever might want to come along while I get cleaned up?"

Excitement danced in Clint's eyes and Jesse didn't want to disappoint him. "Are you sure?" He glanced toward the sun as it dipped below the horizon. "It will be dark soon."

"'Course, I'm sure. Now, skedaddle before we lose any more sunlight," he ordered as he walked into the cabin.

~ * ~

Summer sat upright in the rickety wagon while Clint led the group to the unveiling of his wedding gift to Jesse and Violet. She combed her gaze over the man she'd admired as an older brother, and liked the changes the years had wrought, the slightly longer hair and the large physique. The humorous smile still lit his sun-streaked face that she remembered from five years ago. However, he didn't have his brother's hypnotic eyes. *Thank heavens.*

But no matter how hard she wanted to keep her attention diverted from Jesse, it stubbornly continued to stray to his broad back as he drove the wagon. The fawn colored shirt tucked nicely into the waistband of his pants, and his wide torso tapered down to a slender waist.

Her face grew hot and she snapped her gaze away. Lowering the blue shawl from her shoulders, she tried to cool her body's temperature.

Clint's light chuckle brought her attention back to him. "Summer? What'cha been up to lately? Tried trappin' a man into your womanly web, yet?"

She rolled her eyes and smiled. "This is only my second day back, Clint."

"But the boys around here would be foolish not to notice you." He laughed again. "You're certainly different from when you left."

His gaze moved over her figure, resting briefly on her

bosom, but it didn't send chills down her spine like it did when Jesse looked at her.

"Marvin?" Clint continued. "Can you believe this little runt here has finally sprouted some--"

"Don't say it," she snapped, her face aflame with embarrassment. Everyone laughed while she glared at Clint.

Clint led them over a slope then stopped his horse. When he met Jesse's eyes, he grinned. "Over yonder is your surprise."

Jesse stopped the wagon and everybody leaned up to see. Gasps rang through the air; Jesse and Violet exchanged a surprised look. Not far from a gurgling brook, stood a small cabin with a wraparound porch. Scraps of wood littered the yard, giving evidence to the recent work that had been done. Clint's generosity made the small cabin appear as a grand palace.

"You did this by yourself?" Jesse asked as he climbed down from the wagon.

"Most of it. I had help once in a while."

Tears sprang up in Violet's eyes. "It's absolutely beautiful." Her voice quivered.

Clint dismounted and went over to the wagon to help Violet down. It must have slipped Jesse's mind to do that gentlemanly deed.

"Oh, Clint." Violet's arms wrapped around his neck as she hugged him tight. "You really shouldn't have."

He kissed her on the cheek. "Yes, I should've. I didn't know what else to give you all." He smiled down into her teary eyes.

"It's...the most wonderful...place in the world."

"Yes, it is," Jesse agreed, standing still as he gazed at the cabin.

"All it needs is furniture and some curtains and rugs, but I figured you'd want to decorate it y'rself."

Violet's tears streamed down her face. Her voice must have choked up because she nodded at Clint's comment.

"Can we go inside?" Jesse asked.

Clint chuckled. "Well of course. Let me go in and light some lanterns. It looks as if we didn't quite beat the dusk this evenin'." He led the way into the cabin.

Jesse walked beside Violet. "I still can't believe it. I'm

completely stunned."

"Me, too." She sniffled.

As Clint lifted Pa from the buggy and set him in his roller-chair, Summer studied Jesse and Violet. Summer pursed her lips tightly as she followed behind the engaged couple. Violet's incessant blubbering began to get on her nerves. She didn't know why Jesse and Violet were so dumbstruck. Hadn't they seen a house before? It was just an ordinary cabin.

But her thoughts changed once she stepped inside. Although the rooms were empty, Clint's loving touch was evident throughout the place. A small fireplace centered against the far wall, and above the mantle, he'd carved intricate designs into the wood. Large bay windows opened in the front room and kitchen.

While she walked through the kitchen, she trailed her fingers along the decorative carvings and noticed two closets instead of one. A small staircase in the back led up to an extra bedroom, and the other two were on the main floor.

Seeing all the work that had gone into building the place, shame washed over her from her earlier grumbling. She moved next to Clint. "You've done a wonderful job."

He slipped his arm around her shoulders and gave her a small squeeze. "Thanks, runt."

She laughed. "I think you can come up with another nickname now. Remember, I'm not a little girl any longer."

Jesse walked up behind them, playfully slapping his brother on the back. "Yeah, she's not a little boy, either."

Clint roared with laughter. Glaring, she fired daggers at the man who had made the remark.

Violet still blubbered when the family gathered in the front room, but Summer couldn't criticize her now. If the roles were reversed, she might feel the same.

"I wanted to give it to you on your weddin' day," Clint told Jesse and Violet, "but I couldn't wait for Violet to make up her mind."

Jesse laughed softly, then slipped his arm loosely around Violet's waist. "Violet, honey? I think we really should set a date. Now that we have a house, there's nothin' to stop us."

Violet nodded, but continued to weep in her handkerchief.

Summer studied her sister's reactions suspiciously.

Something about this picture just didn't set right. Instead of being happy, Violet truly looked disturbed. What was going on?

Standing against the wall, Summer watched those gathered in the cabin. Jesse seemed happy enough, but Clint kept looking at Violet. For the first time Summer saw a tenderness in Clint's eyes she'd never seen before. Also, Jesse and Violet acted differently around each other than they had five years ago.

Her mind wandered back to the time she'd left to attend her aunt's school. Although they had always acted proper, Jesse and Violet couldn't stop gazing at each other and holding hands or touching in some way. Now they could actually stay in the same room without exchanging a single glance. Jesse's arm encircled Violet, but they looked as if they couldn't wait to break the contact.

All the way home, Summer pondered on what she had witnessed in the cabin. Could it really be that Jesse and Violet had grown apart in the time she'd been away?

When they arrived home and Jesse lifted her down from the wagon, she stared deeply into his eyes, trying to read his expression. He gave her a tiny smile and his subtle flirtation played tricks with her mind, making her heart flutter.

Once her feet touched the ground, she stepped back and pulled the shawl around her shoulders. That settled it. She had to talk to her sister. But she worried Violet might not appreciate her questions. Would her sister be able to share her feelings with her as she had when they were younger?

She glanced at the couple again and still felt the same nagging suspicion. Well, she'd make Violet confess. There would be no rest until she found out what was really going on between Violet and Jesse.

Four

Full of energy, Summer rose before dawn. She stretched and yawned, then climbed out of bed. In haste, she entered her sister's room and bounced enthusiastically on her bed. "Time to wake up, Violet."

Violet mumbled and turned on her side. Summer frowned and tried again. This time, she provoked a discontented groan from her sister. "Violet? Wake up. We're going fishing. Remember?"

Violet covered her head with the pillow. "Summer, I'm not going fishing. Tell Jesse I'm sorry."

Annoyed, Summer grabbed the pillow and uncovered Violet's head. "Jesse will be disappointed if you don't come."

Violet's eyes opened groggily and she met Summer's stare. "No, he won't. He knows I don't like to fish." She pulled the blanket to her chin.

Summer's heartbeat quickened. Her sister *had* to go. No way could she be left alone with Jesse. One of them might come out with a black eye or missing tooth...or worse.

"Please, Violet. I want you to come this morning. It's very important to me."

"Another time, Summer."

Summer yanked the blankets down to Violet's waist. "Come on, Sis. We don't do that many things together, and I would like to spend some time with you before you're an old married woman."

Violet huffed. "We'll go shopping together this afternoon. Now, leave and let me get back to sleep. I have a terrible headache." She turned her back on Summer, ending their conversation.

Panic snuck up on Summer as she rose from the bed and started for her own room. Usually her sister was an early riser, and everyone knew the best time to catch fish was early morning. But today Violet's headache caused more than one problem. Although

Summer didn't want to cancel the fishing trip, she also didn't want to be held responsible if Jesse came back with any broken bones.

She opened the armoire in her room and stared at its contents, trying to decide what to wear. Her old knickers would be perfect, but ladies didn't wear knickers. Instead, she donned a black skirt and a yellow long sleeve blouse with a cotton lace collar. She pulled back her hair, tying it with a matching yellow ribbon.

She didn't want to examine the reason for her enthusiasm closely, although she felt compelled to look her best. Proving to Jesse that she had indeed matured was top priority. Their horse race had showed her that he'd also changed. For one thing, he wasn't nearly the pest she remembered. Albeit, he liked to taunt her in order to get her to react. And when she thought about his muscular body, crazy little flutters started in her stomach.

She crept out of her room and down the stairs to see if Pa was awake, but just as she neared his door, Ma came out of the kitchen and stopped her. "Summer, don't disturb your pa."

"Why?" she asked. "He's going fishing with me this morning."

"No, sweetheart, not today. He didn't sleep well last night, and I want him to rest."

Summer's hopes for a pleasant morning instantly deflated. "I'm sorry he didn't sleep well. You're right," she said softly, "he needs the rest."

"But I think Pa would be proud if you caught a really big fish for him." Ma gave her a hug, then nudged up Summer's chin with a finger. "But then, he has always been proud of you no matter what you do."

"I'll try my best." Solemnly, she moved toward the door. "I'll be back later. Elizabeth and Nate are going to take care of the stable this morning, but I won't be too long."

"That's fine dear. You go and have fun."

The thought of her father's crippled body dampened her mood, but she did want to go fishing. Maybe Jesse could help her devise a plan to speed Pa on the road to recovery. Of course, she'd have to be nice when she asked.

On the way to get her horse, she snatched her special fishing pole. It still looked in good condition even after five years.

She hurried into the barn and saddled her horse, then rode to her favorite fishing spot. Though Jesse hadn't mentioned a specific place, to her there was only one--a grassy knoll a step or two away from the creek-bed next to a large elm tree. She smiled as she thought of the hours she'd spent there.

She had just arrived and was dismounting when another horse galloped toward her. Her stomach did a wild little dance as Jesse rode over the hill. He was dressed differently. Instead of his Ranger's outfit, he wore a pair of dark blue denims and a chambray shirt.

She inwardly cursed him for looking so good.

"Good mornin', Summer," he greeted, then scanned the area around her. "Where's everyone?"

"Violet couldn't pull herself out of bed this morning, claiming a terrific headache. And Pa had another sleepless night. Ma wanted him to rest."

Jesse dismounted, then tied his horse next to hers. "I'm sorry. Last night's little excursion didn't exhaust your pa, did it?"

Without meeting his gaze, she shook her head as she collected her fishing gear. "No. At least he didn't act as if it did."

She stepped to the edge of the water, noticing how it still mirrored the sky; its borders filled with moss. Reeds grew near the waterline, tall and green; waving in the gentle breeze and sweeping across the land. Wild honeysuckle rode on the wind, reminding her of days in her youth, glorious times she would remember always.

Here and there a frog darted from one lily pad to another, as if playing a child's game of tag.

Moving past him, she slugged to the bank and plopped down by a big elm tree, the same tree she'd carved her name in as a child. She took in a deep breath. Even though she loved fishing, today alone with Jesse just wouldn't seem proper. Things had changed between them. No longer could she think of him as just one of her fishing pals--not that she ever had.

Her pole dropped from her hands and rested on the grass beside her. Pa's affliction weighed heavy on her mind.

Jesse sat beside her and gently poked her ribs. "Hey." She raised her gaze to his smiling face. "Do you want to talk about what's troublin' you?"

"Nothing is troubling me," she lied, then tried to stand,

but he kept his hold on her arm.

"Summer, I can always tell when somethin's botherin' you."

She tried to tug her arm free. "Just leave me alone, Jesse," she snapped.

"You don't want to be left alone. If you did, you wouldn't be here."

It upset her that he could read her so well. She didn't want to appear weak in his eyes. Admitting she needed somebody, especially Jesse, wasn't something she wanted to do.

"I'm fine," she said softly.

He chuckled. "You're not a very good liar."

His comment made her smile.

"No, I have never been a good liar, just an excellent teaser."

His eyes widened. "Oh, is that what you call it?"

"Yes. You were just not a very good sport."

He laughed. "Oh-ho! Are you sayin' I couldn't take your teasin'?"

She gave him her best innocent expression, then shrugged. "Did I say that?"

"You little scamp." He touched his finger to the tip of her nose. "You know exactly what you said, and I'm willin' to bet you're not the least bit sorry."

She shrugged again, this time smiling wide.

His finger dropped to her chin. "Well, at least I brought a smile to your pretty face."

She creased her forehead. *Did he just say I have a pretty face?* Couldn't have. He must have been teasing, but then, why was there a soft expression in his eyes?

For once in his presence, she found herself speechless, content to just gaze into his disturbing blue eyes. They couldn't possibly be this dreamy. Perhaps the sun inching over the hill played havoc with her vision.

"Now, are you goin' to tell me what was botherin' you, or not?" he asked.

The question shook her from her dream. She suddenly realized that though they both liked to tease, Jesse was the one person she knew she could confide in. She could tell him anything and he would understand and give her counsel. Strange she hadn't realized that before.

Liquid formed in her eyes. "I've been thinking about Pa. I hate to see him so helpless. He's always been a strong, active man, but now he can't move to his wheelchair without exhausting himself. At night, sharp pains in his back and legs keep him awake. It just kills me to see him this way."

Jesse swiped his finger across her cheek, drying a stray tear. "I understand. Comin' home to such a shock had to be upsettin', but I've had to watch him wither away before my eyes. Do you know how powerless I feel because there's nothin' I can do to help?"

"Yes," she answered, realizing he felt the same helplessness.

"Come here," he invited, opening his arms and wrapping them around her in comfort.

She went willingly, content to have his strong arms surround her in a protective embrace. Slipping her arms around his waist, she snuggled close to him. Nice.

"Is Pa ever going to walk again?" she whispered brokenly.

It took a few seconds to answer, and when he did, his voice was low and deep. "I don't think so. It'll be very hard on your ma because she's expectin' a miracle. She thinks because she prays every day and goes to church on Sunday, the Lord is going to reward her faithfulness by healin' your pa's legs."

"It's a good thought."

"Yes, but will it happen that way?"

"Ma has a lot of faith."

"True. I guess if anyone deserves a miracle, it's her."

"I know," she said sadly.

Summer drew comfort from Jesse's arms and nestled her head against his chest, pressing closer. The warmth of his body emerged into hers, and the reassuring beat of his heart kept her in place. She swept her hand lightly by his tight waist, and his muscles contracted. Against her ear, the rhythm of his heart accelerated.

His hands moved up her back and into her hair. When he tenderly touched her neck, a wild excitement shot through her. She sat very still and enjoyed the stimulation that made her body come alive, even when his hand slid down her arm.

Jesse's tight muscles interested her, and she skimmed her hand back up to rest against his chest. His muscles flexed and he gave a sharp inhale. Her breath quickened as did his.

She lifted her head and gazed up into eyes that were a heavenly shade of blue. This color was different from before, more alert, yet softer, darker with emotion.

She swallowed the knot lodged in her throat, and noticed his Adam's apple jump. His mouth opened slightly as his tongue darted out to dampen his lips. Her gaze froze on his inviting mouth and the mustache decorating the upper lip. An invisible force pulled her to him.

Her tongue quickly moistened her own parched lips. "Jesse?" she whispered without knowing why.

The beat of her heart was completely out of control, and with her hand pressed against his chest, she could tell his beat just as wildly. His fingers gently swept across her cheek, down her chin, then up to her forehead, very near her wound. Waves of pleasure passed through her body and it was all she could do not to moan aloud.

"How does your head feel? Is the bump still there?" His voice was deep, husky.

"It's still a little sore, but healing nicely, I think."

"I should've told you yesterday, but I think you were really brave when the stagecoach was attacked. Most women would've swooned."

She heard genuine respect in his voice and smiled. "Thank you, but I'm not like most women," she whispered, keeping her gaze glued to his fascinating mouth.

"That's the truth."

His thumb lightly stroked across her bottom lip, causing little flip-flops of excitement in her stomach. Emotion overwhelmed her and clouded her mind. This was all wrong! So, why in heaven's name did she feel the need to be comforted in his arms, and think about pressing her lips to his?

His face moved forward and she had the urge to follow his lead, but common sense warmed her with desire and she forced herself to pull away. Her abrupt movement seemed to jar Jesse to his senses. He withdrew and stood, his eyes reflecting the similar bewilderment.

"Summer...I...I'm sorry. I shouldn't have...um," he stuttered, then cleared his throat. "I...I need to go."

He hurried to his horse, mounted, and was gone in a flash. Confusion rushed through her, but not as quickly as the pleasurable tingles that didn't want to forget his touch.

~ * ~

Summer walked beside her sister that afternoon as they strolled down the main street, window shopping, just as Violet had promised. Today's heat seared through Summer's dress, but she wore a lighter material and didn't feel as suffocated as her sister looked. But nonetheless, Violet's chipper mood gnawed at Summer's nerves. All she could think about was Jesse and what had almost transpired between them at the fishing hole.

As she accompanied Violet into yet another shop, her mind replayed the moments by the stream. Nothing sinful had happened. Not really. Jesse had comforted and shared in her grief. Why then did her heart pump faster and her hands sweat every time she thought about Jesse's enticing lips? And wondering how they'd feel moving with hers?

And even more troubling, why didn't she have the will to stop his exploring hands? She could easily have stepped away from his heated touch. Although there was nothing immoral about the way he had caressed her neck, her arm, and rubbed her bottom lip, the fact remained--he'd touched her and her body had reacted. She shouldn't have allowed it. With her mind preoccupied, she followed behind her energetic companion to the ready-made clothing section of the Merchantile.

Violet held a maroon shawl underneath Summer's chin. "Oh, this color looks lovely on you."

Summer shrugged. "It's all right."

"Just all right? Why it's downright fetching. I think you should get it. You need to spend that well-earned reward money, you know."

"But I don't need a shawl," Summer reasoned.

Violet abandoned the shawl and directed Summer to another table. "How about this?" Violet asked as she picked up a silky pink nightgown with no sleeves and a lacy bodice. Her face flamed as she wadded the gown in a ball. "No, I don't think we should get this for you. This particular garment is used on wedding nights."

Summer's lips twitched as she held back a laugh. Poor, innocent Violet. Thanks to Aunt Lydia, Summer knew a little more about marriage intimacies than most girls her age.

Summer arched a brow. "Why don't we buy it for you? Isn't your wedding next month? Don't you need this for your trousseau?"

Violet folded the garment neatly, then placed it back on the table. "I don't need this."

"Do you already have one?"

Violet didn't meet Summer's eyes. "No."

"Then you need a gown like this."

"No, I don't," Violet insisted. "It's too immodest."

Summer laughed. "Not if you're married."

Obviously uncomfortable with the subject, Violet scowled. "We shouldn't be discussing this." She scurried to another table.

Summer didn't understand her sister's behavior and kept prodding. "Since we are on the subject of marriage, can I ask you a personal question?"

Violet kept pawing at the display of skirts. "Not if it's about my wedding night."

Summer stifled a grin. "It's not. I just want to know how you feel about marrying Jesse."

Violet tossed an answer over her shoulder as she continued rummaging. "How else should I feel? I'm excited, of course. I can't wait."

Her sister's expression didn't show any excitement at all. In contrast, Violet's chipper mood suddenly disappeared. "All right then, if you're so excited, why do you keep postponing the wedding?"

"Because there's a lot of planning and preparing, and…and I don't think I'll have enough time."

Sounded like excuses to her. Summer pressed on. "Violet? Do you love Jesse?"

Her sister dropped the skirt she'd been holding, then turned to Summer. "That's a silly question. Of course I love Jesse."

"Are you certain?"

"Yes. I've loved him since I was sixteen, perhaps even before then. I've known him almost all my life, so how could I not love him? Why, he's like a brother--" She stopped.

Summer understood perfectly, and shock vibrated through her. She gasped. "A brother? You love him like a brother?"

Violet's cheeks flamed as she gave a dismissive wave. "No, I didn't mean that. The feelings I have for Jesse go much deeper than a mere brother. What I meant to say was that he knows me as well as one of my brothers, and well, we've loved each other for so long, it's only expected that we marry."

"Oh." Summer picked up a blouse, pretending to examine it. For some reason, Violet was lying through her teeth.

"Why all the questions?"

Summer shrugged. "I've just noticed a few things that are different than they were five years ago."

"A lot has changed. You have even changed, for heaven's sake."

Summer studied her sister's curious eyes. "I know, but take last night, for example. While we were at the cabin, Jesse put his arm around you only once, and it didn't stay around you very long. He didn't walk around the cabin with you or hold your hand."

Violet snorted a laugh, then quickly put her hand to her mouth. "You've got to be jesting. You're worried over little things like that?"

"It's not a little thing. If Jesse really loves you, he wouldn't be able to stay away. He'd touch you like a precious piece of glass, delicate and tender, and when his eyes met yours, they'd smolder dreamily as if he'd never seen anything so breathtakingly beautiful in his life."

A louder laugh erupted from Violet, but this time she didn't cover it. "Why, Summer, you sound as if you're the one in love."

Panic surged through her. Guilt pricked her conscience. "What?"

"Summer? Have you had those feelings before? During your stay with Aunt Lydia, did you fall in love with a boy?"

Summer released a puff of air between her lips, then

shook her head. "I never found anyone in Brownsville that I could take a liking too. But I did fantasize, and I know when I finally do fall in love, I'll act the same way I've just described."

The smile slowly left Violet's face as she turned back to the clothes. "Jesse and I used to be that way when we were younger. But now that we're adults, things have changed. We know we love each other, but we don't always have to touch or kiss."

"What?" Summer gasped in surprise. "He doesn't kiss you?"

"Shh," Violet hushed her, then pulled her closer. "We kiss, but not often," she whispered.

Summer's hands clasped tightly with her sister's. "Violet, you certainly don't sound like a woman who wants to get married."

"Of course I want to get married. I'm twenty-two years old. If I wait any longer, I'll be considered an old maid."

"But Jesse should be more attentive. I wouldn't want to marry someone I love as a brother."

"Jesse is just acting normal."

Summer lifted her brows. "What is that supposed to mean?"

"It means he doesn't like all that cozying and kissing. He shows his affection in other ways."

In disbelief, Summer huffed. "Are you kidding? I thought all men liked kissing."

"So did I." Violet shrugged. "I guess Jesse is just different."

"For some reason, I find that hard to believe."

Violet's brows drew together. "Be nice. I know you don't like him, but at least give him the benefit of a doubt. Just like his older brother, Jesse is a good man, very loyal, very dedicated, and always trustworthy."

Summer's bark of laughter rang out and echoed through the almost empty store. "Violet? You've just described Jesse as if he were an old, obedient dog."

It took a second, but Violet's mouth twitched into a grin. "Let's drop the subject." She handed Summer a skirt. "Here. I want you to try this on."

"Why are we shopping for me? You're the one who needs

clothes. In fact, we should be buying things for your new home."

Violet shrugged. "We'll do that later. Right now, I want us to be girls again. As you said this morning, we haven't done much together, and it's high time we did. Besides, where else will you spend that reward money?"

"No," Summer replied. "I think maybe I'll save the money for now."

For the rest of the afternoon, Summer kept quiet about Jesse. She didn't buy anything for herself, since Pa was in need of money for a good doctor, and the reward money would be well spent in paying for a doctor who could make his legs strong again. Though she enjoyed herself, she couldn't stop thinking about Jesse at the fishing hole.

Violet's Jesse and the man who held Summer in his arms this morning were two different men. Grudgingly, she admitted he was a caring person. Even when he had hog-tied her to the horse, he'd been worried about her.

She frowned. Finding Jesse's faults were going to be a lot harder than she'd originally thought. Especially if she let herself think nice things about him.

Later that evening, Summer stood beside her sister and dried dishes as Violet washed them. Curious, she studied Violet's aloof profile. Though Violet acted as if everything was normal, Summer could tell something was bothering her. It was obvious that her mind was not on their conversation. Summer tried a couple of times to talk about Jesse, but Violet quickly changed the subject. Something was amiss, but Summer couldn't figure out what.

When the dishes were put away, Violet left the kitchen and locked herself in her room, claiming she needed time alone. Summer didn't argue. This gave her time to check on the livery stable. She hadn't stepped foot inside the barn since this morning, and she felt the urgency to see if Nate and Charles had closed up shop properly.

She didn't want to ruin her dress, so she slipped on another pair of tight knickers, a regular blue cotton shirt that stretched apart at the buttons, and a pair of Pa's old boots. She glanced down at her clothes. Obviously, she couldn't wear these much longer, but since she was going to the livery there was nothing else to wear.

The five-minute walk from the house in the quiet night did her good. The lantern gently swung beside her as she carried it into the barn. Right away, she noticed her brothers had already fed and watered the horses. As she moved from stall to stall, she admired the Quarter Horses that had been brought in this morning for boarding. When she passed by the hayloft her gaze lifted to the rafters and she smiled. She had spent much of her adolescent years up there hiding from Jesse when he annoyed her.

A sudden noise drew her attention to the barn door. Her heart hammered wildly when she recognized Jesse's tall frame silhouetted against the moonlight as he came running in.

When Jesse saw her, he came to a complete stop. "Oh, it's just you." He seemed to control his quick breaths. "When I saw the lantern light, I was concerned. I didn't know who could be comin' in here at this time of night."

"Who else did you think it would be?" she snapped.

"Considerin' your brothers have closed the barn down for the night, I had no idea."

"I came to see for myself if my brothers fed and watered the horses." She tore her gaze from him and scanned the barn. "I must admit, I'm impressed that Nate and Charles kept it looking so good. I didn't think my brothers could be so organized."

"When they first started helpin' after your pa was injured, it was the biggest mess I've ever seen, but they got the hang of it. They're hard workers. You should be proud of them."

"I am."

Jesse's gaze raked over her small figure. His dark eyebrow arched. "So, I see you can't keep away from wearin' your boy's clothes. Figured you'd return to bein' a tomboy again."

Angrily, she planted her hands on her hips. "What did you expect me to wear? I couldn't very well wear a fancy dress while I'm walking around in the hay and unmentionable deposits."

"I thought you were stickin' to the rules of being a lady."

"Well, there are some places where the rules don't apply, and this happens to be one of them."

Jesse stepped closer. His eyes swept over her body again, and his expression softened. Her heart sped, and her body quivered.

He grinned. "Well, if you can't get a better fit than that, I suggest you give them up altogether. Shoot, li'l lady, those trousers look like they've been painted on, and if you keep standin' that way--"

He flipped his finger against one of the opened spaces between her buttons. "--those buttons on your shirt will break loose at any moment. If you're not careful, you might show me more of that mature body than I'm ready to see."

She smacked his hand away and crossed her arms over her chest. Her face heated with mortification. "It's been five years. What did you expect?"

His gaze latched to her frown. "You're angry with me."

She shrugged. "Shouldn't I be?"

Her heart hammered erratically. She hoped he wouldn't mention this morning at the fishing hole. She definitely didn't want to talk about what had almost happened.

~ * ~

Pink colored Summer's cheeks before she turned away and faced the stalls. Jesse bit back a grin. He knew why. Good to see she'd been thinking about this morning, also.

He heaved a sigh. "If it makes you feel any better, I'm angry with myself for what happened at the fishin' hole."

When she picked up an apple from the box by the stall and fed it to the horse, her hand shook. "I don't want to talk about it."

"We have to." He wanted to reach out and pull her into his arms and experience the same softeness he'd touched this morning. Knowing he shouldn't feel this way, he shoved his hands into his pockets. "What happened was--"

"No." She turned and tossed him a heated glare. "I said I don't want to discuss it. It's over and done with. We were both curious, and that was all. Period. End of subject."

"It's not the end."

"Jesse, for Pete's sake, do I need to draw you a picture? You are my sister's fiancé. Forget about this morning. I'm erasing it from my memory, and I suggest you do the same."

Jesse smiled. She was falling back into her hellcat ways. He almost liked it. "No, Summer, you don't have to draw me a picture. But what I want to know is why you're not questionin' my actions? I sure am."

"It's as I said before, we were both curious, so let's leave it alone."

She tried to move past him, but he jerked his hands from his pockets and grasped her shoulders tightly. Knowing full well how she would react, he challenged nonetheless. "Summer, we're not endin' it that way. We're goin' to discuss this like adults."

"I most certainly am not."

Jesse lifted a brow. "What's the matter? Are you afraid?"

Her eyes widened and she pushed his hands away. "Me?" She poked herself in the chest, releasing a button in the process. A hint of creamy flesh flashed at him, and a surge of excitement rippled through him.

"You've got to be kidding," she continued. "I'm not afraid of you. Have you forgotten who you're talking to?"

This was fun. This was the old Summer he remembered. He snickered just to get her goat. "No, I haven't forgotten. I can see you're still a hot-tempered brat." He turned as if to leave, starting to head for the door. "I offered adult conversation, but if you're too immature--"

"Me? Immature?" She moved in front of him. "All right, you want an adult conversation? I'll give you one."

He could have laughed when her hazel eyes blazed wildly, prettier than he'd ever seen. An unexpected grin touched his mouth. "Sure you can handle it?"

She stomped her foot. "Jesse Slade, stop toying with me."

Jesse leaned back against the stall, crossed his ankles and folded his arms over his chest, giving himself time to formulate his words. "You were right. I'll admit, since you came back, I've been curious. I don't rightly know why. Pretty much the whole time I've known you, you've been a pain in my backside. But this mornin' when I saw you upset, I felt the need to comfort you. I shouldn't have been so bold cradlin' you in my arms and touchin' you that way, but I couldn't help it. I really didn't mean to sweep you off your feet the way I did."

Summer's eyes widened and she gasped. "Sweep me off my feet?" Her face flamed bright red. "Why, you no good, swollen headed sidewinder. You haven't changed a bit. You're just as all-fired full of yourself as ever."

She tried to brush past him on her way out of the barn,

but Jesse snagged her arm again. "All right, Miss smarty-pants. Then why did you snuggle up against me nice and cozy like?"

"Well, it sure as the devil wasn't because you swept me off my feet." She tried to pull her arm loose, but Jesse wouldn't let go.

"Then why?" he demanded.

Her chest rose and fell from her quick breaths. "Because...it felt good," she admitted in a soft voice.

A smile touched his lips. "It what?" he probed, wanting to needle her a bit more.

She propped her fists on her hips. "I said it felt good," she nearly shouted.

Jesse's grin faded as an uncomfortable thought crossed his mind. "Tell me, Summer. How many other men have had the chance to hold you like I did?"

"That's none of your business."

"I'm willin' to bet I was the first." At least he hoped he was.

"You were certainly not the first."

He studied her eyes carefully, searching for the truth in her answer, then wondered why it mattered so much to him. "You're a liar."

"And you're nothing but a conceited rogue." She pointed her finger at him. "Next time I'm in need of comfort, you keep your distance, Jesse Slade."

She turned and ran out of the barn, right smack into Clint. Jesse realized that if Clint hadn't grabbed her arms, she'd have fallen to the ground.

"Whoa, li'l lady. What's all the ruckus about?" Clint asked.

Jesse walked slowly toward his brother. "We were havin' an adult conversation."

Clint laughed. "Is that what you call it? From out here it sounded like a cat-fight."

Summer's face drained of color. "You...heard?"

"No, not exactly, but it didn't sound like any adult conversation I've ever heard."

Clint's attention darted between Jesse and Summer. Jesse could tell Clint's mind was working fast, and that worried him.

Clint's gaze skimmed over Summer's outfit. He chuckled. "What's this? Back to wearin' boys clothes?"

"No." She shook free from Clint's hold and stepped back. "I just thought I'd come see if the barn was closed properly, and now that I'm satisfied, I'll be moseying along." She turned and called over her shoulder, "See y'all later."

Jesse's eyes didn't waver as he watched Summer run down the street. He really liked the way those trousers stretched across her cute bottom.

"All right, li'l brother. What's that all about?" Clint probed.

"Nothin'."

"Nothin' my hide." Silence lagged between the two brothers for several seconds. "Summer's gotten under your skin, hasn't she?"

Jesse laughed. "That girl has always gotten under my skin."

Clint shook his head. "Yes, but this time it's different." His gaze followed Jesse's when he turned and looked back down the street. "This argument's different."

"Nothin's different, Clint. Summer and I have always sparked each other's anger." He walked over to his horse tethered nearby. "It's just been a while since you've had the privilege of witnessin' one of our little spats, that's all."

Jesse glanced at his brother and could tell by his expression that Clint didn't buy his explanation.

Clint's eyes widened. "That's it."

"What's it?"

Clint shook his head slowly. "The difference 'tween now and then was back then your li'l arguments never made steam rise from your ears. Before, you never cared whether you hurt her feelin's, but now--" He paused for a moment as if in deep thought. "This time you do care. I can see it in your eyes, Jess."

There was a serious tone underlying Clint's jesting words that bothered Jesse. He turned quickly and mounted the horse.

"Believe what you want, brother.

It was just an argument," he said, not sure if he was trying to convince Clint or himself.

Five

Disguised as drunken old men, Jesse lay beside his brother sprawled out behind a broken down wagon as they watched the bank's activities from across the street. The blasted mid-morning heat baked through his ragged clothing, but he couldn't fidget. He had a job to do. This was the first stakeout with Clint, and the anticipation of capturing the well-known Buchanan gang sent a jolt of excitement through his blood.

Next to him, Clint peered above the over-turned wagon. "Watch that group of men closely. I have a feelin' about them, and my feelin's are usually right."

Jesse's assignment today, along with two other Rangers from Clint's unit, was to watch the bank. The Rangers had been informed about the gang--a group of outlaws known only by reputation for robbing banks and stagecoaches. So far, the gang hadn't killed anyone, and it was up to the Rangers to make sure they didn't start.

Buchanan's gang cleverly planned their robberies, disguised themselves and made successful getaways. Clint was determined to trap them come hell or high water, and Jesse wanted to be by his side when it happened. Of course, the reward money was a great incentive, but mainly he did it for the thrill of the win.

Jesse craned his neck and peered over the edge of the wagon as he viewed the few men scattered along the outside of the bank. "They're doing nothin' out of the ordinary. Are you sure they're part of the gang?"

"Positive," Clint answered as he adjusted his hat lower on his forehead.

"But, Clint." Jesse returned his gaze to his brother. "How do you know these men are part of that group?"

Clint nodded toward a tall man wearing a long black coat.

"Look at that man over yonder standin' by the waterin' trough."

"I see him."

"The trough's empty. Watch that horse. He dips his head, but comes up with nothin'." Clint paused as his eyes stayed on the horse. "There. Did you see that?"

Jesse nodded. "So, if there's no water in the trough, then why is he pretendin' to water his horse?"

"My point, exactly."

Jesse wiped a bead of sweat from his brow. "But how do you know he's part of Buchanan's gang?"

Clint shrugged. "A hunch. Buchanan's right hand man is supposed to be a large man with black hair. I've heard he rides a chestnut horse with orange hooves. Several men fit that description, but few horses have orange hooves." Clint kept his eyes on the man a few seconds longer. "Besides, I've come face to face with that man. There's just somethin' about him that's not right."

"How many other men does he chum around with?"

"There's seven men that I know about. Less than two weeks ago during their last bank robbery, one was wounded in the leg, so be on the lookout for a man with a limp."

Jesse nodded. "Does McClain and Dorsey know this?"

Clint moved his gaze across the street and a couple of buildings over to the other two Rangers standing outside the saloon, visiting with a painted hussy. "They know."

Jesse kept watching the man by the water trough, and the suspected outlaw continued to act as if he were watering his horse. Underneath the brim of his low hat, the man's eyes darted up and down the crowded street. Something was about to happen, and the thought made Jesse's heart pound with expectation, but ten minutes passed with no signs of trouble.

Earlier that morning, Clint had explained Buchanan's cleverness. These outlaws were smart. If they spotted anything out of the ordinary, Buchanan wouldn't go through with his plans. Jesse wasn't worried. Clint could outwit any kind of outlaw.

An odd noise from the boardwalk brought Jesse out of his thoughts. Thump, scrape, thump, scrape. Both Jesse and Clint turned toward the sound. A man with a limp shuffled their way.

Acting in character, Jesse lifted the whiskey bottle filled

with tea colored water and took a gulp, allowing the liquid to dribble down his mouth in the process, giving him the opportunity to study the man as he headed toward the other man by the watering trough.

Jesse peeked from under the brim of his hat. Just as the man passed, Jesse let out an uncontrolled loud belch, then laughed heartily. He elbowed Clint in the side. "Betcha can't top that."

"Wouldn't want to," Clint slurred.

The man with the cane ignored Jesse and Clint as he passed, and continued toward his destination. Reaching the man by the trough, he stopped and the two men conversed.

Jesse kept his gaze fixed on the man the entire time. "Did you see his cane?"

Clint nodded. "It's not just a cane."

"A weapon?"

"Perhaps, but it's too slim t' be a rifle."

Jesse switched positions and glanced at Dorsey and McClain, assuring himself that they were alert.

Five minutes passed before Jesse noticed anything suspicious. A man walked out of the bank, flipping through a small wad of bills. He made eye contact with the two men by the trough as he passed. He signaled by nodding, and the two men returned a nod.

Clint also saw the exchange. "It's about time they made their move. It's gettin' damned hot out here in the sun."

"Do you want me to follow the man who left the bank?" Jesse asked.

"Yes, but don't wander too far away. I want you in my sight."

Clumsily, Jesse stood. Swaying back and forth, he stumbled forward until he could get his rhythm. He held the whiskey bottle in his hand, and every couple of steps he lifted it up to his lips, maintaining his distance for one block.

The gang member stopped by the General Store, leaned up against the outside wall and focused a steady eye on the other gang members. Jesse could either stop near the store--but that might be too conspicuous--or he could keep on walking. He decided not to draw undue attention to himself, and sauntered around the corner of the store.

The man stopped and leaned against the brick wall, so Jesse did the same, trying to keep his eyes on the man, yet still be able to watch what was happening in front of the bank. An out-of-town merchant pulled his wagon to a stop just a half block down from the bank in front of Dorsey and McClain. Jesse narrowed his gaze. The man in black and the man with the walking stick meandered over to the cart, pretending to view the merchandise. Jesse's interest piqued. If by chance a peddler were still wandering the countryside, he'd be heading further up North before winter settled in.

Within minutes, people gathered around the merchant's wagon. Jesse arched a brow. Could this be a diversion? Out of the corner of his eyes, Clint rose and moved toward the wagon. Before Clint got ten feet away, Jesse realized the two men by the trough had miraculously disappeared.

His heart hammered. *This was it.* He felt it like a bad itch crawling over his skin. He glanced over his shoulder. The man he'd followed was still against the wall, wrapping a cigarette as if nothing were happening out on the street.

Damnation. Jesse glanced toward the saloon. McClain and Dorsey stood with their gazes focused on Clint. By their creased foreheads and pursed lips, they were ready to spring at any moment.

Jesse switched his attention back to his brother. Clint nodded toward the bank. Dorsey and McClain acknowledged with nods. Clint staggered across the street and headed toward the bank. With his hat pulled low to disguise his alert eyes, Clint scanned the people still crowded around the merchant's wagon. As he neared the front door of the bank, three masked men burst out of the bank.

"Get out of my way, you drunken fool," the man snapped as he shoved past Clint, knocking Clint to the ground.

Jesse moved to go to his brother's aide, but stopped. Clint wouldn't be hurt. *I must concentrate on the criminals.* He turned, but the grinding click of a gun and the cold barrel pressed against his head made him pause.

"Don't move a muscle," the man behind him commanded. "Y'er just gonna stand right here and watch yer friends get blown to bits."

Jesse's heart sank. Fear gripped his stomach as bile rose

to his throat. From down the road, the thundering of horse's hooves shook the ground, and five mounted men led three more horses on a charge through the center of town. Thankfully, Clint must have spotted them and rolled to the side of the road before getting trampled. A mass of confusion broke out as the screaming crowd scattered for cover.

McClain and Dorsey pulled their revolvers. Shots flew, blasting in all directions and Jesse's hands itched to take his own gun and help any way he could, but the gun pressed against his head stopped him. Inwardly, he prayed the Rangers would win.

Clint sheltered himself behind a stack of barrels. The gang returned fire, bullets exploded through the barrels. Water spilled onto Clint. Jesse's heartbeat hammered against his ribs. When his brother darted toward the bank, Jesse sighed with relief. Clint edged through the opened door and flattened himself behind a wall, drawing his pistol. Cautiously, his brother peeked out the door, found his target, took aim, and fired.

Though gunpowder hung thick in the air, the Rangers took three bandits down. However, the leader and three remaining thieves were getting away.

The man behind Jesse cursed. "Looks like we'll be meeting up with you again in the near future."

Jesse wanted to look behind him to see the man better, but fear kept him still. Before he could do anything, the pressure from the point of the rifle was removed from the back of his head, yet just as quickly, a sharp pain struck his skull. Pain exploded everywhere and caused him to fall to his knees. Fighting for strength, he grasped his head. Warm, sticky fluid coated his fingers mere seconds before he crumbled to the ground. Blackness gathered in his mind and the noises on the street faded into nothingess.

~ * ~

The sultry afternoon heat made Summer feel as if she were stewing in her own juices. Back in the old days she would have taken off her shoes and stockings and cooled herself in the creek. Playing was of little interest to her now, but the thought of cool water slipping over her feet sounded wonderful and she wasn't about to ignore the temptation.

Quickly, before Aunt Lydia's etiquette influenced her to

change her mind, she urged the horse through the shaded woods to her favorite spot just outside town. She dismounted and moved to the huge boulder above the stream shaded by an overhanging limb of an ancient oak, then removed her shoes and stockings and plunged her bare feet into the cool river.

She sighed. Heaven.

This was luxury. Leisure hadn't been on her daily schedule for quite some time, and within a few minutes of doing absolutely nothing, she realized that idleness was difficult to get used to. Especially when a relaxed body seemed only to stir her active mind.

Many things bothered her since returning from Aunt Lydia's. Pa's situation was a major issue, and Violet's wedding still hung heavy on her mind. And Jesse! She slapped her foot in the rushing stream, spraying water in all directions. That good-for-nothing, pompous know-it-all wouldn't leave her thoughts no matter how hard she tried to dismiss his irritating memory.

As she pulled her feet from the water and replaced her stockings and shoes, she thought about how she'd tried to be nice to Jesse. She really had, but his arrogant attitude brought out the worst in her. She couldn't forget about their last argument, and how conceited he'd acted. He thinks he's God's gift to women. Well, he was one gift she wasn't interested in accepting.

Perhaps she needed to tackle the Jesse problem from a different angle. Instead of talking to Violet, maybe she should bring in some help. A third party might be a good buffer, and she knew the exact person. Clint had spoiled her like a little sister. Summer was confident she could enlist his aid.

She mounted her mare and it took only a few minutes to ride home. Tonight she'd go talk with Clint and make him understand her problem.

As she approached the livery, the normally wide-open welcoming doors were closed. Confused, she quickly dismounted and took her horse inside. Her confusion turned to alarm when she saw her brothers and sisters clustered together by the far wall. Judging by the downcast expressions on their faces, she sensed something was amiss.

Her heart dropped. *Did something happen to Pa?*

As she led her horse into a stall, her sister, Elizabeth,

stood. "Summer? Something terrible has happened." Her voice quivered.

Summer temporarily draped the reins over a slat and ran toward her brothers. "Pa?" Her voice wavered.

"No. It's Jesse."

Her eyebrow rose. "Jesse?" She wrinkled her nose. "What's wrong with him?"

"He was wounded this afternoon while he and Clint were out with the Rangers. He's hurt bad."

Summer didn't understand the sudden pain in her chest. She detected tears in her siblings' eyes, and her eyes burned, too. She was almost afraid to ask. "What happened?"

Little Charles wiped a tear off his cheek. "He was knocked around pretty good and his head was bashed in with somethin'. Clint thinks it was the butt of a rifle. There's a huge gash on the back of his head."

"Where is he?"

"At the cabin," Nate told her with a broken voice. "Clint and Violet are taking care of him. The doctor went out, but there ain't nothin' the doctor can do. Old Doc said Jesse will either live or he'll die." Nate moved away from the wall. "I think we should go see if Violet needs any help."

Of course, she had to go. She wanted to go. She didn't understand her feelings, but as irrational as it seemed, she knew Jesse needed her.

Summer glanced at Elizabeth and Emily. "Can you handle the livery while I'm gone?"

"Yes. We'll be just fine," Elizabeth assured.

Kicking her horses into full gallop, Summer and Nate made it to the cabin within ten minutes, then pulled their horses to a stop in front of the porch. She dismounted and touched her aching shoulder. But she didn't have time to worry about her wound now. Jesse needed her. Summer noticed Violet peek out the window, vanish for a moment, then open the front door.

"What are you two doing here?" Violet asked.

"We come to see how Jesse is doing," Nate answered.

The first thing Summer saw when she walked in was Clint with his elbows on the table, his face buried in his hands.

"Clint?" She went over to him and touched his shoulder.

"What happened?"

He stumbled to his feet and wrapped her in a quick hug, then explained the events leading to Jesse's injury.

"How is Jesse?" Nate's voice shook.

Clint combed his fingers through his hair as he sat back down. "He's restin'. Doc has no clue how serious Jess' head is damaged. His face looks like a mule team ran over it, but at least he has no broken bones." He paused a moment. "He's in the bedroom if you want to see him."

Summer followed her brother quietly into the bedroom and stood by the bed. Jesse looked awful and her heart went out to him. His face was colorless except for the grayish-white tones around his lips. Purple bruise marks shadowed his cheeks and his eyes were swollen closed. Scratches marred his handsome lean face and a deep cut marred his bottom lip.

A strange fear surrounded her and she silently prayed this wasn't as bad as it looked. Would he recover from his injuries? Clint acted as if Jesse were on his deathbed. *Will we lose him? Or will he be crippled like Pa?*

For years, Jesse had made her life miserable, but no matter how they fought and argued, she certainly didn't want him dead. She gazed down at him. Heavens, he looked so pitiful and helpless. The very sight of him made her want to cry.

Oh, no! Wouldn't Jesse just love to see her cry over him? Well, that wasn't going to happen, no matter how her heart ached-- yet she couldn't stop the single tear from slipping from her eye. She quickly wiped it away before anyone noticed.

Violet touched her shoulder. "Don't worry. I think he'll make it," she said, comforting. "He's a strong man."

Summer nodded. "You're the one who is strong. You're just like Ma." She smiled.

"Would you like to help me in the kitchen?" Violet asked. "It's getting close to supper, and no matter how much Clint protests, he still needs to eat."

"I'd love to help."

One day of helping turned into three, and Summer stood diligently beside her sister, trying to nurse Jesse back to consciousness, but to no avail. He lay still as death and had yet to open his eyes. Every day the doctor came and repeated the same phrase, *Only time will tell.* Summer was ready to shove his words down his throat because *time* certainly was not *telling* them one darned thing.

Clint left early the morning of the third day. Exhausted, Violet looked wrung out and almost as pale as Jesse. Summer assured her sister that she could take care of him. After Violet left for her walk, Summer checked on Jesse for the hundredth time that morning. He still lay in the same position, looking as pale as that first day. His abrasions were healing nicely, and his bruises looked almost green. Even the deep cut on the back of his head had closed. So, if everything else on his body worked, why wasn't he awake?

After touching his head and finding him slightly warm, she took a damp sponge from the porcelain basin and with gentle care, dabbed his forehead. As she sat on the edge of the bed staring down at him, she couldn't stop the feeling that washed over her. In the last few days, she had silently cursed him for making her sense things she had no business experiencing. For heaven sakes, he was engaged to her sister, though she wondered if the love they professed was habit more than anything else. But she could no longer deny that this man, however arrogant and insufferable at times, touched her in a special way. If only he were a gentleman like his brother.

She laughed inwardly. *Gentleman?* That was about as likely as a Texas snowstorm in July.

As she placed the sponge back in the bowl, the bed moved. She turned back and saw Jesse's hand had wandered to his face where it rested on his forehead. Slowly his eyes fluttered open.

"Oh, Jesse," she said excitedly, "you're awake." She gently touched his hand. "How do you feel?"

Jesse scanned the room for a moment, obviously trying to get his bearings, his eyes coming to rest on her. He blinked, trying to focus in on her. "How do I feel?" He groaned. "Like hell warmed over. My head throbs like a bitch in heat and my body feels like a locomotive hit me head on." He squinted. "And pull those curtains closed. The light hurts my eyes." He shielded his eyes with his hand.

She tried to hide her smile behind her hand. "Oh dear,

that bad?"

"Can I have a drink?" he rasped dryly.

She hurried from the room to fetch him a glass of water, returned and took great care to lift his head gently while he slowly sipped down all the liquid. After he finished, he slumped back onto the bed, exhausted by even that small movement.

He stretched his legs then groaned in pain. "Hell couldn't feel any worse."

He looked at her and she could tell the second he remembered their last rotten moments spent together. He rolled his eyes. "Oh, I am in Hell."

Although relieved there was no damage to his brain--so far--she'd had enough of his surly temper. She considered personally directing him to Hell with a swift kick to his rear to hurry his departure.

She gave him a smile with acid sweetness. She crossed her arms over her chest. "Actually, Jesse, you're not in hell, yet, but a quick transport to that destination could easily be arranged."

His fingers moved to the back of his head. "What happened?"

She shrugged. "We don't know. We were hoping you could tell us."

He scanned his room again with a narrowed gaze, then gave her a quizzical stare. "We? Do you have a mouse in your pocket? As I see it, you're the only person here."

She gritted her teeth, determined not to let him get to her. "Clint and Violet are gone. Clint found you lying in a heap in back of the Amarillo General Store, and he doesn't know what happened. I guess you were hoping to arrest some villains?"

He squeezed his eyes shut and looked as if it pained him to remember. "Yeah, I almost had them."

"What happened?"

"Quit askin' me so many questions," he snapped. "My head's poundin' and my stomach's restin' on my backbone. Get me somethin' to eat so I can gain my strength and go after those slimy--"

"Whoa, slow down there, Jesse. You won't be going anywhere for a while."

"And who appointed you my nurse?"

"Clint and Violet." She straightened her back. "Actually, they are the ones who have taken care of you, but they needed a break. That is why I'm here."

"How long have you been here?"

"Since the first day of your accident, three days ago."

"Three days?" He started to rise. "Ow!" He grabbed his head. "I'm worse off than I thought." He groaned and eased back on his pillow. "So, Miss Nightin'gale, I thought you hated me."

She scowled. "I do," she lied, "but Violet needed my help."

"Why would you be so kind-hearted?"

"Because if you died, I wouldn't be able to personally put you through hell." In a huff, she left the room in a whirl of petticoats.

It was very interesting, how after only five minutes of consciousness, she was ready to bash him in the head again just to get him to shut up.

She stomped into the kitchen and grabbed a bowl from off the shelf, but she was so angry her hands shook. Quickly, she steadied it before it toppled to the floor. All this was Jesse's fault. If he'd acted a little grateful, maybe she could calm her temper a might.

Spooning the broth into the bowl, she slowed her breathing. She would give him the benefit of a doubt. He had to be acting this way because of his injuries. Deciding to give him a second chance, she pasted a smile on her face, entered the room and sat on the edge of the bed.

"Let me help you." She poured on the sweetness.

Jesse's expression wavered slightly, but then he opened his mouth for the first bite. After swallowing the broth, he chocked fitfully. "What is that stuff? Are you tryin' to poison me?"

Her brows drew together as she fought to control her temper. "It's broth that Violet made this morning in hopes that you'd awaken."

"It tastes like pig's scraps."

"Well, it's the only thing your stomach can handle, you ungrateful--" She bit her lip, holding her tongue.

His heated stare locked with hers for several seconds, then he sighed heavily. "You're right. I should be thankful Violet thought to make somethin' gentle for my stomach."

Obviously, he couldn't converse in civil tones, so she kept her lips sealed while she fed him. With his throbbing head, she figured he probably welcomed the silence. The broth would fill his stomach then maybe, she prayed he'd go back to sleep.

After setting the empty bowl aside, she pulled the covers up over his naked chest and tried not to touch his warm, firm skin.

"Are you feeling better?" she asked softly.

His eyelids drooped with fatigue. "At least my stomach is satisfied."

"Are you going to tell me what happened?"

"No."

In irritation, she thinned her lips. "But Clint and Violet would like to know how you got yourself so banged up."

"Fine, when they return, I'll tell them. You don't need to know 'cause you're not concerned about me, or have you forgotten?"

Oohh! She wished she could punch him in the nose. "You're right, it's not my concern."

"Why aren't you at the livery taking care of business?"

"Nate and my sisters have taken over while I've been here with your sorry butt."

"Then leave."

"Gladly." She stood, planting her fists on her hips. "As soon as Violet returns."

"Then you can just stand there while I go back to sleep."

He turned awkwardly to his side, finalizing the conversation. As slumber instantly crept over him, tension as tight as a kite string grabbed hold of her body--annoyance literally vibrating through every bone. She snatched up the bowl and glass and made her way back into the kitchen as liquid pressure gathered behind her eyelids.

That unappreciative, dirty-rotten brute just couldn't say thanks. She hated to admit it hurt, but it did. He didn't care one iota how much time she'd spent nursing him back to health.

As tears streamed down her cheeks, she bit her knuckles and quickly ran outside before the forthcoming sob escaped her throat.

~ * ~

Jesse shielded his eyes from the glare of the afternoon sun as it poured through his open bedroom window. He shifted his position on the hard bed, stretching his aching muscles. His movements would be restricted for a while. Clint, his mule-headed brother, appointed himself Jesse's nursemaid and made sure he didn't get out of bed, except for the necessary. Jesse grumbled, but his protests went unheard.

His brother stacked more pillows behind Jesse's back and propped him up in bed, then fed him a heartier soup today, but it wasn't the steak and potatoes his stomach growled for. When he finished every last drop, Clint placed the bowl on the small stand next to the bed and sat back in his chair, crossing his arms over his chest.

"Let's talk about Amarillo." Clint's brows drew together, lips thinned. "What in the blazes were you tryin' to prove?"

Jesse shrugged. "I wasn't tryin' to prove anythin', I swear. The man left and I followed to see where he was goin'. When he stopped and faced the street, I knew I had to keep out of his vision, so I slipped behind the buildin'. I took my eyes off him for one second and he was behind me, stickin' a gun to my head. He wanted me to watch my friends die, and when that didn't happen, he hit me. I don't remember anythin' after that."

Clint swiped his fingers through his hair. "You could'a been killed. You were told to stay in my sight. Why didn't you follow orders?"

Jesse crinkled his forehead as he met his brother's glare. "Quit talkin' to me like I'm a ten-year-old. I wasn't doin' anythin' foolish and you know it. In fact, I'm willin' to bet you've done the same thing a time or two."

Clint's eyes turned dark, but Jesse knew his brother couldn't deny the truth. After a fair amount of silence, Jesse let the corners of his mouth lift in triumph.

Clint shook his head. "You could've been killed," he said in gentler tones.

Jesse stretched, trying to work his stiff muscles, then rearranged the blankets around his waist. "Thanks for carin', brother, but you know I was only doin' my job, and I'd do it again in a heartbeat. At least I was able to get a good look at one of Buchanan's men."

Clint sighed, then stood and moved to the window, massaging the back of his neck. "Yes, it's good you were able to see his face."

"Did you capture any of the men?"

"Yes. Three were wounded, but two died the next day." Clint glanced back at Jesse. "Unfortunately, the third isn't sayin' a word. I'm waitin' for him to end up dead."

Jesse widened his eyes. "You really think they'd do that to a member of their own?"

Clint nodded, staring out the window. "'Specially if it means keepin' their hideout a secret."

Jesse cursed and punched his fist into the mattress then winced when a pain shot up his arm. "We were so close."

"We'll get them next time." Jesse's head snapped up in interest, and Clint waved his hand through the air. "But without your help."

Jesse scowled. "Oh, come on. You can't do it alone, especially since I've seen one of them."

Clint pounded his fist on the wall and spun around to confront Jesse. "Will you quit makin' sense?"

Jesse grinned. His mind began creating ways to find the bandits, and a couple of wild-haired ideas popped into play, but before he could explain them to Clint, his brother stepped over to the bedroom door and closed it.

"Jess, I have a problem I need to discuss with you. Can I ask you somethin' personal?"

Confused, Jesse drew his brows together. "What's that?"

"How're the plans comin' on your weddin'?"

Jesse laughed. "That's your big problem?"

Clint shrugged. "Well, I've been watchin' you and Violet and the two of you don't look very happy."

"Of course we're happy. Why wouldn't we be?" Jesse's heart hammered as he tried to hide his feelings.

"Jess, listen to me."

Jesse looked down at his finger as it played with the quilt ties.

"I don't see any excitement between y'all," Clint continued.

Jesse looked at Clint and shrugged. "Marvin's accident

has taken away the thrill."

Clint tilted his head and nodded. "That's understandable, but I don't think that's it. I think your love has changed into friendship."

Jesse studied his brother, finding it strange how well Clint could read him. "You know, sometimes I feel that way. Violet isn't the woman she used to be. Now when I kiss her, it's like I'm kissin' my..."

"Sister?" Clint supplied for him.

Silence dragged between them for several seconds.

"So, what do you think that means?" Clint asked.

Jesse shrugged. "I don't know." He turned his attention back to the quilt. "I've tried not to think about it, hopin' it'll go away."

"Has it?"

"No. I still feel like I'm kissin' a relative."

Clint chuckled deeply. "Do you suppose that maybe y'all aren't meant to marry?"

The thought had been eating at Jesse for days, but he'd tried to ignore it. Perhaps it was time to bring it in the open and discuss his feelings with Violet. Before he could say anymore on the subject, a heavenly aroma drifted to his nostrils and made his mouth water, completely clearing his thoughts.

There was a soft knock at the door and then came the soft voices of Violet and Summer as they entered his bedroom, each carrying a portion of his dessert. Summer held a glass of milk and a linen napkin and Violet carried a plate holding a piece of apple pie.

"Ummm, smells wonderful." He carefully took the plate from Violet and set it on his lap.

Violet smiled. "Go ahead. Take a bite. I think you'll be surprised."

Curiously, he jabbed his fork into the crust and lifted a large chunk of apple to his mouth. The pie touched his taste buds and he groaned with delight. "This is the best pie I've ever eaten. Thanks, Violet."

She laughed lightly. "You can thank Summer. She's the one who made it."

Jesse looked at Summer with wide eyes and her face

turned red.

"Yes," she agreed meekly.

He needed to give her a compliment since he knew she had never been a good cook. "You did a heck of a job, Summer." His praise came out with heartfelt sincerity.

"Thank you."

The glare in Summer's eyes challenged him, as if to dare him to say something mean. Jesse refrained for now.

Violet took the napkin away from Summer and placed it on Jesse's lap. "How are you feeling, Jesse?"

"Like I've been caught in a stampede."

"Your color is back, and your bruises are fading. Soon you'll be as handsome as ever," Violet teased.

He chuckled and looked back at Summer. She comically rolled her eyes, but he managed to keep from laughing at her silent comment.

Violet elbowed Summer's arm. "Don't you think he looks better?"

Jesse studied Summer's reaction. Her eyes widened and her throat jumped in what must have been a hard swallow.

Grasping the sides of her apron, she twisted the material in her fingers. "Uh…well, I…uh, sure." She nodded, then swallowed again as she met his eyes. "I think you're recuperating nicely."

Jesse hid his smile behind his napkin when he wiped his mouth.

Summer cleared her throat. "I really should be going now."

"Let me take you home, sweetie." Clint winked.

Summer waved a dismissive. "Don't be silly. I can go by myself."

"I insist." Clint lightly clasped Summer's elbow, then looked at his brother as he edged toward the door. "You get to healin', brother, and build your strength. That Buchanan gang cannot be put off much longer."

"I'll work on it." Jesse shifted uncomfortably as the two left the room.

Violet fluffed another pillow behind Jesse's head. "How does this feel? Would you like another pillow?"

"No."

She reached to his waist and adjusted his quilt. "Are you warm enough? Would you like me to get another quilt?"

"I'm fine, thanks."

She picked up the dirty dishes on the bed-stand. "Are you still hungry? I could get you another slice of apple pie. I can't believe how well it turned out. Summer is finally getting the knack of cooking."

"Maybe later." He patted his stomach. "I can't eat another bite."

Violet turned to leave, but he grasped her hand. "Sit down a minute, will you? I'd like to talk."

She glanced down at the dishes in her hands. "I really should go wash these--"

"Put them down," he commanded in a soft voice.

"Well, all right. I suppose the dishes can wait."

When she sat beside him, he smiled at her. "You've been waitin' on me hand and foot, and I wanted to tell you I really appreciate it."

His fingers softly stroked her cheek, and though they had always shared closeness, he felt her subtle withdrawal. He could see the time of reckoning could not be put off any longer. Violet was just too unresponsive, and he could tell by her expression that something was on her mind.

"We need to talk, Violet--"

"Jesse, we need--" they said in unison.

Violet's eyes widened. They both laughed.

"You go first," she urged.

He briefly examined the woman sitting next to him; straight back, hands neatly folded in her lap, just like a proper lady. Whatever she had to say to him was mighty important.

"Do you know how long we've known each other?"

A smile touched her lips. "Yes. You've been helping my pa for twelve years."

He nodded. "You were sixteen before I really noticed you as a woman."

A light laugh came from her. "Yes."

"I thought you were the prettiest girl in town. You were kind and lovin'--everythin' I wanted in a woman."

"Is that why you asked me to marry you?"

"No."

He turned his body toward her more and a sharp pain shot through his head. Automatically, his hands lifted to his wound. Violet reached out to soothe him, but his wave dismissed her help. Breathing slower, the pain soon passed and he focused once more on their conversation.

"Do you remember our first kiss?"

"Yes." She folded her hands in her lap, her eyes resting on her entwined fingers. "It was on a Sunday. We'd just walked up to Poppy's Meadow to have a picnic, and after we finished eating, you kissed me."

He smiled from the memory. "You were almost eighteen then."

"I remember."

"Do you remember our first fight?"

She chuckled as her gaze lifted. "Actually, it was more like a disagreement, but yes, I remember."

"I'd just told you about the Rangers wantin' me to join. You thought it would be too dangerous."

She nodded. "I cried, but that didn't stop you, so I threatened, and that didn't stop you either." She shrugged. "We made up one month later after you'd come back from a ride to the border."

"But did we ever really make up?"

Her attention lowered to her lap again. "No. We pretended for awhile, but deep down in my heart, I always felt you loved your job more than me."

"I know. By then the town threw us together and it was routine to take you places and kiss you afterwards. It was habit to treat your family like they were my own."

She tilted her head. "Then why did you ask me to marry you?"

He sighed heavily, carefully scratching the side of his head. "The truth is your pa threw the question at me. I was so surprised that I stumbled over my words. He seemed so happy about the idea, and I couldn't break his heart. Marvin is like a father to me and I didn't want to disappoint him."

"So, you don't love me?"

By the look in her wide eyes, he could tell that she was far from upset. In fact, her big brown gaze practically danced with unleashed excitement. He decided to confess.

He shook his head. "Oh, I love you all right, but not like a man who's about to get married."

She grinned. "You mean like a sister?"

"Um...well...yes, like a sister." He studied her briefly. "Are you upset with me?"

Violet let out a deep sigh. "Of course not, Jesse. I feel just the same way."

A gush of air escaped his mouth. "Really?" He chuckled. "You love me like a sister?"

She laughed and shook her head. "I love you like a brother."

Jesse's grin widened. "So you won't be too upset if we call off the weddin'?"

She cupped his face and planted a kiss on his lips. She pulled away and ran her fingertips lightly down his cheek. "Jesse, you've made me the..." She cleared her throat. "Believe it or not, I've been feeling the same way. But--" The excitement in her expression faded. "What about Pa? How is this news going to affect him?"

Jesse sighed, then closed his eyes, stroking his unshaven chin. "I know what you mean. I don't want to hurt your pa, but I don't want to ruin both our lives, either."

She nodded. "Yes, I know."

He glanced out the window, mentally searching for a solution. There had to be a way to make it work. "Perhaps we should wait to call off our weddin'. We've been postponin' it for a while, so what's a few more months?" He quickly looked at her to see her reaction.

She nodded eagerly. "Yes. Ma has found out about a doctor in New Orleans that might be able to operate on Pa's back and heal his injury. Within a few months, we'll know one way or another."

He took hold of her hand. "Should we let anyone else know?"

She gave him a one-shoulder shrug. "I don't know."

"All right, maybe we shouldn't. At least not until we tell

your parents."

The corners of her lips lifted. "Sounds good to me."

He squeezed her hands. "Are you sure you're not angry with me?"

"No, I'm really relieved." She laughed and punched him lightly on the arm. "I'm so glad we had this talk."

"I do love you, Violet." He winked.

"I love you, too." She grinned with a twinkle in her eyes. "Like a brother."

Six

Jesse stared up at the night's shadows dancing across the ceiling as the melting candle flickered on his nightstand. Confinement drove him crazy, and lying around wasn't helping him to strengthen his muscles either.

Carefully, he sat up and swung his feet to the floor. Grasping the bedpost, he lifted himself off the lumpy mattress. His head throbbed and his muscles screamed in pain, but he forced himself to stand. The room swayed beneath his feet and his vision blurred.

Feeling dejected, he sank back in bed and pulled the sheet over his legs. He wasn't a patient man, especially when it came to waiting for his body to heal, but lying in bed did offer him time to think about the happenings of the day. Funny how everything had turned out. For a while, he'd felt like he was digging a hole, falling deeper and deeper into a bottomless pit.

Freedom brought a multitude of feelings with it.

Violet was happy. He was happy. Or was he? He mulled the question in his head for moment. Yes, he was happy, but he no longer had that special woman, and that felt strange.

Then Summer's face appeared in his mind. Lovely Summer--fire blazing from her hazel eyes as she sat hog-tied to the back of his horse; Summer--stubbornly jumping over the fence just to win the race. And Summer--trying to be cordial while she played nursemaid, knowing full well that she would rather rip his head off.

And Summer who could make a heckuva good apple pie.

He stopped when he caught himself smiling. Smiling? He was grinning like a kid in the candy store! He sobered immediately. Why was he thinking about Summer? It would never work. They couldn't even be in the same room without getting into a heated brawl.

Leaning on his elbow, he blew out the candle on his bed-stand and turned over in bed, trying to find a comfortable position and chase the image of a wildcat with auburn hair out of his mind.

~ * ~

Summer bent over the horse's off fore cannon as she forced it onto her lap. The quarter crack on the hoofpick needed to be wielded, but Buck just wouldn't stand still. The horse neighed and belly-bumped into her, making her lose her balance.

"Tarnation, Buck." She growled angrily as she smacked the animal on the shoulder. "If you don't let me fix this, you'll never go out riding again."

She resumed the position, but the ornery horse just wouldn't listen. "Buck, this is your last warning."

From behind her came the gentle laugh of her pa. She swung around. Ma wheeled him in just inside the door. His contagious grin made her smile.

"You ought to tie him off with two clip ropes instead of just one," he told her. "You'll have better control over him that way."

"Pa? What are you doing here?"

"I just come to see what was going on." His gaze combed over her worn britches and faded shirt and he frowned. "I'm sorry I made you return to your tomboy ways."

She dropped her tools on the nearby workbench and ran over to him, the leather apron slapping her calves. Going down on one knee, she gave him a fierce hug. "Oh, Papa." She kissed his cheek. "You didn't *make* me do anything. If you remember right, I chose to come back to the stable."

"Only because I'm in a wheelchair."

Pity laced his voice and tugged at her heart. But she didn't want her pa to see how it affected her. When she pulled away, she tried to give him her best smile. "If you came here to scold me, then you might as well turn back around and head home. I'm not in the mood to take both yours and Buck's ornery temperament."

When the corner of Marvin's mouth lifted in a half-grin, relieved swept over her.

"Is there anything I can to do help?" he asked.

She laughed. "If you can talk some sense into this old

bucket of bones, then you've earned your pay, young man."

Marvin winked and gave her a full smile. "I'll see what I can do." He looked up over his shoulder at his wife. "Ma? Would you push me over to Buck so I can help Summer?"

It was almost like old times again. As Summer worked beside her father, they bantered back and forth and talked about the weather, the other businesses, and the lazy old good-for-nothings in town that Pa had always liked to rile. She smiled in remembrance. Yes, it was as if she had never left.

There was silence for a few minutes as they finished up.

Ma cleared her throat. "Summer, dear, have you heard how Jesse is coming along? Has his head wound healed?"

Summer squeezed Buck's leg and bit her lip to keep the foul thoughts in her head from spewing out. Why did Ma have to ruin such a perfect morning? Slowly, she let out the pent-up air in her lungs. "I'm assuming he's back in the saddle, if that's what you need to know."

"Violet just doesn't talk much anymore, and I can't help but wonder why."

Summer moved the tools back over to the bench while Ma pushed Pa away from the stall and followed. Summer spoke over her shoulder. "Well, Violet hasn't said anything to me either."

"She keeps postponing the wedding and I'm wondering if she's having second thoughts."

Summer shrugged. "Like I said, I wouldn't be the one to ask."

"She's probably worried about the gang the Rangers are looking for," Pa mentioned.

Summer looked over her shoulder at him. "Yes, I overheard Clint and Jesse discussing Buchanan's gang. They sound like a mean bunch of men."

Lillian gasped and placed her hand on her chest. "Well, I would think so. Knocking in Jesse's head like they did, and for no good reason."

Summer chuckled as she untied the leather apron and flung it over the bench. "They had good reason. Jesse was following one of the men, and the bandit didn't like it. Land sakes, even I feel like thrashing him once in a while and I don't have nearly the cause they did."

"Well, I'm just relieved the state of Texas has offered a reward for those bandits," Pa said.

Summer's interest peeked. "A reward?"

"Yes, and a mighty good one, at that."

"Indeed?"

Lillian nodded. "And from what I've heard, the price keeps going up with every bank they rob."

"Seriously?" Summer asked again, more curious than ever. "Are we talking a colossal amount, or really offensive?"

Marvin chuckled. "It's a grand amount, I assure you. I don't think there's anything the lawmen won't do to put a stop to these robberies."

Summer's legs gave way and she sank to the nearest stool. If only she could get her hands on that money, Ma would be able to take Pa to the professional doctor in New Orleans who specializes in back injuries. If only she knew what Jesse knew about this gang, she'd hunt them down like the dogs they were and take them single-handed. If only...

"Thank heavens we have the Rangers to serve and protect us." Pa let out a wistful sigh. "But I just pray no one else gets hurt."

Although Summer nodded in response to Pa's comment, she kept her mind on the reward money. For the rest of the afternoon as she finished her chores, her mind created ways to find Buchanan's gang without getting hurt. They wouldn't hurt a poor defenseless, innocent woman, would they?

A few customers had come in to rent rigs, a few more paid for lodging for their horses, but during her business dealings, she couldn't get the reward money off her mind. She needed that money desperately. More than anyone else! But did she have the courage to go after them? She didn't have all the information the Rangers had, but when she was younger, Pa had taught her how to track down wild animals by studying their hoofprints in the dirt. The gang couldn't be that much more difficult, could they?

If only she could trick Jesse into telling her what the bandits looked like. Of course then she'd have to speak to him, and that was certainly out of the question. If she asked Clint, he'd know for sure what ideas were running through her mind, and she couldn't have that.

Phyllis Campbell

That left one option open. She'd have to follow Jesse. She'd have to tail him and watch whomever he studied. That was the only way.

When Elizabeth, Emily, and Nate came to relieve her, Summer was more than happy to turn things over to them. She had the rest of her day planned within minutes of her walk home. She'd have to find Pa's old black pants and black shirt, and she was going to catch her some thieves.

~ * ~

Summer leaned over her plate of biscuits and gravy as she listened carefully to the conversation at the supper table. Jesse had been invited, which wasn't surprising. Although his presence bothered her, she focused more on his rendition of what happened in Amarillo than how incredibly handsome he looked tonight. She definitely liked looking at him when he wore blue shirts, since it enhanced his hypnotic eyes. His skin color was almost back to being perfect, too. Even the bruises weren't as recognizable.

Jesse proceeded to tell the story, from the moment he and Clint arrived in front of the bank until he was clobbered over the head. But this time, she realized he had described two members of the gang that had not been killed in the shoot-out. Jesse mentioned a man with a limp who walked with a cane. He also mentioned a tall, thin, dark haired man who rode a horse with orange hooves.

Very interesting.

She swallowed the last bite of her meal and leaned back in her chair. Tonight she wore one of her nicer lavender dresses that Aunt Lydia had helped her to make, and she noticed Jesse's attention kept wandering over to her. A shiver of delight rippled up her spine when his gaze swept across the square cut bodice that emphasized her full bosom perfectly. Very few times had she ever felt like a real woman around him, but this was definitely one of them.

"Well, Jesse," Pa spoke. Jesse's intoxicating stare was taken way, when he looked at Marvin. "The citizens in Texas will feel much safer when the Rangers have that gang put away where they belong."

Jesse nodded. "Clint feels like we're gettin' closer to their hideout. He's confident we'll have them soon."

"Jesse?" Summer asked, glad to have his eyes on her

again. "Will you be going out again tomorrow?"

"Yes. Why? Do you need some help in the stable?"

"Well, actually, yes. One of the brakes on the rigs is broken, and I'll need your help, but I can wait until you have the time. It's not that important."

"A couple of us Rangers are goin' to check out Big Springs tomorrow, but I suppose we'll be home later in the day. I'll swing by the stable and help you fix the brake then."

She smiled and she couldn't stop the fluttering sensations in her chest. "Thank you."

Lowering her gaze, she lifted her linen napkin, trying to hide the excitement she knew must be displayed on her face. It'd been awhile, but she'd do a little tracking herself, and with any luck, she'd discover the bandits before the Rangers did.

Bright and early the next day, she left for Big Springs. Nate and Elizabeth covered at the stable, so Summer was able to leave before sunrise. She'd borrowed Pa's old breeches and shirt, because they hid her womanly figure better. She took Nate's cap, sticking every strand of hair up underneath. As an added touch, she smeared dirt on her face to give the appearance of a ruffian.

She reached Big Springs early enough to find a hiding spot, the tallest tree that overlooked Main Street. Nobody noticed her when she took off her shoes and shimmied up the wide tree. Balancing herself on a high branch, she tried to be inconspicuous. This was the perfect spot to spy on Jesse, even though it was a mite uncomfortable.

She stretched out her looking glass and peered through it, thanking the leaves that hid her. Making her rump as comfortable as she could on the thick branch, she pulled her knees to her chest, helping to balance the looking glass. Right away, she spotted Jesse's rugged frame as he rode into town with two other Rangers. Little flip-flops danced in her chest, but she ignored the crazy feeling as best she could. The two other men with Jesse didn't look familiar, and they were certainly not as handsome.

As she studied Jesse through the looking glass, she noticed his keen eye as he eyed every person in town, especially the men. The town people of Big Springs respected the Rangers by the way their smiles stretched from ear to ear, some even going out of their way to stop the Ranger and talk to them. Summer felt proud that Jesse was treated this way. He deserved it.

After a half-hour passed, she tried to find a more comfortable spot in the tree as she situated her legs. She grudgingly tore her gaze from Jesse to the people walking below her. She knew Jesse was on the lookout for a man with a limp, and for the magnificent stallion, but Summer was looking for something different. She wanted to find out how many men were keeping a watch on the Rangers.

Slowly she moved the looking glass to the people on the street, really studying their expressions. A few people she recognized from her past, but she skipped over them and continued her search. When she come upon a cowboy who casually leaned up against the building with his arms folded across his chest, she paused in speculation. Although his hat was pulled low on his forehead, she could tell that by the direction of his head, he had his eyes on Jesse.

The longer she watched the man watch Jesse, the more she suspected he might be one of the gang members. Her heart quickened. *Oh, please let me catch him*. She desperately needed the reward money.

She turned the looking glass back to Jesse, who was now standing in front of the mercantile store, visiting with two women. Her face grew hot with anger. She tightened her grip on the instrument, fearful that she might break it, but at least it was better than jumping from the tree and storming right over to those women and clawing apart their dolled-up faces.

What was wrong with her? Why did it bother her to have Jesse giving those women his knee-buckling smile? Perhaps she felt this way because Jesse was showing signs of being unfaithful towards Violet. Yes. That was it. Now, the question was, should she tell Violet? This might be the key to helping Violet see how unsuited they are.

Jesse laughed, and her chest tightened. *Curse his hide.* And curse her body for feeling such emotions.

When the ladies walked away, Summer breathed a sigh of relief, unaware that she'd been holding her breath. At least Jesse was back to doing what he came here to do. Yet, another hour passed, and Jesse still had not appeared to notice the man leaning against the side of the building.

Soon Jesse and the other two Rangers mounted their steeds and rode out of town. She swung the looking glass toward the stranger by the wall. He tipped his hat on his head, and this time she could tell that he was indeed watching Jesse. The man smiled, a satisfied expression dancing across his face.

He pulled away from the wall and moved over to his horse. She gasped when she noticed his limp. This had to be the man who'd been in Armadillo with Clint and Jesse. He had to be part of the gang.

She quickly slid down the tree, yelping a few times when a branch caught her in the wrong place. Instead of slipping on her shoes, she ran to her horse and leapt on his back. The only thing on her mind was catching the gang member. But then... she slowed her horse, if she just followed this man, perhaps he'd lead her to the rest of the gang. Then the reward would be larger.

Within hours the sun would be setting, and she didn't have much time. But she couldn't follow too close to the stranger. She didn't want him knowing what her business was about. Reaching down by her saddlebag, she felt the length of the rifle, assuring herself that everything would be all right. She was experienced with the weapon and she was quite confident she would prevail.

The ride was long and hot, but she kept on his trail, pacing herself behind him just far enough that he wouldn't spot her. The thief rode down a little knoll. She slowed her horse when she neared the spot the man had disappeared.

Her heart hammered in her ears. Sweat pooled in the palms of her hands, making it hard to hold onto the reins, but she kept on task. As she rose over the knoll, she saw the man. A second rider had joined him. Her heart soared in excitement. *I'll capture two of them.*

She swallowed hard and focused on their activity. Behind her the sun had begun to dip low, creating shadows that were not welcome now. She groaned and moved closer.

The two men had dismounted and moved within a cluster of trees. The orange glare from the sun made it almost impossible to see, so she crept closer until she reached the trees. Keeping her eyes affixed in front of her, she untied her rifle and cradled it in her lap.

Stopping her horse, she listened carefully. The night's insects began their harmonious music, making it more difficult to hear anything. She urged her horse forward. Her nose detected the smell of campfire. She smiled, feeling victorious. She'd march right into their camp, lame them with a bullet if necessary, and hog-tie them together until she could ride for help. Yes, everything was working out according to her plans.

Suddenly, behind her, a branch snapped, and she swung her head to see what had caused it. From out of nowhere, a large frame dropped from the trees and fell into her, knocking her off her horse. She let out a cry and the rifle slipped from her hands. When she hit the ground, the air gushed out of her lungs and the burning in her chest matched the throbbing pain in her head.

The man's large frame had her trapped as he sat upon her, holding her hands into the dirt.

"Who are you, boy?" The gruffness from his voice made her shudder.

She refused to answer, continuing to struggle however useless it was. If she spoke, the man would surely know she was not a boy.

He shook her once. "Answer me. Who are you?"

She tried lifting her legs, but his weight pinned them to the ground. Without her approval, a tearful groan tore from her. The man stilled, his eyes wide with surprise.

"You're a girl," he shouted.

Off to the side pounded the footsteps of the other man. A much thinner man stopped beside her and loomed over her, peering down at her as if she'd grown two heads. The large man grabbed the front of her shirt and ripped it open, revealing her camisole.

"Well, I'll be damned. It's a girl. She couldn't be much older than twelve or thirteen."

Her temper kicked in from the insult, and she scowled. "Bite your tongue, you inbred cowboy. I'm most certainly not twelve or thirteen."

The slender man crouched down beside her and cupped her breast. She squirmed, and when he didn't release her, she spit on him.

"Well, I'll be." He laughed. "The girl's tellin' the truth."

Her stomach churned the longer the man fondled her. Tears built behind her lids and she fought to keep them at bay. She needed to be strong. What was wrong with her? Why couldn't she have let them go on believing she was a young girl? She didn't even want to think of what they'd do to her now.

"Let me go, you imbecile." She pushed her hips up, trying to remove his weight from on top of her.

Confusion marred his ugly face as he looked down on her. "What'd she just call me?"

The heavier man laughed. "Whatever it was, I can guarantee it wasn't nice."

"What should we do with her?" the first one asked.

"I say we have a little fun."

White terror ripped through her, and she could almost imagine what kind of fun they would have. If only she could reach her rifle. If only the large man would get off her.

The large man sitting on top of her pulled the cap from her head then spread out her thick hair. "My, oh, my. She's a real beauty." His hand trailed down her hair to her neck, resting on the other breast.

The other man laughed. "Looks to me like she's tryin' to keep it hidden for some reason." He let go of her breast and roughly moved his hands over her shirt. She squirmed and cried out. "Let's take a look at what's underneath the undergarment."

"No," she yelled as she beat on his chest, but the bigger man just laughed. Her blows didn't even faze him. She reached up and clawed at his face, but the thinner man grabbed her hands and pinned them back down to the ground above her head.

The thin man chuckled as he ripped open her shirt completely, and untied her camisole. "Come on, sweetie-pie, show us what ya got."

From inside the trees, the cocking of a rifle echoed through the air, stilling everyone. The two bandits swung their head around.

"Stay right there, and don't move a muscle or I'll blow your stinkin' head to kingdom come."

Jesse. She sighed with relief and tears trickled down her cheeks uncontrollably.

Jesse continued in a calm, even voice. "Now, nice and

easy-like, I want the two of you to stand. Put your hands in the air where I can see them."

The larger man shook his head. "Come out of the trees where we can see ya. Or are ya a yella-belly?"

"You have to the count of three to get off that woman." Jesse's voice rose. "Unless, of course, you want to find a bullet hole in your chest."

The large man squinted as he tried peering through the shadows. "How many of ya'll are out there? I think we can handle just one of ya."

"You have three seconds. One," Jesse replied bitterly. "Two."

"All right, all right." The man hissed as he jumped off Summer. Both he and his friend stood still with their hands in the air.

"Alrighty, now I want you to move to your right...slowly."

As the men followed Jesse's instructions, Summer scrambled away from them, quickly fastening together the buttons left on Pa's shirt, which weren't very many. She scanned the area, looking for her rifle.

"Ma'am," Jesse said, "please come toward me."

"But, my gun."

"Don't worry about it right now, just step away from the men."

She sighed heavily, and gave up her search. With slumped shoulders, she took a couple of steps in Jesse's direction, then out of the corner of her eyes she saw the glare of the moon that shone from her rifle. "There it is."

In her haste to retrieve the weapon, she tripped over a hidden branch, and went tumbling into Jesse. He stumbled, back and dropped his gun. The two bandits acted quickly and ran toward their steeds.

"Damnation, Summer," Jesse snapped, then grabbed her around the waist and half-carried, half-dragged her to his horse which tethered nearby.

"Let me go."

Jesse practically threw her on her horse, then slapped the animal's rump, giving her a running start. She glanced over her shoulder and saw him mount, then take off after her.

"Ride as fast as you can," he yelled. "I think they're gonna follow us. You know what they look like, and they can't have that."

She dug her heels into the animal's belly and crouched low, holding onto the reins so tightly the leather cut into her hands. But for once she obeyed Jesse's orders and rode like the wind. After a couple of minutes, shots popped from behind her, but the bullets didn't reach her. They must be out of range.

The wind stung her eyes, but she refused to blink, instead focusing her sight on the town ahead as it slowly came into view. The closer they came to civilization, the further away the firing of the rifles sounded. By the time they arrived in town, she breathed a sigh of relief. But when she saw the murderous glare on Jesse's face, her relief turned to fright. She didn't think she'd ever seen him look so angry before. Not even the time when she'd poured honey on his saddle on what seemed one of the hottest days in Waco.

She slowed her horse and Jesse lined up right beside her. His eyes were cold as steel, and it worried her.

"Blast it, Summer," he growled. "Why did you think it was necessary to go after them bandits by yourself? What were you thinkin'?"

Straightening her back, she lifted her chin in defiance. "I was thinking to get a reward."

Jesse let out a gush of air as he adjusted himself on the saddle. "And why would you do a crazy thing like that?"

"Because Pa needs to go see a specialist in New Orleans, that's why."

He shook his head. "Summer, you don't know what you're dealin' with here. Didn't you even realize what kind of danger you put yourself in?"

"Didn't you tell me yesterday that this particular gang hasn't killed anyone yet?"

"Yes."

"Well, that's why I wasn't worried."

He reached over and grabbed her reins, stopping both horses. He leaned in closer to her, and the light scent of cedar and leather mixed with sweat drifted around her. On him it smelled good, and something within her chest stirred.

"I don't think they were plannin' on killin' you, Summer. I think they had somethin' else in mind," he hissed through his clenched teeth. "And I think you know what I'm talkin' about. Summer, they could have... have..."

His voice broke and her face flamed from embarrassment. She was glad of the night's shadows to hide her shame. "Yes, I know they could have...hurt me."

He let out another gush of air, but this time his expression softened. He reached up and cupped her face. "I don't want to think about those varmints puttin' their hands on you. I could kill them for that alone. If I hadn't shown up when I did--"

His jaw hardened and worry etched itself on his handsome face. Her heart picked up rhythm, and it angered her that his touch and emotional stare could make her quiver like a bowl of grits. The tenderness in his words softened her temper, yet she fought it from happening.

"Jesse? How did you know to come after me?"

"I didn't rightly know I was coming after you. I thought I was followin' the bandits."

"But I watched you leave town, and you didn't even look as if you'd seen the man who limped."

He shook his head, keeping his mouth tight when he mumbled. "I wasn't supposed to act like I could see him."

"Well, I'm grateful for you're timely arrival, but I think I would have handled the situation just fine."

His hand dropped and his eyes widened. "You were certainly not handlin' the situation very well from what I could see."

She took control of the reins again, and urged her horse to a trot. "Believe what you will, Mr. Slade, because I know you still think you're everybody's hero. But you'll soon learn I don't need a hero." She threw him a harsh glare. "And I certainly don't need you."

She pushed the horse into a gallop as she left Jesse behind. Her chest grew heavy from her own words, and she wished she could believe them. There was no way she wanted to think of *him* as her hero, but the plain and simple truth was...he'd rescued her and she owed him her life--and her innocence.

Seven

Summer sipped her glass of milk as she tried not to involve herself with the conversation at the supper table. Her attention switched from brother to brother as she listened. She tried casting aside the disturbing thoughts of Jesse, but her loudmouth brothers kept her informed about what Jesse and the other Rangers had been doing this past week. Since her brothers were Jesse and Clint's biggest fans, they also boasted about their exploits and happily discussed the town's preparations for tomorrow's scheduled events.

"Did you see the Mercantile's new picture window?" Charles began. "It took five men to help put it in."

"No it didn't," Nate corrected. "It only took three."

Charles lifted his chin and scowled at his brother. "Yah, but if Jesse hadn't been helpin', I'm sure it would've taken five."

Nate scowled. "But if Clint was there, I'm sure he and Jesse could've put it in by themselves."

A soft chuckle came from the corner of the table as Violet hid a laugh behind her cupped hand. Though no one else had noticed Violet's display, it caught Summer's attention, and she wondered why her sister would act that way. Forgetting her manners, Summer rested her elbows on the table and studied Violet while her brothers rattled on.

"Mr. Smith helped make the sign. I saw'd him paintin' it," Charles piped up, his face smeared with jam as he reached across the table for another biscuit.

"Well, Clint cut out the wood," Nate bragged. "Clint is the greatest builder in the world."

"Clint took me to see the house he built for Violet and Jesse." All eyes turned toward Charles. "I think it's the greatest thing I ever saw'd."

"You have ever seen," Summer corrected automatically

as she flashed a glance his way.

"That's what I said," he snapped, "but Clint says that he built it 'specially for his li'l brother and Violet." He turned to Violet. "Do you like it? Clint didn't know fer sure 'cause he said you howled like a female polecat the whole time you was lookin' through the cabin."

Violet smiled at Charles. "Yes, I really like it."

"Well, I told him that you prob'ly did."

Saying nothing, Elizabeth wiped her face with a cloth napkin, then pulled away from the table. Summer was surprised at her sister's good manners. But then, Elizabeth was in her sixteenth year, becoming a young woman right before Summer's eyes.

"Ma? Can I be excused?" Elizabeth asked.

"Yes, dear," Ma replied.

Nate snickered teasingly. "Where you goin', Lizzy? Goin' ofta meet your boyfriend, Tommy?"

Elizabeth heatedly pushed her chair into the table, making it rock slightly. "It's none of your business."

"Boys," Ma calmly said, "Elizabeth is a young woman now. If she wants to go courtin', it's her own business."

"So just keep your nose outta my life." Elizabeth huffed and stomped out of the kitchen.

The expression on Elizabeth's face revealed the emotion she wanted kept secret, but Summer knew the signs. Inwardly, she chuckled, and even after everyone had left the table, she couldn't help the light laugh that bubbled up from her chest.

Elizabeth was in love.

A strange lonely feeling engulfed Summer and she wished she had someone to love.

As she moved around the table collecting the dirty dishes, confusion boggled her mind when she thought about the man she loved to hate. That blasted Jesse Slade wouldn't stay out of her mind, but sometimes she felt confused by the heated sparks between them.

She emptied the armful of dishes into the sink. Violet smiled at her as she cleaned off a plate. "Thank you, Summer. I haven't realized until just recently how much I've missed you."

Summer laughed. "I think you just like my help in the kitchen."

"No. I've missed you for other reasons." She rearranged the dishes. "I have to tell you, Ma thinks Aunt Lydia sent us home an imposter. Just look at the way you've picked up on domestic work."

Summer smiled. "You know, I never did like this kind of thing, but since I'm not suppose to climb trees and skip rocks with the boys, what else can I do?"

A merry twinkle sparked in Violet's eyes. "I'm just happy you've finally changed."

A tender smile lifted Summer's lips as she reached for a dry cloth. "Here, let me help you."

"No, I'm fine. You go in and visit with Pa."

"Really?"

Violet laughed. "Yes, now skedaddle."

Summer didn't argue, but hurried into the parlor. When she saw Ma helping Pa to the bedroom, she knew the visit would have to wait. Rest would do him good.

Trying to decide how to keep herself entertained for the remainder of the evening, she wandered outside and strolled around the house. When an idea took root in her mind, she smiled wide. She knew Violet felt overwhelmed by the preparation for the wedding, which was why Violet didn't have time to decorate the cabin, so Summer would make Violet some curtains for her new home. Although her talents were not fully developed in that area, she'd still try.

Sneaking quietly, she tiptoed into Ma's sewing room and found the measuring string, then hurried to the barn. Summer saddled a horse and grabbed a lantern before riding to the cabin. As she approached the small house, she couldn't help but feel admiration for Clint's labors. The inside of the cabin was as pretty as she remembered, but as she stepped into the kitchen, the bare walls echoed her feelings of loneliness.

After lighting the lantern, she slowly walked through each room and examined it as a new bride would. She felt painful envy, and she couldn't understand Violet's restraint. If this were her place, she'd be here every day decorating it for her wedding night.

She set the lantern down in the hallway and peeked into the bedroom. Her aunt had told her a little about what happens between a husband and wife, and suddenly Summer's interest was aroused. Stepping into the empty bedroom, she imagined where she'd place her bed if this were her home.

When she thought about some of the things dear Auntie had described about the wedding night, Summer blushed. At the time, it had seemed very shocking, but the more she pondered on the newfound information, she could actually envision doing that with the man she loved.

She remained motionless as she closed her eyes, creating the scene in her mind. She would stand in the bedroom, just as she was doing now, and her husband would come to her and slowly take off her dress. Shivers of delight pumped through her heart and tickled her tummy from the mere idea.

Her husband would be very gentle and loving. She would guide her hands over his wide, leather-tight chest. His skin would be warm. He'd smell like cedar and spice. He'd breath heavily in her ear, and her own breaths would match his. And when he kissed her lips, she'd circle her arms around his shoulders and kiss him back with such tender emotion, expressing all the love she felt for him.

When the man in her dreams became clearer and she could see his face, her eyes flew open. That scoundrel Jesse Slade occupied her thoughts once again. *Why of all people, why did it have to be him?* Dare she admit that he was all she thought about and she actually looked forward to seeing him again?

"Jesse." She sighed heavily in surrender.

"Yes?"

His voice startled her, and she jumped and turned toward the doorway. Her body still screamed with the sensations from her dream, and her mind went numb. Jesse stood with his shoulder propped against the doorframe, his hands folded across his chest. He wore an expression that told her he knew exactly what she'd been thinking.

"What do you want, Summer?"

Her hand covered her pounding heart. "I, uh, I--" she swallowed hard. "What are you doing here?"

"I should ask you the same thing."

"But I asked first."

He cocked his head. "Fine then. This is the place where I'll be livin' soon. Now what's your excuse?"

She unconsciously ran her hands down the waist of her skirt, drying the moisture gathered on her skin, wishing her temperature would cool. "I'm going to measure the windows for some curtains."

"Why?"

"Because I want to do something nice for my sister. I don't know what else to give her for a wedding present."

He nodded. "That's thoughtful."

Her lips twitched into a small smile. "Thank you. The idea just came to me tonight. It might not be the best sewing job in the world, but I'll certainly try my hardest."

He returned a smile. "I'm sure you will, but--" He bent and picked up the lantern she'd left in the hall. "--won't you be needin' some light to measure the windows?"

Giving him a piqued stare, she groaned from her obvious brain shutdown. She rushed to him and snatched the lantern then moved back to the window. After placing it by her feet, she reached into the pocket of her skirt and withdrew the measuring string. She stood on her tiptoes to measure the top of the window, but realized she wasn't tall enough.

As she extended her reach, she felt Jesse's heated stare on her back. An awkward silence stretched between them, and she had a sneaky suspicion that she knew what he was thinking.

"Do you need any help?" he asked.

She glanced over her shoulder and wished he'd remove that ridiculous sensual grin. "No. I can do it." But after a few more tries, she gave a heavy sigh in defeat and lowered her arms. "Jesse? Would you help me, please?"

He laughed. "What did you say?"

She threw him a resentful glare. "All right, this once I'll admit I need your help."

Jesse's laughter grew until he stood beside her. "You're not any good at this measurin' thing, are you?"

She shook her head irritably. "If you had any eyes in your hard head, you'd see I'm not tall enough to measure the top."

"True, but--" He pulled the string from her fingers and stretched it out on the bottom of the window. "--the top is the same size as the bottom, so just measure the bottom. It's easier."

She released a growl-like huff as she snatched the string

from him and proceeded to measure.

Jesse stood close, and his nearness was uncomfortably pleasant, crazily twisting her emotions out of control. Out of the corner of her eyes, she noticed his gaze skimming over her body. Her face burned.

She puffed angrily and lowered the string to her waist. "Would you please stop looking at me?" she asked, continuing to face the window.

"Can't. There's nothin' else to look at."

"Then go some place else."

"You don't like me lookin'?"

"No," she clipped.

"Liar."

She met his stare and lifted her chin stubbornly. "I'm not lying."

His attention moved over her hair, face, and body, and he gave her a cocky grin. "Tell me somethin', Summer. What were you dreamin' about when I first came in?"

She swallowed hard and she knew her heated face gave away her thoughts. "Well, if you must know, I was just fant--um--" She cleared her dry throat. "I mean I was imagining what it would be like to be married and living in a place like this."

His grin widened. "You were fantasizin', huh?"

"No, I was imagining."

"Same thing."

"No, it's not."

Softly, his fingers caressed her cheek. "You were blushin' just now, Summer. Your face glowed like a lighthouse. That doesn't happen very often. What were you thinkin'?"

She knocked his hand away and faced the window. "You startled me, that's probably why my face was red."

He moved closer, bracketing the wall beside her with one hand. "Were you thinkin' about being alone with a man? Were you fantasizin' about how it would be on your weddin' night?" he whispered in her ear.

She forced a laugh. "Of course not. Nice girls don't think about things like that."

He tilted his head and grinned. "But you were."

She spun around and her hand flew through the air to slap

his face, but he stopped it before it could connect with his cheek. He grabbed her other wrist and imprisoned both arms behind her waist, then backed her up against the wall. It only took a second for her to react to the hard contours of his chest as it against her bosom. It felt so right, but this was so wrong.

She struggled. "Let me go."

"No, Summer. I want to know what you were thinkin'."

"I told you."

"No, you didn't. I want you to tell me how you think it'll be on your weddin' night."

"You're an animal," she spat.

"Were his lips touchin' yours in a passionate kiss?" he prodded.

His heart pounded against hers, the rhythm matching perfectly with the beat coming from her. "Jesse, please." Her voice softened. "Why are you doing this?"

His lips hovered over hers as he stared into her eyes. "I don't know. I wish I could make some sense out of this, but I can't."

Jesse's mouth touched her, and she gasped, but surprisingly, she didn't want to pull away. His lips softly coaxed for a response, and she didn't know whether she should give him one. She fought the feelings, but when he hesitantly caressed her lips, she couldn't resist any longer. Her body relaxed, and for the first time in her life she let herself experience what it felt like to be really kissed by a man.

He leg go of her hands, and she let them wander up and stroke his neck, then threaded her fingers through his hair. She kissed him back, thrilling over the feeling of his soft lips touching hers. He pecked first on her top lip, then her bottom, then suckled them one at a time. Seconds later, his tongue entered her mouth. She gasped, but it felt good. A soft moan came from her throat and she stilled, waiting for him to show her the way.

He slanted his mouth over hers, and suddenly the kiss turned wild. She released a throaty moan and clung to him, her fingers digging into the collar of his shirt while her tongue copied the stokes his made in her mouth.

"Summer," he whispered and pulled her closer with an urgency she really didn't understand. She had no desire to stop him. In her mind, she replayed her fantasy and wished for the reality.

His had moved to her breast and then rested. Her nipple stiffened against his palm. As he plucked softly through the fabric of her dress, her nipples responded even more.

She let him caress her for a brief moment until she heard her aunt's cautious voice ringing through her head. It was wrong for her body to experience this kind of pleasure. It'd be different if they were married. But they weren't. And he was promised to her sister.

She tore her mouth from his. "Jesse, no." She tried to pull away, but his tight hold prevented her from moving.

"Oh, Summer." He sighed.

The thrill of everything happening brought another moan from her throat, but she knew she couldn't surrender. The strange feeling began to overwhelm her, but she could not forget he was her sister's fiancé.

She gathered her strength and pushed herself a few inches away. "Jesse, no," she said louder.

He stood and stared at her for a few moments as he held her stare. "Why'd you stop me?"

She frowned, hoping she looked as miserable and confused as she felt. "Can't you see? You and Violet are soon going to be living in this house as husband and wife. This is wrong, Jesse. I can't kiss you like this."

"But, you don't understand--"

She pressed her hands against his chest, trying to move further away, but he held her tight, refusing to let her go.

"Summer, listen to me."

Her temper snapped. "Let me go."

"Summer--"

"No. You're nothing but an insensitive, heartless, lusting...farm animal. If you want someone to kiss, do it to my sister."

She shoved against him with all the force of her body. Knocking herself off balance, she stumbled back. Her foot kicked the lantern, spilling fuel as she fell to the floor. Quick as lightening, the hem of her skirt was licked by a flame.

"Summer," he screamed and flew on top of her, rolling

with her on the ground and beating the flames until the fire was out. Just as quickly, he jumped and stomped out the small fire that had started on the floor.

He knelt down and gathered her in his arms. "Are you all right, darlin'?"

She calmed her panic. "Oh, Jesse," she said out of breath, "I... I... could have burned down your house."

"No, sweetheart. I wouldn't have let that happen." He lifted her skirt and checked her legs.

"I'm all right. The fire didn't touch my skin."

"Are you sure?"

"Yes, I think so."

He cupped her face in his hands, then leaned forward and kissed her lips briefly. "You don't know how terrified I was when I saw your skirt on fire."

"It scared me, too."

"If anythin' would've happened to you--" His voice cracked.

"Nothing happened. You saved me. Once again, you're my hero." She paused, then the thought struck her--he had done it again.

She pushed him away and jumped to her feet. "Curse your hide, Jesse Slade."

Falling back on his heels, he looked up at her, his brows creased. "What did I do now?"

She folded her arms as her temper snapped. "You...you...you always have to be the hero, don't you?"

He stood slowly, shaking his head. "Summer, I don't know what you mean."

"Oh, yes you do, and I'm tired of it. I'm so tired of it that I could...I could--" She paused, searching for her words. Without finishing, she whacked his chest.

"Hey. Whoa. What's goin' on? I don't understand you, Summer."

She continued to plunder him with soft blows even as Jesse deflected them, until her exhausted arms dropped to her sides. "Oh, it's hopeless. You'll never change and I'll certainly never change."

He grasped her shoulders. "Summer, for the life of me,

I can't figure out what you're talkin' about. Will you please tell me what I've done wrong? Why are you so mad?"

Tears gathered in her eyes and her chest felt like bursting. "I'm tired of the way everyone looks at you as if you were some kind of super magical, better than God, hero. You're nothing but a normal man. I hate you."

She stomped toward the door, but he grabbed her by the arm, turning her to face him. "Wait a minute. When did I ever wrong you? How long have you felt this way about me?"

"All my life." She sobbed. "I've always resented you because Pa wished you were his son and not me. I tried so hard, but I could never beat you. I could never show Pa that I'm better than you." Her emotions finally crumbled and the tears fell freely. She covered her face.

"I'm sorry you feel that way," he said softly. "I never had any intention of stealin' your pa's love. But if you'll really look at it, you'll see your pa loves you, Summer. He doesn't want you to be a boy. He's proud of the woman you've become because you're different, and that difference sets you apart from everyone else. Your pa loves you because you're Summer Bennett, not because he wants you to be another Jesse Slade. And no, Summer, I'm not a hero. I only do what I think is right. If others make me out to be a hero, I can't help it."

Tears flowed in streaks, but she lowered her hands and looked into his eyes. He was right. She didn't hate him, she wanted to, but she couldn't. There could only be one other reason this hurt her so bad.

She loved him.

A knot the size of Texas formed in her throat and left her speechless. But then, what could she say? He wasn't hers, and would never be. With her emotions in twisted confusion, she ran out of the cabin and into the night.

Eight

A small children's parade started the Waco Founder's Day festivities in style. Flags waved, banners soared, and people pleasantly visited back and forth. The heavenly aroma of popcorn and peppermint sticks filled the air, stirring Jesse's hungry stomach. In all the years he had attended, today's outing actually brought a smile to his face as he mingled amongst the town folk. At times, he found himself laughing out loud. Dare he wonder over this new attitude? Especially since last night's kiss left him in such confusion?

He leaned back against the street corner post and sighed, watching the hordes of people move from the parade to the displays lining the street. Women gathered around the baked goods and bottled fruits, cackling like proud peacocks over their talents. The men also boasted, but with a mug of beer in their hands. Jesse held back his laughter over their drunken gallantries.

From the corner of his eyes, he noticed another presence, one that confused him greatly. Summer seemed to be copying her sister by looking like the respectable young lady today. The autumn breeze teased the loose strands from the proper bun she had designed, and when she waved at an acquaintance, her glorious smile lit up her whole face. He lifted his lips in reaction.

She stopped by a table of hand-stitched items and touched the delicate crocheted pillowcase, admiring the talent he knew she didn't possess. But with Summer, the wifely talents didn't fit her character, and probably never would. He wondered if it really mattered.

Children darted past her skirts and tilted her off balance, making her angelic laughter ring through the air. His lips automatically pulled wider at the scene. As she crouched to their level and chatted with a few toddlers, a genuine sweetness radiated from her face. A little boy presented her with a daisy, and when Summer bestowed the youngster with a kiss on the cheek, Jesse's heart leapt.

Why can't she be that kind to me?

He closed his eyes and the memory of her kiss returned. His body experienced again the softness of her face and neck. Mentally shaking himself, he tried to force the wonderful sensations out of his thoughts before they drove him insane.

The clicking sound of women's heeled shoes sounded on the boardwalk, snapping his attention back to reality. As Summer and Violet walked his way, his heart accelerated. He took a quick glance at Violet who, as always, looked proper wearing a modest brown dress. Although Summer tried to imitate her sister, the creamy blouse molded better to her womanly figure. The rust colored skirt stretched across Summer's hips, pulling his focus in that direction.

When he realized the direction of his thoughts, he quickly lifted his gaze and met Summer's stare. A tint of pink highlighted her cheeks, and he inwardly cursed his wandering mind. He was sure she knew the direction of both his thoughts and eyes.

"Hello, Jesse," Violet greeted.

"Hello, Violet. Summer."

Summer nodded once and mumbled a soft greeting.

"Are you enjoying this lovely morning?" Violet asked.

"Yessiree. The autumn sun's never felt better."

"I agree." Violet took a quick glance at her sister. "Summer and I are on our way to play a few games. Jesse? Would you like to join us?"

He watched Summer's expression and held his laughter. The look of panic in her eyes told him exactly what she thought of the idea. He should join the two sisters just to antagonize Summer, but after considering the idea, he decided not to take Violet up on her invitation.

"Thanks for the offer, but I'm scheduled to help Clint over at the gunnysack races in a few minutes."

Violet smiled wide. "Oh, that sounds like a lot of fun. What do you say, Summer?" She elbowed her sister's arm. "Should we go support our favorite men?"

Summer studied her shoes and wouldn't meet his eyes.

"Yes. That would be all right."

"Great." Violet clapped. "Jesse, we'll see you over there in a little while."

"I'll be countin' the minutes." He chuckled as the women walked away, loving the sight of Summer's ramrod-straight back and the gentle sway of her skirt. When he felt himself smiling like a kid on Christmas day, he quickly sobered. He had to remember the stubborn woman didn't want anything to do with him.

Hanging his head, he sauntered over to the field where the gunnysack race had been set up. Clint's voice boomed through the streets, inviting everyone to participate. Jesse handed out the sacks and lined up the runners. Clint gave a loud whistle, starting the race.

Putting Summer's attitude temporarily out of his thoughts, Jesse found himself laughing with the others. Time quickly slipped by and before he knew it Summer and Violet stood in front of him, ready to receive their gunnysacks. He smiled politely and handed Summer a sack, then gave one to Violet. It surprised him to see Violet like this, so full of spirit and having fun. It'd been too long since she'd been this cheerful.

At Clint's whistle, the racers geared onward, contestants pushing themselves to their very limits. Laughter throughout the small crowd grew as people began falling to the ground, but not Summer. Of course, the little spitfire always tried to beat everyone. The race ended when Summer crossed the finish line first. Her flushed face and tousled hair made his chest ache with that familiar feeling. He cursed fate for choosing Summer for the woman who could awaken his emotions.

Summer joined in the next race and succeeded in winning again. When she paid for the following race, he decided she needed a lesson in humility. He grabbed a gunnysack and stood in line beside her. When her eyes met his, he gave her one of his self-assured grins, silently communicating his intention. She read his expression perfectly and lifted her chin, accepting the challenge.

He tried to remember that he was upset with her, but watching her only made him feel giddy.

"On your mark," Clint began loudly. "Get set. Go!"

Jesse put his full effort into the race, staying right next to Summer. Her determined glances let him know that she would not give up, but then again, neither would he.

Neck and neck he jumped beside her, making his way to the finish line, enough ahead that it looked as if he'd win the game. Mere feet before he reached the finish line, a nagging thought entered his mind. Their conversation from last night at the cabin hit him full force, her voice echoing loudly. *"I've always resented you because Pa wished you were his son and not me. I tried so hard, but I could never beat you. I could never show Pa that I was better than you."*

A pain sliced through his chest and he knew he couldn't beat her now. He had to forfeit the game.

Faking a fall, he tumbled to the ground just inches away from the finish line. The crowd cheered as his opponent crossed first. He looked up and saw triumph on Summer's face and his heart melted. He'd made the right decision when he noticed her happy expression.

He stood and climbed out of the sack then brushed the dirt off his jeans. With the game over, the crowd drifted away and he took the opportunity to go over to her. She held a different look in her eyes when she faced him this time. Dare he hope her feelings have changed?

He smiled and stretched forth his right hand. "Congratulations, Summer."

Her humble smile softened when she placed her hand in his. "Thank you."

He didn't know if she thanked him for handing over the race or for his kind praise, but suddenly it didn't matter. Her expression was enough. His hand warmed against her skin.

She withdrew her hand, and with a light heart, he watched her walk away. For the first time he could remember, he didn't feel upset over her competitiveness because now he understood why she had this drive to win.

Somebody's strong grip clutched his arm and he turned. Clint stood behind him. "That was a good thing you did. I'm proud of you."

Jesse gave his brother a blank stare. "Proud of me for what?"

"For fakin' the fall. I don't know if anyone else could tell, but I knew what you were doin'." He nodded. "Good job, li'l brother."

Jesse shrugged. "Well, a guy's gotta do what a guy's gotta do."

The loud bell from the middle of town captured their attention. The afternoon event would be starting in a few minutes. In the past years, Jesse hadn't been excited about the picnic, but today he couldn't wait. "Come on, Clint. Let's go."

Clint chuckled. "Well, I'm not rightly a young'un any longer and this picnic's just for you young folks."

"Oh, that's hogwash. You're just as available as I am."

Clint's brows creased. "Whatcha talkin' about? You're engaged, aren't you?"

Jesse hesitated, unable to confess what has transpired between him and Violet. Playfully, he slugged his brother in the arm. "You know what I mean."

Clint nodded. "I suppose."

Side by side Jesse and Clint meandered over to the grandstand, then stood by as the single adults gather around for the auction. The advertised purpose for this year's picnic was to help raise funds for the new church, but everybody knew the real reason was to match young couples together.

Jesse studied the eager young women who'd baked and decorated their lovely baskets all morning, hoping to snatch a young man who would make the highest bid for their lunch. Twenty-five baskets displayed for auction and the same amount of giggling females stood sneaking peaks at the men who clustered together on the opposite side.

Out of all the young ladies, Jesse's attention held to one particular female. Summer couldn't help but outshine the rest. Her hair had fallen out of her tidy bun and was pulled back with a rust colored ribbon. She looked prettier than all the other girls.

This was Summer's first year entering the picnic, but she didn't seem as eager as the others. Of course, she wouldn't. She didn't have a special man in her life to place a bid on her basket. He wondered if she even cared about such things. Did she want to become a wife, a mother like the other girls?

When the auctioneer picked a basket, the young girl who owned it blushed profoundly. It was easy to see which basket belonged to whom. Jesse rolled his eyes over the girl's childlike antics. Halfway through the proceedings, the auctioneer picked a basket whose owner didn't turn red as a beet. Jesse's curiosity had been aroused and his gaze studied each of the remaining girls.

The auctioneer started the bidding. "Who'll bid for this tastey basket of food? Do I hear ten cents?"

Clint chuckled softly then raised his hand. "I'll bid two bits."

Jesse raised his brows. He thought he knew his older brother, and lately he wondered if Clint might have a secret love. Jesse's interest sparked and he looked forward to discovering the lucky lady.

Mr. Banks grinned. "Fifty cents? That's a good bid, Mr. Slade. Do I hear fifty-five?"

Another man in the crowd reached out his hand and waved. "I bid fifty-five."

Mr. Banks' smile widened. "Good, good. Do I hear sixty cents?"

Clint nodded. "Sixty."

"Thank you, Mr. Slade. Do I hear sixty-five? Does anybody want to go against Clint Slade?"

Jesse laughed and nudged his brother teasingly, then shouted, "I'll bid eighty cents."

Gasps echoed throughout the crowd and Jesse realized everyone suspected that he would bid on Violet's basket like he had every year. This particular basket wasn't Violet's because she always decorated hers in the same material as her dress.

Clint glanced down at Jesse and winked. "You think so, do you?" he whispered. "I bid one dollar," he said louder.

Gasps exploded all around and Jesse kept his attention on the girls, but he still couldn't figure out to whom the basket belonged.

Mr. Banks' full smile showed his enthusiasm. "Oh, Mr. Slade that is an excellent bid. Remember men, we're thinking about the funds for a new church. So let's loosen our moneybags and dig in a little deeper. Do I hear one dollar and ten cents?"

"How about one dollar and fifty cents?" Jesse called.

"One dollar and fifty cents? Do I hear more?" Mr. Banks asked.

"Two dollars," Clint yelled.

"Do I hear two dollars and fifty cents?" Mr. Banks looked over at Jesse.

Jesse shook his head and held up his hands in surrender. As much as he wanted to tease his brother, he couldn't embarrass Violet by winning another basket.

Mr. Banks ended the bidding as he smacked his pallet down on the small wooden box in front of him. "Sold to Clint Slade for two dollars," he exclaimed and the crowd cheered.

Jesse couldn't wait any longer. He had to know what lady held his brother's interest. "Who does the basket belong to?" he yelled.

Mr. Banks glanced at the name on the card, then his eyes widened. "It belongs to Miss Summer Bennett."

Immediately pain gripped Jesse's stomach and all his excitement vanished. He kept his eyes on his brother when he joined Summer and the look of pleasure on Clint's face explained he'd known the true identity of the basket's owner all this time. Jesse's gallant brother drew Summer's hand around the crook of his arm and escorted her to a spot just inside the trees. Both Clint and Summer wore wide grins.

Jesse didn't like it one bit.

~ * ~

Summer smiled up at Clint when he claimed her for the afternoon. Her escort's mouth lifted teasingly as if he played the part of the cat, and she, the canary.

"You'll regret paying that much for my basket," she warned. "I assure you my lunch doesn't taste anywhere near a two-dollar dinner."

He laughed and picked up the basket. "But you must remember, Miss Bennett, the money goes to help the new church."

"True, but I still think you should not have bid so high."

"Awh, Summer. Your company is well worth two bucks."

She tilted her head and looked into his handsome face. "Why, thank you, kind sir."

She led Clint over to a spot she had previously chosen for their picnic, then laid out the blanket with Clint's help. She felt comfortable with Clint and they bantered back and forth lightly as the afternoon slid by. She enjoyed Clint's company. He complimented her on the meal and he actually ate every bite. She prayed he wouldn't get sick afterward.

During the meal, her gaze strayed across the field to her sister and Jesse. They sat on their blanket looking as if they enjoyed their friendly lunch, except they were not supposed to be friends. They were supposed to be in love. Why would two people in love not look at each other or touch hands? At least they could smile at one another. Plain and simple, Jesse and Violet looked absolutely bored.

"So, Summer," Clint said, forcing her to take her gaze away from Jesse. "Whatcha been up to lately? I really haven't spoken to you much since you came home."

"True, but you've been busy. I'm sure it was no little task building a cabin."

He grinned. "I didn't build it all by m'self, you know."

"I seriously doubt that. I know you, and you're too honorable to admit it was all your doing."

He laughed and leaned down on the blanket, his elbow holding his weight. "But we've gotten off the subject. Are you back for good or do you plan on goin' back to your aunt's again?"

"I'm back for good."

"What do you plan on doin' now?"

She shrugged. "I haven't thought about it."

"I'm thinkin' you will do what every girl your age does. Find yourself a man, get married and have a litter of kids."

She laughed. "That's not what all girls my age do." She playfully pushed his shoulder, rocking him back on the blanket.

"That's right. I forgot that you're different." He righted himself fully. "Your purpose in life is to irritate my brother."

She looked down at her lap and absently picked off a biscuit crumb. "Maybe, maybe not."

Clint reached over and nudged her chin up with his finger. "Hey runt, what's wrong? Did I say somethin' outta turn?"

"No." Her gaze rose and met his, and the resemblance between him and Jesse disturbed her. "I don't know what has gotten into me lately, but I can't carry on a decent conversation with your brother no matter how hard I try. He just loves to get my goat, and he doesn't care if it hurts me."

He leaned forward and took hold of her hands. "Summer, tell me somethin'."

"What?"

"Why would he hurt you now when he's never hurt you before?"

She looked across the field to Jesse. "I can't explain it." She shrugged. "Maybe it's because I'm a woman now and I have tender feelings."

Clint laughed and withdrew his hands. "Or maybe it's 'cause you don't want to see Jess marry your sister?"

Her head swung back to Clint. A brief silence passed between them as she studied his serious expression.

She nodded, hoping she didn't give her true feelings away. She must led Clint to believe that she still disliked Jesse. "I don't think my sister should marry him. I think Violet deserves better."

"But my brother's a good guy."

"I hold a different opinion." She folded her arms across her chest. "Maybe it's pure selfishness, but I don't want him as my brother-in-law."

"Whatcha goin' to do about it?"

Her eyes widened. "Why do you think I'm going to do something?"

Clint howled with laughter. "Because, my dear runt, I know you well."

She smiled fully. "Would you hate me if I did something to stop the wedding?"

He looked at her quizzically. "Don't rightly know.""

"Will you help me?"

He shrugged. "I'll have to really think about it."

He gave her a wink, and it reminded her of Jesse again. The uncomfortable feeling surfaced inside her chest, and although she sometimes got might angry with Jesse, the attraction was still there. Curse that irresistible Jesse Slade!

~ * ~

Summer welcomed the setting sun because it brought the cool night air, and for the barn dance it was certainly a refreshing treat. This would be her first dance since she was an adult and excitement filled her when she thought about showing the town just how much she'd changed. Before she had moved in with Aunt Lydia, she attended the dance, but because of her young age, she went home before dark.

Although she tried to impress all the young men, there was really only one man her gaze searched for, curse his hide. Since she couldn't get Jesse off her mind, she went about flirting with every man who danced with her, hoping to forget about the man who had kissed her so passionately last night. But tonight she decided not to think about that, the effect of the homemade brew she consumed aiding her greatly in the decision.

She felt so pretty in the new shimmering blue dress that fit her bodice and waist perfectly. It showed off the tops of her shoulders, and a fair amount of bosom. The bustle even accented her slender hips. Yes, she felt beautiful and very feminine. Of course, when most of the men fought over her to see who would be her next dancing partner or who would go fetch her another mug of brew, it boosted her ego tenfold.

The gallantry of the young gentlemen almost took her mind off Jesse, who danced with many girls and looked to be enjoying himself. His intoxicating blue eyes sparkled when he laughed at something his dance partner said, but she tried not to notice. She also couldn't help but notice that he didn't dance that often with Violet. In fact, for a man in love, he was not around Violet often enough.

Summer's surprise expanded when Clint showered her with constant attention. She liked his focus only because it made the younger men try harder. But Clint would always be like an older brother to her. His facial features looked much like Jesse's-- chiseled cheeks, square jaw, straight nose, perfectly sculptured lips. His hair was a much darker color than Jesse's, and thankfully, Clint's eyes were not as baby blue and dreamy.

"My dear, Miss Bennett." Clint grinned and mocked a small bow. "Would you give me the pleasure of this next dance?"

She smiled and slid into a half curtsy. "Why certainly, you handsome devil." She took his arm and went with him to the center of the barn floor.

The dance was a quick, toe-tapping, knee-slapping rhythm, and the dance floor filled quickly. Clint's capable hands led her around the floor with ease. His quick feet kept the beat and didn't step on her toes even once, which relieved her, since most of her dances were spent moving her feet from under her partner's.

She laughed from exhaustion when the dance ended. She followed Clint off the floor and over to the water bucket. She accepted the water, almost wishing it was the beer, but it eased her parched throat and helped to cool her temperature.

"That was fun." He laughed and took another long drink.

After setting her cup down, she daintily wiped her moist brow with a handkerchief. "Yes, it was. You're a really good dancer. Wherever did you learn? I thought all you ever did was ride with the Rangers and chase outlaws."

"I'll never tell my secrets."

"Confess, Clint. Do you leave broken hearts in every town you visit? Are there a string of women who wait for you to return? Could one of these lucky women be the one who taught you to dance?"

He leaned closer. "I'll never tell."

She swatted his arm playfully. "You're cruel, absolutely cruel."

"And you're as cute as a bug." He slipped his arm around her waist and pulled her next to his side. "Would you like to go outside for some fresh air?"

She gave him a sideways glance. At first she thought he was teasing, but his eyes held a streak of seriousness. She wondered about his intentions. Hopefully, it wasn't the same reason most boys wanted to take girls outside in the dark. Clint had always thought of her as the little sister he never had. "I guess I could use a little fresh air."

Without taking his arm from around her waist, he moved them toward the barn doors. Just as they reached the opening, another man approached, moving in front of her and Clint. She didn't react right away, but Clint did.

"Hello, Jess," Clint greeted. "Are you havin' a good time?"

Jesse smiled at his brother and a familiar ache grew around her heart, darn him.

"Yessiree. Tell me one person who isn't?"

Jesse moved his gaze back to her and his eyes swept over her body. His boldness stirred her blood and she trembled with wanting.

"Summer?" he asked. "Would you honor me with the

next dance?"

She was taken back. She looked to Clint. "Is it all right if we take a walk afterward?"

Clint winked. "It's alrighty by me."

She cautiously slipped her arm around Jesse's elbow as he escorted her to the dance floor. Once the fiddle began singing, she realized this was the worst possible dance to have with him. Why did it have to be a waltz?

Jesse curved his arm around her waist and cradled her fingers in his large hand. "You look mighty pretty tonight," he said softly.

She blushed, but hoped he would think her flushed face was the result of the heat in the barn. "Thank you. And I think you look exceptionally handsome."

His eyebrow rose and he missed a step. "Oh, really? I didn't think you noticed."

"Why wouldn't I notice you?"

"Because you've been too busy flirtin' with other men."

Her eyes widened. "Have you been spying on me, Jesse?" She shook her head. "Tsk, tsk. Shame on you. Don't you know that it's rude to ogle your fiancée's sister?"

He lifted an eyebrow. "I wouldn't exactly call it oglin', Summer."

"What would you call it?" She leaned closer and lowered her voice. "Would you call it...lusting?"

His arm tightened around her waist and he stared into her eyes. The heat from the barn had nothing to do with the rise in her temperature now. She realized how comfortable it felt to be in his arms and she hoped this dance would last forever.

"Do you want me to lust after you?" His voice turned seductive, which made her heart pump madly.

What had she gotten herself into this time? Couldn't she remember what it did to her insides? "That wouldn't be a good thing to do to your fiancée's sister."

"You're right. It wouldn't be a good thing to do at all."

Straightening her posture, she concentrated on her steps, but as hard as she tried, she couldn't keep from staring into his intoxicating eyes. Unfortunately, none of the other men could compare to Jesse. The poor lost souls couldn't even compare to Clint.

"Summer? Can I ask you a personal question?"

"Depends on how personal it is."

His lips turned up into a lopsided grin. "I'm sure you'll think it's very personal."

"Ooh, now I'm curious."

Silence lasted a few awkward moments as he struggled with his words. "I want to know...well, shoot, how can I say this without soundin' like some over-protective father?"

She laughed lightly. The look of agitation on his face told her of his discomfort.

He took a deep breath. "Why is Clint suddenly payin' court to you?"

The question startled her, making her miss a couple of steps, but she quickly recovered. "How would I know? I thought you could tell me."

"So, it's true? He's payin' you court?"

"I don't think so. He's being extremely friendly and he's giving me more attention, but I think he just likes my company."

"Yes, I think he likes it a little too much."

She wrinkled her forehead. "Jesse, just what are you implying?"

"The way I see it, Clint is flirtin' with you, and you're flirtin' right back."

"What's so wrong with that?"

"Because, he's practically a brother to you."

"So. Clint and I are not related, as you well know, Jesse Slade."

"There's a thirteen-year age difference."

"So. What difference does that make?"

"It's just not right." His voice rose.

"Oh, but it's all right for my sister's fiancée to flirt with me?"

She knew her voice was loud, but really didn't care who overheard. Apparently, Jesse did. He glanced around them quickly, then glared at her as his arm tightened around her waist. "Summer, I'm not talkin' about me. I'm tryin' to figure out what my brother's doin' and put a stop to it."

She gasped. "That's the most ludicrous thing I've ever heard. You want to put a stop to your brother's fun? Do you want him to be as miserable as you?"

"What makes you think I'm miserable? I'll have you know I'm havin' a heapin' good time tonight."

She rolled her eyes. "Oh, sure, with every woman but the one you're engaged to. You can't even put your arm around my sister and show her a little affection." She huffed. "Good heavens, Jesse, you're going to be married. Why don't you start acting like a man in love?"

"I thought I said," he bit out slowly and deeply, "that I don't want to talk about me."

"On the other hand," she snapped, "I happen to think this whole conversation is about you. I don't know why, but I think you are jealous of your brother. He is unattached and carefree and you feel as if you're drowning because you are about to get married. Yes, Jesse, I do think this is all about you, but if you are so unhappy with my sister, why don't you do something about it?"

The music stopped and she turned sharply on her heels, leaving Jesse standing on the dance floor. Steam threatened to rise from her ears. Summer was suddenly in great need of some fresh cool air. Nothing and nobody was going to stop her from going outside with Clint now.

Nine

Summer let out an exhausted sigh when the cool night air touched her face. She gazed up into the star-filled sky and replayed the conversation with Jesse in her mind. Anger threatened to consume her once again, but she glanced at Clint and allowed herself to be calmed by her walk with him.

"It's a lovely night," she told him. "Thank goodness the weather is cool."

Clint nodded. "'Specially since we're all worked up over dancin'." He paused and looked at her. "But I don't think you're as worked up over dancin' as you are over Jess."

She stopped and faced him with hands on her hips. "What is that supposed to mean?"

"It means," he said as he moved closer and gently grasped her elbows, relaxing her stance, "the dance you shared with my brother has left you very upset."

"It doesn't matter what I do with Jesse, I'm always left extremely irritable."

He chuckled and shook his head. "Nothin's changed between you two. I remember when you'll were younger, and after every argument, you'd come lookin' to me for comfort."

"You were someone to release my frustrations on because I couldn't take them out on Jesse."

"Why not?"

"He wouldn't let me." She chuckled. "Just when I was about to give him a piece of my mind, he'd turn and walk away. I never did get the final word."

"He didn't have much patience for you back then."

Her smile quickly disappeared. "He still doesn't."

"Oh, no, he can now. You've changed, Summer."

She shook her head. "Not around him. I don't know

what it is, but every time I get around that man, it doesn't matter how hard I try to be nice, he always rubs me the wrong way."

Clint circled his arms around her waist and pulled her close. "Lucky man."

His comment took her by surprise. She tried to read his expression, but couldn't. "Why?"

He grinned. "Cause he can rub you, and I can't."

"Oh, Clint, you're funny."

"What's so funny about wantin' to rub you?"

His eyes scanned her face, down her neck and chest, making her feel a slight discomfort.

"I'll admit that you have the kind of body most men dream about touchin'," he continued.

Bluntness had never been a problem with Clint, but this time it sounded so improper. Heat from her embarrassment touched her cheeks. "Clint, really."

His arms tightened. "I'm sorry I shocked you, but it's the truth."

"Are you saying I have the kind of body you dream about?"

He lifted his chin. "I don't think I'll answer that one." He smiled. "I wouldn't want to embarrass you anymore."

She rather liked his flirtation. Didn't mean it would go any further, but that was all right with her. She placed her hands on his chest and admired his muscular build as her fingers absently played with the string-tie hanging from his neck. "Well, since we're confessing secrets right now, I'll have to admit that you, too, have the body most girls dream about."

"Good girls or bad girls?"

She laughed. "Both."

"Didn't know good girls dreamed 'bout men's bodies. Didn't think that naughty thought even crossed their innocent minds."

"Well, I consider myself a good girl." His brows rose in question, so she hurried with, "No matter what you seem to think." He laughed as she continued, "But there have been a few occasions where I've let my imagination run rampant."

"Oh, really?"

"Yes. Of course, it helped to have an aunt who told stories

about her own romantic escapades."

"Your Aunt Lydia?"

"Yes."

"What kinda stories?"

"Let's just say I'm not as innocent to the secrets of marriage as most girls my age."

"Not from experience, I hope."

Her cheeks burned again. "Oh, no. But my ears have been scorched to the core."

His arms tightened until her body pressed intimately to his. "So, can you tell me what I'm thinkin' right now? What kinda signals are you receivin'?"

The kind she didn't like--at least, not from him. Although their flirtation had been fun, she didn't think she'd liked to be kissed by him. "I think you're trying to tease me."

"Wrong answer." His face moved closer to hers. "Dare to try again?"

Her heart hammered quickly, but not from excitement. What was she doing with him? And why did he want to kiss her? "Clint, I don't think--"

"Then don't," he whispered right before his mouth covered hers.

This wasn't their first kiss, nor would it be their last, but this kiss was far different than the kind he used to give her when she was a child. This was the kind of kiss lovers shared. Like the one she'd shared with Jesse. His lips were soft and gentle as they moved upon hers. Too bad he was Clint and not another man. She didn't think she could ever have passionate feelings for Clint.

He drew back slightly. "Summer? You're too stiff. Relax and enjoy." His lips moved back to hers and suckled them.

She closed her eyes and tried to follow his request, but she still felt as if she were kissing her brother. Strange that she would wish Clint was Jesse right now. Why couldn't she think of Jesse as one of her brothers? Shoot, he was as bad as a pesky mosquito. The thought brought a silent chuckle to her throat.

Clint pulled back, confusion evident in his eyes. "Now that's a first. Never in my life has a woman laughed while I tried to seduce her."

Her face heated. "Oh, Clint, I didn't mean to laugh."

"Then why did you?"

Her mind scrambled to think of an excuse. She could never confess that she had been thinking about Jesse. How could she explain her feeling for Jesse when she couldn't figure them out herself? "It's funny because you're like a big brother to me."

He grinned. "True."

"And kissing you feels like I'm kissing my own brother."

His eyes widened. "Do Nate or Charles kiss that good?"

A bubble of laughter escaped her. "Certainly not. But it doesn't matter. The situation just struck me funny."

His fingers moved to her mouth and stroked her bottom lip. "So, you didn't get excited in any way?"

"Your lips felt nice and I liked the way you kissed, but I couldn't help wishing you were somebody else."

One of his dark bushy eyebrows rose. "Who?"

"Just somebody besides the man who I've looked upon as a big brother pretty much my whole life."

He sighed heavily and relaxed his face as a smile touched his lips. "You're a good kisser, Summer, but you're right. I didn't get excited, either."

"See? It's not right for us."

"Darn. I was hopin' to get to know you a little better t'night."

"You have, just as I've gotten to know you. But Clint? We'll always be good friends, and I want that more from you than I want a beau right now."

It took him a few seconds before he nodded. "You're right. I don't know what I'd do without you as my friend." He rubbed his knuckles on her cheek. "Now I need to confess somethin'."

"What?"

"The main reason I brought you out here was to make somebody jealous."

Although she should have punched him in the nose for that, she laughed instead. "Now it's my turn to confess."

"You, confess?"

She nodded. "The main reason I came out here with you was to make somebody jealous, too."

He laughed as he hooked her arm through his and turned

them back toward the barn. As they drew closer, Jesse's muscluar body caught her attention. He stood by the open double doors as he peered out into the night. She didn't know if he could see what she'd been doing, but he looked very upset--so, yes, he probably did see her. She silently groaned.

She glanced at Clint. "I think we better go in before your brother decides to act like an arrogant hero again."

"You think he will?"

"Yes. He has been acting strangely tonight."

"Really?"

She nodded. "He seems to think I've been flirting too much. He also can't understand why you have become attracted to me."

Clint looked at his brother with a wide smile. "Then we better go in. I'd hate to have Jess thinkin' badly of you."

She laughed. "Too late. He already does."

~ * ~

Jesse's mood declined the longer the night wore on. The heat from inside the barn warped his mind, which led him frequently to the refreshing breeze coming from the open doors. He scanned the shadows in the night, and when he couldn't see Clint and Summer, his temper escalated.

He'd been counting the minutes since he saw them leave. So far it'd been twenty, and his patience thinned. He lingered by the barn doors, waiting for their return, but the wondering only increased his foul mood.

After what seemed like an eternity, they finally emerged into the light, and he stepped back into the barn's shadows before they noticed him. About to burst from anger and afraid he might let his emotions get the better of him, he quickly distanced himself from his brother.

Another cup of Jed Hansen's homemade brew would calm his temper. He marched over to the table, filled his cup to the brim, and quickly gulped down the scalding liquid. Within seconds, he refilled his empty cup. Out of the corner of his eyes he saw Clint coming toward him, but Summer wasn't with him. Jesse breathed a sigh of relief, then mentally tried to shake off his anger.

Clint reached Jesse's side. The grin on his brother's face was a testament to his happy mood. Jesse's blood boiled.

"How are you enjoyin' the dance?" Clint asked.

"It started out fine, but it's endin' rather miserably," Jesse grumbled.

Clint's eyes widened. "What's wrong? Seems to me like it's the same as last year's dance."

Jesse glanced across the crowd. "No, it's not the same."

"What's so different?"

Jesse turned away from his brother and leaned against the table with another drink in his hand. As his gaze skimmed the dance floor, he found Summer with another man. Even through his jealous anger, he still thought she was the prettiest woman at the dance. She smiled while she danced with this man, and her eyes sparkled. Would she ever look at him that way? His heart dropped. Probably not.

Ignoring Clint's last question, he quickly changed the subject. "So, what's the story with you and Summer?"

"There's no story."

He looked at Clint and arched a brow. "Oh? Didn't look that way to me."

Clint leaned his hip against the table and folded his arms across his chest, wearing that all too cocky grin that Jesse didn't like.

"How did it look?" Clint asked.

"Well, considerin' you bid quite high on her picnic basket, and the way you danced with her and then took her outside for a breath of fresh air, I'd say it looks as if you're smitten with the girl."

Clint threw back his head and laughed. "All right, so I'll admit I find the girl irresistible t'night. She's quite beautiful, or haven't you noticed?"

Jesse ignored the last question. He didn't dare confess aloud how lovely he thought she looked, and especially what kind of feelings shot through his body. "Does that give you the right to pursue her?"

Clint shrugged. "She acts like she enjoys it."

"Of course she enjoys it." He moved closer to his brother. "It's probably the first time anyone ever treated her like a woman."

Clint's smile stayed on his face as he looked out across the floor. "She also didn't seem to mind the kiss I gave her."

Jesse gritted his teeth so hard he thought they'd break. The need to drive his fist into Clint's face almost overwhelmed him. He tightened his grip around the mug of homemade beer and threw his brother a glare.

"You took advantage of Summer Bennett?" he asked then quickly gulped down a swallow to cool his temper.

Clint shook his head. "No. I kissed her, that's all."

"And she didn't resist?"

"No. She, too, was curious."

"And?"

"And what? We kissed. That's all."

Jesse slammed his empty cup on the table. "No, it's not all. I want to know if there will be other kisses?"

"Li'l brother." Clint moved over and placed his hand on Jesse's shoulder. "If I didn't know you any better, I'd think you were jealous. You're not her father nor her brother, so quit actin' like it. 'Sides, you have no claim to her. You're engaged to Violet, or have you forgotten?"

Jesse pushed Clint's hand off his shoulder. "No, I haven't forgotten." He quickly filled his cup again.

Silence sliced through the air as Jesse fought to keep his anger from reaching its boiling point. He breathed deeply. "So, are you going to kiss her again?"

Clint slid his hands into his back pockets and rocked back on his heels. "Don't rightly know. If the occasion arises, I might. But what business is that of yours?"

"I'd hate to have you break her heart. You've been around, Clint. You know things she doesn't understand. Summer's a country girl. It'd crush her to think you cared and to have you break her heart."

Clint's eyes widened. "What makes you think I'll break her heart?"

"I've seen the way you leave women cryin' after you. You're a love'em and leave'em kind of guy, and Summer needs a forever kind of man. Somebody who'll commit to her."

A grin touched Clint's lips. "Just like yourself, right?"

"Yes, like me--uh, I mean, not like me, but sorta like me." He brought up the brew up to his mouth and tossed back the liquid, hoping it would cover up his fuzzy mind.

Clint hid a smile behind his hand, and Jesse gnashed his teeth. Didn't Clint have any feelings? Didn't he understand? This was not a joke.

"Well, li'l brother." Clint patted his shoulder. "If I think I'm breakin' her heart, I'll let you know. I'm sure you'll be there to pick up the pieces."

Jesse nodded. "And don't think I won't." He set his cup down gentler this time. "I mean, um...she'll need a shoulder to cry on, and I have big, solid shoulders."

"Yes, and you're just the kindhearted man that the girls go to cry on."

Jesse nodded, but his hazy mind didn't quite understand what Clint had just said.

Clint walked away chuckling. Jesse had to find Summer and warn her about Clint's intentions. He didn't want Summer to fall in love with Clint, only because his brother would surely break her heart. But what bothered him more was thinking that Summer would actually have feelings for his brother. *Why does she want Clint and not me?*

His focus stayed on his brother, even when Clint went over to Violet and asked her to dance. That was all right, because this gave Jesse the chance to locate Summer and warn her. But as he glanced out across the dance floor, he didn't see her anywhere. Damnation. What if another man decided to take her outside and steal a kiss?

It looked as if Jesse was going to play hero again. He sauntered out of the barn, bumping into a few people on his way. But he had to save her cute little hide and especially, her virtue.

~ * ~

Summer drew in a deep breath and let the cool air clear her lungs. The unbearable heat in the barn overwhelmed her. So did Jesse. He'd been watching her all night, just as she couldn't stop watching him. As the night wore on, his mood declined rapidly. His heart-warming smile had disappeared and lines of sadness marred his handsome face.

Summer had abandoned her friends and left the barn unnoticed. Privacy was what she needed, and maybe a moment of solitude would clear the confusing thoughts lingering in her head. There was definitely a growing attraction between her and Jesse, but he was the one engaged to her sister--so then why did he watch her with his dreamy stare?

She walked behind the barn and passed the haystacks, the bright moon lighting her path. After finding a comfortable spot to sit on the ground, she looked to the stars sprinkled in the darkened sky. She frowned. It would be a perfect night for lovers.

Jesse, oh Jesse, she sighed and squeezed her eyes shut. What could she do about her feelings for him? And how could she control her anger whenever he was around? It was actually a good thing she exploded so easily. It kept her from doing things with him she knew were wrong. She didn't want to hurt her sister, and going behind Violet's back and kissing Jesse was definitely wrong.

But, what if by chance, something were to happen to change Jesse and Violet's mind about getting married? She opened her eyes and straightened. Could she prevent herself from arguing with Jesse? Could she actually go through a whole conversation without getting mad?

Probably not.

A loud thump from the other side of the barn snapped her out of her thoughts. A man cursed and groaned, then came another loud kerplunk against the wall. She rose and dashed to see if somebody had fallen. She turned the corner and stumbled over the body lying in her path.

Kneeling beside the person, she turned him over to see if she could help. The man groaned as his arm fell away from his face.

"Jesse?" she asked in amazement.

"Oh, sheeeet," he slurred.

She didn't disguise the laughter in her voice. "Jesse? Are you drunk?"

He pulled himself to a sitting position and rubbed the side of his head. "Yup. Think so."

He looked at her, blinked a few times as if trying to focus on her face. When recognition finally struck, he grinned.

"Summer, darlin'? What's a haystack like you doin' out here in these fields of women?"

She smothered another laugh with her hand. "Jesse? What happened?"

His fingers drew circles on his forehead. "I'm not rightly

sure. I was walkin' along, and suddenly the side of the barn jumped out and smacked my head."

Her laughter echoed through the night. "Can you get up?"

"I think so." He moved to stand, tilted and fell. He blinked a few times. "Maybe I'll have to wait until the bright stars leave my eyes first."

"I declare, Jesse, I think you are very drunk."

"Nah." He brushed his hand through the air.

She glanced toward the barn. "Where's Violet? Does she know how drunk you are?"

"No." He grabbed her arm, pulling her down beside him. "Don't get Violet. She doesn't need to see me this way. 'Sides, she's happy right now and I'd hate to ruin her mood." He let go of her arm and slumped against her. "It isn't very often I see her happy."

"What are you talking about? You make her happy."

"No, I don't." His head rolled and his face fell into her chest.

Senstaions stirred within her bosom and she pushed against him, but his dead weight kept him in place. "Jesse, please."

"Nobody loves me," he mumbled. "Nobody cares that I'm unhappy."

"Jesse, you're talking nonsense." She pushed him upright. "Come on, we need to get you home and sober you up. Is Clint still at the dance? I'll go get him and he can help."

"No," he shouted again, his gaze colliding with hers. "I don't want his help. You don't need his help either. He's bad news, Summer. He'll hurt ya and break yer heart in two." He drunkenly held up three fingers.

Feeling confused, she shook her head and tried not to grin. "For the life of me, I wish I knew what you were talking about."

"You can help. You can take me home." He swung his arm around her neck and tried to stand. He wobbled against her, so she helped him to his feet and held him until his legs were steady. Leaning on her for support, he slipped his arm around her shoulders. It took great effort to get him to the buggy, but determination guided her every step. It was embarrassing to see Jesse so drunk he could hardly walk, and she didn't want the town to see him like this.

"Summer?" his voice whined slightly.

"Yes, Jesse?"

"Have I told ya how purty ya are ta-night?"

His face was too close, and she really didn't want to look right at him, so she continued to watch their feet as she drug him to the carriage. "Yes, I think you mentioned it while we were dancing."

"And have I told ya what a good dancer ya are?"

"No."

His face fell into her hair as he breathed deeply. "And ya smell just like honeysuckle."

"Thank you." She tried to ignore the tingles spiraling through her body and took careful steps, but he still lagged beside her. "Would you quit talking and concentrate on moving your feet? I can't carry you."

"Oh, Summer, do ya know what y're doin'?" He looked into her eyes and grinned. "Y're rescuin' me. Y're my hero."

She rolled her eyes heavenward and kept walking. Once they were at the buggy, she pushed him into the seat then climbed in beside him. Urging the horses forward, she hurried to get home before he lost consciousness. The ride went smoothly, even when she dragged him out of the rig and into the house. After depositing him on his bed, she stepped into the kitchen and lit the stove to heat the kettle for coffee.

When she walked back into the room, the scene she witnessed stopped her in her tracks and made her want to laugh. Jesse sat on the edge of the bed, pulling off his boots. He'd managed to lift one foot over the other, earnestly trying to accomplish the task, but it was his comical expression that made her smile. His forehead creased as he concentrated, his tongue caught between his teeth and lips, and his face crinkled with the effort it took. The absolute strain etched on his face reminded her of a little boy diligently trying to complete a complicated task. Through his grunts and groans, she could tell his effort was getting him nowhere.

"Here, let me help." She moved beside him, bent and grabbed his boot. "I swear, Jesse, you're the most obstinate person I know. I don't know why you decided to get yourself drunk tonight, but it's the most idiotic thing you've ever done. I hope you have a tremendous headache in the morning."

She pulled off the boot and raised the other foot. Glancing into his eyes, she noticed a tender expression when he looked back at her. Gone was the boyish look, replaced with one she didn't want to define.

"Thank you," he said softly.

She smiled. "You're welcome."

"You didn't have to help me."

"Yes I did."

"Why?"

"Because if I didn't, you could've been discovered by Violet, and I didn't want my sister to see her future husband in this condition."

His fingers grazed her cheek. "You do care about me, don't you?" The drunken slur had left his speech.

Her attention switched back to his boot. She didn't want to answer his question, so she concentrated on her task. Luckily, she didn't have to answer.

"You do, I can tell." He sighed heavily and his hand dropped to the bed.

The boot came off and she placed it next to its companion on the floor. Jesse had a faraway gleam in his eyes and she assumed he had drifted into a drunken stupor.

"Let's remove your shirt and make you more comfortable for bed," she mumbled.

As her fingers fumbled with the buttons of his shirt, his dopey expression changed as he stared openly at her. His tender stare made her nervous and she wished he had stayed in his drunken coma. Her heart jumped. Of course, knowing she was actually undressing this man didn't help matters.

"Will you give me a hand, Jesse? I can't remove your shirt by myself."

He slowly slid his arms out of the sleeves and she managed to strip it off him. Her smile completely disappeared when she became aware of his broad, muscular chest. Golden tan skin colored his frame, and her hands itched to run across his warm flesh. She clenched her hands into fists in resistance. Very little hair sprinkled his chest, but it didn't take the masculinity away. In

138

fact, it made him more irresistible, more desirable. She suddenly wished she'd left him on the ground by the barn. She quickly turned away.

"Summer? Look at me."

"No." She moved, but he grabbed hold of her hands and held onto them. Without asking her permission, he placed her hands on his bare chest then sighed.

"Your touch heats me."

Shock forced her to look at his face. His eyes no longer had the effect of liquor. They were lucid. A knot formed in her throat and she swallowed hard, fighting the desire creeping into her body. She couldn't remove her hands. They felt so good next to his fiercely beating heart.

"Touch me, Summer. Move your hands all over my chest and feel me."

Her breathing became harsh, and for the life of her she couldn't figure out why she didn't stop him from moving her hands over him. Somehow, he'd put her in a spell and she couldn't pull away. She didn't want to.

He held her hands prisoner as he directed them over his hard frame. Slowly and softly, her fingers floated across his skin, down his chest, across his ribs to his hard stomach. He retraced the path back up and his head dropped forward, his breath against her ear.

"This feels so good. I like the way I feel when you're touchin' me."

Her knees weakened as she knelt in front of him, her fingertips brushed against his soft hairs, and pleasure shot through her. He nudged his knuckle beneath her chin, gently raising her face until she had no doubt of the warmth and emotion she saw there. Heady sensations coursed through her body.

"I never imagined it would feel like this," he told her.

"How long have you been imagining?" Her voice was low, sedated.

A small smile appeared on his face. "Since I almost kissed you by the fishin' hole."

"You almost kissed me then?"

He grinned. "You know I wanted to."

A gush of air escaped her mouth. "Yes, I knew."

"Do you like me fantasizin' about you?"

"No, I mean yes--I don't know. You confuse me. Why have you been imagining me touching your chest when it should be my sister?"

He shrugged. "Don't know."

Silently, their gazes connected and a single question haunted her. She couldn't put it off any longer. She had to know. "Jesse? Are you sober enough to answer me truthfully?"

"You make me feel a different kind of drunkenness, my darlin'."

Her heart thumped harder against her chest. "Jesse? Are you in love with my sister?"

His hands stopped hers from their soft travels over his skin, but his eyes remained focused on her. "Not in the way a man should love a woman who is about to become his wife."

Her eyes widened. "How long have you known this?"

"A while before you came back from your aunt's house."

"Why then are you still going through with the wedding?"

"Everyone is expectin' us to wed. Violet and I have been courtin' for several years now, and the engagement sort of just fell together. I do love Violet, but not in a husbandly way." He paused then continued. "I think she feels the same way."

"Is that why you think she isn't happy?"

"She's not happy. Can't you tell?"

"Then make her happy, Jesse. Let her go."

His fingers tenderly stroked her hands, and then he lifted one to his mouth and placed a kiss on each of her fingers. "Will that make you happy?"

Her heart quickened. "That's irrelevant." She tried to pull away, but he wouldn't let go. He placed her hand back on his chest.

"Don't leave. I like the feel of your hands on my skin."

"Jesse, this has gotten way out of control."

"Please don't go." He leaned forward and brushed his lips on her cheek. "Please stay with me."

His hot breath and even hotter body tempted her, but she didn't want to lose herself in passion like she almost had in the cabin. "I can't, Jesse."

"I need you," he mumbled.

His lips moved across her cheek to her mouth. Scorching heat sparked through her and she pressed her lips to his. He suckled her top lip then repeated the gesture to the bottom. His mouth slanted across hers and the kiss turned urgent, creating a greater excitement inside her. Jesse's tongue entered her mouth and caressed, and she moaned deeply.

She didn't know what had taken over her body and mind, and right now she didn't care. She enjoyed kissing him this way no matter what strenuous efforts it took to push away the guilt.

His kiss was just as she remembered it--soft and hot, tender yet wild. She touched her tongue to his and her body exploded once again. Her chest ached with that unknown feeling. Her nipples hardened, and she suddenly wanted his hands on her breasts, kneading, shaping them, and filling his hands. The urge to run her hands all over his chest overwhelmed her, and just as she freed them from his guide and ready to direct them on her own, a noise came from outside.

Clint was home.

She quickly pulled away, breathlessly. "Jesse? It's Clint."

"Clint?" he asked, dazed.

"Yes, Clint."

The front door opened and Clint's voice boomed through the house, startling Summer to her senses.

"Jesse? Are you here?" Clint called.

Jesse groaned and fell back on the bed, flinging his arm over his eyes. "Yes, I'm in the bedroom."

Summer stood and quickly ran her shaky hands over her dress, then over her hair, patting it in place. She hustled out of the bedroom and met Clint just outside the room. Clint's eyes widened.

"What's goin' on here?" he asked warily.

She swung her arm toward Jesse. "Your brother got himself stinking drunk. He was walking into walls and embarrassing himself, so I took it upon myself to help him home." She tried to calm her hurried speech. "I would have come to get you, but he didn't want any help."

Clint's gaze moved over to the bed then back to Summer. Her cheeks burned hot as coals, and she hoped he didn't notice when she bit her swollen lips.

Clint smiled sheepishly. "Thank you. I'll take care of him now. Do you need a ride home?"

"I'll just borrow the wagon, if you don't mind."

"No, that'll be fine." He walked her to the door.

"He'll have a tremendous hangover in the morning, I'm afraid."

He nodded. "I'm sure he will."

"Good night, Clint."

"'Night, Summer." He placed a light kiss on her heated cheek. She stepped out and he closed the door.

By Clint's mischievous grin, she surmised he'd guessed what was happening before he entered the cabin...but she hoped to God she was wrong.

Ten

The early morning sun peeked over the hills and shone into Summer's bedroom window, waking her from a most refreshing sleep. She stretched and yawned, then turned and slid her feet out of the bed onto the cold wooden floor. Although the heat was almost unbearable during the day, at least the morning proved that a new season was nigh.

She rubbed the sleep out of her eyes, then stood and went over to the closet. She pushed through the gowns hanging on the rod, contemplating what to wear for the day. Her hand brushed across the dress she'd worn last evening and she paused. *Jesse.*

She really shouldn't have touched his bare chest and kissed him so passionately. Never would she forget the way her body had tingled, but guilt overrode her excitement, and her heart grew heavy. Violet would never forgive her. Summer didn't think her sister would understand that Jesse was on her mind constantly, that all she thought about was being held by him, feel his tender lips upon hers and press her body against his hardness.

Yet...did Jesse feel the same? Did he have the same bothering feelings as she had? Could he be thinking of her this very moment as she thought about him?

Once she'd washed, she slid a yellow dress over her head and arranged it around her body. She glanced in the mirror as she fastened the buttons and liked the way the bright sunflower material lit up the auburn highlights in her hair. Before leaving the room, she brushed out the night's tangles in her hair and pulled it away from her face with a matching ribbon.

Unable to control the giddy feeling from last night's kiss, and especially, Jesse's confession, she smiled wide. He had enjoyed her touch, and she knew he enjoyed kissing her. She skipped down the stairs on her way to see Pa, but as she entered the kitchen Violet stepped from the other room and stopped her. The solemn expression on her sister's face made fear clutch Summer's chest.

Tears glistened in Violet's eyes. "Something happened to Pa."

Summer gasped. "What?"

"Late last night, Pa tried to walk while Ma was out of the room. He fell into Ma's vanity and his hands slid right into the glass on the mirror. The glass cut his arms pretty bad."

"Oh, no." Her breath caught. "How is he now?"

"He's sleeping, but not very peacefully. Ma says he feels worthless, and his depressed mood is worrying her. She's afraid what he might do."

Summer slumped in the nearby kitchen chair, covering her face as the tears gushed forward. "There must be something we can do."

"We all feel helpless, especially Ma."

"If we could just get that reward money, it would pay for the doctor in New Orleans." Summer didn't know how, but she had to capture those bandits. She could think of no other way to get the money.

Kneeling down by her side, Violet circled her arms around Summer's waist and cried with her. This was the first time Summer had been this emotionally close to her sister.

Summer withdrew and wiped her eyes. "Where is Ma?"

"In with Pa."

"Well, come on." Summer slapped her knees and stood. "We've got a household to wake and chores do. We can't let Ma do anything today but take care of Pa."

Violet's eyes widened, and even Summer couldn't believe she'd actually said those words. This was the first time she could remember ever wanting to take charge of the household work.

The corner of Violet's mouth lifted. "Yes, we do."

"I'll have Nate run and put a sign on the livery door, and if any customers happen by, they can come do their business here at the house."

Along with Violet, Summer helped wake her brothers and sisters and then prepared the breakfast meal. Summer wrapped an apron around her waist and went about the house preparing for the day. In the kitchen she scrambled eggs, fried bacon, and cooked biscuits. After feeding the family, she cleaned the table, washed the dishes, and even swept and mopped the floor. In the front room, she and Violet straightened, swept and dusted, even aired out the rugs and curtains.

During the day, Summer visited with Pa for a few minutes before he dozed. Pain kept him from talking, so she let him rest. She hurried about the hourse, doing her chores with a smile, which surprised Ma greatly, especially because this was a side of Summer nobody had seen before.

After supper, Ma informed the boys they were going to do the dishes and clean up. Summer was exhausted and grateful for the break. This also gave her another chance to visit with Pa. He seemed more awake than he'd been earlier, so their visit lasted longer.

"Summer, my dear." Marvin smiled at her. "I'm so happy to see you helping your sister around the house. I know how much you'd rather be down at the stable, and it thrills me to see you taking over some of the household duties."

She knelt by the side of his bed and rested her hand on his chest. "It was nice to be with my sister today." She chuckled. "It's not very often I'm this way."

He laughed. "Your ma was just about to give up hope of you ever becoming a genteel lady."

"And now what does she think?"

Lifting his bandaged hand, he brought it to her cheek and barely touched it before he set it back down to the bed. "She's not worried. She's sure you'll make some man very lucky one day." He looked over at Violet who sat on the chair next to the bed. "Just as your sister has."

Violet smiled and touched his shoulder. "Thank you, Pa."

"You're getting a really good man, my dear," he continued as he kept his gaze on Violet. "I like Jesse very much. He'll make you very happy."

"Yes, I know, Papa."

Summer noticed Violet's expression waver. Could her sister possibly have the same kind of doubts as Jesse?

"Jesse Slade is a good man." He paused, his attention returning to Summer. "And one day, you'll find a man just like

145

him."

Summer couldn't have replied if she'd wanted to. Her constricted throat and achy heart threatened the cry of anguish already gathering on her tongue. She nodded and gave him her best smile. Deep down inside she knew she shouldn't entertain the idea of Jesse loving her when Pa obviously wanted Jesse to marry Violet.

"Girls?" Lillian poked her head inside the bedroom. "Why don't you let your pa get some rest now?"

Violet stood and gave Pa a kiss and left the room, and Summer followed soon after. Summer wanted to speak to her sister, but Violet excused herself and went up to her room, closing the door behind her.

Feeling as if she also needed solitude, Summer decided to go to the livery stable. Instead of changing into her brother's breeches and shirt, she stayed in her dress. During the day, she'd switched to a coffee colored skirt, minus the slips underneath. The round neckline of the beige blouse cooled her as she worked around the house, and loose bell-shaped, see-through sleeves helped the air circulate around her arms. Tonight's weather was chilly, so she grabbed a shawl before leaving the house.

She walked slowly to the stable, and once inside with the animals, comfort settled in her chest. This would always be her haven. She smiled and patted Buck's nose. No matter what her problem, she could always come here and find peace and solace. Just like now. Buck had been bedded for the night, but she still picked up a brush and stroked his mane.

She smiled. "Hello, handsome." He whinnied and she laughed.

"Have you missed me? I've certainly missed you." She leaned forward and nuzzled the side of his head. "Yes, I've missed you terribly."

A rustling came from behind her, and Jesse's voice purred in the quietness of the barn. "I wish you'd be as sweet to me as you are to that horse, Summer."

Letting out a gasp, she swung around and faced him, her hand flying to her chest. "Land sakes, Jesse." Her heart jumped. "Why in the blazes do you insist on sneaking up and scaring me all the time?"

"Didn't think I was sneakin'. A corpse would've heard me a comin'. Hell, even Buck heard me, so why couldn't you?"

She shrugged. "I guess I was in deep thought."

"Your pa?"

"Yes. Did you hear what happened last night?"

He took a step closer. "Yes. How is he today?"

"He has a faraway look in his eyes as if he doesn't care what's happening to him. He has no ambition to get out of bed and get dressed, and he's always talking to Ma about how useless he is to our family." She stepped away from Buck and closer to Jesse. "I heard him tell Ma, he wished he were dead." Her voice broke and she covered her mouth. She fought the tears gathering in her eyes.

"That kind of attitude will slow his recovery."

"Yes, it will. Oh Jesse, I'm so afraid he won't ever recover."

"Is there anythin' he needs? Anythin' I can take care of for him?" She shook her head. "How 'bout your ma? Is there somethin' I could help her with?" Negative response again. "Your brothers? Your sisters?"

"No, Jesse. My family doesn't need anything."

"How about you?" His fingers grazed her cheek softly. "Is there anythin' Summer Bennett needs?" His gentle smile warmed her. "Anythin' I can do for you, my darlin'?"

Her heart lodged in her throat again, and his touch shot waves of desire throughout every part of her body, but she couldn't let him know. Pa wanted Jesse to marry Violet. There was nothing she could do--or would do.

"No, I'm fine." She stepped back and broke the contact. "How are you?" She managed a teasing grin. "Did you have a splitting headache this morning?"

"Yes." He leaned back against the stall and stuffed his hands in his pants pockets. "And I want to thank you for bringin' me home last night. I really don't know how you did it."

"I've never seen you so drunk. Actually, I've never seen you drunk at all." She shook her head.

He shrugged. "I know it was stupid, but I just couldn't stop drinkin' Mr. Perkins' beer. I shouldn't have, but it actually dulled my senses, and I needed that last night."

"Why did you need it?"

"I think you know why."

"Maybe I do." She turned and went back over to Buck, picking an apple out of the crate on her way. "Why were you jealous of all the boys I danced with, especially your very own brother?"

"Because my brother is not a boy, Summer. There's a difference between boys and men, which I'm certain you've already discovered."

She wouldn't turn and look at him, even though she heard him come up behind her. The heat radiated from his body and joined with hers, and his musky cedar scent nearly made her knees buckle. She fought the urge to turn and press herself against him, get swallowed by his comforting embrace.

"You shouldn't be jealous. Not of Clint. And you shouldn't feel this way toward me," she said softly.

"I thought I explained things last night. My mind was a little fuzzy, but I'm quite sure I expressed my feelin's." His fingers took a lock of her hair and caressed it. "My body still burns from your touch last night, and whenever I think about the kiss we shared, butterflies dance in my stomach. I've been waitin' all day to come see you, but the Rangers had me runnin' all over the countryside."

Confusion made her mind swim, and she wanted to cry and kiss him at the same time. She'd do neither.

Leaning her face against Buck's neck, she sighed heavily. "Oh, Jesse. What are we going to do?"

"What do you mean, my darlin'?"

She spun around. "Quit calling me that. I can never be your darling."

His arms circled around her and heat consumed her again, scattering her thoughts. "I can't help what I feel, because yes, Summer, you are my darlin'."

"But...but Pa wants you to be Violet's darling." Her voice choked again. "It's what Pa wants, and I cannot take it away from him, especially now."

He released a heavy sigh and rested his chin on her head. His hands moved across her back in small circles. "I'm torn, Summer. I don't want to disappoint your father, but at the same time, I can't live a lie." He withdrew and looked down into her eyes. "Do you remember last night when you told me to let Violet go so I could make her happy?"

She nodded.

"Do you still feel that way?"

She nodded again.

"So do I."

Her brows lifted. "Are you going to break off your engagement?"

"Fact is, it's already been done."

Her jaw dropped. "Really? What did Violet say?"

"She agreed with me. She only loves me like a brother. I finally realized the mistake I made in askin' her to marry me. We don't love each other the way two people gettin' married should. I love her, but I've never desired her. She's always been a really good friend."

"You know the difference?"

He grinned. "Yes. You seem to forget, I don't stay in Waco every moment of the day. I've traveled to many different towns and met an assortment of women. Usually, they're the ones Clint sees regularly."

She gasped. "You don't mean...prostitutes," she ended in a whisper.

A shout of laughter rang from his throat. "Hell no! Those women scare me to death."

Relief swept through her. "I'm glad to hear that."

He tightened his hold and pulled her body up against his. She liked the feel of his strong arms around her. It made her feel safe. Comforted. Protected. Loved.

"I happen to like a different type of woman," he said huskily.

"What kind is that?"

"I think you know."

She grinned. "Humor me."

"Well, I happen to like women with dark auburn hair, big beautiful hazel eyes, and skin as soft as rose petals. I also like my women to be very shapely." His hands slid down the sides of her body, over her hips and briefly touched her legs before moving to her waist again. Heated shivers folled his touch.

His face registered with surprise and his eyes widened.

"Summer? Where's your corset?"

"I've been doing housework all day, and the dagum thing was too uncomfortable."

His grin widened. "Ummm, nice. Very nice."

He lowered his mouth to hers and the kiss was soft and meaningful. She responded, even opened her mouth to feel his tongue sweep through her, but then guilt overrode her emotions and she turned her face away. His lips caressed her cheek.

"Jesse? Please don't do this. You make it so hard to refuse."

"Then don't."

"I have to."

"No you don't."

"Yes. It's Pa's wish that you marry Violet."

"But I don't want to marry Violet and she doesn't want to marry me. Your Pa will understand."

His lips trailed down her neck, leaving feathery soft kisses on her skin. His hands moved underneath her arms, holding her just far enough away so that his mouth could continue its descent. When he kissed the exposed skin on her neck, her erratic heartbeat pounded against his lips. She held her breath as he brushed across a rigid point. Explosions erupted in her body, and the unfamiliar warmth made her wary. He moved his mouth back and forth against the bead and her nipple tightened. One of his hands joined his lips and cupped her breasts. *Could passion really be this wonderful?* She dared hope.

"Oh, Summer." He sighed. His kisses became wild, his hand pawed at her bodice while the other hand found the buttons and quickly released them.

Turmoil and confusion amid pleasurable tingles clouded her thoughts. Her mind had constantly fought her body since she'd returned to town. But how could she get her mind and her heart to agree? She wanted the same thing Jesse did, and she didn't want to feel guilty about it.

"Jesse, this isn't right."

"Nothin's ever been more right, darlin'."

He was certainly an expert at undressing a woman. Cool air touched her breasts as her bodice fell open. His hand pulled aside the thin material covering her bosom, while his mouth frantically searched for skin. She couldln't tear her gaze away from his eager mouth--and heaven help her, stopping him was the furthest from her thoughts. Her breasts were bare to his stare and for some strange reason, she didn't feel a bit embarrassed. How could she when his admiring gaze looked at her as if she were more precious than gold?

"I never thought--" His mouth swept down to cover a tip.

When the liquid heat of his tongue touched her nipple, an animal-like sound escaped her throat. Had she made that sound? His hot mouth and wild tongue forced throaty moans to erupt from her. Even Jesse groaned.

"Jesse...Jesse..." She enjoyed the sound of his name being murmured in passion as she held his head to her bosom.

Carefully, he lifted her in his arms and carried her into one of the empty stalls. She didn't protest when he laid her down on the hay, she just tightened her hold on his shoulders. His mouth moved back and forth across her lips, then roamed once more to her breasts. The position allowed him better access, and for this, Summer was grateful. His mouth lapped first one nipple and then the other before he yanked the material down until her whole chest was bare of any kind of restriction.

She released a pleasurable sigh. Aunt Lydia's stories had not prepared her for this. Never in her wildest dreams had she imagined it would be so wonderful.

She kept her attention on his mouth and hands as they glided over her skin. The passion written on Jesse's face told her he was as aroused as she was. He expressed it in the way his lips caressed her skin, the way his tongue touched her nipple, and especially the way his hand fondled her fullness.

Her body came alive and each part of her cried out for his touch and his kiss. She didn't know exactly what she wanted, but she knew she wanted more. Much, much more. Did Jesse know? Could he help her? Could he be her hero once more?

His hand left her breast and moved down her stomach, down her hip to her leg, his fingers pulled up her skirts and headed underneath. It frightened her, but once his hand touched her pantaloons, the unknown fear passed, leaving her in a pool of intoxicating bliss. His hand didn't hesitate as it moved to that spot where she craved him most. Although he had not removed her underclothing, his fingers pressed against her most tender spot through the material, and she released a loud moan.

Yes, this was what her body craved, and she wanted it from Jesse.

"Summer?" He kissed the tip of her breast then touched it with his tongue before lifting his head. "I want you, and I know you want me."

His eyes were a deep blue...an intoxicating blue. "I do want you."

"I want you, now."

"Here? In the stable?"

"I don't care where we are. I want to lie naked next to you and fit your body with mine, and make love until we're both satisfied."

Luckily, her mind still worked...barely. She swiped a lock of hair off his forehead. "If I let you take me now, like this, it will be wrong." *How can I be so rational when Jesse's hand feels so good where it is right now?*

"It's not wrong. Not this. Not us." He pressed his hand harder between her legs and she couldn't hold back her moan.

"Jesse? Are you...willing to do the right thing by me? If I let you take me, are you going to..." She couldn't say it. She couldn't even believe she thought it.

His brows drew together. "What?"

"I'm not that kind of girl, you know. I can't do this without..."

He stared at her face for a moment before his forehead creased and eyes narrowed. "Are you talkin' about marriage?"

She hesitated, wondering if that was really what she wanted. "Yes." She didn't retract the words after they left her mouth, but as mixed emotions crossed his face, she wished she'd never said it.

Raising up slightly, he looked down into her eyes. "You expect me to marry you?"

"I can't give my body to anybody but my husband," she defended.

His hungry stare devoured her breasts as his hand pushed between her legs again, his fingers moving over the moist spot on her body. Heat coursed through her again, but she forced herself to stay strong.

"I--don't--know. Summer, I want you so much."

Bending his head, he captured her breast again, but she pushed him away with the heels of her hands. A pain like no other ripped through her heart at his clear refusal.

"Wrong answer." She rolled away and sat up, letting her temper fly in an unsuccessful effort to douse the pain he'd cause. "Jesse Slade! You're the most ignorant man on Earth, and I hope you live a lonely life in Hell."

She pulled together her bodice and jumped off the ground. Tears swam in her eyes as she darted away from him. She wouldn't let him touch her ever again. And she didn't know how, but she would not think of the excitement he'd brought to her body. Now she knew what kind of man he was, there was no way she would be able to look him in the eyes and see him as her hero.

~ * ~

"Damn women! Can't live with 'um, can't shoot 'um," Jesse muttered for the hundredth time as he rode through the hills on assignment. He couldn't stop replaying in his mind the events that had unfolded the night before, and the unbelievable mistake he'd made. Passion had never been so wonderful, and Summer had been so responsive. Why had he acted like such a fool when she asked him about marriage? It really wasn't such a far-fetched idea.

But then this is Summer Bennett.

Pushing back the brim of his hat, he swiped the cuff of his shirt across his sweaty brow. That hard-headed woman made him crazy. She could get his loins in an uproar and her kisses could melt an iceberg, then two minutes later, her glare could slice through him, tearing a painful hole in his heart.

He urged the horse into a gallop, shoving aside all thoughts of last night as he scanned the deserted land. The Rangers have been hell-bent on finding Buchanan's gang, and while he was laid up with head injuries, they had come across some leads on the outlaw's hideout. He'd been sent to check out the locations.

So far, Jesse had been running blind. Although this trail led him nowhere, he decided to go one more mile before heading back to town. Buchanan's gang would have more sense than to camp out this close to civilization, anyway.

His thoughts returned to Summer, and he sighed heavily.

That woman confused the hell out of him--yet he couldn't really imagine his life without her. Although he loved to rile her, it was more than that. He loved the way she could stir his emotions with just her sweet smile, and she could certainly stir the desire inside his body. He admired the way she'd taken control over her pa's business when she came home from Brownsville. And he really loved the way she melted in his arms and kissed him like there was no tomorrow.

No, he couldn't see his life without her in it, and the idea made his heart pound out of control. He loved her, dagnamit. And he didn't care who knew.

A familiar scent drifted through the air and stopped his thoughts, making him rein his horse to a complete stop. Sausage. Somebody cooked over a fire, and the aroma caused his stomach to rumble. The smell came from over the next knoll, so he quickly dismounted and crept on foot to the top.

Several horses blocked much of his view of the five men who clustered around a campfire, but they weren't close enough to identify. From where Jesse crouched behind a bush, they all looked the same; dark dusty coats, dark pants, and very wide brimmed hats. If only he could get a closer look, but in order for him to do that, he'd have to come out of hiding.

Straining his neck, he searched further down the hill to see if there was any kind of cave, but didn't spot one. He didn't think the bandits would stay out in plain sight, but it sure looked like he was wrong.

Because they were too far away, he couldn't tell if he recognized any of the men. Were they ones involved with the bank robbery last month in Amarillo? His hands itched to get a hold of the man who whopped him over the head with the rifle, and especially the bastard who'd laid his hands on Summer.

A rustle came from the trees behind him...then a rattle. *A snake!* His horse whinnied frantically. Jesse cursed under his breath as his attention wavered between his horse and the men around the fire. Within seconds, all heads turned his way. He jumped to his feet and pulled the horse back down the hill.

Shouts came from behind and bullets whipped around him. This was no time to be on foot, so he mounted and pushed the horse into a run. Luckily, he still had the lead, but he wouldn't leave anything to chance. He and his horse rode as one. *Don't let me down.* The closer he got to town, the safer he'd be. He hoped Buchanan's gang wouldn't chase him that far.

Glancing behind him, he saw that they were gaining speed. He dug his heels into the horse's belly and urged him faster. The pop from a gun exploded behind him, and a bullet whipped past his ear. Too close, he thought as he crouched lower, riding like the devil was behind him. But the devil seemed to be on the bandits' heels, also, and that worried him.

Another rifle blasted, and the bullet pierced the back of his shoulder. He had no time for this! Biting his lip, he fought back the pain. Holding tight to the reins, he prayed his horse would deliver him to town soon. Sweat poured off his brow as the pain reached deeper into his back. Dizziness overcame him. His shirt quickly dampened with his own blood.

Just a little further...just a little further. Blinking, he tried to keep the darkness from taking over his mind. He pictured Summer's face and it soothed his pain. Love swelled in his heart. He must make it back to town to tell her how he felt.

Up ahead were the tops of buildings. Help was in sight. Gritting his teeth from effort, he looked behind him just as the others pulled away. The race had ended and he'd won. Through the pain, his body relaxed with the knowledge that he'd be home soon. Slowly blackness seeped in around him, shutting down his senses completely.

Eleven

Summer hefted the laundry basket in her arms and carried it out across the back porch to the clothesline. Squinting up into the afternoon sun, she wiped away a bead of sweat from her forehead. The morning chores were exhausting. Instead of helping Violet take care of Jesse this time, she'd chosen to stay home and assist Ma.

Summer wouldn't waste any more of her affection on that scoundrel. Her heart just couldn't take it.

Poor Jesse wasn't having very good luck lately. Although this recent injury caused him to lose a lot of blood, the doctor had easily removed the bullet. Jesse's arm and shoulder would be extremely stiff for a while, but he would live. Apparently, his horse had led him right down the center of town. He'd been spotted and helped within moments after being shot. But Summer refused to help her sister care for him. Violet had begged, telling Summer that Jesse was asking for her, but Summer wouldn't risk her already damaged heart on that polecat.

Pushing away her broken feelings resulting from the humiliating night in the barn, she focused on her chores. Before she'd gone to help Aunt Lydia, Ma couldn't get her to wash clothes no matter how hard she tried, but Summer actually enjoyed doing it now.

Funny how time changed her.

From around the house, voices floated through the air. Someone was at the front door, but she didn't want to go inside to see who'd come calling. Ma was in the house and could take care of things.

Within minutes, Ma called her name. Grudgingly, Summer set down the clothes and wiped her damp hands on her apron.

When she stepped inside the back door, Ma seized her by the arm and dragged her further into the kitchen. Ma's hands practically ripped off her apron, then moved up to Summer's hair, arranging it around her head neatly.

"Ma? What are you doing?"

"Shh," Ma whispered. "You've got company, and I'm making sure you're presentable."

Ma pinched Summer's cheeks and made her wince. "Who's here?"

A smile stretched across her mother's face. "One of your beaus from Brownsville."

Summer crinkled her forehead. "I didn't have any."

"Now, sweetie, don't be shy. You can tell your Ma."

"No, seriously. I don't have the slightest idea who you're talking about."

Ma planted her hands on her hips. "Albert Kendal, that's who."

Summer widened her eyes. "Albert Kendal?" She laughed. "But Ma, he was never my beau--"

"Well, he is now." Ma grabbed her arm and pulled her toward the parlor. "Albert's come courtin', so let's not keep him waiting."

Summer didn't have time to prepare herself, because before she knew it Albert Kendal stood in front of her, wearing his Sunday best. He held his bowler in the crook of his arm and an assortment of flowers in his other hand. He smiled.

What is he doing here?

"Hello, Summer." Albert's deep voice stirred the awkward silence in the house.

"Hello, Albert. What are you doing this far from home?"

"I was riding through town, and when I took my horses to your livery to be stalled, I ran into your brother and sister. I couldn't pass up the chance to come and say hello."

"Well, what a surprise." She laughed lightly, not really knowing what to say.

Ma laughed, too. "Summer, dear, why don't you ask him to sit down?"

"Of course. Albert? Would you care to sit?" She motioned

to the couch. "And would you like a glass of fresh lemonade?"

He nodded. "That'd be wonderful on a hot day like this." He glanced down at the flowers then held them out to her. "And these are for you."

She smiled. "Thank you." She took the flowers and turned to get her guest a drink, but Ma moved in front of her.

"Let me fetch the drinks." Ma grabbed the flowers out of Summer's hands. "I'll put these in a vase. You two just sit and visit for awhile."

Uncomfortable, Summer moved to the single chair as Albert sat on the couch. He looked the same. Of course, it hadn't been that long since she'd left Brownsville. Albert's blond hair seemed lighter, and his mustache was longer than she remembered, but other than that, nothing had changed.

He really hadn't courted her in Brownsville. Aunt Lydia had invited him to supper a few times, and he'd sat next to her at church, but nothing more.

"Albert, it really is a shock to see you."

"Well, Pa sent me out in the world to make my living." He shrugged. "Although, I'm not sure of what that'll be just yet."

"I thought you were going to follow you father and go into the banking business."

He shook his head. "That kind of work doesn't interest me."

She offered a polite smile, remembering back when she'd had a small crush on Albert. He was the kind of man she'd dreamed about marrying. He came from a wealthy family and even worked at the bank his father owned. His charm could sweep any girl off her feet, and his manners were impeccable. And as unbelievable as it seemed, he was here to see her. So, if he was such a great catch, why didn't she feel like reeling him in?

"You're looking well," he commented after a lengthy silence.

"Thank you, and I think you're looking well, too."

"I missed you after you left Brownsville."

She lowered her gaze, her cheeks heating. "Albert, I really don't know what to say."

"Say you'll go for a ride with me this afternoon. I'll rent a buckboard from the livery. Your ma has invited me for supper, but

I'd like to spend a little time with you before meeting your family."

She really had no reason to turn him down. Her heart didn't belong to anyone--although it had its weak moments around Jesse until he'd made it clear he'd rather get caught in a barn with a skunk than marry her. Well, she didn't need that kind of man. Perhaps she should give Albert a chance to turn her feelings around.

She looked up at him and smiled. "I would be delighted."

His handsome face brightened. "Wonderful." He stood and reached his hand out for her to take. "Shall we go?"

Hesitantly, she placed her hand in his and rose. "I better tell Ma where we're going." She looked toward the doorway and Ma entered with a tray of lemonade filled glasses.

"I heard every word," Ma answered with a laugh. "Quickly, drink this to quench your thirst before you leave."

Albert swallowed his drink in two gulps, then pinched in his cheeks from the bitter taste. She tried not to laugh out loud as she took her time with the drink. When the glass was half empty, Ma took it away. "All right, you two, skedaddle, and I don't want to see you back until supper time."

"Don't worry, Mrs. Bennett, I'll have your precious daughter back before sundown," Albert charmed.

By the twin peaks of color on her mother's cheeks, Albert had already won over one member of her family. Would Summer allow him to capture her heart as well?

Albert Kendal proved to be the perfect gentleman. Throughout the afternoon, he only went as far as to touch her hand as he helped her in and out of the buggy. Once in a while, his leg brushed against hers on the bumpy ride, but he quickly apologized and moved away. His brown eyes only stayed on her face, never wandering any lower than her lips.

Certainly a change from the feeling she experienced when she was around Jesse.

The afternoon didn't go fast enough for Summer, but finally evening arrived and the dreaded moment of introducing him to her family came. *Would they like him?* Pa seemed perky as he sat at the supper table with the family, which pleased her, but when her family warmed up to Albert, her heart sank. Even Violet accepted him, and her brothers' wide eyes couldn't get enough of the new man at the table, especially when Albert told stories of Brownsville. Funny thing was, Albert's stories were not as interesting as Jesse and Clint's, but her brothers acted as if Albert had just walked off a golden cloud. Both Elizabeth and Emily wore starstruck expressions, and Summer knew what her sisters were secretly dreaming about.

Too bad Summer didn't feel that way about him.

As the evening wore on, she pasted on a grin that she knew didn't quite reach her eyes. Only when Albert announced it was time to leave did she manage a truly genuine smile. When she walked him to the door, he thanked her for a lovely evening, then took her hand and placed a chaste kiss on her knuckles. Summer waited for the shooting waves of pleasure that always happened when Jesse had kissed her, but they didn't come. Inwardly she cursed herself for comparing the two men. Then she silently scolded Albert for not being Jesse, and herself for wanting him to be.

"Can I call on you tomorrow?" he asked.

His question startled her out of her thoughts. "Uh...sure."

"I'm staying at the Waco Hotel here in town, and I'd feel honored if you'd join me for a picnic tomorrow afternoon. I'll have the hotel's restaurant cater."

Automatically, she conjured up excuses, but before she could think of one, she stopped. *What am I doing?* Prince Charming stood in front of her. Would she throw it all away for a frog like Jesse?

She smiled. "I'd love to go on a picnic with you."

He squeezed her hand then stepped out the door and over to his buggy. As his lithe body climbed into the seat, she stubbornly decided to let him woo her. She'd let Albert erase Jesse from her mind.

~ * ~

Jesse cursed aloud. He rubbed his achy shoulder and fell in defeat against the headboard on his bed. Those stretches the doctor insisted he do with his arm were not helping the pain at all. Was the old Doc trying to punish him for some unknown reason?

"Jesse, quit using such filthy language in front of a lady," Violet complained as she carried in his lunch. "I swear, you're sounding more and more like your brother."

"So, what's wrong with that?" he snapped.

"If I have my way, I'll clean up Clint's speaking, too."

"Women."

Violet placed the tray of food in front of him. "I think you're feeling better. If your rotten temper has anything to do with your quick recovery, I'm sure you'll be back on the saddle in no time."

"You bet I will." He flexed his arm again and winced from the pain. "Just wish it didn't hurt so much."

"What do you expect?"

"My head injury healed quicker than this."

She rearranged the pillows behind him and he sank back onto his mattress. "No it didn't." She turned and left the room, effectively ending the conversation, and annoying Jesse that much more.

His temper was at the boiling point, and his injury had nothing to do with it. For three days he'd been without Summer's company. He repeatedly asked Violet to have her sister come see him, but Violet told him Summer refused. Little by little, his heart broke. Obviously, she was angry with him for the way he'd behaved when they'd been together in the barn. Had his actions finally pushed her away for good? He kicked himself in the rear for reacting the way he had, and to make everything worse, he'd heard a rich man's son from Brownsville was courtin' her. That really chaffed Jesse's hide! Who did the man think he was courtin' *his* Summer?

Violet raved about the very handsome man who rode into town and swept Summer off her feet, and her brothers couldn't stop talking about how rich the man was. Even Lillian and Marvin approved. Unfortunately, there wasn't a cotton pickin' thing he could do about it until his wound healed. His shoulder wouldn't let him ride his horse, and to Jesse, that put him totally out of commission. Why had his luck changed for the worse? If only he could talk to Summer alone. He wanted to confess his love for her, but the stubborn filly just wouldn't come to see him.

"Are you about done?" Violet called from the kitchen.

"No."

"Well, hurry."

He glanced through the doorway into the next room. "What's so all-fired important about finishin' my meal so fast? You gotta date?"

Violet stepped into view. "No. Summer is bringing Albert over to meet you and Clint, and I want you to look your best." She crossed her arms over her chest. "I also want you to be on your best behavior."

"Picked the wrong day for that."

Her stern expression wavered. "Please, Jesse. This is important to Summer."

His gut twisted. "Why?"

"Because getting your approval is important to her. She thinks of you and Clint like her family."

He knew Violet was wrong, but he didn't argue the point. "What's so special about Mr. Rich Pant's son?"

She cocked her head. "His name is Albert Kendal," she corrected, "and I can't explain. It's just something you'll have to see for yourself."

"He can't be that perfect."

Her smile lifted. "Summer thinks differently."

His gut wrenched tighter and his heart dropped. "But Clint isn't home yet."

"He should be home shortly."

"When is Summer bringin' her beau?"

"Anytime now, I believe."

"Damnation." He gulped down the last bite of the stew. "I'm done."

Violet hurried over to his side. Her smile widened as she took the tray. "Please try and be civil. Don't get my sister's temper up, either."

"Why?" He climbed out of bed. "Hasn't ole Kendal heard her foul mouth, yet?"

"Jesse, you know she only acts that way around you."

He shrugged his good shoulder. "Yeah, aren't I the lucky one?"

The clip-clop of a horse and churning of wagon wheels snagged his attention. "Damn. They're here already and I'm not even dressed." He glanced down at his bare chest as his hand brushed over his stomach. "I need to find a shirt." He looked further down to his bare feet poking out from his jeans. "And put my boots on."

"I'll go let them in." Violet hurried into the other room.

Blast it all, but his movements were as quick as an old woman in a mud pit with the wind blowing against her. How could he prove himself a better man in Summer's eyes when he was still an invalid?

He grabbed his shirt off the back of a chair then flipped it once through the air, releasing some of the wrinkles. Summer's sweet voice drifted from the other room, making his heart hammer. It'd been three very long days since he'd last seen her, and although it was his fault she hated him, he still anticipated seeing her angelic face again. If only he could get her alone, he'd apologize for his behavior and tell her he loved her and *did* want to marry her.

A man's deep baritone voice mingled with the two feminine ones and grew louder the closer they came to his room. He turned his back to the door as he tried to slip on his shirt, but his injured shoulder stiffened and pain shot through his arm, restricting his movements.

From behind him came Summer's soft gasp, and before he knew what was happening, she stood by his side and lifted the end of his shirt.

"Here, Jesse, let me help you."

Her kindness startled him and he turned and looked at her. Their gazes met and his breath held. The ocean blue color of her dress softened her face. She'd even fixed her hair differently, pulling back the sides, letting the fullness cascade down the middle of her back.

Land sakes she's pretty.

He smiled and tried to express his love through his stare. "Why, thank you, Summer."

She stepped in front of him and began fastening the buttons of his shirt, her gaze dropping to her fingers.

A grin tugged at his mouth. "Darlin'? I think I can handle the rest myself."

Her cheeks darkened and she stepped back. "Oh...of course."

Silence lasted only a brief moment before the man behind

her cleared his throat. When Jesse assessed Summer's new beau, his heart wrenched. This man was definitely no cowpoke. Albert Kendal couldn't be more perfect, and the mere thought left a hollow feeling in the pit of his stomach.

Summer turned, took hold of Albert's arm, and pulled him further into the room. "Albert, I want you to meet Jesse Slade." Her gaze lifted to Jesse's. "And Jesse, this is Albert Kendal from Brownsville."

A charming grin appeared on Albert's face. Jesse's jealousy intensified.

Albert gave Jesse's hand a hearty shake. "It's good to finally meet the man the Bennett family can't stop raving about."

Jesse managed a grin. "So, Summer, what have you been tellin' this man about me?" His grin widened as he teasingly stepped over and slipped his arm around her small waist, pulling her to his side--mainly to get her away from Albert Kendal.

Summer's body stiffened. "Just the truth." She gave him a pasted smile. "My brothers have been putting you up on your pedestal again. After all, you are the town hero."

"Me? I thought you were."

She chuckled. "No, Jesse, you are."

"What's this?" Albert interjected. "Why would Summer be the town hero?"

"Haven't you heard?" Jesse asked.

"Jesse, no," Summer warned in honey-sweet tones, but her stare blazed through him.

Jesse continued as though she hadn't spoken, "Let me tell you, then."

Keeping his arm around Summer, he proceeded to explain to Albert about Summer's stagecoach rescue. During his lengthy and very descriptive tale, Summer struggled to free herself from his hold--in a subtle way--but he wouldn't let her go. No, he liked her this way. Liked it almost too much. Her rose scented soap tickled his senses and made him ache, and all he wanted to do was kiss her endlessly.

As he finished, he glanced down into her angry eyes and winked. "It just makes me so proud my girl acted that way. She's so brave."

From out in the hallway, Violet's laughter rang through

the cabin. He tried to ignore it.

"Jesse, you've stretched the truth quite a bit," Summer bit out slowly.

"Heavens no." He glanced back at Albert. "If you doubt my story, ask anyone in town. They'll tell you what happened."

Albert laughed. "I'm sure you're telling the truth. Back in Brownsville, Summer was the only girl I knew who'd dare take on the town bully. He was younger than me by a year or so, but his strength made him a legend in our town. Summer didn't care. She showed him right away she was a girl not to be messed with."

"That's enough." Summer held up a hand, still trying to wiggle out of Jesse's hold. "I wish you two would stop talking about me as if I were not here."

"I'm sorry, darlin'." Jesse bent and kissed her forehead, letting his lips linger longer than they should. He grudgingly released her and stepped back. She almost fell to the floor, but quickly regained her footing.

"So, Mr. Slade? How are you feeling?" Albert asked. "Summer and Violet have told me about your escape from the bandits--with a bullet wound to show for it. They also mentioned the head injury you received a while back. You're lucky to be alive."

Jesse flexed his sore arm, mainly to show off his acquired muscles, which were considerably more than Albert had. "Yes, I'm extremely lucky. Each and every day I feel a little better, thanks to Summer's lovin' care."

"What?" Summer gasped, her eyes wide as she stared at him.

Albert turned and looked at Summer. "You didn't tell me you took care of him."

Her face flamed. "I helped Violet take care of him the first time, but it was mainly while he was unconscious."

"Come now, darlin', don't be modest," Jesse teased.

"I'm not. Violet is the one who deserves all the credit. She's the one who nursed you back to health."

"Yes, Violet is certainly a Godsend." He chuckled and moved over to the single chair in his room and sat. "I hope you don't mind, but I really need to sit."

"Maybe we should leave," Summer suggested with

anticipation in her voice.

Jesse quickly extinguished her hopes. "No, stay a little longer. In fact, Summer, why don't you go into the kitchen and fetch a couple of chairs for you and Albert. I'd like to get to know Albert a little better before you leave."

Jesse stared at the man who'd captured Summer's interest, and with a sinking heart he knew Albert Kendal was the perfact man for her. It injured Jesse's pride knowing he'd never be rich like the banker's son, and he'd never have the acquired manners this man possessed. In every way Albert was perfect, and Jesse should let her go--just like he'd let Violet go. That was the only way Summer would be happy. With a tight chest, he realized Summer's happiness was what mattered most.

~ * ~

Summer marched into the kitchen like an obedient dog. Did she act this way so Albert wouldn't see her bad temper? Who was she trying to impress, Albert or Jesse? And why in heaven's name would she want to get hurt by Jesse again?

She grabbed two chairs and dragged them back to the bedroom. When she entered, Jesse was in the middle of telling Albert about his life. Albert kept his attention on Jesse, but he looked completely bored. She groaned in silence, knowing she'd have to change the subject onto something more interesting.

Albert took the chairs from her and placed them across from Jesse, and they sat.

"So, Albert," Jesse kept talking, "I heard you work in a bank?"

"Albert's father owns the bank." Summer lifted her chin proudly, hoping to get a rise out of him, but Jesse's expression didn't waver. It bothered her to see him look so composed. Why wasn't he jealous like she'd hoped he'd be?

Jesse nodded. "Let me ask you, Albert." He leaned forward in his chair. "Has your father's bank ever been robbed?"

Summer gasped. "*Jesse.* I think that is none of your business."

Jesse shook his head. "I beg to differ, darlin'. Because I'm a Ranger and we've been after a gang of bank robbers, I think it's necessary to know if we'll be needin' to check out the bank in Brownsville. You never know, but Mr. Kendal's bank just might be the next target."

Albert shifted in his chair. "Well, if you must know, the answer is yes. My father's bank was robbed a long time ago."

"How long?" Jesse scratched his newly acquired whiskers.

"About two years or so."

"Well, it might be beneficial for the Rangers to check it out anyway."

Annoyed, Summer folded her arms and glared at Jesse. His manners were far from normal, and it worried her what he might say next. Her mind scrambled to think of a way out of here before Jesse said something that would really embarrass her.

Jesse relaxed in his chair, grinning in that knee-buckling way of his. "So, Albert," he began.

He quickly glanced her way. Summer paniced. *Oh, no! Here it comes.*

Jesse looked back at Albert. "How serious are you about courtin' Summer?"

"Jesse," she snapped.

"Will we be hearin' weddin' bells in the near future?" Jesse continued.

Albert choked on a laugh and hid his smile behind his hand, but she didn't think it was funny at all. With anger firing her actions, she stood and pulled Albert with her. "I think we need to leave now. Jesse, you'd better get more rest so you're not as rude to whomever else might want to drop in on you."

Jesse stood, still grinning from ear to ear. "If you must." He stretched forth his right hand. "Albert? It was certainly a pleasure meetin' you, and it's good to see our little tomboy has finally captured herself a beau."

Mortification washed over her, and if there was a hole big enough, she'd crawl into it--either that or take a gun and shoot Jesse Slade. Without saying goodbye, she dragged Albert out of the room and out the front door.

Violet and Clint stood on the porch very close together, and when Summer charged out, they quickly pulled apart. Clint took a step toward Albert. Summer breathed a fortifying breath and regained control of her emotions. Straightening her shoulders, she forced a smile even in this stressful situation. "Clint, I would like you to meet Albert Kendal."

As Clint politely conversed with Albert, Summer's thoughts escalated into rage. How dare Jesse treat Albert that way? And why was Jesse acting as if he were her Pa? Why did she even care what Jesse Slade thought? She hated him.

Unconsciously, she followed Albert to the buggy, and with each step her anger intensified. Jesse had to be put in his place once and for all. She couldn't allow him to treat her new beau with such rudeness.

Albert's hand clutched her elbow, preparing to help her into the carriage, but she withdrew. "Albert? I forgot something inside the house. Stay right here and I'll be back."

She marched back into the cabin and by the time she reached Jesse's bedroom, she felt like a cannon ready to explode. She'd let Jesse feel the brunt of her thoughts and give him what for.

As she walked into the room, Jesse was sitting on the edge of his bed with his hands covering his face. The wilted way his shoulders hunched while he rubbed his forehead made her pause, but when the floor squeaked beneath her feet, he jumped up. All expression was wiped clean from his handsome face, and she thought she'd just imagined his sorrow. His shirt had been unbuttoned and hung open, and she tried not to look at his bare chest.

"Did you forget somethin'?" he asked.

"You have no right." She walked up to him and pointed her finger to his chest. She tried to ignore the heat seeping through her skin. "I think you owe Albert an apology."

"Why?"

"You know why. You were extremely rude to him."

"Was not. I thought I was quite polite."

"Fine then, you were very rude to me."

He chuckled. "No, Summer, I wasn't."

"You have no reason not to like him. He's a wonderful man."

He nodded. "Albert seems like a true gentleman."

She pursed her lips together. Nothing was sinking through his thick skull. Sighing heavily, she dropped her hand. "Why don't you like him? Is it because you're jealous?"

"Jealous? Why would I be jealous?"

"Because he's a gentleman and his father owns a bank, and because...because he likes me."

Jesse crossed his arms over his masculine chest, covering the spot her gaze couldn't stay away from. "Listen sweetheart, I'm not jealous in the least bit. So his father is a banker, whoop-tee-do. And so he's a fine gentleman. I'm happy for him. I'm happy for you. He's exactly what you need, Summer. Grab him while he's still interested."

Anger flowed through her body, but her heart ached. Jesse acted as if he didn't care at all whether or not she fell in love with Albert. Whether he knew it or not, Jesse actually gave his permission for her to marry Albert. Her heart cracked a little more. She'd wanted him to be jealous. She still sought a marriage proposal from him even though he'd shown her time and time again what kind of man he was.

She straightened and lifted her chin. "You're right. Albert is exactly what I need in a husband. He respects me and treats me well, and he's not so full of himself he cannot see other people's needs. Albert is everything you're not, and I would be stupid to let him go."

Jesse held the same blank expression on his face, but his jaw tightened. She wished she knew what he was thinking.

"Then go get him, Summer," he said calmly. "Hurry and go claim your hero."

Tears threatened her eyes, so before she embarrassed herself anymore in front of Jesse, she turned and ran out of the room, running to the man she hoped would be able to take Jesse from her heart forever.

Twelve

Jesse swallowed another bite of Violet's apple pie, and realized once again, it didn't taste as good as Summer's. He threw the fork on the plate and cursed. Why couldn't he stop thinking about her? What had he done in his life to deserve this kind of punishment?

Violet's laughter floated in from the kitchen, then the deep rumble in Clint's voice as he spoke to her. Their happiness gnawed on Jesse's nerves, and he couldn't stand to hear anymore. Lately he'd wondered why Violet still stuck around. Was she here for him or for Clint? It seemed like everyone was happy nowadays--everyone except him.

"Will you two be quiet in there?" he shouted. "Can't you tell a man's tryin' to be miserable in here?"

Staring at his plate, he frowned. How much more of this torture could he take? Although his heart cried out for Summer's love, he knew Albert was the right man for her.

When his bedroom door opened, his attention pulled toward his brother walking in. A smile stretched across Clint's face as wide as the Mississippi River. Jesse boiled inside. *Why can't I be that happy?*

"So, what have you found out about Buchanan?" Jesse snapped.

Clint shrugged. "Not a whole lot. Buchanan's gang has moved their hideout again."

Jesse hit his fist against the mattress and cussed.

"But I think Buchanan's hired more players," Clint continued.

"Really?"

"Yes. During their last robbery, the Rangers took out three of their men, so Buchanan would need to replace them.

He needs the help."

Jesse shrugged. "True."

"I wish I knew what bank he was settin' his sights on next. Knowin' Buchanan, he's goin' to let us stew awhile."

Setting the empty plate aside, Jesse scooted over to the edge of the bed. "What have the Rangers been doin' this past week?"

Jesse listened to his brother's detailed schedule, but soon his mind wandered and, as they always seemed to do these days, his thoughts turned to Summer. What was she doing? Was she with Albert? Had Albert kissed her--and if so, did Albert's kisses excite her? Although he'd practically told her to marry Albert, deep inside, Jesse hoped she'd come back to him. In his mind he created ways to win her back so he could watch her melt in his arms. Her lips would meet his in passion, and she'd allow him to hold her tight against his body.

"Jess? Are you payin' attention to me?"

Jesse quickly snapped out of his thoughts. "Uh, yeah."

"Then quit lookin' as if you're in another world."

"Sorry." He shrugged. "Just tryin' to think of ways to help the Rangers," he lied.

"Well, ye've been helpin' out just fine by getting' yourself better. I'm assumin' you're well enough to ride a horse?"

Jesse stood and stretched out his sore shoulder muscle. "I've been out ridin' little by little the last few days."

"Good, then maybe you'd like to ride with us tomorrow?"

His eyes snapped back to his brother. "I'd love to. Do you have any idea how borin' it is to sit around the house?"

Clint laughed. "Yes." He wandered over to the window and looked out into the night. "So, Jess? How's things goin' with Summer?"

Jesse mocked a laugh and shook his head. "Things aren't goin' between Summer and me."

"Why not?"

"Case you haven't noticed, Summer has a new beau."

Clint turned and ran his finger over his mustache. "Well, li'l brother, when you and Summer get together, sparks fly and it's celebration day all over again. It's obvious to anyone who knows the two of you that you have some kind of feelin's for each other."

Jesse chuckled. "Yes, it's called a death wish."

"Jess, I'm serious."

"So am I. You've seen us together so you know she hates me."

"She thinks she hates you because you force her into feelin' that way." Clint shook his head. "Why do you always make yourself look bad? Why do you keep provin' what an ass you are when I know you're not?"

Jesse walked over to his armoire and fumbled with the handle. He opened the door and grabbed his coat, preparing to go out to the barn and get the horses down for the night. "I don't want her fallin' in love with me." After he said the words, he wished he could retract them. He did want her falling in love with him--as soon as possible so his heart would quit aching.

"And are you sure she is?"

"Yes."

"Why? What's happened for you to suspect?"

"I've kissed her." Jesse kept his voice low as he glanced at his brother. Clint's grin widened.

"You don't say." Clint chuckled. "And, has she responded to your kisses?"

"Yes. She seems to enjoy them."

"And how about yourself? Do you enjoy them, also?"

Jesse scowled. "What's with all the questions?"

Clint shrugged. "Why are you so touchy? Can't you just answer the question?"

"Clint," Jesse warned, but his brother just laughed.

"Jess, are you havin' certain feelin's for Summer?"

Jesse sighed and ran his fingers through his hair. "What if I am?"

"I don't blame you, brother. She's a very beautiful young woman. But what I'm wonderin' is, if *you're* fallin' in love with her, too?"

Jesse waved his hand through the air. "Don't wonder any longer. Why would I fall in love with a woman who makes me madder than a rabid skunk?"

"Makes me wonder if she's as passionate when she kisses as when she argues."

When he recalled their last heated kiss, his face relaxed.

"Yes, she is."

"But you don't want it to get serious?"

"No, Clint, I don't. Albert is husband material. I'm not. Albert comes from a fancy home, and wealthy upbringin'. Isn't that what all women want in a husband?"

Leaning against the wall, Clint's fingers continued to outline his mustache as he stared out the window. "You know," he said after a few minutes, "I'm not totally sold on Summer's new beau. There's somethin' about him that rubs me the wrong way."

Jesse laughed. "I can say the same, but that's cuz I don't like to see her with another man."

"Nope, there's somethin' else."

"Yeah, Albert is too perfect with his cocky swagger and his uppity manners."

Clint looked at Jesse and nodded. "Exactly. He thinks the sun came up just to hear him crow."

Jesse laughed. "Are you serious? You feel that way, too?"

"But you received the same first impressions I did, right?"

"Well, yes."

"Then somethin' must be wrong with the man."

"Of course somethin' is wrong with the man," Jesse snapped as he grabbed his boots, "he's courtin' Summer Bennett."

"No, there's somethin' else, and I'm goin' to find out what it is."

"Leave it alone, Clint." He slipped on his boots and moved over to the door. "Summer needs a good man, and she deserves someone like Albert, not the likes of me."

Clint nodded. "The problem is, I have a feelin' Albert's not a good man at all."

Jesse shrugged and walked out. In the back of his mind he wanted to believe Clint, but he knew Albert was perfect for Summer. She deserved Albert--end of subject.

~ * ~

Summer sat ramrod straight in the horse and buggy as Albert drove them to Poppy's Meadow. The past week had gone extraordinarily slow, and she anticipated the day Albert would leave. He hadn't mentioned anything about moving on...she just hoped he would. But until that time, she'd play the part he wanted. She'd act as if she enjoyed his attentions. Besides, it seemed to make Pa happy that she was finally courtin'.

She hadn't seen Jesse since she and Albert had been at his house. Her spirits dropped lower, and she silently cursed her thoughts for wandering where they didn't belong. But at least she knew Jesse had graciously backed down. He'd accepted her decision to see other men. She could tell he wasn't happy about it, but it's what she'd wanted.

"Summer," Albert spoke, breaking the silence. "I've noticed your sister has been looking at me a lot. Do you know why?"

"Which sister? Violet?"

"No. Your younger sister, Elizabeth."

She loudly blew out a gush of air between her lips. "Don't think anything of it." She flipped her hand through the air. "Lately, Elizabeth has been looking at anyone that wears long sideburns." She laughed. "I'm even worried for the old widow Larsen. She's gotten to be very hairy."

When she met his gaze, a withered expression creased his forehead; his eyes dull with hurt. Perhaps she'd spoken out of turn or had been too blunt. Trying to cover up her blunder, she waved her hand through the air again and laughed. "But this time, I must admit that Elizabeth has chosen a fine looking man to dream after." She gave him a grin. "That is, if it's all right with you that she's looking?"

He shrugged. "Well, she's a little young for me."

"Yes, she's still in her sixteenth year."

His expression warmed. "Besides, I'm in the company of a beautiful woman, so why should I be thinking about another?"

She refused to comment, not willing to make another blunder.

When he pulled into the meadow, Albert stopped the buggy and set the brake. "This looks like a wonderful place for a picnic."

"Yes. This is one of my most favorite spots in all of Waco. See over there--" She pointed to a small stream. "When I was a child, I'd take off my shoes and stockings and go wading." She pointed in the opposite direction. "And over there in that small group of trees is where I used to play hide-and-seek with my sisters. I always won because I was a better tree climber."

Albert laughed. "You sound like you had a fun childhood."

She nodded. "I did. Especially the times I spent with my pa in the livery. He taught me everything from shoeing a horse to repairing a wheel for the rigs."

Albert turned and jumped down, then reached up and lifted Summer out. She didn't know if it was because of his puny strength, but he seemed to struggle with holding her, and she bumped into his body. When she noticed the gleam in his eyes, she realized he'd done it purposely. She held her tongue this time and when her feet touched the ground, she politely pushed away.

"Do you want to grab the blanket?" she asked as she stepped over and lifted out the picnic basket.

"Let me get the basket." He reached out and took it from her. "You can take the blanket."

He remained suspiciously quiet as he followed her over to a spot just under a tree. She flipped out the blanket and covered the small spot of grass. Continuing to play the part of a gentleman, he helped her unpack the basket, but she noticed he bumped against her a little more than necessary; brushing next to her and touching her hand. She hoped she wouldn't be fighting him off before the end of the meal.

She filled her plate with the cooked chicken and freshly baked rolls and cheese that her Ma had prepared this morning. Summer even noticed her favorite pie was packed in the basket for dessert. Ma thought of everything.

As she ate, Albert's stare gnawed on her nerves. Couldn't he look someplace else?

She swallowed her bite of roll. "So, Albert, what are your plans for finding employment?"

He shrugged. "I thought about going into banking, but I don't rightly know exactly what I want just yet. I wish my pa had provided for my schooling, but he seemed to think I'd just waste the money on something frivolous."

"Do you have money now?"

"Yes. Pa gave me a little to survive for a while, but it's running out quickly."

"What will you do when you run out and you haven't found work?"

He grinned. "Well, I thought about trying to capture that famous gang the Rangers are looking for."

Her heart caught in her throat--or was it the bite of chicken she'd just took? She swallowed hard. "You're thinking about capturing them? By yourself?"

"Yes."

"Do you know something the Rangers don't know?"

"Not yet."

She nodded. "Personally, I think the Rangers will capture them. From what I've heard, they are hot on Buchanan's trail."

"And I think Buchanan is sending the Rangers on a goose chase."

"Why?"

"No reason, really. But don't you think it odd the Rangers haven't captured them yet?"

She shrugged. "I never thought of it like that." She took another bite of her chicken.

"When I get the reward," Albert continued, puffing out his chest with arrogance, "I've thought about opening a saloon."

She snorted a laugh. "A saloon? Don't you know your pa will skin you alive? Why would you want to own a saloon?" She flipped her hand through the air. "Besides, Waco has enough already."

He shook his head. "In my opinion, no town could have enough." He met her gaze, and his confidence annoyed her. "I'll be making a living, and providing for the family I'll soon have. Aren't those necessary?"

Summer didn't think that much of Albert as it was, but now she thought even less of him. He definitely did not impress her, and she realized they had nothing in common. But she really didn't have a lot of things in common with Jesse, either. Yet with Jesse, it was exciting to banter back and forth. It thrilled her to see his eyes ablaze with heat whenever their conversations went out of control, especially when the fluttering in her stomach couldn't stop dancing, making her want to be held by him and kissed to distraction.

When she found herself gazing across the field in a dream-like state, she quickly pulled her thoughts back to the man sitting across the blanket from her. With a sinking sigh, she realized Albert would never be able to take Jesse out of her heart. Maybe no man could. But did she really want Jesse out of her heart?

"Thank your Ma for fixing this meal," Albert commented. "I just love her cooking."

She forced herself to smile. "I'll tell her. She'll be happy you were pleased."

She set the plate of food down beside her, unable to eat another bite. Albert did the same, then scooted closer to her. She panicked. There was no way she wanted to get closer to him.

"I have an idea," she said, quickly jumping to her feet, "let's walk down by the stream."

"Sounds good to me." He smiled and stood.

As she led the way, Albert's hand slid behind her, just above the waist of her skirt. One inch lower and she'd give him a what for with her elbow. With each step, her anger grew, and she'd have to end this afternoon of leisure very soon or she'd forget her manners and punch him in the nose.

From the corner of her eyes, something in the group of trees not far from the stream caught her attention. She glanced in that direction, and as she withdrew, she realized there was a man hiding in the trees. Could her eyes be deceiving her, or was that man Jesse Slade?

They reached the edge of the stream and stopped. She moved her gaze in that direction once again. Sure enough, standing behind a tree, she detected the side of Jesse's face. Trying to act casual so Jesse would not know she had seen him, she let her attention move slowly away from the trees until it had surveyed the whole field. When she settled her sights back on Albert, her lips tugged into a grin, and she didn't fight off the urge of excitement building up inside her.

She should be angry. Why, that dirty rotten polecat was spying on her and Albert. Yet, this made no sense. Why was Jesse spying on her when he acted as if he wanted her to be with Albert? He hadn't seemed a bit jealous that afternoon in his house. He'd all but encouraged her to be with Albert. Could she have read him wrong? Was he indeed, jealous?

She wanted to be upset, but she couldn't garner up any anger for Jesse. Instead, she was in the mood to tease. Taking in a big breath of air, she moved beside Albert, displaying her widest smile, for not only Albert's sake, but for Jesse's. She hooked her arm through Albert's and gazed up into his eyes.

"Albert? Have I told you how much fun I've had this past week? I'm so glad you decided to drop by and see me on your way through Waco." She raised her voice a bit, hoping that Jesse could hear her.

Albert's grin broadened. "I, too, am enjoying myself."

"I really hate to see you leave."

"Like I said before, I don't really have any plans to leave in the immediate future."

Going one step further, she rested her head on his shoulders, noticing right away that he was not as muscular as Jesse. Such a shame for Albert. He wrapped his arm around her shoulders and his body relaxed.

"This is nice," he said huskily.

"Yes. I just love watching the water run over the rocks. It's so soothing for the soul."

"No, I was talking about us. About this." His arm tightened around her shoulder.

She rolled her head back just enough to look over to the clump of trees again. Jesse's body leaned away from the tree while he practically strained his neck to see what was going on by the stream. Summer bit her lip to keep from laughing out loud.

She tried not to appear as if she was watching Jesse, but she also wasn't very comfortable in Albert's arms, either. And for some unknown reason, her legs itched. Casually, she reached down her leg and scratched. Within seconds, her other leg became irritated, and she had to rub that limb, too.

The longer she leaned against Albert, the more her legs burned with soreness, and the uncomfortable feeling seemed to crawl up her legs. Beside her, Albert shifted his stance, then he reached down to scratch his leg, too. This was too coincidental, but she couldn't let Jesse know that something was not right in her and Albert's cozy little embrace.

She pulled away slightly and turned fully toward the trees. Jesse quickly ducked and stumbled backwards. In that direction came a loud cuss from him. Even Albert jerked his head toward the trees.

"Is somebody over there?"

"I'm not certain."

She stepped away, and the itching on her legs increased. She could stand no more of this. Bending, she lifted her skirts just enough to scratch her ankles. She let out a loud gasp. Her legs were covered with tiny red ants. They were standing in an ant hill.

"Awh." She screamed and stomped fiercely, trying to get the ants off her. Behind her, Albert screamed like a child bit by an angry dog as he stumbled into the water, falling on his back and rolling around like his body was on fire. If not for the intense pain in her legs, she would have laughed out loud over his candid display.

She looked back to the trees again. Jesse ran along side his horse, almost in a limp as he held his pants. She couldn't be sure, but from back here it looked as if he'd been attacked, too, but by a cactus instead.

Forgetting her pain for a few seconds, she did laugh out loud, not caring who heard her outburst.

~ * ~

Albert pulled the horse to a stop and Summer released her tight hold on the seat of the buggy. Her attention swept across the area Albert had chosen, the gentle brook flowing over the rocks, keeping rhythm with the sounds of the afternoon's chirping insects. Overhanging trees shaded their spot, and a grassy knoll sloped down the hillside nearby.

This was their second outing, and this time she suspected he wanted to be alone with her. Of course, she was almost thankful to the ants which had interrupted their first outing, painful as it had been. Both she and Albert had bites on their legs and itched for the following two days. Inwardly, she chuckled when she thought that her pain was nothing compared to Jesse's. Why that poor man could not sit down for twenty-four hours due to the cactus welts on his arse.

Albert set the brake, then jumped down. "Nate tells me that this is another spot you enjoy visiting."

She smiled. "I used to come here with my brother to play in the water. We skipped rocks and had mud fights."

He laughed, grabbed her waist and lifted her down. "Do you miss being a tomboy? From the way your family talks about you, I get the impression you used to wear pants more often than dresses."

Once she found her footing, she pulled away from his hold. "It's true. I used to be a tomboy, but I really don't miss it as much as I thought I would."

"Why not?"

She shrugged and watched the water cascade lazily around the boulders of the stream. "It's rather nice being treated like a lady. I like the attention the boys are giving me now."

He turned her chin toward him, his fingers caressing her skin. "So, you prefer the boys over the men?"

"I've not had very many men pay attention to me."

"How many?"

Jesse came to mind, but she quickly dismissed the idea of trying to explain her feelings about Jesse to Albert. Confusion was still lodged in her head and heart where Jesse was concerned. "Only one, really. Of course, now that I think about it, I really don't think he was being serious with me. I think he just wanted to know what it would feel like to kiss me."

"Who was it?"

"Clint."

Albert's expression quickly changed to surprise. "Clint kissed you? I thought he was like a brother to you."

She nodded. "He is. I think Clint was bored that night and needed a distraction. He kissed me and I laughed. It felt as if I were kissing one of my brothers."

"And how did Clint feel?"

"Luckily, he felt the same. We know each other too well to be anything but good friends."

He moved closer. "I hope you don't feel that way about me."

She waved her hand. "Of course I don't think of you as a brother. We hardly know each other. When I lived with my aunt, you only visited on a few occasions."

"True, but those few occasions were enough for me to know that I really liked you. I was absolutely miserable after you left Brownsville."

Fear crept inside her, but she still managed a smile. Albert had been the perfect gentleman, but her feelings for him didn't rise above friendship. There couldn't be anything stronger, and Jesse was the cause.

"Ma and Violet have kept me so busy I don't have time to miss my friends in Brownsville."

"I bet the men in this town have been lining up at your door." He chuckled. "Do I have to fight off any of your beaus?"

She laughed. "Nope. Sorry to disappoint you, but nobody has been pounding at my door lately."

"Are the men around here addled? You're absolutely adorable, Summer. You're the prettiest girl I've seen in a long time."

He stroked her cheek again, but let his fingers trail down her neck. The sensations were unpleasant and she stepped back, but the buggy blocked her way.

"I've always been just one of the boys around here, and I think that's the reason they don't come courtin'," she said.

"Then luck is certainly on my side." Albert moved closer and slid his arms around her waist. "I like having you all to myself."

Why couldn't she feel the excitement with Albert she experienced whenever Jesse held her? Why couldn't Albert thrill her the way Jesse could? It wasn't fair! Her body just would not allow her to have the kind of feelings with Albert as she had with Jesse.

"You're too sweet, Albert. Believe me, I don't deserve your admiration."

He leaned his forehead against hers. "I just wish I could show you more attention, but unfortunately, I'll be leaving tomorrow."

Surprise washed over her, and she widened her eyes. Happiness welled up in her chest. Just the other day, he said he didn't have plans on leaving. He must have changed his mind.

"I understand." She tried not to look too thrilled about the news.

"So, I was thinking," he said, pulling her body against his, "that maybe you might want to give me something to take along the trail so that I'll think of you all the time."

By the look in his eyes, she knew what he wanted. She also knew he wasn't going to get it. She acted innocent. "I don't think I have a miniature portrait of me, but I'll try to find one."

He laughed huskily. "No, my sweet, I was thinking more on the lines of this--"

He crushed his mouth over hers, and right away she stiffened. It was hard to let him kiss her. His lips were not gentle, and the throaty sounds coming from him were making her nauseous.

Albert withdrew slightly. "Come on, Summer. Open your mouth for me. I'll show you what kissing is all about."

She turned her face. "Albert, no. I can't do this." She tried to pull back, but he held her tight.

"You're just frightened of the unknown. I'll teach you the different ways of kissing."

She squirmed and avoided his kisses the best she could without being too rude. "I don't think I want to learn from you." His hold tightened. Panic set in. "Albert, please let me go. I don't feel right about doing this with you."

"Oh, but Summer, you certainly feel right to me." He moved his hand to her breast and squeezed.

Hot anger shot through her and she pressed the palms of her hands against his chest. He still wouldn't move. She gnashed her teeth and let her hand fly through the air until it connected with his face. "Albert, no!"

She waited for his reaction, but he grinned haughtily and pressed his mouth to her neck, moving his slobbery kisses downward.

"You just need to learn how to please a man, Summer, and I'm going to be that lucky man."

"Over my dead body," she snapped. "Albert, I'm warning you, if you don't let me go this instance, I'll do something you'll soon regret."

Without moving his descending mouth, he chuckled. "You couldn't harm a flea."

Nobody, but nobody talked to her like that, especially this man with only one thing on his mind! Were all men this way? Jesse didn't even talk to her in such a tone. Thank heavens Jesse wasn't anything like Albert. Jesse's kisses were so much sweeter, and she ached for that gentle treatment. Suddenly her perfect image of Albert was shattered, and hatred for him boiled through her blood. When his hand became wilder as it pawed at her breast, bile rose in her throat. It was time to get physical. She'd show this man exactly how tough she could be.

Pushing her hands against him as hard as she could, she moved him back just enough to bring up her knee. Luckily he wasn't as tall as Jesse, and the point of her knee met perfectly with his groin. As he fell away, a loud gurgle exploded from his throat and he clutched his crotch in a bent position. Pain etched itself on every line of his face, but she didn't care. She was going to add insult to injury.

Not very often was she privileged to punch a man in the face, but she wouldn't pass up the opportunity when presented to her. She doubled her fist and let it fly until it connected with the end of his nose. This time a sickening crunch echoed. Summer was sure she had broken his nose. Blood poured down his face. He held his groin with one hand and with the other covered his bleeding nose, which didn't stop the flow of blood very well.

Before climbing back to the buggy and leaving his sorry butt there, she reached in her wrist purse and pulled out a handkerchief.

"Here, this might help stop the bleeding." She tossed it to him, then turned and climbed into the carriage. "Next time, maybe you'll think twice about pawing at a lady," she snapped, then urged the horses forward in a fast trot.

She didn't feel like laughing, although the picture of Albert's bloody nose and twisted body stuck in her head. Her hopes were shattered of ever finding the perfect man. Albert certainly wasn't, but he had given her that impression. So if he couldn't pass the test, what man would? And if that man ever came along, would he take Jesse out of her heart?

She rode about a mile before a rider on horseback galloped toward her. At first she thought it was Clint, but as he rode closer, she recognized Jesse's lean frame. She slowed her horse and waited for him to join her.

When he stopped his horse, she asked, "What are you doing here?"

"Are you all right?" His voice was laced with worry.

"Yes." She creased her brow. "What's wrong? Why are you here?"

184

"Where's Albert?"

She really didn't want to explain, but it looked as if she had no other choice. "He's back that way about a mile." She tossed her head in the direction. "He wasn't playing very nice, so I let him know how I felt about it."

Jesse's sober expression quickly changed. His lips twitched until a broad smile stretched across his mouth. Throwing back his head, he howled with laughter. "I should have known you'd be all right."

She folded her arms across her chest. "Now, will you tell me what's wrong?"

He leaned forward on his horse. "Nate came over to the house a little while ago. He mentioned that Albert had taken you out here to be alone. Clint and I didn't like it. We just didn't feel good about you bein' alone with him."

She scowled. "You didn't think I could take care of myself?"

He shrugged and his smile disappeared. "Should have figured you'd be upset."

"Well, I am. You had no right sticking your nose into my business."

"Summer, I was worried about you. In fact, from your comments, it seems Albert Kendal really isn't a perfect gentleman, is he?"

She tapped her toe on the floorboard, hesitating in answering. But she could read Jesse well. His know-it-all smugness oozed from his handsome face.

He grinned. "Thank you would be an appropriate reply right now."

She shot him a glare. "Why? You didn't rescue me."

His smile quickly disappeared. "No, I guess I didn't." His voice softened. "But now that I know you're all right, I'll leave." He turned his horse around and rode off.

Her heart dropped and tears pooled in her eyes. When would she ever understand him? And why couldn't she stop loving him?

Thirteen

The gentle, late Autumn breeze swept through the open window of the kitchen and caressed Summer's face, stirring the few tendrils that had fallen loose from the stylish knot on the back of her neck. She sat at the table with Ma and Violet, helping to prepare dinner. As she chopped the carrots and onions, the faces of two men appeared in her mind. The one she loved to hate, and one she hated to love. The more she thought about Albert's false gentlemanly manners and Jesse's stubborn hide, the harder her knife struck the cutting board.

It had only been a week since Albert's quick departure, but Summer's boredom consumed her mind and left her restless. Even working at the livery didn't help to calm her aggravation. She stayed away from Jesse, knowing if he released even one syllable in her presence, her temper would explode, and in the process, leave her with a wounded heart. Yet, life was not the same without him.

She put all of her effort into keeping books for the livery and trying to increase their clientele, yet she couldn't keep her head occupied for very long. She prayed for a release of her turbulent thoughts, but her prayers went unanswered. The only thing good happening in her life so far was the miraculous improvement of her father's attitude. He seemed more chipper and more communicative. She'd even heard him laughing.

Albert's hasty departure entered her mind again, and she viciously chopped off the end of the carrot. Her family had wondered what went wrong, but Summer wouldn't speak of it. She didn't want to ruin the image they held for him, mainly because she was afraid they wouldn't believe her if she confessed the truth. Albert had done such a good job sugar-coating himself, her brothers practically idolized him, and poor Elizabeth couldn't stop walking around with that dazed love-sick expression. Even Ma and Pa thought he was an angel sent from Heaven. How could she tell them that Albert's one-track mind was far from that exalted place?

Just thinking about the roughness as he'd forced his slobbery kisses on her and pawed at her breast, made her whack the knife on the cutting board, totally missing the carrot. She hadn't realized she'd made such a racket until she looked up and saw the horrified stares from Ma and Violet.

Lillian gasped. "My dear, what in Heaven's name is wrong?"

Summer laid the knife on the table and gave an innocent smile. "Nothing."

Violet tilted her head and studied her. "I'm afraid to ask what pictures are lurking in that head of yours."

Summer laughed. "It's nothing, really."

Lillian relaxed and smiled. "So, my dear, have you heard from your Mr. Kendal lately?"

Summer's hand tightened around the handle of the knife and her brows furrowed together. "No, Ma." She quickly laid another carrot on the cutting board, and chopped it into uneven slices. "Besides, he's not *my* Mr. Kendal. Why? Have you heard from him?"

Lillian chuckled. "Why would he contact me?"

Summer shrugged.

"I got the impression he was sweet on you," her mother continued.

"Ma, we're only friends."

"That's what Violet and Jesse used to say." Lillian turned to Violet. "Now look at them. They're getting married."

Summer glanced across the table at her sister. Violet picked up a potato and quickend her hand as she peeled, her eyes downcast and her lips pursed together tightly. What could her sister be thinking?

"Besides," Lillian went on, "Pa wants to know why Albert hasn't been coming around lately."

Summer shrugged. "I didn't want Albert bothering Pa."

"Oh, horse manure. He wouldn't be a bother. Pa likes to meet the men who court his daughters."

Violet set her knife on the table and leaned forward and

touched Ma's arm. "Ma? I think Summer is worried Pa will do to Albert what he did to Jesse."

"What is that, Violet, dear?"

Violet took a deep breath and squared her shoulders. "Pa came right out and asked Jesse when he was going to marry me," she explained. "It not only embarrassed Jesse, but forced him into doing something he didn't want to do."

Summer let out a loud gasp and stopped the knife in mid-stroke as she stared wide-eyed at Violet.

Lillian's brows furrowed. "Now, what is that suppose to mean? Your pa didn't force Jesse."

Summer kept her stare on Violet's expression, hoping her sister would tell the truth. Summer's heart hammered in anticipation.

Violet took another deep breath. "Ma? I have a confession to make, and I seriously hope it doesn't affect your feelings for Jesse."

Lillian reached out and grasped Violet's hands. "What is it, my dear?"

"Jesse and I...don't love each other any longer."

"*What*?" Lillian blurted, and Summer clutched the side of the table to keep from sliding off her chair in shock.

Violet patted Ma's hands. "Would you lower your voice? I don't want Pa knowing this yet." Violet stood and walked over to the sink. "Jesse and I were in love at one time, or at least what we thought was love. But I know now it was only a schoolgirl's crush, and after a while of seeing each other on a regular basis, everybody just assumed we were in love. Pa even assumed, and that was when he asked Jesse when he was going to marry me. Jesse really wasn't planning on it, but because Pa seemed so elated, Jesse couldn't deny Pa's wishes." She paused. "I kept going forward with the wedding because I was too afraid to tell Pa. I didn't want to break his heart, especially now."

"Oh, my poor dear." Lillian moved to Violet and wrapped her arms around her in a hug. "You'll never be able to break his heart. Your pa wants to see all of his daughters happy, and if it means breaking the engagement with Jesse, then he'll approve."

"Ma?" She pulled away. "Jesse and I have already stopped our plans. We were just waiting for the right time to tell

Pa."

"How long have you known you weren't in love with Jesse?"

"For a while now." Violet's smile widened as a tint of pink painted her cheeks. "Ever since I fell in love with somebody else."

Lillian's eyes widened, and Summer thought for sure she'd fall off the chair this time. She gasped aloud, and questioned before her mother could. "You're in love with another man?"

Violet laughed. "It was easy for me to fall in love with Clint, because I was never really in love with Jesse."

Summer laughed. "*Clint*?"

"Clint Slade?" Ma blurted.

"Yes."

"Oh, my lands," Lillian shrieked giddily as she hugged Violet again. "I don't think you'll have to worry about disappointing Pa."

Tears gathered in Violet's eyes as she returned her mother's hug. Over Ma's shoulder, Violet's happy eyes met with Summer's and she smiled.

Lillian pulled away. "Let's tell Pa tonight."

Violet frowned. "No, Ma. Jesse wants to be with me when I tell him. It's only fair."

"All right." Lillian turned to Summer. "Go find your brothers and have them fetch Jesse right away. I want him here tonight as soon as possible."

"But Ma," Violet interjected, "they're at the stable closing for the night." She turned to Summer and grinned. "Summer? You go get Jesse."

Suddenly, Summer's happiness disappeared. Heat rushed through her, and made her hands clammy. She *couldn't*. She'd have to be polite…or would she spout hateful words? Or worse, would she fall into his arms and beg for his love?

Ma yanked Summer's arm, bringing her out of the chair toward the back door. "Hurry, child, we don't have time to waste."

Ma wouldn't let her dally. The older woman was right on Summer's heels, pushing her until she was out the door. Summer sauntered to the barn and hitched the one horse buggy, but Ma ran out behind her, shooing her slowness. "Hurry as if fire were on your heels."

With a heavy heart, Summer nodded then climbed into the buggy.

She stretched the ride to Jesse and Clint's house and arrived in ten minutes, even though it only took half that time if she rode quickly. The quick beat of her heart told her she actually looked forward to seeing him again--and seeing his reaction to Violet's confession.

A small light shone through the front window. She stopped the vehicle, then set the brake. Taking a deep breath, she jumped from the vehicle. On wobbly legs, she walked to the front door and knocked.

Jesse opened the door and the sight of his handsome face knocked her senseless. Curse his hide for looking so incredible in bluejeans that molded to his muscular legs, and the beige shirt tempting her with a hint of skin at his opened neck. His eyes widened and a smile appeared on his tempting mouth. Although his smile made her knees weak, she kept her lips pursed in a solemn expression. Soon, his smile disappeared and worried lines claimed his face. He took her hands in his and pulled her inside the warm cabin.

"Has somethin' happened to your pa?"

His kindness nearly shattered her defenses. Her heart melted. "No, Jesse. Pa is fine."

He breathed a heavy sigh. "Oh, good." He crinkled his forehead. "Then what's wrong?"

She pasted on a smile as she tried to calm down her madly beating heart. "Ma sent me to get you. Violet has finally told her about your engagement being canceled, and Ma wants the two of you to tell Pa tonight."

His brows lifted. "Violet finally confessed? I can't believe it. How did Lillian take it?"

Summer chuckled. "Believe it or not, she's ecstatic. It shocked her to think the two of you didn't love each other, but she was happy to know that Violet is in love with Clint."

Jesse's eyes widened and his jaw dropped. "What?" His voice escalated. "Violet and Clint?"

"You didn't know either?"

"I suspected, but then I dismissed the idea." He hesitated,

then whooped a loud shout of joy, picking Summer up and swinging her around once. "Can you believe it? My brother and Violet?"

She laughed over Jesse's enthusiasm and rested her hands on his shoulders. Pleasure filled her the longer she remained in his arms. Curse her hide, but she didn't want this emotion to end. "No, I can't believe it."

"But I'm glad my brother has finally found the right woman. That's a relief off my mind. Let's just hope your pa takes it as well."

"Ma seems to think he will, which is the reason she sent me here to get you."

"Wait for me. I'll grab my duster."

When he released her, the loss of his warmth sapped her strength. Closing her eyes, she breathed deeply, trying to calm her racing heart. Once she felt in control, she straightened her stance and opened her eyes. Without a doubt, she would fall into his arms tonight and beg for him to love her. As weak as her heart was right now, she knew it would happen. But she couldn't let it. She'd never been helpless in her life.

"Jesse?" she called out. "I'll just meet you back home."

"No. If you leave, I won't be able to get there. My horse threw a shoe earlier this evening."

She cursed under her breath. "Where is Clint?"

"The Rangers have him stayin' in Amarillo for the next couple of days." His voice came down the hall.

"What's in Amarillo?"

"Leads."

"Leads?"

"Yes, information leadin' us to that gang we've been after."

"I really hope the Rangers catch them soon," she said, inwardly wishing that she'd be the one to capture them and take the reward.

Jesse walked back into the room. Frozen in place, she stood as her gaze roamed over him, loving the way his shirt tightened around the cords of muscles in his arm when he slipped on the russet duster. He'd always look handsome no matter what he wore.

Slowly, he walked toward her, but she remained still. When his gaze moved down to her gray dress, shivers of delight coursed through her blood. Nothing had changed, especially the way he could always make her heart pitter-patter. She loved him, but she was destined for a lonely life without him by her side. He stepped in front of her and the pounding of her heart echoed in her ears.

"You look beautiful tonight, Summer."

She smiled as her face flamed. "Thank you. You look very handsome, too. How are you feeling? Is your shoulder healed completely?" She hesitantly touched the fabric of his coat by his injured shoulder.

"Yes. I'm back to normal. I've even started movin' some of my things into the new cabin."

"Really? Clint still wants you to live there?"

"Yes."

"That's good."

"How about you?" he asked. "How have you been farin'?"

"Fine."

He glanced down at the floor and shuffled his feet. "Are you still seein' Albert?"

"No."

His gaze jumped up and met with hers. "I'm sorry he wasn't the man you wanted him to be."

Her smile disappeared. "I don't think there is a man who can fit that mold."

"What mold is that?"

Dare she tell him? She wanted to--oh, how she wanted to blurt out, *I love you, Jesse, and I always have. I'll probably love you until the day I die.* But, her stubborn pride held back the confession.

"Albert didn't respect my wishes."

He shrugged. "Perhaps he'll change someday."

His nonchalant attitude made her want to cry, so she quickly turned and stepped toward the door before he noticed her threatening tears. "Maybe he will," she snapped. "We better go. We shouldn't keep Ma waiting any longer."

He grabbed hold of her arm, stopping her. Heated tingles

shot through her body from his touch.

"Summer, wait." He stepped in front of her, and for the first time she noticed sadness in his ocean blue eyes. Her heart broke a little more. "Summer? What do you want from me?"

She breathed deeply, mainly to control her tears. "I don't want anything from you."

"Then why--" he paused, staring deeply into her eyes.

"Why what?"

He gently caressed the fabric on her sleeve, then ran his knuckles up and down her arms. "I keep getting' mixed signals from you, and I'm very confused."

"I'm not sending you signals, Jesse."

"Then why do your beautiful eyes light up when you look at me?" He moved his hand and softly stroked the side of her face. "Sometimes I catch you studyin' me, and the emotion written on your face is so tender I can feel it clear to my soul." His tongue wet his lips. "And why does your body shiver every time I touch it?"

Her body responded from his comment, making her heart rate increase. The conversation was getting out of hand, and her control would break any minute.

"I'm sure I don't know what you mean," she whispered, afraid her voice would crack. She took a step back, but once again, he grabbed both of her shoulders, pulling her body up against his. When that familiar spark ignited in her bosom, she gasped.

"Yes, I think you know exactly what I mean. Just like now. You can feel it. I can see it in your eyes. I can feel it through your body."

She couldn't deny it, but yet what good would it do to admit her true feelings? He'd never be able to think of her as a woman. She'd always be the little tomboy to him.

"Does it matter? Does it really matter, Jesse?" Her voice broke. After moistening her dry throat, she started again. "Fine, if you want to know the truth, I'll tell you, but I promise you it won't solve a thing."

Gathering all the courage she could find, she took a deep breath and prepared her confession, but just as she opened her mouth to speak, the clip-clop of a horse's hooves in the yard broke her concentration. Jesse cursed before he stepped to the front door and pulled it open.

Nate jerked on the reins and stopped the horse in front of the porch and jumped down. "Ma sent me to see what was taking so long."

Summer quickly stepped past Jesse and ran to Nate's horse. "Ma is very impatient, isn't she?" she spoke over her shoulder. "Well, she'll just have to keep her pantaloons on because we're on our way."

She lifted her skirts and mounted the horse, not caring that it didn't have a sidesaddle. "Nate? Will you bring Jesse in the buggy? Right now I'm in no mood to argue."

She mounted, grabbed the reins and pushed the horse forward, struggling with her tears and praying Jesse would not see.

~ * ~

Summer stood with her back against the wall in the living room, leaning her head against the wood's hardness. From the moment the family had gathered to listen to Jesse and Violet's confession, Summer was unable to take her eyes off Jesse's handsome face and powerfully attractive body. As the words from the conversation flitted through the air, Summer's mind didn't register what was being said. All she could think about was hiding her own feelings. She loved Jesse, but she couldn't go through another heartbreak. He'd made it clear what he wanted--and marriage was not part of it.

She'd ignored the yearnings of her heart because of Jesse's engagement to Violet, but that was no longer necessary. Jesse held some kind of feeling for her, the night he was drunk and the time at the barn proved that. But could he ever accept and love her for the woman she'd flourished into and want her as his wife? And was she willing to risk rejection, yet again? She didn't want him to think he could treat her as anything less than a lady

Shadows danced across Jesse's face from the few lamps in the room, making him appear ruggedly handsome. Whenever his eyes moved her way, their hypnotic power sent tingles through her body clear down to her toes. As always when he studied her, her stomach fluttered in giddiness. This time, she wanted to feel this way, and so didn't try to push away the emotion.

Staying in the same room with Jesse was pure torture. She needed to leave. Hiding in her own bedroom wouldn't solve anything, but at least her skin wouldn't tingle when his gaze slid over her, and his masculine scent of cedar and leather wouldn't make her weak in the knees.

Banishing her out of control thoughts, she quickly decided when Jesse and Violet were finished talking to Pa, she'd sneak up to her room for the remainder of the evening--mainly because she worried that Jesse would want her to finish their conversation. Under no circumstances could she do that. She'd been weak back at his cabin, and she couldn't let herself get that way again.

When Pa showed signs of fatigue, the talk with Jesse and Violet ended. After many hugs and kisses between Ma, Pa, Violet and Jesse, Ma ushered Pa into his bedroom for some rest. Because of everyone's ecstatic mood, Summer couldn't find the right moment to sneak away. Every time she took a step toward freedom, Violet maneuvered herself between Summer and the stairs, keeping Summer from slowly fading out of the room.

Her younger brothers, who idolized Jesse, were disappointed that he wasn't marrying Violet, and so kept Jesse at the house. The longer the night wore on, the more impatience gnawed on Summer's nerves. Finally, Lillian entered the room and announced it was time for the boys to go to bed. Summer sighed with relief, but before she could summon the courage to make a quick getaway, Nate jumped up and spontaneously volunteered his help. "Ma, I'll go with Summer to take Jesse home."

Summer's heart dropped, and she desperately thought of a way out.

"No, Nate," Lillian instructed, "it's time for bed. Summer can take him home by herself."

Summer shook her head, ready to argue her point.

"But Ma," Nate whined, "it's late and Summer needs somebody to protect her when she comes home from Jesse's house."

Summer met Jesse's laughing eyes, then suddenly, every person in the room shared the humor. Jesse moved over to Nate and ruffled his shaggy brown hair.

"Have you forgotten about your sister's special talent for defendin' herself? I think I'll be the one needin' protection tonight."

Jesse's comment didn't upset her like it might have

before, and she laughed. "Just the same, I like the idea of being protected like a lady."

Nate grimaced. "Ewww! I don't want to even think about that."

Jesse chuckled. "Maybe I'll let you ride with me at another time, buddy," he told Nate. "Tonight I'd like to have a talk with Summer. Is that all right?"

Summer's heart sank and anxiety surrounded her. She shook her head, and opened her mouth to say something, but was interrupted.

"Why?" Nate complained. "All you and Summer ever do is argue. 'Sides, if she takes you home, she'll ruin your night."

Summer held her breath and waited for Jesse's reaction, silently praying he'd agree with her brother. Instead, Jesse glanced at her and grinned. In three long strides, he was by her side, playfully nudging her elbow.

"I guess I'll just have to take my chances," Jesse told Nate over his shoulder. "It's really important I talk to her tonight."

She sighed a defeated breath, knowing she couldn't get out of it this time.

"Golly gee," Nate grumbled. "I'm fifteen years old and I still can't stay up late." He turned and stomped into his bedroom.

Summer looked back at Jesse and found his gaze still remained on her. When a tender expression crossed his face, her heart twisted.

"Is that all right with you?" he asked.

She shrugged. "Well, actually, I had different plans--"

"Of course it's all right," Violet stepped forward and interjected, tugging gently on Summer's sleeve. "She'd love to take you back home, Jesse."

Summer glared at her sister, but Violet just gave her a teasing grin.

With Jesse by her side, Summer turned and walked toward the door.

"Summer, dear?" Lillian called. "Don't be too long. We have a busy day tomorrow. If we plan to get Violet and Clint married before the end of the month, we'll need as many hands as possible."

"Ma." Violet stepped over to her. "Shall we wait for Clint

to ask Pa for my hand first?"

Summer chuckled over Ma's confused expression. "Don't worry, Ma. I won't be long."

Violet leaned over to Summer and whispered in her ear. "Take as long as you want. You and Jesse have a lot to discuss."

Summer turned and met Violet's stare. *How did she know?* Were her feelings so easily noticed? She hoped not. "Thanks...I think."

Violet winked, then moved back inside the house and closed the door.

Summer's heart pounded with each step to the one-horse buggy. Both she and Jesse were quiet except for the crunching from the dry leaves underneath their shoes. When they reached the buggy, Jesse took her hand and helped her up into the seat then climbed in to sit beside her. He took the reins and urged the horse forward.

She sat straight, trying her hardest not to bump against him, but the rickety springs on the seat made it next to impossible. It took more strength to keep herself from touching him than it would if she just surrendered. But that she could not do.

Jesse cleared his throat. "So," he began after a few awkward minutes of silence. "I think the talk with your pa went well."

"Yes. Pa was elated to hear Clint would be joining the family."

"Clint's a good man. He'll be a good husband for Violet."

"I agree."

Jesse turned his attention to her. "See, that wasn't so hard."

She crinkled her brow. "What wasn't so hard?"

"Agreein' with me."

The teasing expression on his face made her grin, which relaxed her slightly. "You are correct again, Mr. Slade. That wasn't hard at all."

He looked back on the road, keeping his smile. "Thanks for not puttin' up a fight when your ma volunteered you to bring me home. Thought I might have to drag you out of the house kickin' and screamin'."

She shrugged. "You almost had to. My refusal fell to deaf

ears and I had no other choice but to come."

He glanced at her. "Why didn't you want to take me home?"

"Because I'm confident you could make it home safe and sound on your own."

He chuckled. "Oh, so it wasn't to avoid our unfinished conversation?"

She sucked in a quick breath. "Well, yes, that's another reason."

His hand moved and covered her clasped hands resting on her lap. "Can you honestly tell me you'd rather not speak openly about your feelin's?"

She lifted her chin and squared her shoulders as she stared ahead on the road. "I would appreciate it if you wouldn't bring this up. I feel the same as I did before Nate interrupted us earlier this evening."

"But you never told me how you felt."

She scowled. "My feelings haven't changed, Jesse. Now leave the matter alone." She focused on the road.

Jesse withdrew his hand and didn't say another word. With a heavy heart, she blinked, fighting back the tears. She would not let him break her heart again. When they drove to the front of the cabin, she sighed. Finally, she'd be free of his overpowering presence…and be able to control her weakened heart.

He stopped the horse then set the brake, but he didn't climb out. The reins dropped from his fingers as his elbows rested on his knees. His stare focused on the back end of the horse as he sighed. His shoulders wilted.

The constrained silence became uncomfortable, but finally Jesse jumped out of the buggy. Keeping her aching heart under control, she reached for the reins. Suddenly, Jesse swore, grabbed her around the waist and yanked her out of the seat. She gasped, more from the shock of having her body slide down his hard frame than the surprise of his sudden movement. His heated gaze bore deeply into hers as he held her close.

"Why do you keep pullin' away from me?" His voice choked with deep emotion. "Don't you think I care about you?"

She swallowed hard. "Sometimes I wonder."

"What's to wonder? Can't you tell how I feel?"

She turned her head from his intense stare. "It's no use, Jesse. It doesn't matter how I feel about you or how you feel about me. It'll never work."

His labored breaths fanned her cheek and she fought her body's weakening restraint. Strong arms pulled her tighter against him. She couldn't stop the pleasurable gasp from escaping her throat.

Several minutes passed, and Summer allowed herself to enjoy being in Jesse's arms. But soon the moment would end. She'd go home, and things would be the same as it had been before. Things would never change between them. She knew it, and she thought he knew it, too.

He withdrew slightly and looked down at her. The shadows played across his face. Seriousness touched his saddened expression through his frown.

Jesse's brows creased and his jaw hardened. "No. I won't let it end like this. Damn it, I'll make it work."

Fourteen

Summer stood frozen as Jesse's mouth moved downward. In one gentle motion he pressed his lips to hers. She tried turning her head, but his hand bracketed her chin and kept her still while he tasted her lips, again and again.

"I can't let you go," he whispered.

Then his tongue outlined her stiff lips before he slipped his velvety hot tip inside. She surrendered, weak kneed and clinging to his shoulders.

His hand moved down her neck, caressing, then stroking when it curved over her breast. Heat poured through her, making her lose control. She moaned and arched, giving him more of her fullness. When he squeezed, tingles of excitement darted up her spine. He rubbed the pad of his thumb over her hardened tip and she moaned.

Swiftly, he lifted her in his strong arms and carried her inside the cabin, heading straight for his bedroom. The full moon shinning through the window created carnal shadows, turning the mood passionate. He laid her on his bed, then joined her. His mouth united again with hers as his hand moved down to cover her quivering womanhood. Automatically, her legs stiffened when fear of the unknown swept through her.

"It's all right," he whispered encouragingly. "I won't hurt you."

As she let her thighs relax she threaded her fingers through his hair and pulled him closer. He rolled halfway on top of her. His rigid arousal pressed intimately against her hip and an unladylike crow of pleasure emerged from deep within her soul.

"Oh, Summer," a reverent utter escaped his lips. "I've loved you for so long."

So have I, her mind screamed, but she couldn't speak the

words her heart was singing--her wandering lips over his prickly jaw wouldn't rest long enough. Kissing him was just too enjoyable.

His hands released the row of tiny buttons down the front of her blouse, then jerked the material free from her skirt. As her lips continued caressing his mouth, jaw, and neck, she helped him remove all the barriers, even undoing the satin tie holding her chemise together.

When his hand covered her bare flesh, her insides melted to hot butter, her restraint was abandoned as she fell back on the bed. Jesse bent over her, his ardent kisses impatient across her bosom, as he made his way to the tip of her breast. His tongue lapped at the taut nipple, then sucked.

She held his head, moving it to one breast and then the other, as a hungering need for more grew inside her. Going with her feelings, she lifted her hips and pushed against his arousal. Liquid heat rushed through her.

"Jesse," she whimpered.

When he pulled up the material, her skirt rustled. He rested his hand on her bare thigh and she quivered in anticipation.

He lifted his head, flames of desire dancing in his eyes. His hand moved between her thighs and touched the spot that ached for him. Closing her eyes, she murmured his name again. Moisture had gathered beneath his wandering hand. His palm pressed in the juncture, and she let out a throaty moan. He lifted himself slightly as both hands pulled down her bloomers, discarding them on the floor.

The stroke of his fingers was feather light as they touched the swollen bud high between her legs, and an assault of spasms rippled through her. His breaths came out ragged, as did her own.

While his fingers explored, his mouth fastened back onto her breast. An exquisite pleasure erupted between her legs in the area where his fingers were doing maddening things to her senses. She squirmed and rubbed herself deeper into his hand.

The sucking motion of his mouth and the rhythm of his fingers accelerated, and her body experienced things she had never imagined. She savored the newfound feelings.

"Jesse, Jesse," she repeated, her voice clogged in her throat.

"Yes, my love?"

"Please."

"Please what?"

His fingers pushed into her again and she moaned deeply. "Do you love me?"

"Oh, yes."

"Then make love to me."

Disappointment washed over her when his hand left her, but his fingers pulled apart her clothes, urgent to remove them. She sat up and helped, and within minutes she lay naked. His gaze devoured every inch of her flesh, and cascades of pleasure flowed through her, building upon the sensations still racking her body.

She reached for his shirt and released the buttons, but impatience won and he ended up ripping it apart, buttons flying to the floor, rolling to the wall and under the bed. Boldly she put her hands on his trousers. The shape and size was fully noticeable through his jeans, huge, hard, and pulsing. She glimpsed a hungry look in his eyes that sent her heart racing.

"You're so hard." She labored in speaking. "Aunt Lydia didn't tell me about this."

The side of his mouth lifted, giving her his sexy grin. "Then let me teach you."

"Yes, oh yes."

She opened his trousers and helped him pull them down. When his rigid member popped out--magnificence surrounded by curly black hair--she gasped. By the time he was as naked as she, her mouth had turned dry. Her body quivered with anticipation, yet nervous for what was about to happen.

He crawled back on the bed and lay fully on top of her, his hands ahead of him guiding the way. When he stroked her thighs, they trembled and opened. He guided himself to her swollen femininity and slid inside. Sharp pain sliced through her and she gasped. She stopped and held her breath.

"It's all right, my love," he whispered. "The pain will disappear."

Just as he promised, within moments heat poured back into her and she relaxed. Slowly he began to move, in and out, until he filled her completely. His warmth spread through every limb, fulfilling her every need. She leaned up and pressed her mouth to his, then pushed her hips against him.

His hands cupped her bottom as he drove in deeper, murmuring her name mixed with words of endearment. The emotion in his tone tore at her heart, and tears of happiness sprang to her eyes. Spasms built within, and with each thrust, her mind and soul spun, soaring higher and tighter. With shuddering soulful cries, she went over the edge and slowly tumbled back down until the last of the spasms left her sated and complete.

"Jesse, I love you." The emotion in the words came from her heart.

"Oh, Summer," he groaned. "I love you, too."

As the last word tore from his mouth, he shuddered. Their breathing gradually returned to normal, but their bodies remained connected. She fit with him perfectly and didn't want to ever leave.

Turning her head, she kissed his moist brow. "Thank you."

He lifted on his elbows, his smile of satisfaction evident. "No, thank you."

"I mean thank you for loving me."

He shook his head. "It was out of my control. I think I fell in love with you that time at the fishin' hole."

"Me, too."

He kissed her mouth. "Summer? Would you do me the honor of becomin' my wife?"

Tears filled her eyes again and streaked down her cheeks. "It's...about...time."

She flung her arms around him and kissed him soundly, then she softened her lips and pecked lightly at his. She rested her forehead against his, and sighed deeply.

"This is so cozy," he whispered. "I think I'll keep you here all night."

She giggled and snuggled closer. "What would Ma say if she saw us like this?"

"She'd say, *Pa, get your gun.*"

Her laughter rang through the quiet house.

"Oh, Jesse." She sighed and caressed the side of his face. "I really can't believe I'm here, like this, with you."

"I know. I still think I'm dreamin'."

"I've been dreaming for so long, I'm glad it's finally come true."

He took her head in his hands and pulled it to his waiting lips. His mouth moved slowly over hers, but the passion flared quickly and the kiss turned urgent. His tongue swept through her mouth and her tongue copied the movements. Hesitantly, he pulled away and burrowed his face into the hollow between her cheek and shoulder. Her uncontrolled breathing matched his.

"If we get started again, I'll never let you leave."

"Then Pa will definitely get his gun."

"Marry me tomorrow. Now that I've tasted you, I won't be able to wait very long for another preview of our weddin' night."

"I have an idea. Let's see if we can have a double ceremony with Violet and Clint?"

He grinned. "Let's talk to them tomorrow."

She nodded. "First thing."

~ * ~

She was in a dream world. It was the only explanation for her happiness right now. The lulling sway of the buggy as she rode back home, and the gentle autumn breeze against her flushed face put her thoughts on a cloud as she replayed in her mind everything she and Jesse shared together. Never in her life did she think her mind and body would be completely controlled by a man, but she liked it. She wouldn't change her life right now for anything.

It was so hard to leave Jesse's side, but she didn't want her family suspicious, although she figured Violet knew what was going to happen. But Jesse had helped her dress and gave her another lengthy kiss before sending her on her way. Feeling star struck, she hardly knew where she was going.

From inside the cluster of trees, a noise pulled her from her dreams. The full moon helped light the darkened night. Shadows danced in certain areas. Prickles arose on her arms and the back of her neck, warning her of danger.

She slowed the buggy and listened to the night sounds. Too quiet. Something was not right. Someone was out there trying to keep hidden. She hoped it was only one of her brothers, but eeriness overwhelmed her, and cold fear shot up her spine.

Automatically, her shaky hand reached over on the seat for the rifle she'd always carried whenever alone, but the seat was empty. With a fearful sigh, she remembered leaving it in the barn this afternoon.

Feeling an urgency to flee from this spot, she urged the horse faster, reassuring herself that everything was all right. Whoever was in the trees was not out to get her. But the quicker the horse galloped, the harder her heart pounded, and the more she felt as if trouble brewed, and she might be caught in the middle. Unfortunately, her feelings were usually correct.

Taking a deep breath, she willed herself to calm down. She may not have a gun, but her quick wits could help her in any situation. However, no ideas were springing to mind right now. Helplessness washed over her...which was the worst feeling in the world.

Another few minutes passed, and she slowed the buggy to a stop, listening again to the sounds of the night. This time, the chirps from crickets and the croaking of frogs sang through the stillness. Relief poured through her, knowing she hadn't been followed. But then, whoever was out there, was still further back by Jesse's house.

Jesse was in trouble.

Without thinking of what the consequences might be, she jumped out of the buggy and quickly removed the harness from the horse. It had been awhile since she'd ridden bareback, but it wouldn't bother her to do it tonight. Thank heavens the horse was Buck, and he responded when she urged him to a gallop and took off for Jesse's house.

Her eyes were alert, her ears focused on the night sounds and anything else that might be out of the ordinary as she rode through the darkness. Light glowed through the trees, looking as if it came from a lantern. It was still a distance away, so she slowed her horse until she was closer, then stopped him completely. Several voices came from within the trees.

"Now that the light's off, it's time to make our move. Joe? Do you know what you're gonna do?"

"Yeah, I'm gonna dump gun powder around the house, then torch the place."

"Billy? Do you know what you're gonna do?"

"If the bastard comes out, I'll shoot him 'tween the eyes."

"All right, let's go."

Summer's heart dropped to her feet and tightness took

hold of her chest. Jesse's house was the only thing nearby, and she could only assume they were talking about her beloved. Jesse wasn't aware of what was going to happen, so she had to be the one to stop the bandits. But how could she? She didn't even have a gun.

It didn't matter. Jesse's life hung in the balance. Something had to be done.

When rustling erupted through the trees, she knew the bandits were heading out, so she kicked her horse forward as fast as she could toward Jesse's house. Getting there before the others was her plan, but she had to think of something to do to alert Jesse in case she didn't make it.

As she pushed her horse to his limit, ahead of her, the bandits still held the lead. She screamed at the top of her lungs, making a horrendous amount of noise, calling Jesse's name and bellowing for Jesse to run, that danger was near. Hopefully, Jesse could hear, but then, so could the bandits. They turned and came her way quicker than irritated hornets.

She couldn't see faces, just shadows. When they neared, black and red bandannas hid their identities. A man rode next to her and grabbed her arm, pulling her from her horse and falling to the ground. A blazing pain ripped through her shoulder, but she didn't concentrate on the affliction. She kept screaming.

"Damn you, lady, shut up," the man snapped as he tried to cover her mouth, but Summer fought, kicking and clawing to avoid him. She wasn't going to give up easily. With all her might, she shoved until the man was off her, then she scrambled on hands and knees to get away. But just as she moved, another man attacked her.

"Let me go!" Summer continued screaming and punching, thinking she was succeeding because the buffoon who held her down wasn't doing a very good job. Before she had a chance to wiggle out of the imbecile's grasp, another man was helping to hold her to the ground. Since her legs were free, she kicked him in places men did not like to be kicked.

"Ouch! Damnation, woman."

"Would ya grab her feet?" one shouted. "Tie her hands, too. And while you're at it, stick something in her mouth. She's making too damn much noise. She'll alert the whole town."

While one man tied her feet and hands, the other stuffed his sweaty bandanna in her mouth. The salty taste made her gag. She dug her teeth into his fingers. He cried out, but continued stuffing until the cloth blocked any sound. She couldn't move, but what frightened her more was wondering if Jesse had heard her at all. What if she hadn't been loud enough? These men were going to burn down his house tonight no matter what ruckus she'd caused.

She prayed Jesse had heard and escaped. The men left her on the ground while they hurried off to burn down the house. From where Summer lay, she could see the smoke, then the flames, and heard the crackling of wood.

Tears streamed down her face as the sky lit up, and she wondered if the Lord was going to punish her by making her stay here and watch the heartbreaking sight. She prayed even harder the good Lord would somehow deliver Jesse from his burning house so he could save her. But the Lord must have been busy, because she could do nothing but watch the flames dance high in the night air as the poisonous smoke filled her lungs.

There was no sign of Jesse.

Fifteen

Morning sunlight streamed through the filthy window onto Summer's face. She turned her head on the pillow to avoid the irritation. With the subtle movement, a cloud of dust stirred in the air and with a sneeze, she came fully awake. When she opened her eyes, the brightness in the room sent a splitting pain pulsing through her head. She groaned.

Last night's events had sapped every fiber of strength from her body, and she'd fallen asleep as soon as she laid on the bare mattress and rested her head on the meager excuse for a pillow in the abandoned room. She did, however, get a clear picture of the ranch house, and the high wooden fence that guarded the surrounding land.

When she remembered the fiery flames leaping throughout Jesse's cabin, her heart cried out in angry protest. Although the proof of his death was the fire, she refused to accept that the man she loved was dead. Jesse had heard her. She had to believe it. He escaped, she was sure of it, but by the shouts of victory from the men who'd kidnapped her, they believed otherwise. She clung desperately to her hope that Jesse had escaped his intended fate.

She had no clue who her kidnapers were, but she was determined to solve that problem right away. They couldn't hide from her forever. She'd make sure of that. And she'd make them pay.

Twisting her hands, she struggled with the ropes around her wrists, but only managed to tear her flesh. She kicked her feet, but the ropes were securely tied. With a defeated sigh, she ceased her attempts. Gathering the small amount of liquid in her mouth, she moistened her dry throat, which still tasted like stale sweat and smoke, but at least the bandits had taken out the bandanna before throwing her in this room last night.

Now was a good time to start complaining. They'd soon regret they took her prisoner.

"Is anybody out there?" she shouted. "I know you're there because I can smell you." She paused in hopes of an answer, but heard nothing. "Hello, you mangy animals, you can't ignore me. I'm hungry, and I have certain womanly necessities that have to be taken care of quickly."

From outside the closed door, nothing was heard, so she tried again, this time, louder. "Listen to me, you good-for-nothing jackasses. I know you're there. And don't think ignoring me will make me shut up, because I'll keep on making a racket until I get some food and water."

A movement from outside the room quieted her shouts and the clanking of dishes came from out of nowhere. Heavy footsteps boomed on the floor toward the room, so she rolled on the bed and faced the door. It opened and a man stepped in, still dressed in black wearing a red bandanna around his throat. She recognized this man as one that had attacked her not too long ago when she'd followed him and his friend into the woods.

When recognition struck, her whole body vibrated from fear. She remembered their intent before Jesse had rescued her. Who would rescue her now? Would these men touch her where only Jesse had touched her before? The taste of fear clung to her tongue as her stomach churned. She mustn't let them see her fear.

The deep wounds on his face resembled the vicious claws of a wild animal, showing that her struggles last night had not been entirely in vain. Big gaping wounds scratched up his cheeks and neck, still red with a hint of blood. He must have been the one she kicked between the legs, too.

"Well, li'l missy. Looks like we meet again."

Sickening waves of terror rolled through her stomach at his suggestive comment. "That is most unfortunate."

"Let's meet proper this time, shall we? My name is Joe."

"So."

He chuckled lightly. "You're a stubborn filly, that's for sure. I might have to finish what me and my partner started the last time we met."

"Over my dead body," she growled.

He shook his head. "No. Your death will not solve a thing right now. We have plans for you, sweetheart. Big plans."

"The Rangers are going to find you, and they'll not rest until all of you are dead."

A smile touched his face and he chuckled. "I don't think so. You see, I know something you don't."

"And what might that be?"

"The Rangers are headed for a trap. Tomorrow, in fact. You are the bait, and those stupid fools have fallen right into our clutches." He pulled at the bands holding her wrists and proceeded to untie them.

Fright consumed her, squeezing her heart, making it hard to breathe. But she tried to stay strong. "What do you mean?"

"They're trying to find you at this very moment. They'll come close, and because of their devotion, they will be killed."

"Why? Why are you doing this?" She panicked, her voice breaking again.

Joe dropped the ropes from her hands and moved to her ankles. "Because they have to be stopped. Buchanan is in charge now, not the Almighty Rangers."

She willed herself to stay in control. Now was not the time to show fear. Buchanan must not win. Justice had to prevail.

"Why...why did you burn...Jesse's house?"

A pleasant expression crossed his face, and she wanted to tear out his eyes.

"Jesse Slade double-crossed the gang, so he had to die. It was a pleasure watching his house burn to the ground."

She fought her slowly building tears. "What do you mean he double-crossed the gang?"

"There are a few secrets Jesse kept from everyone, especially the Rangers. He was part of Buchanan's gang, and has been for a while. Because of his stupid mistake a couple of weeks ago in Amarillo, two of our men were killed and one was captured. Buchanan doesn't like his men to make mistakes, and he kills those who do."

Her mind tried to reject the idea, and she couldn't stop the tears falling down her face. "Are you sure that Jesse is...dead?"

"Yessirree. His place burned to ashes, don't you remember?" Joe chuckled. "It's a good thing he lives so far from town or else people might've come to help. Though I'm sure once help arrived, it was too late."

"No. I don't believe you." Her voice cracked. "Jesse is alive...and he's not part of your gang."

"Sorry, sweets, but although you tried to save your lover, it didn't work the way you planned. When Buchanan makes a point, he doesn't mess up. Nobody wants to cross Buchanan. Too bad you risked your neck for the wrong man." He bent over her, his face too close. "And to think, I could have been your man that afternoon in the woods." His hand cupped her breast for a quick squeeze. She slapped him. He pulled away then left the room, shutting and locking the door behind him.

A knot of pain formed in her stomach, and her hunger disappeared. Could she believe this man? Was her beloved Jesse dead? She watched the flames consume the house last night, and knew that by the time her family would have arrived, it would have been too late to help. And, if Jesse was alive, she was sure he would have rescued her by now.

In bewilderment, she tried to think why Jesse would be part of a notorious gang. If he were part of Buchanan's group of men, wouldn't Clint have suspected? But apparently, none of the Rangers had actually seen one of Buchanan's men--except Jesse.

Pressing the palms of her hands against her temple, she tried squeezing out the mind-boggling thoughts, not wanting to believe any of it. She couldn't possibly accept that the man she loved was actually a criminal.

~ * ~

Dazed, Summer sat by the window and stared across the acres of vast desert plains, looking past the dirt smudges on the glass. Her head rested against the wall, not caring if her filthy clothes melded with the unkempt room, or that she hadn't eaten since before she was kidnapped.

She had no idea where she was. Nothing looked familiar from outside her window. For two days, she'd waited, hoping for somebody to come get her. As each day passed, her hope of rescue decreased. She couldn't eat, for her stomach refused it. She couldn't sleep, because every time she closed her eyes, her mind played back the flames that danced around Jesse's house as it burned to the ground. All day and all night she stared at the grungy walls in the small room that held her captive. Outside, the peaceful land brought a wave of terror to her soul when as each hour passed, the chance of a rescue dropped from slim to none. It frightened her that her captors would come in and manhandle her like they promised, and she wondered why they were holding back.

Her family surely thought she was dead. The last thing they knew, she was with Jesse in his house. So, if everybody thought she was dead, she might as well be. Why then, was her body taking so long to wither away?

Three times during the day the foul smelling bandit, Joe, entered her room with a tray of food, which she left untouched. His words were minimal, for which she was grateful. The third day when he came into her room, he looked much happier than before. His irritating whistle scraped on her nerves like fingernails on a chalkboard.

"I just thought you'd like to know, Buchanan has won, yet again. Our plan worked and all twenty Rangers were killed in a bloody battle just outside Becker's Pass. The Rangers were led into the pass like blind men. We trapped and shot them. Not one Ranger was left alive."

Joe shook his head. "Your friend, Clint, was one of the last to die. He was a tough old bird, though. We thought for sure he'd never give up. It was such a touching sight to see. You should've been there."

Summer heard, but she didn't let it register in her head. Not until the man left the room, then her chest restricted in pain and the tears she thought she didn't have anymore came rushing through. She sobbed brokenly, wrapping her arms around her waist as she rocked back and forth. She didn't know what happened to her will to live, but she couldn't understand why her life would be spared to suffer through all of this heartache.

The day passed slowly. She dozed a few times, but horrid pictures of Jesse's burning body filled her mind and kept her from resting. When she tried putting aside those thoughts, she envisioned Clint and the other Rangers being shot, and it sapped away the small amount of strength her body had left. When the room darkened at nightfall, the door opened again and in walked Joe, but this time another man followed who carried her dinner.

Joe looked at the untouched tray of food left from lunch,

and shook his head. "Why aren't you eating? Don't you know you need to keep up your strength?"

She didn't answer, just continued to stare out the window.

He moved by her. "You're probably wondering what's going to happen to you, right?" He waited for an answer, but she didn't reply. "Well, it just so happens that Buchanan has taken a liking to you. In fact, he sent me to make you an offer."

Summer slowly lifted her eyes to his face, but she still refused to speak.

"Buchanan wants me to tell you that if you give yourself to him and become his woman, he'll set you free once he tires of you. It might take a couple of months, but he'll eventually get bored. I've warned him about your stubborn temper, and he thinks it's intriguing. He's looking forward to taming you."

Summer boiled with anger, and somewhere left in her body she found the strength to voice her opinion. "You can tell him to go to hell. I'd rather suffer a long agonizing death than to give myself to a murderer!"

Joe shrugged and stood. "All right, I'll tell him. He won't like it and might decide to take you anyway, but at least he gave you a choice."

Joe left, but the second man remained in the room. He stood against the door, his arms folded over his chest as he stared at her. Although he tried to appear impassive, she detected a glimpse of sympathy in his expression. The urge to persuade him to her side nudged at her, but she didn't have enough vigor.

The man stood by the door for another few minutes, then walked to her. He squatted to her level so she could look right into his smoky eyes. "Miss Bennett? Ya need t' eat somethin' and gain your strength."

She blinked, but didn't respond.

"I realize ya don't know me, and ya certainly don't trust me, but I'm tellin' ya everythin' will be all right. Ya just have'ta eat."

She swallowed, then licked her lips. "I want to die," she whispered.

The man hesitantly touched her hands, folded in her lap. "No, Miss Bennett. I won't let ya die. People are waitin' for ya t' come back home."

A tear slid from her eye. "They think I'm dead."

"No, they don't."

"Jesse...is dead. Clint is dead. I want to die, too."

The man glanced to the door, then his gaze met hers. "Clint's not dead."

Confusion tugged at Summer's brow. "What did you say?"

"Clint's not dead."

All at once, the rhythm of her heart sped up just a notch, and blood rushed to her head, bringing with it a slight pound. "Are you certain?"

"Yup."

Her lifeless body remained still as she studied his face. "Why are you telling me this? You're one of them. You helped kill the Rangers."

"No, I didn't."

"But, why are you telling me this?"

"I'm tryin' t' give ya some hope. I'm tryin' t' help ya gain your strength just in case someone comes t' rescue ya."

She blinked. "Will someone come to rescue me?"

"If I know Clint, he will."

"Who are you and how do you know him?"

"My name is Frank, and I've been friends with Clint for a while. He saved my hide quite a few times, and so I decided t' repay him for his friendship. I was the one who warned him about the trap Buchanan set for the Rangers."

"How did they escape?"

"Clint's fiancée devised some concoction that looked like blood. I put blank bullets in their pistols, so when the showdown began, it looked like a blood bath, but none of the Rangers were seriously wounded." He chuckled. "We fooled Buchanan but good."

Her hopes lifted. "But, what about Jesse? Is he alive, too? And was he really one of Buchanan's men?"

"I'm sorry t' say he was one of Buchanan's men, and since Buchanan doesn't take kindly t' men who cross him, he made sure that Jesse's house burned to the ground, and that Jesse didn't leave alive."

"But what about you? By helping Clint, you double

-crossed your leader."

"But that was before. Now I know that the Rangers will capture Buchanan, and he won't have time t' punish me."

A noise came from outside the door, and he stopped and jumped to his feet. "Miss Bennett, please eat. Clint will need your help in the rescue." He moved out of the room, closing the door behind him.

Her mind struggled in torn affliction. Should she believe this man? He acted sincere. She wanted to believe Clint was still alive, but the way Joe talked, he made it sound as if Clint were dead and buried. But what if he lived?

And to think Violet helped. Certainly different from the shy, plain sister Summer thought her to be.

With all of her heart she needed to believe. Her soul told her to keep the faith, and she would be rescued soon. So, finding a small amount of strength, she moved to the tray of food and nibbled lightly on the piece of bread. After a couple of bites, her empty stomach growled, her head pounded, and her body shook from hunger. She began to eat faster, and soon she devoured every last bite.

Yes! She was going to gain her strength, and yes, she was going to be rescued by Clint. He had to be alive. Her heart told her to believe Frank. Unfortunately, she knew when all of this was over, he'd crumble from the knowledge of Jesse's deceit. But now she had to think of the family that seriously needed her. Pa needed her, and she certainly needed him.

Summer pulled herself away from the window and paced the room, mainly to strengthen her legs and keep her heart pumping. She would request a basin of water, a wash cloth and soap, and hopefully her spirits would reenergize when she washed away the caked on dirt that layered her skin.

After several hours passed, her exercise was put on hold when the door to her room opened and Joe walked in. Frantically, she searched the room for some kind of weapon, but he had been careful about leaving any sharp or heavy objects behind.

His cheerful grin worried her. "Buchanan wants to see you."

She glared at him. "I'll not give myself to him. He'll have to take me by force if he wants me."

Joe grinned, running his fingers through his hair. "That's the way he likes it, but I think he just wants to talk to you right now. You're still very weak, and he's waitin' for you to gain back your strength." He glanced at her empty breakfast tray. "By the way, what made you decide to start eatin'?"

Stubbornly, she folded her arms across her chest. "I'm not going to let a bunch of dim-witted bandits get the best of me."

He laughed. "Hardheaded woman." He grabbed her elbow and pulled her out of the room.

They walked down a hallway, and the expensive furnishings in the other rooms made her gasp in surprise. The scent of pine and freshly lemon-waxed tables lingered in the hallway. The place was nothing less than a rich man's castle--except for the room she was staying in. After passing five more rooms, he led her down a few stairs into a spacious room. A small fire crackled in the far corner, and a table not far away had a deck of cards laid out, looking as if a game had been interrupted. Along the other side of the room, a glass-plated liquor bar lined with whiskey bottles stood out.

A tall man leaned against the bar with his back toward her as he poured himself a drink. When she entered, he turned. In fright, she gasped. His height made him appear domineering, and his square jaw gave him the authority he demanded. *So, this was the man they called Buchanan.*

He took a sip of his drink, eyeing her up and down. "Joe, you may leave us now."

Joe nodded, then backed out of the room, closing the door behind him.

Summer stared openly at the man, hoping she didn't give away the sheer white terror slicing through her right now. "Are you Buchanan?"

"Yes, that's what my friends call me, although it's not my real name."

"What is your real name?"

He laughed lightly. "It's not wise to give you that kind of information."

She let out a ragged breath. "Are you going to kill me?"

"Of course not, my dear." He stepped to her and took a lock of hair that fell across her shoulder. "There are so many more uses for your delectable body. Killing you would be a terrible waste."

She stood still, praying that he wouldn't hurt her. Praying that he'd set her free.

"Would you care to sit?" He motioned toward the couch.

Summer slowly moved to the chair, keeping her eyes on the man next to her.

"I have many plans for us, my dear." He sat next to her. "Now that the Rangers are out of the way, I'll be free to live my life the way I want." He took another sip from his glass.

"Running from the law? What kind of life is that?" She shook her head. "Have you no smarts at all?"

"Smarts, you say? Who really has the smarts, my dear Summer? I now live in a home big enough to be a palace, while those stupid Ranger friends of yours scrape the streets just to put food on the table."

"Yes, but they don't have to hide in fear for the rest of their lives."

"True, because they're dead."

She gasped and held her tongue for now. It was still hard to believe Clint was alive and coming to rescue her, but she willed herself to believe. That was the only thing keeping her strong. "Are you certain?"

"I helped check their bodies. Every last one of them was covered in death's blood."

She clasped her hands together on her lap as she fought for control. "Will you tell me about Jesse? Was he really one of your men?"

"Oh, yes. He was one of my best men, in fact." He chuckled. "A shame he had to turn on me."

She didn't think her heart could break any more, but the ache deep within her chest proved differently. "No...not Jesse," she mumbled as tears threatened to spill from her eyes.

"Yes, Jesse. Sorry to sully the last memories you have of him, but someone needed to inform you. Jesse Slade just wasn't the hero everybody thought."

"When...how long...had he been working with your gang?"

"I'd say about five years or so."

"How'd you meet?"

"We met at a saloon. We were into our cups, drowning our sorrows the best way we knew how, and Jesse began telling me he needed to find a way to make money. The man he worked for at the time wasn't paying him enough, and Jesse needed to make more money."

"Why? Did he say why he needed more money?"

"Said he and his older brother were tired of living in a shed. It was about time they built them a real house." He shrugged. "Couldn't blame him there. I know how it feels to live like a scrapper."

"Then what happened?"

"I told him of a way he could make more money. He liked the idea immediately."

She snorted a laugh. "I really don't think Jesse would go for that bank robbing thing. He's more of a man than that."

"Apparently not. Jesse was real excited about robbing banks, and he went with us the next time we hit one." Buchanan's smile broadened. "Jesse's been with us ever since, and he was able to have a house built for him and his older brother because of his share of the money."

In the back of her mind, she thought of when Clint and Jesse had moved into their house--and Buchanan was right. It was about four years ago. She bit her bottom lip to keep from sobbing aloud. She had to stay strong. She didn't want Buchanan to see how this news had affected her. "So, what are you going to do with me?"

His eyes turned dark when a grin touched his mouth. "I think you already know."

Her stomach turned. "I'll not give myself to you," she slowly bit out. "I loathe the very ground you walk on."

"But Summer, don't you know that becoming my mistress is the only way you'll be able to stay alive?"

"Then I'd rather die!"

He chuckled and leaned over to her. His hand touched her chin softly. "You know I can force you, don't you?"

She slapped at his hand, but it only served to tighten his hold on her chin. "It will be rape."

"Haven't you heard? That's the way I like it." He laughed

again.

His hand slid from her chin down her neck, and her stomach lurched. No matter how weak she was, she'd fight him all the way. She slapped his hand away and jumped to her feet. He stood right beside her and grabbed her hands, forcing them behind her back. In one jerk, he pulled her body against his.

He smiled triumphantly as one hand slid over her breast. "As much as the idea tempts me to take you now, I'd rather wait until you're stronger. I hate overpowering weaklings, and right now you're no stronger than a fly."

Pushing her away, she fell to the ground, but he stepped over her and out of the room, calling for Joe to come get her. Once she was alone in her room, she let the damn of tears open and they streamed down her cheeks. When was Clint going to rescue her? She really didn't think she could handle any more of this torture. All this information about Jesse was hard to swallow, and closing her mind was the best solution. Call her a coward, but she couldn't deal with the pain.

Summer realized she wasn't the hero everybody had thought, either, and right now, she didn't care. Now she had to come up with a plan or Buchanan would ravage her. Death was certainly preferable.

Sixteen

Six o'clock the next morning an ear-piercing cannon blast exploded outside the house. The loud eruption shook the ground, bringing Summer instantly awake and into an upright position. She scrambled out of bed and ran to the door and pulled on the knob, but Joe had kept it locked. A group of scurrying footsteps clammered outside her room as the men screamed frantic instructions. Although she was anxious to know what was going on, deep down she had the feeling this was her rescue.

Unfortunately, there was no way to get out of her room to find Clint, and waiting patiently wasn't one of her virtues.

She paced back and forth in the small room, and within minutes, someone came to her door. Keys rattled as they tried to unlock it. Her gaze fastened on the doorknob, hoping to see her rescuer, but when the door opened, her heart sank. It wasn't Clint as she had hoped, but Buchanan.

"Come with me," he commanded, grabbing hold of her arm as he pulled her out of the room.

She stumbled on her ragged skirts. "What's happening?"

He didn't answer, but Summer could tell by his angry expression, he hadn't planned on this attack. Anticipation jumped in her chest. She was going to be rescued!

The scent of gunpowder hung heavy in the air, filling her lungs with the smoke. She coughed and rubbed the sting out of her eyes. All around her men in long underwear scattered like chickens. They held guns and rifles as they headed in one direction of the house, but Buchanan dragged Summer the opposite way.

She panicked. "Where are we going? What's happening?"

"We're under attack, and if you don't want to get shot, you'd better shut up and stay close to me."

Clearly a battle had started at the ranch, and the popping

of gunfire was all around her. "Who's attacking us?"

"I have no idea."

"Maybe it's the law coming to rescue me."

"I seriously doubt it, Summer, considering I have most of the Sheriffs in Texas on my payroll."

She placed her hands over her ears, mainly so she wouldn't have to hear anymore of his so-called truth right now. It was hard enough to accept the fact that Jesse had been a part of a gang all this time.

In one of the rooms on the south side of the ranch-house, Buchanan led her inside and slammed the door. A musky scent thickened in the damp, cold storage room. He pulled her over to the other side then stopped and released her. He lifted the rug hiding a trap door.

"We're going under."

She shook her head and backed away. "No, we're not!"

"Oh, yes, we are. I'm going and you're coming with me. We can do it easy or we can do it hard."

"I'll just slow you down, because I won't go willingly."

He reached out and roughly grabbed her by the arm. "You're my insurance, sweetie, so you're coming."

She struggled, but knew in her weakened condition, he would overpower her. She scanned his body and noticed only one gun in his holster. With what little strength she had, she quickly decided to put up a fight. Did she have any other choice?

Anger consumed her. She clawed his face with her free hand, and when that didn't work, she used her teeth to bite into his flesh. He yelped and released her hand, which gave her the freedom to claw at him again, this time she used her legs and kicked his shins, then aimed for more tender parts of his body.

"Damn it, Summer." Buchanan yelped as he struggled to get control over her. "You'll not win."

"I may not win, but I'll inflict as much pain upon you as I can before you take me away."

He slapped her hard across the face and she cried out. Although the pain knocked her senseless for a few awkward seconds, it intensified her anger and she continued to fight. His hand balled into a fist, and she prepared herself for the next jolt of pain. When his fist connected with her jaw, it snapped her head back and she fell in a heap on the floor. Her head swam, and she fought to stay conscious.

He knelt beside her. "Dammit, Summer, I warned you to stop. Now I'll have to carry you."

She refused to comply. Her mind screamed at her to fight, but as he lifted her limp form in his arms, she couldn't raise her hands to stop him. Heavy footsteps boomed right outside the door, then the cracking of wood echoed through her throbbing head when somebody kicked in the door.

"Don't move, Buchanan, the game is over. You're under arrest." The familiar voice swam in her head as she struggled to stay conscious, but blackness filled her mind.

Did she hear Jesse's voice speaking from Heaven or Hell?

~ * ~

A sharp pain penetrated through Summer's head. She tried to open her eyes, which only intensified the agony. As she turned her head against a pillow, an excruciating throb exploded in her jaw. She didn't want to awaken, but she had to get her bearings. The whispering sounds around her seemed familiar. In fact, the soft bed cradling her injured body felt familiar, too. Pa's faint cigar smell and Ma's freshly laundered spring-flower scent lingered through the bed sheets, arousing nostalgic memories.

I'm home!

She tried again to open her eyes, and the painful movement made her moan.

"Summer? I'm right here, dear."

"Ma?" Summer's voice squeaked, and she managed to peel open her eyes. At first, everything around her was unfocused, but she laid blame on her extreme headache.

"Don't talk, Summer. You're going to be all right now. You are safe at home."

Once her vision cleared, she glanced around the room. Her family stood around her bed; Pa in his roller chair on one side, Ma on the other. All three sisters and both brothers stood down at the end of the bed.

She touched her throbbing jaw and quickly withdrew her hand from the pain. "What happened? I don't remember much after he hit me."

Pa stroked her hand. "The Rangers attacked the fort and

killed most of Buchanan's men. Clint captured Buchanan himself."

She smiled, although her face ached from the small movement. "One of Buchanan's men, I think his name is Frank, he told me the Rangers were still alive and that Clint was going to rescue me."

Violet moved from the end of the bed to her side. "Clint didn't rescue you. It was Jesse."

The pain in her head pulsed stronger, igniting the beat of her aching heart. "That can't be right. Jesse is dead. I saw his house burn down."

Violet smiled. "No, Summer, he's alive. He heard your screams the night of the fire and escaped just in time."

Tears sprang to her eyes and she turned away from Violet, burying her face into the pillow. "No...no," she sobbed.

Pa squeezed her hand. "Summer, what's wrong?"

"Leave me alone. Let me be." She cried harder, clutching the blanket up to her mouth. She didn't think there was much of her heart left to break, but the slicing wrench in her chest told her different. Jesse was a traitor. She knew everything about his sordid past, and he had lied to everybody, especially her.

"Everybody out," Ma instructed. "Summer needs rest."

"I can't understand what's wrong." Violet whispered. "I thought she'd be elated to hear Jesse was alive."

"Perhaps Clint and Jesse can help us figure out what's bothering her," Pa suggested. "When will they be back from the jail?"

"I don't know, but Jesse is dying to see Summer, so I know they'll hurry," Violet answered.

After the door shut, Summer released her misery as sobs wracked her sore body, but she didn't care. Of everything she'd been through the past few years, nothing was as painful as this. Falling in love wasn't worth all the heartache.

She tried to fall asleep and forget, but her mind remained alert and her ears heard every little footstep, every word and breath her family made. She didn't know how many minutes passed, or how much of the day had gone by, but soon came the squeak of the door as it opened. Violet tiptoed inside and walked to the bed.

Violet knelt and touched Summer's hand, then smiled. "I didn't know you were awake."

"I can't sleep," Summer mumbled, not feeling the strength to talk.

"Summer? Will you please tell me what's wrong?" Tears formed in Violet's eyes. "I can't stand seeing you this way, and it tears me apart to hear you cry."

Sighing deeply, Summer moved her hand and entwined her fingers with Violet's. She swallowed, then licked her dry lips. "When I was being held prisoner, I learned some things. Things I didn't want to hear. The first day of my captivity, I thought Jesse was dead. I tried to save him that night of the fire by screaming, but I didn't think it had worked. The next day when I awoke in my prison, they said that the Rangers were going to be killed in an ambush."

"Yes, that was what they wanted Buchanan to believe."

"After that, I didn't eat or drink. I wanted to die. When Clint's friend told me that Clint was alive and would come to rescue me, it gave me the strength to eat. I believed Clint would save me, so I ate to gain back my strength. When Buchanan called me to his room, he told me something that I just could not accept, but he made me believe it. Of course, this whole time, we both thought Jesse was dead."

"What did Buchanan tell you?"

Summer's extremely heavy heart wouldn't let her confess. Her body was too exhausted to be put through anymore torture. She stiffened her trembling lips. "I don't want to talk about it, Violet. Maybe another day, but now all I want to do is rest."

"All right, I'll leave." Violet kissed her gently on the cheek.

Just before Violet left the room, Summer asked, "Violet? Will you do me a favor, though?"

"Anything."

"I don't want to see Jesse. Please don't let him come here. I'm not ready to face him."

"But Summer--"

"Violet, no. Please don't ask, just do as I wish."

She nodded. "All right. Go to sleep, now. When you awaken, you'll feel much better."

~ * ~

Summer pulled herself out of bed and forced her stiff

legs to her vanity. She struggled with her rigid body and sat on the chair. Through the mirror, Buchanan's handiwork captured her attention. She gently touched the bruise on her cheek and flinched. The whole left side of her face was swollen, which left a ghastly purple mark. She didn't think it was possible, but she looked worse than she felt.

Leaning her elbows on the tabletop, she linked her fingers and rested her tender chin on her knuckles, then sighed heavily. It was still hard to believe Jesse had rescued her. Her mind had struggled to believe he escaped the fire, but when Buchanan told her those horrible things, she forced herself to accept Jesse was dead, only because it made it easier to hate him. But now...how could she look at him knowing how he'd deceived all those he claimed to love? When Buchanan had made the accusations against Jesse, it seemed impossible to accept, but the more she thought about it, everything made sense.

Jesse had gone behind everybody's back with his lies. Didn't Jesse care that Clint devoted his whole life to the Texas Rangers? Apparently not. There were times when Clint risked his neck for his brother, yet still, Jesse continued to delude everybody. Jesse certainly fooled her into loving him. And even if he had come to love her as he claimed, she could never allow herself to be with someone who held himself above the law.

A couple of knocks sounded at the door, making her jump. "Are you decent, runt?" Clint cracked the door open and stuck his head inside. He grinned.

Summer couldn't help but smile. Clint had always been able to brighten her day. "And if I wasn't decent, would you still come in?"

"Damn right." He stepped into the room. "It's not every day I get to see you in your skivvies."

She launched herself into his embrace, throwing her arms around his neck for a big bear hug. "Oh, Clint, it's so good to see you." Then she remembered about his house, and stepped back. "Oh, Clint. I'm sorry I couldn't stop Buchana's men from burning down your house."

He shrugged. "Don't worry your pretty li'l head. Jess had pretty much moved into the new cabin by then, and now I'm going to be gettin' my own ranch."

"Really? You're going to start a ranch?"

"Yes. My dream's finally comin' true."

She smiled. "Thank goodness Buchanan's men didn't know about the cabin you built for Jesse."

His knuckles softly brushed her cheek as his gaze narrowed. "Look at you. Always a tomboy, aren't you? Can't seem to get rid of the bumps and bruises?"

When she laughed, a slight pain sliced through her jaw, and she tried to ignore it. "If you think I look bad, you should see the other guy," she joked.

"I did. Hauled his ass to jail, in fact, and you're right, you clawed his face pretty good. He's goin' to have some serious scars because of your fingernails."

"You were there at his ranch? You saw me?"

"Yes, only seconds behind Jess when he entered the room. He went straight to you, and I had the privilege of capturin' Buchanan myself."

She could tell Clint wanted to talk about Jesse, and since she didn't, she quickly changed to another question. "Were any of the Rangers hurt during the rescue?"

"No."

"Frank told me about Becker's Pass. Did anybody get hurt then?"

"A few, but most of them received just minor injuries." He chuckled lightly. "That sister of yours concocted a potion that looked like blood, so when they fired at us, it made us appear as if we'd been shot. Thanks to Frank, none of the guns had real bullets, 'cept, of course, when we broke through the ranch."

He paused and shook his head. "Thought for sure my li'l brother was goin' to get a bullet through his chest the way he stormed that fort lookin' for you. He was hell-bent on findin' you, and he didn't care who he shot."

She frowned and backed away. "Clint, I don't want to know about Jesse."

"Why in the world not? If not for Jess, you'd--"

"Clint, please. I don't want to hear about his heroics." She turned and walked back to her vanity table and sat, placing her hands over her face as her fingers massaged her temple.

"Summer, honey." He moved behind her and gently

rubbed her shoulders. "Violet tells me that you've refused to see Jess."

"Yes."

"Will you tell me why?"

"I'd rather not."

"Please. I can't understand what's happened. The last thing I knew, the two of you were gettin' all cozy like."

"Clint, please," she begged, meeting his stare through the mirror. "I don't want to talk about him."

"But I do." Kneeling beside her, he turned her body toward him and took hold of her hands. "I don't know what has made you so mad at my brother, but it's tearin' him apart. Your refusal to see him has made him miserable. He loves you so much-
-"

"Clint, stop." Her voice broke. "I don't want to hear that. I've learned some things about Jesse that has ruined my love for him."

"I can't believe that."

"It's true. He's not the man we think he is."

"What did you hear?"

"I...can't...tell you." She sobbed harder, covering her face with her hands.

"Summer, honey? How do you know what you heard is true?" She nodded, without replying. "Have you searched through your heart about this? Summer, your heart will never lie to you."

She still didn't answer...couldn't.

"Who told you these things?"

The tears didn't stop flowing no matter how hard she wiped them. By now, she thought she would have run out.

"Please, Clint. I need a little more time before I can talk about it."

He kept silent for a few awkward moments, he let out a heavy sigh. "All right, I'll give you a little more time."

She lifted her head and looked at him. "Thank you." She kissed him on the cheek, then reached on the vanity table and grabbed a handkerchief.

"So, Clint?" She daintily blew her nose, trying to remember her manners even in this horrible situation. "When are you and Violet getting married?"

"Funny you should ask, 'cause just today we've decided on a date. How does November sixteenth sound?"

"That's two weeks away."

"I was hopin' it'd be sooner, but your ma was insistent about that date."

"She just wants to make sure everything is ready for Violet's big day."

"Yes, but I've waited too long now. I'm afraid to wait any longer. I don't want to lose such a wonderful woman."

"You won't." She caressed the side of his face. "You're a good man and Violet won't let you go. In fact, if Violet hadn't grabbed you, I might have."

"Naw. You're too much like a sister to me. 'Sides, you and Jess were made for each other."

At the mention of his brother's name, she pushed away from Clint and stood, moving over to her bed. "Clint? Could you please leave now? My headache is coming back and I need some rest."

"All right."

"Clint? Before you go, could you do me a favor?"

He stopped before reaching the door. "Sure, runt. What is it?"

"I know my family has told your brother that I don't wish to see him, but could you relay a message to him for me?"

"'Course."

"Tell Jesse that I've changed my mind about our future. Tell him I don't want to be his wife."

Clint bit his cheek, his eyes darkened as he frowned. He nodded. "I'll see you later, Summer." He turned and left her room.

Heaviness grew in her chest, but telling him was something that had to be done. Turning off her feelings for Jesse would be hard, but she had to start a new life no matter how difficult. And she didn't know if she should turn Jesse in or if she should tell Clint and have him do it? And if she confronted Clint, would he be able to handle it?

~ * ~

The hardest week of Summer's life stretched before her in a slow daze. Her face healed, the purple bruises on her cheek turning yellow as they aged. Each day, she walked a little more, slowly building her strength, allowing her body to return to normal, yet things would never be normal again.

The town had named both Clint and Jesse as their heroes because of catching Buchanan's gang, and a small celebration was held for the Rangers and their families. Summer didn't attend, blaming her head injury. Afterwards, Clint came over for dinner and made an announcement that shocked the Bennett family. Cattle ranching had always been a dream of his, so after the wedding, he was going to quit the Texas Rangers. He'd already purchased the land and had the cattle ordered, and with help from Jesse and the other Rangers, he was building a cabin for him and Violet.

Summer's heart cheered for her sister. Violet and Clint deserved to be happy. Too bad Jesse didn't.

Clint granted Summer's wish, because Jesse's name wasn't mentioned in her presence, and at times she was grateful to hide her scarred emotions. When she overheard bits of conversations from her brothers, her heart twisted in a deep aching need for resolution. But it was still too soon to talk to him.

Undoubtedly, she wouldn't be able to avoid seeing him, and it worried her that when she looked upon his chiseled features and agile body after all this time, she'd change her mind and forget his past sins. If that ever happened, she'd remember his deceit..the lies he told not only to her and her family, but also to his own brother.

She kept herself busy helping Ma with the planning of Violet's wedding, but her spirits sagged in self-pity. As the wedding drew near, Summer's anxiety ate away inside her, and she withdrew. The wedding would force her to face her wounded feelings for Jesse.

The weather turned chilly, so Summer wrapped a heavy shawl around her shoulders before venturing outside. She stepped around the house, peeking in every corner so she wouldn't accidentally run into Jesse, although she'd heard he was with Clint in Dallas today overseeing the final trial of Buchanan's gang. She damned herself for feeling so afraid of her emotions--of her own heart. Had love changed her into a ninny?

Feeling more assured about her privacy, she ventured to the flower garden and kneeled in the rocky soil to pull some weeds. She arched her back and breathed in the fresh air, enjoying the way the warm rays of the sun caressed her skin as the small breeze teased her free flowing hair.

Her brothers and sisters had been taking care of the livery, and at times Summer didn't feel needed there. She felt as if she had nowhere to go and nothing to do, but yet she had to do something. Pa still needed surgery. Making him well was the only way to save the livery.

Just as she pushed her fingers into the dirt, clip-clop of horses came from up the road, and turned to see if Ma and Violet had returned from town. Using her hand, she shielded the bright glare from the eyes as the sun bounced off the buggy. Soon, the vehicle came into view.

Surprise registered in her when she recognized the visitor, and she jumped to her feet. "Aunt Lydia," she shouted, running to the buggy as it came to a halt. "What in the blazes are you doing this far from home?"

Lydia hopped down and laughed. "Isn't there a wedding in a few days?"

"Yes, but I didn't think you'd come because of the school and all." Summer pressed her cheek against her aunt's.

"Of course I'd come. You're my family." Lydia pulled away, her eyes combing over Summer's attire. "You haven't changed since the last time I saw you, except--" The corners of her mouth lifted. "You are a little dirtier than I remember."

Summer grinned. "Even ladies need to do yard work."

Lydia's attention shifted to Summer's face again, and her aunt's smile disappeared. She must have noticed Buchanan's handiwork. Lydia softly touched the bruise on her cheek.

"Have you turned back into your tomboy ways and wrestled with some boys?"

Summer shook her head. "A man hit me."

Lydia gasped as her hand flew to her mouth. "What happened?"

Linking her arm with Lydia's, Summer led the way back into the house as she shared her story.

The rest of the afternoon with Aunt Lydia went well, but by evening, fatigue weakened Summer's mind and body, though she remained diligent in her household chores. After dinner, Summer stood beside Violet and helped her with the dishes. Just as

Summer sank her hands into the warm water, Nate scrambled in through the kitchen door, huffing and puffing.

"Summer? Lizzy needs... Lizzy..." he trailed off, taking in big gushes of air.

"What about Elizabeth?"

"She wants...to talk to you...down at the stables."

"Whatever for?"

"I don't know. She's uh, cryin' and she says she don't want to talk to her stupid brothers, but needs to talk to you instead."

Summer grinned. Her sister was probably having girl trouble and needed advice. Summer had to go, no matter how tired she felt. She looked over at Ma. "Can you finish these dishes for me?"

"Yes." Ma moved beside her, taking over. "Lydia and I can handle the rest."

"Are you sure?"

Ma laughed. "Yes, now get out of here."

After Summer folded her apron and laid it on the counter, she grabbed her heavy shawl off the hook by the back door and left. She walked slowly, breathing the brisk evening air into her lungs and enjoying the season's cool weather.

She entered the stable and stopped. She listened for her sister, but didn't hear a thing. The barn was abnormally quiet, especially since Nate, Elizabeth and Emily were supposed to be here closing things down for the night. She spotted a lantern illuminating the area next to Pa's old office. Elizabeth must be there.

"Hello? Elizabeth?"

Summer's voice ricocheted off the walls in the large barn, but she didn't hear her sister's reply. She moved toward Pa's office, glancing around the spacious center of the stable.

She stepped inside the office. "Lizzy? Where are you?"

A noise came from behind, and she jerked her head back toward the middle of the stable, but the horses in the stalls next to her shuffled lightly in the hay, snapping a few straws in the process.

She took one step out of the room. "Lizzy? Are you here?" she asked again, louder this time.

The lantered buzzed overhead, and the horses snorted, but she didn't hear anything from her sister. Where was she, and what kind of game was she playing? Whatever it was, it was she was not amused! It was dangerous to leave a lantern in the barn with no one inside.

Plopping her hands on her waist, she huffed. "Elizabeth Bennett. If you don't show yourself right now, I'm going home. I'm in no mood to mess around with you tonight. I'm very exhausted, and if you don't--"

"Summer."

The moment she heard Jesse's voice, the words stopped in her throat. Gasping, she swung around toward the deep intimate tone. Jesse stood in the shadows off to her left near the door. Why hadn't she seen him? Her heart sunk to the pit of her stomach and dizziness washed over her.

With shaky legs she stepped back to retreat, but he took three long strides and reached to grab hold of her. "Summer, don't go."

His manly scent of cedar and leather surrounded her, making the palms of her hands moist. She couldn't swallow, she couldn't breathe, and now she couldn't move.

"Jesse, please let me go. I...don't want to see you. I don't have anything I want to say to you."

"Don't tell me that. I miss you so much." His voice broke.

His face was full of pain through his wilted brows and liquid eyes, but that wasn't her fault. It was his. He was the one who'd been lying. "Jesse, I have nothing to say to you," she repeated.

"Can't you at least tell me why? What have I done to make you hate me?"

Her heart clenched with that familiar anguish. She wished he didn't look so hurt, and she wished his baby blue eyes were not so dreamy. His thumb stroked her upper arm and she wished her body would remain cold instead of heating up every time he touched her.

"I think you owe me an explanation, Summer. The last time we were together, I was kissin' your sweet lips and touchin' your body. We were talkin' about getting' married, and lookin' forward to relivin' the passion on our weddin' night. We were talkin' about how much we loved each other, and how happy our lives would be as husband and wife."

She had to stay angry with him. She forced her mind to hear the words Buchanan had spoken so surely. Jesse had been a part of his gang. "Things have changed. I don't feel that way any longer." Her voice quivered.

"I don't believe that. You can't change your heart so quickly." He closed the space between them and pulled her into his arms. "You're afraid of somethin', and I want to know what it is. How else can I help you?"

She struggled in his hold, but it was useless. Without her consent, her body began to melt, her mind turning to mush with each second she stood in his masculine embrace. "I don't want your help."

"Tell me, Summer," he whispered, lowering his head as he brushed his lips across her cheek. "I want to go back to the way we were before the kidnappin'. I can't understand what's happened to change all that."

His tongue flicked the lobe of her ear, sending chills shooting down her body. *Remain strong*, she repeated, but she knew she was fighting a losing battle. History was repeating itself because she was in Jesse's arms, feeling that exciting burn in every part of her body. Her breasts tingled, her loins ached, and she wanted to feel his lips against hers.

"Oh, Summer," he mumbled as he touched his tongue to the sensitive part of her ear. "I love you so much."

She squeezed her eyes closed and fought for strength, but she didn't stop his wandering lips as it pecked lightly on her earlobe, then moved up her neck to her face as he trailed kisses toward her mouth. Before she could protest, his mouth covered hers. His lips were hot, yet soft and gentle. Her heart seemed to stop beating all together only to jolt back into an erratic rhythm.

She responded with an unknown hunger that she didn't know she possessed. Her hands slid over his shirt, around his neck, and she forged her fingers into his thick hair. Her body melded to his, contouring to his hard, male form. A blast of need, of pure desire blossomed inside of her, making her body remember how it'd felt to make love to him.

His tongue traced the seam of her lips and she opened for

him. The feel of that part of him inside her cast away any restraint she might have had left. She tightened her hold and kissed him harder. She pressed her hips more firmly to his and he groaned. He slid his hands down to her buttocks, wrenching a moan from her.

He nipped at her bottom lip, then slowly, seductively, licked at it. He withdrew only enough for her to see the dark passion in his eyes. The need to make love to him was a raging force inside her. Her conscience dictated to her she should stop...but she couldn't. Not now. Not when he could fill the aching need she'd kept hidden since they'd last made love.

Seventeen

Jesse stared into Summer's intoxicating eyes, expecting her to stop his wandering hands and sultry kisses. He didn't know what had caused her anger, but all he wanted to do was replace it with her captivating smile. The only way he knew to do that was to make love to her and remind her of their passionate joining in his cabin and the love they'd shared--of the way things had been before she was kidnapped by Buchanan.

Just when he thought she would pull away, she tilted his chin and covered his mouth with her own. Her kiss was frantic, hungry, and drove him wild. His groin grew heavy with arousal, and the need to make love to her overwhelmed him.

Her soft fingers traced his face, then slid back around to his neck as they threaded through his hair, holding his face to hers. He felt more alive with each touch. As she dragged her fingers over his body, every inch of skin ignited with fire. He trailed his own fingers down her neck, over her shoulders, and lower still until he found her breast. Her firm mounds filled his hands, and he said a silent prayer of thanks she wasn't wearing her corset. He squeezed gently. She moaned into his mouth and arched her back. His thumb rubbed across a nipple and she shuddered in his arms. His body hardened to the point of pain.

He cupped her bottom again and lifted her to better align their bodies. He pushed her up against the wall for support before lifting her skirts and pulling down her petticoats and bloomers. She kicked her garments free, then he encouraged her to wrap her legs around him. His arousal throbbed in anticipation. The hot feel of her scorched him, even through the fabric barriers standing between them. He quickly unfastened his jeans and pushed them down until he was free.

Summer made a tiny sound of distress as she pushed her hips against his pulsating organ. He didn't make her wait, but slid his thickness up into her liquid heat. As they joined, her cry of pleasure matched his.

Although this wasn't exactly the place he wanted to make love to her for the second time, the danger of being discovered added a certain thrill. Hopefully, Violet would make sure the family stayed away.

He drove into her, deeper, stronger, faster. Summer kept the rhythm, riding him like a wild stallion. Finding her mouth again, he buried his tongue inside and hungrily kissed her. She responded the way he'd hoped she would, passion driven, taking him on a ride he'd never forget.

When little cries of delight erupted from her throat, he tightened his hold on her buttocks and pounded into her harder, bringing her to her climax as he reached his. Within moments, his groans of satisfaction matched hers as he spilled his seed into her.

He continued to kiss her until his breathing returned to normal, pecking lightly at her lips, gradually riding down the wave of pleasure. He smiled and leaned his forehead against her as he untangled her legs from around his body and set her down. She wobbled slightly, and he held her until she was steady. As he pulled up his pants, she pushed her skirts down her bare legs and slid her pantaloons back on. A flush of color erupted on her face. Jesse assumed she was embarrassed at her passionate display.

He kissed her forehead, down the side of her face, and she tilted her head back to give him access to her neck. She was exactly as wonderful as he'd remembered. And he couldn't wait to make her his wife.

"Summer, darlin'," he said, lifting her chin with his knuckle. "There's nothin' to be feelin' ashamed about. What we did was natural. It's what two people do when they're in love."

She shook her head slowly, her eyes fluttering open as she looked at him. A pink color still tinted her cheeks, and her swollen mouth begged him to kiss it again. He leaned down and pecked lightly, but she pressed her hands on his chest and moved him back.

"No, Jesse."

"No?" He stroked her cheek, moving his hand down her

neck, over the swell of her breast, and then rested there. His thumb rubbed across her beaded nipple.

He didn't know what he'd said this time to snap her ire, but she suddenly slapped his hand away, the fire blazing in her hazel eyes giving evidence of her anger.

"Jesse Slade." She pushed her hands against him again, moving him away. "You have no idea how ashamed I feel right now, and what we did was *not* natural. We acted like a couple of rutting animals."

"But Summer, it's all right. I love--"

"I don't care," she shouted and stepped around him.

He reached to grab her, but she slid through his grasp. "Please Jesse, if you have any feelings for me at all, please grant me this one wish and stay away."

Tears streaked down her cheeks before she ran out of the stable. His heart breaking, he let her go.

~ * ~

Violet's wedding loomed nearer, and Summer's misery increased. Jealousy consumed her very being, and she couldn't grasp the fact that Violet had found happiness and she could not. She thought about the intimacies Violet and Clint would soon share, and in her mind she relived the exquisite feeling that raced through her when she and Jesse joined their bodies in passion--a feeling she'd never know again.

She spent the day hiding in her room, wishing she could get out and ride Buck. Ma and Violet and her other two sisters were busy putting the finishing touches on Violet's wedding dress, and Summer couldn't stand to be around such joy.

She glanced over the orderly array of brushes, combs, ribbons and hairpins that lay on her vanity. She chuckled. Three years ago, this paraphernalia would certainly not be displayed for everyone to see. Sling-shots, fish hooks, and her collection of rocks would be scattered on the table top. Her fingers glided over her hair ribbons, wondering which to wear at the wedding. Since it was too late to have a dress made for the occasion, she'd wear her newest--the one she wore to the celebration dance during Waco days. The gown was still in good condition, and the men treated her special when she wore it.

She recalled Jesse's reaction with a hint of sadness. She

also remembered they'd talked about a double wedding.

As soon as she thought of him, she quickly dismissed him out of her mind. Why couldn't she just forget about that man? Perhaps she still loved him and couldn't make those feelings disappear. But how could she love a man who had been part of a thieving gang? How could she love a man who'd have such little respect for his own brother or for the law? But then again, after all they'd shared, how could she not love him?

"Awh," she hissed and dragged her fingers through her hair. She needed to get outside or she'd go mad. She needed to saddle up Buck and ride as fast as she could, leaving her worries behind. Just like she did three years ago before she left to go to her aunt's school.

She marched out of her bedroom and out of the house. She quickly scanned the area to make sure Jesse wasn't around, and when she was satisfied, she ran to the livery stable. Nate and Charles were wide-eyed when they saw her, their smiles intensifying as she went over to Buck's stall and began saddling him up.

"Where ya goin', Sis?" Nate asked as he and Charles came closer.

"I'm going for a ride."

"Are ya all right, Summer?" Charles asked.

"Yes, I'm fine. I just feel the need to ride Buck." She glanced over her shoulder, down at her youngest brother. "Don't worry. I won't be long. When I get back, I'll help you with the stable."

"Yippee!" Charles cheered.

She mounted the horse, adjusting her long skirts to fit, then she urged the horse into a gallop. Once again, she surveyed the area to make sure Jesse wasn't around. Not seeing him, she breathed a sigh of relief.

Kicking Buck into a run, she enjoyed the wind blowing through her unbound hair. Her heart felt lighter, and she allowed herself to smile. Yes, this was exactly what she needed.

After riding around for about fifteen minutes, she found herself at her favorite spot. Poppy's meadow. The gurgling stream beckoned her to come and wade through it with her bare feet, but she denied herself that luxury for now. The weather was turning chilly, and the water would be, also. She didn't want to chance catching pneumonia.

Slowing Buck, she walked him beside the bank of the water. Watching the way it trickled over the rocks and down the creek bed relaxed her, calmed her, and made her think clearly. When her thoughts turned to Jesse, she didn't curse herself this time. She realized she had to tell someone. She had to tell Clint about the lie his brother had been living the past four years. And if Clint didn't believe her, then she had to confront Jesse. Maybe she could make him feel guilty enough to turn himself in.

Over the sound of the water came another sound. A horse approached. She glanced over her shoulder and recognized the rider immediately. The way his rugged frame sat upon the horse as he moved perfectly with the galloping rhythm, made her heart sigh from loneliness. At this moment, she knew she'd always love Jesse, but she couldn't bring herself to marry a lying criminal.

She should have left right away, but she hesitated, wanting to watch him just a little while longer. His hair seemed longer when he wasn't wearing his hat. As he drew near, her heart hammered frantically, and suddenly, she knew it was still too soon to talk to him. Just the thought of confronting him with her knowledge scared her to death, and she didn't like feeling this way. She hurried and yanked on the horse's reins, pulling him around in the opposite direction. Kicking her heels in his belly, she pushed him forward into a run.

From behind her, Jesse called out her name, but she kept riding. The sound of approaching hooves let her know that he wasn't giving up the chase. It frightened her, yet at the same time, the feeling was exhilarating. She wished confusion would leave her mind soon so she could think straight.

She crouched low over Buck, gripping to the reins as she pushed him faster. Even through the strenuous circumstances, she smiled from the knowledge she was winning the race. Race? What was she thinking? This wasn't another one of their competitions. Yet, it was, because she didn't want him to catch her. If she allowed him to win, he'd take her in his arms and hold her...and her body couldn't resist his glorious lovemaking.

She growled from the thought of her traitorous body, and urged the horse faster.

"Damn it, Summer," Jesse yelled from behind. "I'll not let you get away this time."

Her smile widened, but she fought it the best she could.

"Summer, you'd better stop, or I'll..."

She glanced over her shoulder and couldn't believe how close Jesse was. "Go away."

"Not this time."

Ahead of her was the same fence she had tried to jump awhile ago. Could she jump it again? She had to. Jesse was too close behind her.

Gearing herself for the jump, she crouched lower, and between the reins and her legs, she led her horse in the direction of the fence. "Don't let me down, Buck."

The moment came, and she held her breath. Closing her eyes, she prayed Buck would make it over the fence. He jumped. Within seconds, her body jerked when she and Buck landed safely on the other side. Relief gushed out of her mouth in one big breath.

The sound of hooves pounding stopped and the sickening thud when his body hit the ground rendered through the air. She threw a glance over her shoulder to see Jesse lying still on the ground, the horse standing near. Had he been knocked unconsious- -or worse? Her heart dropped. What if he'd hit his head on a rock and it had killed him? No matter how she felt about him, she didn't want him dead.

Quickly, she pulled Buck around and rode over to Jesse. His right leg was bent at the knee and underneath his left leg. Dust colored his face as it lay on one side, his eyes closed. He lay deathly still.

She gasped and jumped off her horse, flying down beside him. "Jesse?" she asked as she gently touched his face. His chest looked still. He wasn't breathing.

"Jesse," she screamed and shook him once, then laid her head on his chest to hear his heart.

Before she had time to think, two strong arms circled around her as Jesse rolled them over. He was now on top, his eyes were open, and a big smile displayed on his tempting mouth. Oooh! How dare he trick her.

"You do care," he said.

She pounded her fists on his chest, but he didn't budge.

"You dirty rotten...dog. How could you trick me like that?"

He shrugged. "Just wanted to see if you still cared."

She scowled, and breathed a heavy sigh. She had been defeated by his cheating antics, and now she knew she couldn't get out of telling him what she knew. In fact, she almost looked forward to it. A great weight would be lifted off her shoulders.

"Yes, unfortunately, I still care."

He chuckled lightly. "Don't look so broken up about it, darlin'."

She pushed him off her and sat up. "If you only knew how broken up about it I really am, you wouldn't be teasing me."

He removed a twig from her hair. "Summer? Will you talk to me now? I think I have the right to know why you've suddenly changed your mind about our weddin' and about lovin' me."

She nodded, then glanced down at her hands resting in her lap, not wanting to meet his intoxicating blue eyes. "Yes, I'll talk to you. I need to get it off my chest. It's been eating me alive trying to deal with it on my own."

Tears sprung to her eyes and she blinked, trying to fight them away. Her emotions had been on the edge for so long, she didn't know how to hold them back anymore. "While I was being held prisoner, I learned some disturbing things about you."

"I gathered as much. Was it somethin' Frank said?"

"No, although he didn't deny it when I asked him about it later."

"Tell me," he urged.

She breathed deeply, trying to keep her emotions in control--long enough to get the story out. She looked up into his saddened eyes and her heart wrenched.

"The first person to tell me this terrible news was Joe. When I asked him if you were really dead, he told me you were because Buchanan doesn't take kindly to men who double-cross him. Apparently," she paused briefly before continuing, "you had double-crossed Buchanan that day in Amarillo."

Jesse shook his head.

"Think, Jesse, think really hard and I'm sure you'll realize what I'm talking about."

"Can you give me a hint?"

She rolled her eyes. "Good grief, which sin should I pick? How about Buchanan's gang? Can you possibly think of what I might have learned while being held prisoner? Joe told me that you were one of Buchanan's men," she said slowly. "And that you have been for about four years."

Her chest heaved with each breath she took, her hands balled into fists on her lap, but she kept her chin erect, ready for his denial. She studied Jesse really closely for his reaction, but she didn't expect to see the tug of his lips as he tried not to grin. He must not have heard her correctly.

"Jesse, you're an outlaw. You should be taken to jail along with Buchanan and his other men."

"Oh, really?"

His humorous response sparked her anger more. "Jesse, I mean it. If you don't turn yourself in, I'm going to."

He chuckled and rose to his feet. "Don't like the fact that I'm an outlaw, huh?"

Her eyes widened. "What do you think? You lied to everyone. What would Clint say if he knew? What would Pa say, for that matter?"

"Can I ask you a serious question?"

She pulled herself up and stood in front of him. "Oh, you want to get serious now?"

"Yes."

"Fine. What do you want to ask?"

"What was your first reaction when you heard this?"

"Oh, let's see...I was overjoyed?" she snapped sarcastically. "How do you think I reacted? I couldn't believe the man I loved was part of a gang."

"So, what made you change your mind?"

"Not only did Joe tell me, but Frank said it too, and then Buchanan, of course, couldn't wait to tell me the whole sordid story. He told me you helped rob a bank, and that's how you paid for yours and Clint's cabin."

Jesse shook his head and frowned. "Yes, good ole Buchanan. Such a trustful, law abidin' citizen. Such a carin', loyal, upstandin' man in the community."

She gasped. "How can you say that about him? He's none of those things. He's nothing but animal droppings!"

"But he must be a good man in order for you to believe every word that came from his mouth."

Confusion made her hold her tongue as her mind struggled to keep alert. Could she have been wrong? Jesse's statement made sense. Why was she so willing to believe a man like Buchanan?

She tilted her head. "Are you denying the accusations, then? Are you saying that you were never part of Buchanan's gang?"

He shook his head as he walked over to his horse, adjusting the reins. "I'm not denyin' I was a friend to Buchanan, but I'll deny I was ever an outlaw."

She laughed harshly. "You can't deny one thing and not the other. They go hand in hand. If you were friends with Buchanan, you were most certainly an outlaw."

"No, I was never an outlaw." He paused then met her gaze. "Are you ready to hear the truth?"

A rush of adrenaline shot through her body and made her dizzy. Her heart hammered so irregularly, she thought she'd keel over and die any moment. Could she have been wrong? "Fine. What's the story?"

"Are you sure you're ready? Aren't you afraid I might say somethin' you don't like? After all, my credibility isn't as good as Buchanan's."

Jesse was being stubborn, but he was reacting to her distrust. "Just tell me," she said calmer.

He folded his arms. "Four years ago I met a man in a saloon. I was feelin' poorly, feelin' like I wasn't makin' enough money, and so I was heavy into my cups when Buchanan came up to me. As we talked, Buchanan hinted at a way to make money." He shrugged. "I couldn't help but feel excited." When she scowled, he held up his hand. "And no, it's not because I thought of myself. I was actually thinkin' of Clint. My brother was part of the Rangers, and I knew this kind of information would be helpful. So that's when I became part of the gang, sorta. You see, I never went in with them when they hit a bank, yet I tried actin' like I was one of them."

He sighed heavily and ran his fingers through his hair. "When I went to Clint and informed him about Buchanan, he told me to join the gang and collect all the information I could. Funny thing was, Buchanan thought I was givin' him information about the Rangers."

"I don't understand something," she cut in. "If you were part of Buchanan's gang, then why couldn't the Rangers ever find them? Why has it taken four long years to finally capture them?"

"Buchanan is clever. That's one good thing I can say about him. Although I was part of the gang, I never rode with them. Most of the time, Buchanan's gang was out of Texas, anyway, so, I never knew from one week to another where Buchanan was located. It was only by coincidence I ever caught up to them here in Texas."

"But Buchanan said that you were one of his best men."

Jesse nodded. "That's because Buchanan thought he was gettin' information about the Rangers. Usually, I would just give Buchanan the Ranger's location. I worked undercover for the Rangers."

She grasped the sides of her skirt, hiding her shaky hands. "So what happened in Amarillo that made Buchanan think you double-crossed him?"

"They recognized me, and I was with Clint. I was helpin' the Rangers, and Buchanan didn't like it."

With every word from his mouth, her heart dropped a fraction lower. She studied his expression, and could see he was telling her the truth. His face remained serious, and she felt lower than dirt. How could she have been that gullible to believe Buchanan over the man that she claimed to love?

After a few minutes of silence, Jesse cleared his throat. "If you don't believe me, you can ask Clint. He'll tell you exactly what I just did."

She stood in stunned silence for a few minutes as her mind began to work properly. It'd been quite a while since she allowed herself to feel anything more than hurt, but now regret stabbed painfully inside her chest, hurting just as much as when she'd thought Jesse had lied to her.

Covering her face with her hands, her shoulders sagged in relief. "Oh, Jesse," she sobbed, "how could I have been so foolish?"

Jesse moved over to her, taking her shoulders gently.

"Look at me." She didn't move, so he lifted her chin until her eyes met his. "I should've told you, but it had been a secret for so long, I was used to keepin' it to myself. Please don't hate me for that."

She shook her head. "But how could I have believed those terrible lies about you? You were the man I proclaimed to love, yet at the first test of my devotion, I didn't trust my own heart, and I believed someone else."

"Summer, remember the condition you were in then? Half-starved, weak as a kitten? Your mind wasn't sharp then. Once the idea took root, it just grew. I understand." He pulled her closer, laying her head to his chest. "The truth is out in the open now. Everythin' is fine."

"No, everything is not fine." She looked up at him. "I can't believe you don't think I'm the worst woman in the world. How will you ever believe me now? I don't deserve your love."

"Please don't do this to yourself, darlin'."

"Jesse? Will you ever be able to forgive me?"

"I already have." He kissed her forehead. "Summer, I want to know one more thing. Do you still love me?"

Tears streamed down her face as she nodded. "I never stopped. That's why I didn't want to see you. I thought if I broke all contact with you, it'd be easier to hate you."

Gathering her closer against his body, he pressed his face in her hair. "I've been so miserable without you. I couldn't figure out what I'd done wrong." His voice broke.

"You didn't do a thing. I'm the one to blame. I should have trusted you. I shouldn't have believed Buchanan." Her sobs increased and all she wanted to do was bury her head in Jesse's neck and cry while he held her. But Jesse wouldn't let her cry any longer. His mouth moved down and covered hers, silencing her sobs. The moment their lips met, she kissed him with all the love she could muster, hoping he would forgive her for being so gullible and untrusting.

"Oh, Summer," he mumbled against her lips. "I love you so much."

She sighed deeply, finally able to admit her feelings instead of trying to hide them. "I love you more than you'll ever know." She paused, then asked, "What can I do to make it up to you? How can I make up for all this time I refused to see you?

How can I let you know how sorry I am?"

He gave her a tender smile. "By marryin' me tomorrow."

"Tomorrow? But that's when Clint and Violet are getting married."

"They want us to share it with them. They were hopin' we'd work things out and have a double weddin'."

She smiled fully, something she missed doing. She stared into his eyes, then relaxed her body against his.

"Does that mean yes?" he asked.

She laughed and briefly kissed him on the lips. "Of course that means yes. I'd be a complete fool if I turned you down now."

"Summer, darlin', you've made me the happiest man alive, do you know that?"

He kissed her again, and he showed his love through his kiss. The tender way his lips moved across hers, and the caressing way his tongue swept through her mouth was so sensual, exciting, arousing. When his hands wandered over her back, her buttocks, around her waist to cup her breasts, every touch was designed to tell her how he felt. She arched, pushing her breasts into his hands, and he groaned deeply, unable to hold back how much it affected him, also.

"Summer?" His mouth left hers and traveled down her neck. "I don't think I can wait until tomorrow night," he told her in a low, sedated voice. "I want to feel your body against mine again. I want to touch your nakedness and kiss every inch of you."

She giggled. "You can't wait one whole day?"

He raised his head and met her eyes. "No. Can you?"

"No, I can't, but I will. The wait will make our lovemaking that much more enjoyable."

The corner of his mouth lifted. "And how do you figure that?"

"Because we won't be making love in the stable, or hurrying before someone discovers us. We'll be in a nice soft bed and we'll be able to lay in each other's arms all night long."

He leaned his forehead against hers. "You're right. I'll wait."

"Thank you for forgiving me."

"Darlin', I'll do anythin' to keep your love. There's nothin' in this world that will pull our love apart. Not ever again."

"Promise? Swear to it?" she asked.

"Oh, yes. Every damn day for the rest of my life."

~ * ~

That night Jesse and Clint joined the Bennett family for dinner. Jesse couldn't keep his eyes off the most beautiful woman he'd ever seen, and thankfully, Summer also stared at him with star-struck eyes. He reached under the table and grabbed her hand, linking his fingers with hers. Life was finally good, and it would only get sweeter from here on out.

A conversation was going on at the table, but he and Summer were doing their own kind of communicating. Through his gaze, he tried to tell her how much he loved her, and as his fingers softly stroked Summer's fingers, he tried to let her know that he couldn't wait to become her husband--and especially couldn't wait for their wedding night. By the twinkle in her eyes and the gentle lift of her lips, she understood him perfectly.

Just before supper was completed, a knock came on the door. Ma excused herself to see who had come calling at supper time.

"Well, Mayor Tubbs. To what do we owe this wonderful surprise?"

"I was told that the Slade brothers were here."

Both Jesse and his brother stood and moved away from the table. They strode into the front room, and within seconds, the rest of the family followed.

Mayor Tubbs smiled and stretched his right hand out in greeting. Clint shook it first, then Jesse. "It is my privilege to present you with the reward money for the capture of the Buchanan gang."

In unison, the whole room echoed with gasps.

"I know most of the banks in Texas have already given their rewards to the Texas Rangers," the mayor continued, "but I believe because of Clint's determination and Jesse's willingness to go undercover, the reward should go to the two Rangers who did the most in planning the downfall of Buchanan's gang."

Jesse glanced at Summer. A frown marred her face. She had hoped to catch them herself so she could pay for her pa's surgery. But in a way, she helped more than anyone.

"Actually, Mayor," Clint spoke as he stepped closer to

him. "I think you're wrong. I was just doin' my job with the Rangers, and I think someone else deserves this reward more than me." He glanced over at Jesse. "What do you think, li'l brother?"

Jesse could read his brother well, and he agreed. "Yes, we were just doin' our job."

Chuckles rang through the room. The mayor shook his head. "You're being stubborn, just as I was warned you'd be."

"No, Mayor, I'm downright serious." Clint turned his attention to Summer. "I think Miss Bennett deserves my share. She did more in helpin' us find those varmints than anyone else I know."

Summer gasped. When Clint took the bag of money from the mayor and brought it over to her, Jesse's heart picked up rhythm.

"Here, take it." Clint held the bag within her grasp.

Tears filled her eyes as she stared at the reward money, then she lifted her eyes to Clint. "Really? You think I deserve this?"

"Hell, yes, li'l lady. If it hadn't been for your kidnappin', the Rangers wouldn't have known where in the blazes that Buchanan gang was located. And if it hadn't been for my li'l brother tryin' so hard to rescue you, I don't think Buchanan's gang would have been caught." He smiled. "Take the money, Summer. I don't need it."

Her hand shook when she grabbed hold of the bag. Tears streamed down her cheeks when she turned and walked over to Pa. She knelt to his level and kissed his cheek.

"You can go to New Orleans now and get that surgery." Her voice cracked.

Pa's eyes filled with tears. When he smiled, his lips quivered. "Thank you, Summer. Thank you so much."

The family gathered around Summer and Pa, and each took their turn in hugging and kissing. Summer stepped away and went directly into Jesse's embrace. He held her tight and kissed her forehead.

She looked into his face. "Everything is going to be perfect now."

He nodded. "Yes, it will."

Eighteen

"Damn," Jesse snapped as he walked across the wooden floor in front of Clint, who lounged on the sofa. Jesse stopped in front of his brother and glared at him. "Why aren't you actin' nervous? Tomorrow is your weddin', too."

Clint stretched his arm across the back of the couch and laughed. "Because, dear brother, I've already made Violet my bride, if you know what I mean."

Jesse folded his arms across his chest and cocked his head. "Yeah, well, I've made Summer mine and I'm still actin' like a nervous groom."

"When was the last time you made love to Summer?"

"Two days ago."

Clint exaggerated his grin. "That long, huh? Explains why you're actin' like a horse who's stepped on a rat'ler. Should've done somethin' about that itch in your pants before now."

"Yeah, I know," Jesse grumbled, walking back across the floor. "But Summer wanted to wait. Said it'd make our weddin' night more special."

Clint shrugged. "Maybe, maybe not."

Jesse shot his brother another scowl. "So what do you think I should do? Go get her tonight and take her behind the bushes?"

Clint laughed. "No, now it's too late."

"Argh." Jesse growled and walked into the kitchen and over to the stove. He picked up the kettle and shook it, testing to see how much water remained in the pot.

"If you're thinkin' about coffee, you'd better think again," Clint hollered. "It'll keep you up all night."

"Double damn." Jesse slammed the kettle back on the stove, then marched back into the front room and plopped himself down on the sofa beside Clint.

Jesse sighed heavily and rested his head against the wall. "I don't think I'm goin' to get any sleep tonight anyway."

Clint chuckled. "I don't think you're goin' to get any sleep t'morrow night, either."

Jesse smiled. "I never thought I would feel like this. I'm scared to death, yet I know I won't be able to live without Summer."

"I know 'xactly how you're feelin'."

"You have a hell of a way of showin' it."

"Oh, believe me, deep in my heart, I'm a li'l nervous, but I know I'm doin' the right thing. I love Violet more than life itself."

"Guess you do feel like me." Jesse studied his brother a moment, then asked, "How long have you been yearnin' after Violet?"

Clint's eyes widened, then he straightened in his seat. For the first time Jesse could remember, his brother blushed. "Does it matter?"

"I'm just curious."

"Promise you won't be mad?"

"I won't be mad."

Clint's smile touched his face again. "I think I've liked her all along. When you first started workin' for Marvin, I liked her, but she was too young for me then. By the time she had matured into a woman, she only had eyes for my li'l brother. It was too late then."

Jesse grinned. "Funny how things have changed."

"Amen to that. It just goes to show that Violet is made for me just as Summer is made for you."

"Yeah, that's another thing I don't understand, but I'm not goin' to waste time figurin' it out." Jesse chuckled. "Heaven only knows how I fell in love with the little tornado, but nothin' will change my feelin's for her now."

"Good for you."

Jesse folded his arms and stared up at the ceiling, his thoughts taken by Summer--as always. He thought about the last time he'd made love to her at the stable, against the wall, and he grinned. Passion had taken right over for the both of them, and he hoped their love-life would be like that forever. She was as passionate in her temper as she was in kissing him. She lived her life being fervent about everything she cared for.

His loins tightened, and silently cursed. He glanced over at Clint, and luckily, Clint seemed to be consumed by fantasies of his own. But damn it, Jesse didn't think he could wait until tomorrow. He knew he'd have a constant stiffness in his trousers during the wedding tomorrow, not to mention that damn gathering the Bennett family would have afterwards that would last for hours. No. Jesse couldn't wait. He had to go to her tonight--even if it meant taking her behind the bushes.

He lifted himself off the couch, stepped to the door, and yanked his jacket off the hook on the wall.

"Where are you goin'?" Clint asked, wearing a wide grin.

"I have things to do before tomorrow," he snapped before slamming the door closed. Clint's rumble of laughter rang through the house, and Jesse heard it all the way out to the barn.

~ * ~

Summer fastened the buttons on her old shirt before tucking it in the waist of her knickers. It'd been a while since she'd worn these clothes, but she couldn't possibly climb out the window and shimmy down a tree in a dress.

She tiptoed over to the window and carefully opened the shutters, then lifted up the pane. The cool brisk air touched her heated cheeks, teasing the loose curls around her shoulders. She breathed in the night air and gained more courage as she thought about her plan to see Jesse.

All right, so she admitted she couldn't wait. She just had to be lying in his arms tonight no matter what the consequences.

She poked her head out the window and listened. The silence convinced her that the coast was clear. She picked up her brother's boots and threw them into the yard, then listened again for any stirring. Everything remained still.

Glancing straight ahead to the wide oak tree mere feet away from her window, she rubbed her hands in nervous excitement. It had been ages since she'd climbed a tree, and even longer since she'd sneaked out of her own bedroom window. But she couldn't rest tonight until she'd made love to Jesse.

Cautiously, she climbed out the window and onto the

ledge. She'd had a lot more courage in her younger years, and now her heart created frantic rhythms in her chest. Would she fall if she made the leap to the tree?

She took a big breath, swung her arms and jumped, reaching for the limb that had always caught her before. Awkwardly, her hands fastened on the branch until she could pull herself up. Once she settled her feet on the tree, she sighed with relief.

She looked at the ground. Funny, but it wasn't as far as she remembered. Of course, she'd been much smaller back then. As she turned to climb down the tree, she touched around the limbs with her toe.

"What do you think you're doing?"

Summer gasped loudly and glanced toward Violet's window. Her sister leaned out, a scowl pulled her eyebrows together.

"It's not what you're thinking," Summer replied quickly.

Violet tilted her head. "You're wearing your old boy's clothes, and you've just jumped from your window to the tree. It looks like you're running away." She paused briefly. "Summer? Do you, by chance, have cold feet?"

Summer creased her brows. "Well, of course I do, but it's only because I climb better without shoes. And if you haven't noticed, the weather is quite nippy tonight."

Violet rolled her eyes heavenward. "I didn't mean it that way." A grin touched her lips. "Are you ditching your own wedding?"

Summer hitched a breath. "Of course not. Whatever would make you say that?"

"Then why are you escaping out your window in the middle of the night?"

Summer chuckled lightly. "Because I miss Jesse."

Violet's smile widened. "And you're going to meet him somewhere? The stable, perhaps?"

"Well, no, not exactly. You see, I'm going to ride out to our cabin and well...uh, well…"

Violet laughed, but kept it low. "Summer, I know exactly what you're planning." She withdrew back into her room. "Just be careful this time. Don't forget to take a gun," she ended before closing the window.

Summer rubbed her forehead. Violet knew what she was doing, and didn't stop her. That could only mean one thing. Her lips stretched into a wide smile. Violet wasn't innocent any longer either.

After landing safely on the ground, she slipped into her old boots, and crept to the barn. She quickly saddled a horse, grabbed a rifle, and mounted. Before she left, she glanced back at the house to make sure nobody else had spotted her. When the house remained dark, she sighed.

She trotted until she was a fair distance from the house, then urged the horse faster. When she imagined being in Jesse's arms, urgency swept over her. As she neared the cabin Clint had built for Jesse, her heart hammered out of control. Jesse's bedroom light was still on. Could he be thinking about her in the same way?

She stopped the horse, dismounted, and ran around the side of the house toward his window, but when she noticed the man in the room was not Jesse, she came to a stop. What was Clint doing? And more importantly, why were Clint's brows drawn and his lips pulled into a frown as he read a piece of paper?

Jesse's opened window beckoned her nearer, so she quietly crept closer. A twig snapped underneath her boot, and Clint's head spun around. She was caught.

"Summer?" Clint moved over to the window. "What are you doin' here?"

She thanked the quarter moon tonight, or Clint would be able to see her heated cheeks. By the amount of embarrassment that had consumed her face, she was sure she looked like a turnip.

"I...I...came to talk to Jesse."

Clint blew out a gush of air, but his expression remained worried. "Oh," he mumbled.

Something was wrong. The prickly sensations crawling up her spine were undeniable. She stepped over to the window. "Clint, where is Jesse?"

He stared at her for a few long seconds, then motioned his head. "Come inside. I think you should read this letter."

Her heart pounded with each step into the cabin until she met Clint in the front room. When he handed her the letter, she took it with shaky hands.

"Clint, I'm sorry I didn't have the courage to tell you face to face, but I finally realized tonight that I'm not ready to get married. I've decided to head out West to start a new life. Please tell Summer that although I love her, I'm just not ready. I hope, in time, she'll forgive me."

Numbness spread over her body and the letter fell from her fingers to the floor. Tears gathered in her eyes as she stared right through Clint. *This can't be happening!*

"Summer." Clint took hold of her cold hands. "I'm sorry."

A tear slid down her cheek. "I don't believe it."

"Neither do I. Jess and I were just talkin', and he was tellin' me how happy he was to be marryin' you. Sure, he acted like a skittish horse in a briar patch t'night, but that's to be expected. I had no idea Jess felt that way about marriage."

Her knees weakened and she collapsed, but Clint caught her and kept her from falling. "Let me help you over to the couch."

She didn't feel a thing when he sat her down, then covered her legs with a blanket. "Let me go fetch you a cup of coffee." He turned and hurried into the kitchen and within minutes came out with a cup of steamy brew and placed it in her stiff hands.

She slowly shook her head. "He can't be gone. He loves me. He wants to marry me."

Clint sat beside her and touched her chin. "He does love you. In fact, I think he'll still be there for the ceremony tomorrow."

"And what if he's not?" Her voice chocked as she turned and buried her face in his shoulder.

"Honey, I don't know what to say. I'm in shock, too."

She raised her head and met his eyes. "Why would he decide this tonight? Why couldn't he have figured this out earlier?"

Clint shrugged. "You're askin' the wrong person. I wish to hell I knew."

She stared at the cup in her hands, not caring that the coffee slowly cooled. Her heart crumbled, and it was on its way to dying a slow and painful death. Emptiness consumed her mind, and she hoped when she awoke, she'd discover this had all been a dream.

"I'll ride out and talk to your parents. We'll postpone the weddin' until--"

"No," she snapped, finally finding the strength to turn her head and look at him. "I'll not let Jesse ruin my sister's wedding."

"But Summer, it's your weddin' too."

"Not anymore. Tomorrow, you'll arrive at the church, just as planned, and you'll walk my sister down the aisle and make her your bride."

"But what are you goin' to do?"

Good question. She stared back down at her cup. She could admit defeat, go home and lock herself in her room until she was old and decrepit, but that wouldn't accomplish a damn thing! Back five years ago, she wouldn't have let Jesse get away with this. What kind of simpering female had her aunt changed her into?

Full of determination, she handed Clint the cup of coffee, then stood. "What am I going to do, you ask?" She marched over to the door, speaking over her shoulder. "Well, I'm certainly not going to sit on my backside and let this happen without a fight."

She flung open the door and turned to Clint, whose wide-eyed expression showed his surprise. "No, sir-ree! Summer Bennett is not going to cower this time."

Clint slowly rose to his feet. "What are you goin' to do, Summer?"

"I'm going to hunt him down like the side-windin' animal he is and bring him back--hogtied if necessary. Nobody breaks my heart and gets away with it. He can tell me to my face that he doesn't love me." She marched to her horse and quickly mounted.

"Summer," Clint called after her. "It's the middle of the night and the moon isn't very bright. How're you gonna find him in the dark? Wait a minute, and I'll go with you."

She lifted her chin. "Oh, don't worry about me. I'll find him." She kicked her heels into the horse's belly and rode away.

~ * ~

She could have been a Texas Ranger.

The thought flashed through her mind as she rode across the plains searching for that rotten polecat, Jesse Slade. She picked up his trail easy enough--the fresh piles of horse droppings were a dead giveaway. She headed Southwest toward the Brazos River. He'd need to water his horse while heading toward the border, and

Brazos was the only sensible river to follow.

Before starting on her journey, she dropped back by the house, still creeping around in silence, and grabbed a few leftovers to munch on. She also collected some rope, knowing she'd probably have to tie Jesse and forcefully bring him home.

Clint had warned her about the quarter moon, but she put all of her other senses to work. The flapping wings of the disturbed night birds still hovered in the sky, and the night insects had stopped their singing. Yes, she would find Jesse before morning, she was sure of it.

As she munched on an apple, her keen eyes, now accustomed to the near darkness, scanned the plains, spotting the tumbleweeds, a few jackrabbits, but nothing that would put her in danger's path. She looked out across the horizon and spotted a campfire in the distance. Her heart leapt into her throat. It might be Jesse. If not, she'd brought her rifle. Her hand moved beside her leg to the long iron fastened to the saddle, and just in case, her pocketknife was hidden away in her boot.

When she approached the sparse trees, she slowed, and then stopped. Not too far ahead, she could see the silhouettes of two men, one sitting at the base of a tree, and the other crouched beside the fire as he stirred a pot. Her heart hammered. Maybe this wasn't Jesse, and if it was, who was he traveling with?

She dismounted and tied her horse to the nearest tree, then crept toward the fire until voices grew louder. When she recognized Jesse's her heart thumped crazily, but the tone in which he spoke was not pleasant. She moved closer, then noticed Jesse's hands were tied behind his back.

Prickles danced over her skin. *Something was wrong.* She kept low and listened.

"You know, Albert," Jesse snapped, "Clint was right. You are one addled man. Definitely not the perfect fellow you led us all to believe."

Summer gasped, then quickly covered her mouth. *Albert Kendal?* What was he doing here?

Albert belched a loud laugh that rang through the night. "Count on some stupid Ranger to point out my flaws."

"Well, you could've proven us all wrong, you know."

"Shut up," Albert shouted. "I didn't kidnap you to pass

the time."

"Then why did you kidnap me?"

Albert pulled the pot off the fire and set it on a nearby rock. "I have my reasons."

"And it has somethin' to do with the reward money, right?"

"Damn straight." Albert reached in his pocket, withdrew his knife and whittled on a stick. "That money was meant for me, and it would've been mine if you and your stupid brother hadn't ruined my plans." Albert walked over to Jesse and bent toward him. "But I still have the upper hand. I'm still in control."

Summer held her breath as she continued to watch. What in God's name was Albert thinkin? Obviously, his head wasn't on right.

Jesse blew out a gush of air. "So, what are your plans? If you think my brother or the Bennett family is goin' to come lookin' for me, you're sorely mistaken. That farewell letter you forced me to write explains it all." He shrugged. "They think I've ditched my weddin'."

Albert let out an eerie laugh, and Summer's terror multiplied. Albert Kendal was one very ill man.

Albert plopped on the ground next to Jesse. "Oh, if I know that little hellion of yours, she'll come looking for you. And because she's so stubborn, your brother will come with her." He flicked his knife on the piece of wood. "You forget, I know Summer Bennett quite well."

Jesse let out a harsh laugh. "And I know her even better. If she thinks I have run off on my own weddin', she'll give up on me for good." He shook his head. "No, Albert. Don't plan on seeing Summer anytime soon."

Albert scowled and reached in his holster, pulling out his revolver. He cocked it as he aimed straight at Jesse's heart. Summer gasped, then quickly covered her mouth again.

"If you kill me," Jesse said calmly, "then how will you get your reward money?"

Albert's lips stretched into a wide grin. "It doesn't matter because I know your precious sweetheart and brother will come for you."

Jesse slowly shook his head. "What if you're wrong?"

Albert let out a growl as he pushed himself to his feet and turned away, staring at the low burning fire. "We'll just have to wait and see what happens. One way or another, I'll get that reward money from Summer. She'll pay handsomely to have her lover back in her life once she discovers I've kidnapped you."

"Don't count on it. I've broken her heart too many times."

Albert spun and kicked Jesse in the stomach. Jesse groaned and slumped over, and Summer's heart stopped. When he sucked in a quick breath of air, relief swept over her.

"If she doesn't come after you, I'll convince her to give me the money, even if it means riding back to Waco to collect your woman and finish the seduction I'd started on her."

Jesse's head snapped up. "Don't you lay a finger on her."

Albert laughed. "Oh-ho. I've found your weak spot." He knelt beside Jesse and pushed him to an upright position. "Perhaps that's the key, here. Maybe I can have both. Summer's just the woman to fill my sexual needs."

"You touch her, and I'll kill you."

Laughing, Albert sauntered over to his bedroll and flipped it out on the ground next to the fire. "Not if you're already dead." He shook his head. "Oh, you're so stupid. You must have inherited that from Clint." He lay down and folded his arms behind his head as he stared up at the stars.

Summer waited for Jesse's reply, but he kept silent. Minutes passed and the quietness bothered her. She stayed still in fear that Albert would hear her. She'd left the rifle tied up to the saddle, and her only weapon was the small knife in her boot.

Silently, she watched and waited. The fire slowly burned down to coals, making the area darker. Off in a distance, a wolf cried and she shivered in fear. She had to help Jesse, but Albert would undoubtedly put a stop to her plans if he heard her. Oh, what to do?

"Pssst. Albert, are you awake?" Jesse called out softly.

Albert didn't answer.

Summer's head snapped toward Jesse, her heart pounding fiercely. What was he doing?

"Summer?" he whispered.

She sucked in a breath. "Yes."

"I think Albert is asleep. Sneak over to me, if you can."

She crept behind the tree he leaned against and stopped, squatting close to him. "How did you know I was here?"

He turned and looked at her, a soft smile bracketing his handsome face. "Because I know you."

She smiled.

"Did you bring a gun?" he asked.

"Yes, but the rifle is tied to my saddle."

"Can you get me untied?"

She reached into her boot and withdrew the pocketknife. "I brought my knife."

"That's my girl. Now cut the ropes around my wrists."

In the darkness, she felt for his hands. He squeezed her fingers briefly, then she concentrated on slicing through the rope. Her eyes moistened with emotion, but she'd put aside those feelings for later. She had to release Jesse.

"Summer? Is Clint comin'?"

"I left without him. Why?"

"Because I don't know if Albert is actin' alone. If he is, I'll be able to handle him. If not, I might need help."

"But Jesse, you're not alone." She leaned closer to his ear. "I'm here."

He squeezed her fingers once again just as the ropes gave way. He rubbed his wrists, then pulled her to him and gave her a quick hug. "I'm so grateful for your help, but now you need to go back to your horse and get the gun."

"What are you going to do?"

"I need to stay right here."

"But why--" A rustle came from the other side of camp, and she paused. Both of them swung their heads in that direction. The lump where Albert was sleeping was still visible through the small glow from the coals.

"Summer, just do as I say. I have to stay right here, just in case Albert wakes up. Do you understand?"

"Yes." She moved quietly out of the trees, her adrenaline pumped from the danger, but her heart soared with the knowledge that Jesse had not ditched her before her wedding.

~ * ~

As Summer disappeared through the cluster of trees, Jesse's heart soared. His little tornado had come to his rescue once again.

With a controlled sigh, he rearranged his thoughts and focused on Albert. He glanced across the camp to the roll, which conspicuously hadn't moved, and his curiosity arose. Even in sleep a man might move a bit. Slowly, he lifted to his knees, his eyes on the still form, when behind him, a twig snapped. He swung his head and saw the shadowed figure of Albert beside him.

An eerie cackle slipped from Albert's throat as he raised the thick tree branch above his head. "You still think I'm stupid, don't you?"

With a swift movement, Albert struck Jesse's head. Fighting the threatening cloud of darkness, Jesse forced himself to remain conscious. Summer's life depended on it.

Albert quickly stepped past him, going in the same direction Summer had gone.

"Summer..." Her name barely left Jesse's lips before he slumped back against the tree as thick darkness consumed his vision and his mind.

~ * ~

When Summer spotted her horse, she broke into a run until she reached Buck's side. Buck appeared skittish, and she prayed the wolf she'd heard earlier hadn't come closer. Holding her breath, she listened, but she didn't hear any sounds, so she reached for the rifle. Just as she touched it, somebody seized her hand from behind and whipped her around.

The man in front of her stank like stale whiskey and heavy cigar smoke, but she couldn't quite see who held her.

"Hello, my beautiful."

She turned her nose away from his bad breath. "Albert?"

"You're very perceptive."

She tried to study his shadowed face. Strange, but he didn't look anything like the man who'd courted her for those few weeks. Probably because his demented mind was in charge now.

"I thought you were on your bedroll a few minutes ago."

"No, you saw something lumpy."

She glanced over her shoulder toward the fire, searching for Jesse. His laughter sent a sickening wave down her spine.

"If you're looking for your lover, I've knocked him over the head with a log. He should be out cold for a little while longer.

Either that or he's dead."

A sob escaped from her and she struggled, trying to release her wrists from his grasp.

"Come back to the fire with me. I have a little surprise waiting for you."

Her stomach churned, and she hoped to God his surprise wasn't going to be something vile.

He pulled her along with him, practically dragging her to the camp as she stumbled over bushes and rocks. When she passed Jesse, his head was slumped forward, resting on his chest, and a trickle of blood ran down the side of his face.

Albert gave her one last push and she dropped to her knees on his bedroll. He cackled. "Exactly where I want you."

She scrambled to get up. He withdrew his pistol and pointed at her heart.

"You really showed up at the right time, you know. Jesse here wasn't being a very good hostage."

She straighened her back. "Jesse will never do your bidding. He has more intelligence in his little finger than you have in your whole body. He's just stringing you along, and soon you'll be behind bars waiting for your hanging."

He sneered, and she cringed, hoping she hadn't gone too far with her words.

"You are the one he's stringing along, sweets. Do you really think he's going to marry you?" He laughed louder. "Think again."

"He loves me!"

"Perhaps, but I won't let him have a wonderful life." He crouched beside her, still holding his pistol. "Jesse stole the woman I had planned to have for my wife, and I'm stealing her back."

She gasped. "You wanted to marry me?"

"Yes." He touched a lock of her hair and she swatted his hand away. He scowled. "Jesse also took the reward money that was mine."

"That money was never yours. You did nothing to aid in the capture of Buchanan's gang."

"But I would have if Jesse and Clint hadn't stopped me."

"When did they ever stop you?"

A scowl covered his face. "I was the one hiding behind

the building when Jesse was in Amarillo. I was the one who whopped Jesse over the head with the butt of my rifle that time they watched the bank. And it was the bullet from my gun that hit Jesse's shoulder not too long ago."

She shook her head. "It was one of the bandits who shot at Jesse."

"No, but I made him think it was. I had a couple of friends with me, and we were searching for Buchanan's hideout when Jesse came galloping into our camp. We were close. I knew it. I didn't want Jesse to know how close I was, so me and my friends chased him down."

She rolled her eyes. "Quit making up stories, Albert. Why can't you just admit you're a failure? You'll never be as good as the Slade brothers." She shook her head. "You may have tried to bring them down, but as you can clearly see, they have survived and are back on top. You've failed, Albert. You're a miserable excuse for a man."

Even through the darkness, fire shot out of his eyes. He jumped to his feet and pointed the gun at her. "I haven't failed yet, dearie." He cocked the rifle. "My plans are still in motion. Although, I still have some unfinished business with you."

"What are you talking about? You couldn't possibly still harbor thoughts of marrying me."

He laughed. "Not any more. You're considered a used woman, so I'll do to you what I do to most used goods. I'll take what I want, and then throw you away."

Her eyes widened as coldness crept throughout her body. "If you lay a hand on me-- "

"You'll what?" His loud chuckle echoed through the night. "I'm the one holding the gun, or have you forgotten?" He grinned, and it sent sickening chills all over her.

He loosened his belt and her body froze. His tongue drew across his lips in a disgusting manner as his gaze moved over her body. She would not let him touch her.

He pulled out his shirttails and knelt beside her. She tried to scoot away, but he grabbed hold of her arm. "Play nice, and I won't hurt you too badly."

"Go to hell, Albert."

"Not before I have my way with you."

His hands were upon her as fast as lightning and he laid his body on top of hers. She squirmed, but he was too heavy to move. When one of his hands connected with her breast, anger vibrated through her body, from the tips of her toes up to her head. Her breathing became harsh, and she balled her hands into fists, ready to unleash her fury if the man tried to go any further.

"Show me what you've given to Jesse," he snickered. "Show me the little whore beneath all of that fancy learning."

"You bastard," she shouted. With strength she didn't know she possessed, she pushed him off her and sprang to her feet. Her fists pummeled the air, aiming for anything solid. Although he slapped at her hands to stop them, her knuckles met his nose, his lip, then his neck, and he gurgled in painful protest.

He lunged toward her, wrapping his arms around her as they stumbled to the ground. The gun flew through the air and landed mere feet away. She elbowed him in the chest and rolled on her stomach, crawling to get the gun, but he grabbed her ankle. She turned again, aimed the point of her boot, and struck him in the face.

Cursing, he rolled on his back, and landed closer to the gun. He grabbed it and aimed at her. The explosion rendered the air and the bullet whizzed by her head, but she continued striking and kicking at whatever she could. He aimed the gun again. She kicked it out at his hands. With the gun gone, she jumped on him and continued to strike as hard as she could. His grunts and groans only intensified her onslaught.

"Summer, get off him." Jesse's voice boomed from over her shoulder, but her rage pushed her to the edge and she continued to pummel Albert.

"Summer, that's enough." Jesse's strong arm circled around her waist and lifted her. She finally noticed Albert's bleeding face and pained expression. *Good, let him suffer.*

"Summer." Jesse turned her to face him. "I have the gun now. Everythin' is all right."

She looked back at the man who had curled like a babe on his side, holding his crotch. "Damn right."

"Sit up, Albert," Jesse commanded. "Get on your knees and put your hands behind your back."

Albert cursed Jesse, his luck, and the Almighty God

above, but did as he was told.

Jesse quickly tied him, then nudged his boot into Albert's back. "Now stand, you flea bitten varmint. It's a damn good thing you didn't take your boots off when you laid down earlier, or you'd a been walkin' back to town barefoot."

Summer led the horses into the circle around the fire. A sense of pride filled her chest as Jesse tied the rope that bound Albert's hands to the saddle horn of his horses. She squeezed him around the waist. "Good job, Ranger Slade."

He gathered her in his arms and kissed her forehead. "Are you all right?"

"I am now. What about you?" She looked up and gently touched the gash on the side of his face.

"I'll be fine. Don't worry."

"Did you hear he was the one who shot you and hit you on the head with a rifle?"

"Yes, I heard, although everything was sort of foggy."

"Oh, Jesse." She slumped against him and pressed her face to his chest. "I can't believe..." She sniffed back a tear. "I wanted to kill Albert."

He stroked her hair. "I know, darlin'. I still want to."

She lifted her head and gazed into his handsome face. "Let's take him back to town. I'm tired."

He smiled and kissed her forehead. "You need to rest before our weddin', or you're goin' to fall asleep durin' the ceremony."

She caressed his chin. "Only if you're lying beside me."

"Are you talkin' about tonight?"

She smiled. "Yes. After what has happened, there's no way I'm going to let you go."

His face softened. "Promise?"

She lifted the corners of her mouth. "Every day for the rest of my life."

Epilogue

Leaning on the porch's wooden pillar, Jesse gazed out across the magnificent rolling green acres of his property, then back at his beautiful wife who knelt with her sister beside the flower garden, doing more talking than weeding.

He smiled and his chest constricted with that wonderful feeling of love. Both Summer and Violet's bellies were exactly eight months round with child, and he anxiously anticipated the arrival of the new additions to his family.

A peal of laughter rang from the stables nearby, and all heads turned to see what excitement had just occurred. Marvin and Nate ran out of the barn hoopin' and hollerin'. Jesse smiled. It was sure good to see his father-in-law walking and running like he'd used to.

"Buck just became a father," Nate shouted.

Summer and Violet awkwardly rose and waddled toward the barn. Marvin's back and legs carried him perfectly, his face beaming with enthusiasm as he slipped his arms around both daughters. Marvin's operation had turned out better than the doctors had expected.

"Can we see, Pa?" Summer asked.

"Of course, go right in." Marvin ushered his daughters inside. Marvin turned his head and looked at Jesse. "Are you coming, son?"

"Yes, I'll be right there." The smile stayed on his face as he watched the people he loved--a family he thought he'd never have.

Clint meandered out of the barn, his arms covered to his elbows with mucus from the mare's birth. He walked over to the pump to wash. "Hey, Jess? You need to come see. Birth is such a wonderful miracle."

Jesse pulled away from the post and skipped down the three stairs onto the grass. "Our life is a miracle, Clint. I mean, look at us. Fifteen years ago, I never imagined we'd end up like this."

Clint shook the excess water from his arms and strode toward Jesse. "You are right, li'l brother."

Jesse walked with Clint toward the barn. "God's certainly smiled down on us."

Clint nodded. "Don't think Heaven could be much better."

"Yes, it could."

Clint stopped and looked at him through a narrowed gaze. "Yeah? How do you figure?"

"We could have dozens of kids, most of them boys, of course, and we'd teach them everythin' they need to know about bein' Rangers and Ranchers."

Clint's roar of laughter brought Summer and Violet waddling out of the barn and over to them. Summer stopped beside Jesse, slipping her arms around his waist.

"What's so funny?"

Clint shook his head. "You're gonna be one busy lady, Summer." He turned his attention to his own wife. "And you'll be right beside her."

Summer sighed and rested her head against Jesse's chest. He put his arm around her shoulders and pulled her close. "All I care about is making my husband happy." She smiled up at him.

Jesse's chest constricted again, and he loved the feeling. "You've already done that."

"Swear to it?" she asked with a twinkle in her eyes.

He laughed. "Every damn day."

About Phyllis

Phyllis Campbell does what she loves best – writing love stories. An award winning, critically acclaimed, romance writer, she's devoted to writing to finding that 'happy ending'. She's been an avid reader of romance since the first year of her marriage in 1985, and she still can't get enough of a great story. She works daily at writing that next romance novel that will please her fans.

Other Titles By Phyllis:

My Heart Belongs To You
My Knight, My Rogue
Always, My Love
Ten Ways To Melt A Man's Heart
Crazy Cupid (in Stupid Cupid)
It Must Have Been The Mistletoe (in Mistletoe Magic)

Visit our website for our growing catalogue of quality books.
www.champagnebooks.com

On Eagle's Wings
by
Rebecca Goings

ISBN 1897261446

Will Eagle's Wing be able to fix the time-line he's derailed without losing his heart in the deal?

Also available in paperback

Fraternity by Lori Derby Bingley

ISBN: 1897261497

One man. Six women. And a fraternity of brothers who will do anything to keep their secrets.

Operation Heartstrings by Rayka Mennen

ISBN: 189726156X

In a world of intrigue and conflict, two agents find their hearts linking. Will they escape with their lives and hearts intact?

Braless In The Buick by Jenna Leigh

ISBN: 1897261608

An undercover agent's investigation into mob contacts leads to titillating revelations about a single mom.

Ten Ways To Melt A Man's Heart by Phyllis Campbell

ISBN: 1897261675

When love and friends collide, the outcome can be humorous...and disastrous.

Printed in the United States
130196LV00001B/11/A